The applause dies down. Th
quiet. Natalie takes her cue. She's w
hair, pulled into short pig tails on the
washes over her. She steps forward ⟨   ⟩......, her bare feet
padding lightly on the old polished stage planks. Each footstep is careful
and deliberate, bouncing lightly on the balls of her feet as if she were
perched on low dance heels. The murmurs hush around the theater as
she begins her monologue. She stalks the stage, swinging her hips with
a grossly inappropriate confidence, true to the character. Camp Director
had trepidations about giving Natalie the part of Val Clarke from the start
and this was exactly why. Men around the theater start looking around
nervously, sweating, shifting around uncomfortably, cussing lightly under
their breath, covering with indifferent smiles at the people around them,
looking around uncomfortably. Her Latina accent slips out a little as she
remembers on the fly to clean up a vulgar line, one the first of many in a
risque song.

"I didn't give a fu-get about the red heels!" she shrieks with joy.
Camp Director shoots her a look. Nostrils flare, eyes wide, *Clean up the
song*.

"Merry Christmas!" Natalie sings falsetto with a twinkling of her
fingers in time with a bell in the orchestra pit.

"I was ugly as sin!" She pouts and slithers and runs her hands
over her body like a temptress,

"Flat as a pancake!" She gives her budding, albeit stage padded
chest a quick bouncy, shamefully sexy little boost,

"Get the picture?" She sashays around the stage, telling her
story. "It was the way I looked, so I said 'Forget you!' to the Rockettes,"
To the Camp Director's relief. The music chimes in and the song picks
up from her monologue on the beat - no rest.

"Dance: Ten, Looks Three…" she begins to sing, Camp Director
knows it's coming.

"To buy…" The Camp Director holds her breath…

"This and That…." Camp Director is relieved but it's short lived as
Natalie's teenage body bounces across the stage. It doesn't seem to
matter that she's cleaning up the lyrics. Women around the audience
glare at the men next to them, some even smack them. The music
exaggerates it all as an implicit accomplice. Natalie breathlessly giggles

along to keep pace and when the tempo slows her performance takes on a red light district aura. She's too young to be perceived as this sex kitten, performing this song. To the audience's horror and shameful titillation Natalie moves with the professional expertise of a stripper jiggling around,

"Had the bingo bongos done," She pouts. One more comically censored refrain goes by. "This and That…" but Camp Director realizes just how much censoring the song didn't matter. Natalie is pointing directly at "This" and "That." *She's pointing right at them!* To her credit, Natalie *did* point that out in rehearsals when she protested censoring the song in the first place. *I shouldn't have let her have this part,* Camp Director thought, *damn it!* Natalie is now leaning towards the audience to share a dirty little secret to an uncomfortable front row.

"Didn't hurt my SEX life either." Some of the other kids on stage giggle as the big S word coils around the audience like a snake offering forbidden fruit. Camp Director clasps a hand over a gasp.

"She was supposed to say *Love Life!*" she hisses at her assistant, her daughter, who just shrugs and rolls her eyes.

"Fix the chassis…" Natalie bumps her booty out and adjusts her leotard suggestively. Camp Director tenses up, winces at the loud *smack* the elastic bodysuit makes when it snaps back into place on Natalie's perky teenage…That.

"This and That!" Red stage lighting and a sexy drum beat - more big miscalculated mistakes weighing on Camp Director's mind - accompany Natalie through the choreography for the instrumental piece. The dance number seems to go on forever. Camp Director is sweating, it's a nightmare she can't wake up from. Natalie proudly swishes to the front of the stage, smirking knowingly, bathed in spotlight. Per the script she breaks the fourth wall and leans forward, teasingly.

"You're looking at my tits." She breathes at a man in the front row. He blushes and tries to spontaneously combust rather than face the shame. She's right - he is. He's looking right at her tits. He knows it, she knows it. Everyone around him knows it. The crowd gasps collectively as does Camp Director and some of the other performers. They nervously look around, whispering to each other, giggling, "she was supposed to say *Assets.*"

A young impressionable Courtney steps forward on cue. "I would kill to have just one of yours." She delivers, beaming in the uneasy laughter she gets. Camp Director shakes her head in her hand. The torch horn blares another torturous sexy stripper beat breakdown. Camp Director jumps, nerves shot, nasty stares and accusatory glances pelting her from the audience as Natalie grinds across the stage. The audience sits silent, aghast, uncomfortable. Natalie plays innocent, plays oblivious to their discomfort with her sexuality. But she knows. She knows what she's doing. She knows how uncomfortable they are and she doesn't care. *Everyone here wants to fuck me*, she thinks proudly, *I want everyone here to want to fuck me.*

The song rises toward the show tune's show-stopping crescendo ending,"Tits and ASS!" she belts out a deep bellow from below the abdomen. Mouths fall open. Camp Director's mouth hits the floor. "Tits and Ass will change your life, they sure, changed, miiiiiiiiiiiiiiiiiiiiiiiiiiiiiiine!"

Silence. Natalie stands at attention center stage, beaming, proud as can be, basking in the shocked dead silence. She gives a cute head nod, hip bump and a flirty wink to the guy she'd embarrassed in the front row and saunters back into line. Boards creak lightly under her stride, the sound of her feet padding across the stage make a small tacky noise as her bare feet pull against the polyurethane coating. The audience sits silent, every eye fixed on Natalie's slow-twitching butt cheeks. You can hear people blink. Shocked. Horrified by her overly sexualized performance, by the scantily clad teenage temptress. Shocked and horrified by their own dirty titillation. *The little tramp.The Lolita!* Everyone in the theater feels touched when she improvises a goose to the butt of the young man next to her in line as she spins around to face front. In that moment of dead silence, a young Elizabeth in the crowd knows as sure as Natalie smacked that boy's ass, she wants to be up on that stage next year getting that kind of attention and adulation. The lights drop, a delayed applause erupts, now safe, anonymous in the dark shadows. Her performance was inappropriate. But she nailed it.

Aprils, Full

By, C.J. Rush
9/11/16-4/8/19
Book 8

"Not every performance with music is a musical. In a musical the lyrics in the songs further the plot and serve as dialogue." J.E.R.

The Full Moon in April of 2018 was a Pink Moon

Copy Editor, Rockstar & Advisor:J.Sukup-Robinson
Script Supervisor, Editor, Advisor: J.K. Thompson
Contributing editor: K. Bova
Photography Department Advisor: E.Mayer
Additional thanks to K.C and K.G.

It's Sex and the City but with porn, drugs and gambling.

"A room full of sweaty naked straight men with semi erections and eye contact issues…"

To Natalie, wherever you are.

Act 1 Scene 1

Int:ALLISON'S CAR-MORNING

ALLISON, a sturdy Midwestern girl in her early 20's, chain smoking as she drives.

ALLISON:
Fucking bastard!

She slaps the steering wheel in a fit of rage.

ALLISON:
I don't know. New York is so flat out this way. It's so high up you can see for miles but the whole landscape seems...sheared off. Flat. It's weird to me too, I know, but the quickest way South from here is North.

Allison lights another cigarette off of her cigarette.

Allison is twenty-two years old. Thankfully, in four years of marriage she and Louis have no children. That would make all of this that much harder. She can only imagine.

Allison's a fairly tall girl, not noticeably, not extraordinarily, just tall enough to be self conscious about it but not enough for it to be defining. Or useful. Taller than the average broad. Top of the middle. Her father had always joked about Allison resembling a 'sturdy midwestern gal' Allison was never sure 'Sturdy' was a compliment though dad seemed to think it was. "All little blond girls look alike," her father would laugh whenever he had to pick her up from a bus stop or a school function as a kid. "And they all sound like they're from the midwest, why is that?" he would ask Mom who always just said she didn't know with a fake curious interest like it was the first time she was hearing this information, that he's never posed this question before. *Sturdy*, Allison thinks, glancing around at herself while keeping an eye on the road. Her grandmother always said she had 'those child bearin' hips'. *A little busty too, eh, grandma?* In proportion. They always embarrassed her as a budding teen. Her tits. Boobs. Knockers. Fun Bags. Her tits always embarrassed her so she kept them pinned down with clothing and hidden behind loose sweaters or baggy button down plaid shirts. *I did look like a farm girl didn't I?*

Louis stands in the doorway getting smaller in the rearview mirror in the background, a shadow in the doorway. His Cheshire grin glints in the morning sun. His smile is an awkward line, like he isn't completely comfortable doing it. Smiling.

Driving home to Mommy and Daddy. Not sure how I got here. How did it come to this? Allison is beaten mentally. The drive from upstate New York to her parents house in Yorktown is lonely and taxing. The full color of fall peaked in the last weeks and now there are big holes in the brilliant urgent reds and soft yellows. Big ragged brown scars, bare branches speed by, clawing at her. Divorce inevitable, pending. She pieces together the collapse, rolling through their timeline a slideshow of memories. *Where did the poison set in? When did it go wrong?* She never liked that girl. She smelled homewrecker on her right away but Allison was still polite to Louis's new friend. Even when she came to visit with her boyfriend from back home. *Just friends indeed.* A teenage student. Then again, in hindsight, Louis had started working on Allison when she was about twelve. Subtle. Allison screams,"Fucking bastard!"

Allison shifts through thoughts without segue, clutchless from Louis to landscapes to topical news.

"I don't know," She announces to the empty car, "New York is so flat out this way, it's so high up you can see for miles but the whole landscape seems sheared off flat. It's weird to me too, I know...but the quickest way South from here is North." Allison lights another cigarette and tries to amuse herself with her own little inside jokes.

"The quickest way south from here is north." She repeats with a chuckle imitating the crazy old man that gave her and Louis directions the first time they came up here. "North to I-90 East, much quicker those Interstates than the state roads, Look at a map and you think State Route 20 is the way to go but in the long run, for a long haul ole' lucky 13 North. That's how you get south from here." Allison's stomach rolls in a growl. She left in a hurry of emotions, forgot to eat. *Maybe Louis was right, I am losing my...what am I saying?! I'm not crazy, that man was trying to make me feel crazy! I believe the term is gaslighting though I have no idea why.* The image of a dirty 1880s main street, lined with kerosene lamp lights flashes before her. Allison thinks about the move up here from Yorktown to Madison county. She'd read the sign at the county line aloud.

"Like as in the bridges of?" She'd asked excitedly.

"Yes as in the bridges of," Louis added, "You know L. Frank Baum was from here, the author of…"

"*The Wonderful Wizard of Oz*! I know!" Allison finished exuberantly. "Did you know the yellow brick road was in Peeksk…"

"Oh Allison, that's just a myth." Louis had said with that smile, that weird line that runs crookedly across his face when he's amused.

Now she follow follow follows the double yellow line to no place like home. Her belly rumbles again and she resigns to get off the next exit and eat whatever's there.

"Of course." She says dryly as she pulls into the lot of the Syracuse Hooters complete with the fluorescent sign, "Late Breakfast Served." It wouldn't be the first boobs in Allison's face.

"Ah, Sonja…" She thinks aloud. Before Louis, when he was still just the guy across the street, before Tommy, there was the summer of Sonja. Allison lights a cigarette. With Louis, he made her feel safe, secure. And she guessed that was what she had wanted: Safety. But when she had been with Sonja, Allison felt beautiful and sexy. And loved. To this day Allison isn't sure why she separates and groups those things together, sexy and loved or safe and secure, but she does. And she got what she wanted, or needed, or both from Sonja and Louis whenever she wanted or needed. *Like how we crave salt.* Allison hadn't thought much about women since Sonja, she hadn't even known until it happened that she could be into women like that. Hell, now? In the late 90's? Most chicks are bi, but Allison doesn't really think of herself that way. She did think Louis was going to try to get her to hook up with that little tramp when he first brought her home. Turns out he was saving her for himself. He'd been developing an odd sense of sexuality since they moved to Gore but it was weird. Off, somehow, almost… devious? Louis had always been practically asexual, it had surprised Allison when they first kissed and that was after he proposed to her. She thought about that moment on his porch, he didn't even really propose to her, more like *told* her to marry him. It hadn't come off that way but now in hindsight, the words mean more now. Indicative in context. It seemed being in Gore had awakened something in him, some deep devious demons. He started hanging around with teenage students and he even learned to play guitar. *For Christ's sake he's an English teacher. An English Teacher!* she sings in her head automatically, recalling their drama camp production of *Bye, Bye Birdie*. "The English teacher's wife," she'd sung to herself happily on the drive up to Gore when Louis took the English professor position.

Allison walks into the Hooters and is seated at a small round table, one of those higher tables around the bar. The stool is a tall round swivel, her feet are a full foot off the carpet on a metal foot rest that reminds Allison of the antique barber's chair her father used to sit in every Sunday. Sometimes Allison would go with him to get his haircut. She would sit quietly and read *Highlights* or *People* while dad got a haircut and a shave and talked to the old barber about sports or politics. She looks around at the Hooters girls. None of them are Sonja. Then again she just isn't that Allison anymore either though. Is she? She's not one hundred percent sure who Allison is anymore. Allison who?

"I'm incognito." She puts on a Russian accent "Inka. Inka Cockneedo." She giggles to herself. "Sounds like a porn name, Inka Cockneedo, Russian spy slash whore. You can call me Inka."

She'd changed her name when she got married to Louis. Now what? Does she go back to her maiden name? *Can I just drop his name and just be Allison? Probably not. I'm not even sure who I would ask. 'Who did Cher pass that by?* "Yeah, just Inka."

Allison notices a man outside the window smoking, feels the taste. The taste that happens in a smoker's mouth that says *Why yes, a cigarette would be delightful right now.* She orders a plate of wings and a soda, drapes her coat over the chair and goes outside for a cigarette. Seems like only yesterday you could still smoke in most restaurants. These family -- sort of -- corporate chains were the first to go smoke free.

Allison takes a long drag on her cigarette and looks at the glowing tip, *I feel like Louis somehow introduced me to Sonja.* She looks back down her smoke and thinks the same thing. *Or was it Carol?* She takes another long drag, blows it out slow, nodding her head

"Yup, you too…" She thought about all the times she'd cried on his shoulder, he always had a smoke for her. He doesn't smoke. *He had those cigarettes just for me,* It dawns on her like a sunrise. When she gets back from her smoke and epiphany a big steaming plate of hot spicy chicken wings is waiting for her in her spot. She eats. She eats and she thinks. While she noisily slurps Buffalo sauce off meat, meat off tiny bones, she continues to think. It makes her feel wild, she indulges in it. Allison gawks hungrily at a large-breasted waitress, peering over two fists of bones with orange teeth and lips. She shakes her head a little, unsure if she's joking or serious, leering. She catches Allison checking her out. Allison gives the bubble-breasted server an exaggerated, silly wink. Offering a thumbs up, she can feel a glob of blue cheese dressing stuck to her cheek. Her lips and tongue stinging from the authentic Frank's Red Hot, she imagines her face is stained the same orange as her fingers. Her daddy used to make a hot sauce with peppers from his garden that made her face sting the same way. It's the Capsaicin. Gotta amuse yourself somehow. *Even if you're down and dumped.* Allison chuckles slightly at her terrible corny word play. *Down and dumped.* It reminds her of a joke her father might say. "Down and dumped huh?" she hears him in his dad voice, then he'd laugh a belly dad laugh and go mow the lawn or something. Had to look good for the annual block party. Allison looks over at Bubble Tits and giggles, isn't this why guys come here? *Git that fat ass over here, baby.*

"Excuse me, miss…?" Allison calls to the waitress, "Can I have some more blue cheese and some napkins?" Feeling reality, she puts a hand over the blob on her cheek and looks away in shame. *What if someone opened a place like this but with the dudes walking around in booty shorts and half shirts. They could call it Tube Steak Charlie's. I wonder if any guys would cry discrimination if we only hire girthy 8 inchers or better? Gotta fill out those banana hammocks, son.*
When she finishes her wings Allison goes and sits at the bar. Bubble Tits is the bartender. Allison nurses a Ginger Ale in a souvenir Hooters glass and gives serious consideration to the juxtapositions of the gross commercialization of sex and chicken. Back and forth, chicken, crisp golden brown sizzling chicken and marketing and the bartenders bouncy Hooters. Allison sips her drink slowly, watching cash flow back and forth, hand over tits.

On the TV behind the bar a skinny blond in a bikini slides across the wet hood of a car seductively.

Carol and her minions teased Allison relentlessly about her tits and the boys just wanted to grope her in the dark at the makeout parties. They never wanted to talk to her in school after though. It wouldn't be until she'd grown taller and into her hip and bust line that she could have felt less self-conscious but that's not how it works. It's a vicious cycle and that damage is hard to undo. We're all the personality we develop between 11-17. Allison has these deep rooted body image issues.

On the TV behind the bar burger juice dribbles seductively down an under dressed young ladies chin.

I guess that was one of the most comfortable things about Louis. He was so asexual her body had never mattered. He was like sweatpants and a baggy sweatshirt.

Act 1 Scene 2

Interior;Kitchen-evening,

the phone rings, ALLISON picks
up on the second ring,

ALLISON:
Vonderlande residence,
Allison speaking

The house is empty. Allison's father still works late, same as when she was growing up. She always thought it was to get away from her mother, all that working late. Mom told her she would be out herself until later also and to go in through the back door. Like when she was a kid. The back door is open, as promised. She walked in and stood there for a minute looking around the room for the first time in what seemed like a lifetime. That's when the phone rings. An old rotary style on the wall next to her. Phone Rental is still a charge on the monthly phone bill from when they first moved in and hooked it up, original number and everything. Nobody owned a phone back then, you rented one from the phone company. As soon as Allison picks up the phone she regrets it.

"Oh my Allison! I heard you were coming home, it will be so nice to see you!" It's Carol's mother across the street. When they were kids Carol set Allison up for humiliation every chance she got. Carol's mother knows damn well Louis threw her out, probably knows she got traded in for a newer model too. She can hear the Rub Your Nose In It tone in her voice. *Your daughter tortured me relentlessly when we were kids, you old witch.*

"Carol is so excited to get to see you…" She sings. *That bitch. No she isn't, she's a terrible hag and so are you.*

"OK I'll tell my mom you called," she chokes through a fake smile, "Tell Carol Hi," she lies, "It was nice talking to you too." Allison hangs the receiver back on the cradle and gives a tug down on the springy phone wire like she did as a girl. She watches it bounce, bobbing and springing like springs do, longingly, far away. And she can't help feel Carol's mother knew her mother is out and she just got here. She looks down the hall at the front door, through the window in it. Louis' parents still live across the street, next door to Carol's parents. Her fists shake, anger fills her for a moment. Allison walks slowly down the hall with a whitening chill of doom. She moves dreamlike, slowly re-familiarizing herself with the creaks and groans of the of the old hardwood planks that haven't changed, beneath the antique knit throw runners. She walks into the door, the window inches from her, she runs her gaze up the door along the grain lines, oddly familiar. Reliable old grain lines in the front door. She fixes her gaze to the glass looks through the square pane. There it is. Louis' house. Just the sight of it hits her in the gut. Not so hard but even a light gut shot takes your breath away a little. Even just a tap will give her pause. Allison smoked her first cigarette with Carol at the bus stop right there. She watches young Allison take the cigarette from Carol. She coughed, tried not to cough too hard, she wanted to be cool too. It was harsh, but she recalls it not being as harsh as she thought it would be. She talked to Louis about it later that evening after school, he gave her more, showed her how to hold it, how to inhale and not die coughing. He showed her how to ash and keep her ash head neat. At the time the detail that Louis didn't smoke didn't even occur to her. She watches young Allison begin her path to nicotine addiction.

Upstate Louis closes his eyes and breathes in deep his small victory, exhales slow. His hands clasped, fingers touch lightly at the tips. He looks in prayer in his brown leather easy chair, though nothing Louis ever says or does can be mistaken for prayer. It's more like contemplating prey.

Allison turns on her heel out of context and walks abruptly back into the kitchen where she'd left her purse on the island. She plucks out a cigarette from the pack. Upon further thought takes a second one and goes out to the back steps. The front porch has a chair and a roof but that view. She would rather not sit there and look at Louis and Carol's houses. The back concrete steps are uncomfortable and she just sat for hours and there's no shade back here though there's no sun either and the view out back is of her old swing set, not Louis' house. Allison lights one cigarette and places the other down next to her, the lighter beside it. The cigarette rolls out of line a bit and she straightens it. She gently taps her ash off in a tight pile next to her lighter. The delicate ash pile sits unafraid against the breezeless evening. When the cigarette reaches the last drag and the yellow filter paper turns burnt red she uses it to light the second one then slowly turns the butt out next to the ash pile, carefully leaving the butt standing on end. Slowly she pulls her hand away and takes a long drag on her smoke watching the balancing butt for any signs of wobble. The swing set her dad put in for her when they moved in creaks a rusty whine. The rust flakes into the tall grass that grows around the legs and under the swing for two. It's there. The swingset, the yard, the neighbors. Yorktown is all here. All the yards and basements they played in. The basements where the teen makeout parties happened. It's all here. Out there beyond the yard. The dark damp thin carpets over poured concrete floors, the wood paneling, the home-built bars in the corners, the musty mismatched scratchy loveseats and couches where they groped and dry humped. The shag carpets and mirrors and refilling the old man's liquor bottle with water or ice tea. Yorktown. It's all still here and now Allison is too. Again. "Here I am," she seethes, closes her eyes, breathes deep, exhales, squeezing her butt in a tight shaking pinch. The wave of intense anger passes, she turns out her second cigarette, grinding out the ember in a tight shaky grip. *It still feels like I'm visiting.* She blows the Ash Puddle to the wind, gathers up the butts and tosses them in the trash can by the door on the way back in. *Here I am.* She climbs the stairs, each creak and groan greeting her home, catching her up. Mocking her. *Here I am.* She stands in the doorway of her childhood bedroom. *Just visiting. Crash in the guest room. My teenage bedroom for the weekend then I'm going home. I don't have a home anymore. This is my home now. Again.* Allison picks up her Snow White Snowglobe and shakes it. Holds the globe to her face, watches glitter snow swirl. When the storm subsides she shakes it again and sets it back down. Allison sits on the bed. They left her room exactly as it was. *I was married, not dead.* It's not exactly a holy shrine to Allison, it's still considered the guest room. With 80's teenage girl decor, complete with her old Wiccan bible, Guns 'N Roses, Poison, and My Little Pony posters. There was some crossover. Allison thinks she might try to take a nap but she lays down and her eyes refuse to shut. She lay staring at the ceiling. In elementary school her friend Debbie had a Kirk Cameron poster on the ceiling over her bed. He had come to the mall to sign autographs and promote Growing Pains. He was giving all the girls kisses and Debbie was excited to kiss him. A guy in the back of the crowd yelled out to Kirk, "You're gonna get Mono!" Everyone laughed including Kirk. He blushed and said he was "not gonna get Mono" then winked at Debbie, scribbled his signature across her poster and gave her a kiss. She put that poster over her bed and was a little too vocal, if you asked Allison, about touching herself looking up at Kirk. Allison is embarrassed now about how naive she remembers being about it, asking, "You rub yourself looking at it…?"

"Oh Debbie, if I had your confidence now." Allison whispers hoarsely, "Kirk Cameron?" Allison lays there unable to sleep for what feels like years. She can hear the clock in the hallway ticking loudly in the quiet empty house. Tick, tick, tick. Off into infinity. She rolls on her side, her eyes falling where they may. On the side with her desk, the snowglobe, the door, a Bret Michaels poster. They all stare back at her. She rolls to her other side. It's not much better -- the window, the dark backyard with the rusty swing-set in the tall grass. Her eyes are open but she isn't seeing, she's seeing but not really registering. "I don't think napping is going to work," she says and rolls back on her other side. She thinks about childhood, falling asleep looking into her Snow White snowglobe on the desk. She got it in Disneyland in California when she was young. Life was so simple then, before...before she reached that age when girls couldn't be "chunky" without someone saying something about it. Before she was a piece of meat with child bearing hips, before she was "that girl with the boobs." She's not that big in the chest now, she was just busty early. Other girls hated that. Carol hated that. Allison sensed that right away. She was surprised when Carol wanted to hang out and then she'd do something horrible to her. Every time.

Allison thinks about Louis. The last few flakes of glitter snow slowly sink, twinkling, swirling, reflecting. *Where did it go wrong? Could it have been right from the start?* Allison was so young. She lays motionless, awake but not really, as the last flecks of glitter fall to the bottom, so too does Allison fall out of wake and consciousness. Now as the water stops spinning, the glitter lays flat and Allison has sunken into her bed, into herself. Awake but Off. The clock spins out of control in the hall. Her wind up alarm clock with the two bells beside the bed stopped ticking years ago. Nobody winds a clock in a guest room. Time passes without it. Allison hears Mother come home, but she still doesn't move. It's fully dark now. Allison rolls, gaze fixed out the window out into the darkness. She can feel her mother's eyes burn holes into her back as she peeks through the cracked door. Allison can hear her mother breathing in that way people breathe in their voice. If she doesn't say anything Allison thinks she'll let her think she's sleeping.

"Allison? Are you awake?"

"No." Allison says flat and joyless. She still lays motionless, her mouth hardly moves. She says nothing else. Mother comes in anyway, sits at the foot of the bed, puts her hand on Allison's hip. She says nothing as if the laying on of hands should say it all but it too says nothing and neither does Allison. Mother seems to think it's enough and stands up.

"I'll fix you a plate." She says, standing up straight and curt, needlessly brushing nothing from her lap and straightening her Mom Uniform. Her costume. So she can run off to perform her part, her Mother role. The Martyr. She leaves. Allison continues to lay still for some time. *She's so fake,* she thinks, *Superficial.* She ponders searching for just the right adjective. *Mother is a nurturer. And it's fake. Not so much fake as it is an act. It's a play she puts on, a part she plays faithfully. Never Break Character.*

Dad comes home a while later. He peeks his Dad head in and says "Hello" with a hint of awkwardness. He has no words of comfort. He's not a cold man but he's an old-fashioned one and as such is often unsure how to handle feelings and women in most situations involving the same. "Umph, kiddo…" Is about all he can manage to mutter. Mother and Dad eventually go to bed, Allison hears their door shut. Her belly rumbles the memories of spicy chicken. Silently Allison sits up, stands, walks downstairs to the kitchen. The plate Mother made up for her is on the top shelf of the refrigerator. Two roasted chicken legs, seasoned the same way they always have been, a serving of buttered noodles and a heaping scoop of canned green beans. One of mother's standard dishes.

Allison stands before the microwave and watches the plate spin. The hum of the microwave being the only sound besides the *clunk* the carousel plate makes at the predictable spot in the rotation. *Clunk.* She sits at the kitchen table and eats in silence staring at her plate. The lone bulb in the ceiling light over the table seems harsh. It bathes the kitchen in a stark hospital white, baring all for analysis in full high-definition life.

"You're awfully judgmental. For a lightbulb." She says with no joy, squinting at the bulb. Abruptly she lets out a maniacal burst of one laugh. She finishes her plate, washes it and places it by itself in the drainboard. She looks at it.

"To think about what you've done." She says, adding "Slut" so abruptly it startles her and she lets out another burst of laugh. She takes her joyless jokes and metaphors back up to bed. She glances at the useless alarm clock, contemplates winding it. Clicks off the bedside lamp instead.

"Tomorrow. Tomorrow I'll start keeping track of time again." Sleep finally comes for Allison.

Catatonic
Act 1 Scene 3

Interior:bedroom, morning

Allison feels the spring
tension against her fingers
through the key as she winds the
clock. It's a classic. Two brass
bells on top of a round clock
face like shiny ears.

ALLISON:
Are your ears ringing?

She puts the clock down on
the nightstand and watches it
thoughtfully

A rage tremor shakes her, she wants to pick up the clock and hurl it against the wall. It passes. Tick tock. With her finger she pushes the minute hand around until the time is correct, according to her best guess, based on the clock in the hallway a few minutes ago on the way back from the bathroom. She'd felt intrusive in the bathroom. Pissing in someone else's toilet, her feet cold to numb on the tile.

Louis stands in the window of the upstairs living room of the old farm house, watching the sun rise, waiting for a trap to spring. A little blue three-door car with a 'Born Again Voodooist' bumper sticker approaches from off in the distance, under a cloud of dust along the long straight farm road. He's been expecting her. She's right on time. Headed straight for the jaws of his trap. Snap. Guided by long come-hither fingers, the long slender fingers of the shiny crocodile drawing little fishies into his waiting jaws, slither like a snake, draw in prey to feed on, to bite down on, to inject his poison into. Venom to render his prey. Catatonic.

Baby timber rattlers can be especially deadly should you stumble across one in the forest. They have not yet developed control of their venom and will unload their deadly arsenal. Louis has experience. Expert control of the venom he releases into his prey. Catatonia sets in slow.

There. Clock set. Allison holds the clock back with a sigh and watches the second hand creep around the face. Keeping track of time, counting each second from here to eternity, from now till then, here to there. This and That. Allison pantomimes the choreography automatically, always does out of habit ever since camp. Every time she hears the phrase "This and That" in any context she can't help point to This and That, a perversion of genuflection.

From Divorce till what? Death? Second Marriage? Is that redundant? Why? Do I really need to be married? That's what she's supposed to do, isn't it? Make up one half of a pair? The Fair Half, the submissive half. Unequal Halves? Is that a thing? From a pair into a family, a set and growing. *Look good to us ladies, so we want to put babies in you.* That's what we're for. Putting babies in. Here, hold this,

Catatonic
Act 1 Scene 3

Interior:bedroom, morning

Allison feels the spring
tension against her fingers
through the key as she winds the
clock. It's a classic. Two brass
bells on top of a round clock
face like shiny ears.

ALLISON:
Are your ears ringing?

She puts the clock down on
the nightstand and watches it
thoughtfully

A rage tremor shakes her, she wants to pick up the clock and hurl it against the wall. It passes. Tick tock. With her finger she pushes the minute hand around until the time is correct, according to her best guess, based on the clock in the hallway a few minutes ago on the way back from the bathroom. She'd felt intrusive in the bathroom. Pissing in someone else's toilet, her feet cold to numb on the tile.

Louis stands in the window of the upstairs living room of the old farm house, watching the sun rise, waiting for a trap to spring. A little blue three-door car with a 'Born Again Voodooist' bumper sticker approaches from off in the distance, under a cloud of dust along the long straight farm road. He's been expecting her. She's right on time. Headed straight for the jaws of his trap. Snap. Guided by long come-hither fingers, the long slender fingers of the shiny crocodile drawing little fishies into his waiting jaws, slither like a snake, draw in prey to feed on, to bite down on, to inject his poison into. Venom to render his prey. Catatonic.

Baby timber rattlers can be especially deadly should you stumble across one in the forest. They have not yet developed control of their venom and will unload their deadly arsenal. Louis has experience. Expert control of the venom he releases into his prey. Catatonia sets in slow.

There. Clock set. Allison holds the clock back with a sigh and watches the second hand creep around the face. Keeping track of time, counting each second from here to eternity, from now till then, here to there. This and That. Allison pantomimes the choreography automatically, always does out of habit ever since camp. Every time she hears the phrase "This and That" in any context she can't help point to This and That, a perversion of genuflection.

From Divorce till what? Death? Second Marriage? Is that redundant? Why? Do I really need to be married? That's what she's supposed to do, isn't it? Make up one half of a pair? The Fair Half, the submissive half. Unequal Halves? Is that a thing? From a pair into a family, a set and growing. *Look good to us ladies, so we want to put babies in you.* That's what we're for. Putting babies in. Here, hold this, oops, touched it last. Two and growing, barefoot, naked in the kitchen under just an apron showing off that cute butt. Wooden spoon in hand to stir up a piping hot serving of traditional values for her nuclear family man. Allison looks over at the Snow White snow globe. Walt always said, "Keep Moving Forward." *Where though, Walt? They say space is always expanding, but into what? Where, Walt? Sure Aunt Catherine knows, she takes it all on faith but I don't get it.* Allison melts flat like a puddle of glitter snow, trapped under the pressure of the water trapped on top of her. Under a giant dome. *Never Break Character,* Allison hears Camp Director telling her. Problem is she doesn't know who she is anymore - her whole life is a question. On pause. Pending definition. Pending divorce. The spotlight is blinding, all eyes on her but she can't see out, can't see *it*, just knows it's there, the first row, the mezzanine, the balcony, the lobby. It's behind the glare. Behind that blinding light at the end of the tunnel, they're watching, waiting to boo and hiss or laugh at her pain or offer love and approval with their applause. Love and hate can be so close. A standing ovation for ovulation. I bet they call it menopause because that's where the men all pause. No longer of use to them. On pause. The spotlight is blinding, nobody told her her lines, is she even in costume? Aren't we going to rehearse this?! Line please? Is this it? Is this...did I get it? Did I get the part? Who am I?! What's my line?! Allison sits and stares, her mind racing while the clock spins. When the bell starts ringing she picks up the clock and winds it up again. Tick. Tock.

Home For The Holidays

Act 1 Scene 4

Interior:Living Room, day

ALLISON is sitting in a chair in the middle of the room.

The chair they pull out for holiday visitors. Dark stained antique walnut with the ornate back. Allison always thought it looked like a harp. The small one that angels play. Allison sits still. The second hand on the two-bell alarm clock next to the Snow White snow globe upstairs pounds a slow, deep, echoing beat but the world speeds around her, a fast-forward montage. Halloween, Thanksgiving rush past her in the stiff wooden chair with the hideous red knit pillow on the seat. It's deceivingly useless, the pillow, as you can really feel every grain of the wood in your ass and the lip around the edge that holds in the useless pillow digs into the backs of your thighs like a medieval torture device. Good God, why on Earth do we give this God-awful chair to our guests?

Allison watches as the holidays speed past. Parades of gifts and bouquets of polite society in the suburbs. Tin foil covered dishes and cousins you've never heard of. Allison watches it all go by quietly, on VHS fast-forward on an old black-and-white tube with only one channel knob and a suspect at best vertical hold. Once it starts going you could wait it out. Sometimes it'll stop the endless scroll on its own, but not always. Sometimes you have to stomp on the floor or smack the top of the set. And when smacking it around doesn't change it's behavior you have to get down on the floor and fiddle with the V-hold knob.

Allison does not stomp her foot. She does not smack it. She sits and watches. She watches the scary masks parade by, the blood reigns, the candy showers. She's unphased by the neighborhood kids in their innocent costumes, nothing like the real masks we wear everyday, hiding the real monsters lying for applause,

"He's fucking a student." Allison bluntly tells her uncle's cousin's wife twice removed. Turkey legs swirl around doing the can-can dance. Frolicking, posing, stripping and dripping with brown-yellow fat-butter gravy. Allison licks her lips, chapping in the cool dry breeze of visiting relatives and dead leaves. She wipes the crumbs of Mother's famous Graveyard X-Mas Cookies, Mother's little holiday crossover joke that she tells when serving them with a lighthearted laugh as if it's the first time it had occurred to her. Allison stays detached. She would like to have less questions to answer. So far it isn't working as well as she'd like.

"Sure Uncle Whoever, my husband threw me out and tried to have me committed so he could fuck a student. Pass the nog."

"Hey Aunt Bea, 'the Hell are you? Yup, fucking a teenager, traded up for a newer model, Happy Kwanzaa, pass the chocolate chip pumpkin bread, please…?" Allison's extended family talk about her politely behind her back, behind their hands right in front of her like she isn't there.

"The whole thing was scandalous…" Mother laughs with a fake airy grace and smile. Mother defends Allison but with a coy and playful tone so nobody can tell if she's joking or not or who's side she's really on. *Her side. Her own side, so non-committal of you, thanks Mom.* "Merry Christmas…" a million Val Clarkes' sing, Carol caroling, doors slamming, swing open to cheers, chimneys, *Chim chiminey, chim chiminey, chim chim cher-ee.*

The party is starting to slow and it's just as well as Allison wants to get off. The tips of the floorboards slow against the deck, the bigger kids step off with pride and confidence out onto the blare of the midway before the carousel even slows down, before it can come to a complete stop. Every year on the carousel Allison tried to get off earlier than the year before. She watches as her antique torture chair and the living room floor slow to meet the deck, the carousel, the brass ring. *It's a new year, I'd better get an early start!* Allison quietly stands, softly apologizing to nobody, needlessly excusing herself. Invisible, she slips from the living room "Ten, nine, eight…" She counts down quietly to herself along with the bustle she withdraws from. "Seven, Six, Five…" She counts down the last steps to bed along with the party downstairs and Dick Clark on the black and white tube. "Four, Three…" The vertical hold lets go, is fixed with the stomping of revelers unnoticed over the handshakes and empty promises and resolute lies, "TWO!" Allison falls toward the pillow in her darkened room, Bret Michaels and Snow White watch silently. The moon twinkles off of a lone flake of glitter snow, "ONE! Happy New Year!!" They cheer from below. Allison sleeps.

Act 1 Scene 5

ALLISON sits down at the counter. An amplified voice from the back of the shop welcomes,
(v/o)
"...Roze to the stage."
A short Bohemian girl with red hair and heavily tattooed walks slowly to the microphone. Swinging her pale red locks in front of her face she sits on the stool, shyly reads a poem.

Allison laid about through the holidays. What began as family caring and sympathy has turned into cold denial. By the end of February Dad is done pretending she got in yesterday and is leaving tomorrow. Mother is simply overlooking it all. Allison's overstayed her welcome. She can feel it, in snide little comments, backhanded compliments and not-so-subtle directions out of here. When you need help your family will help you but eventually you have to start helping yourself. Allison needs a job. The coffee shop in Mohegan Lake, Cafe Ine, has a Help Wanted sign in the window. It's in a little strip mall with a Texas smoked meat joint, a hair salon, and a flooring outlet. It has all the contours and colors of a strip mall including the retail chum spots that turn over every couple of years featuring kitch clothing and such. There is also a pizza place because you really can't put up a strip mall without one. Not in New York anyway. It's in the building codes. This one has a notable quirk, which skyrocketed it to instant local infamy: A drive up window. A brilliant accident, the window wound up on the passenger side of the car due to the direction traffic needs to flow through the small parking lot. Convenient, as a pizza box can be difficult to pass over a steering wheel. Local legend suggests the building was designed to have a bank but a passenger side drive up window for banking doesn't work quite as well.

Allison had always felt like a visitor in her own house even as a kid, now it's much worse. Her relationship with them was always an awkward sort of strain, sort of like, well, trying to pass a pizza over a steering wheel. As an only child, once Allison was old enough to understand such things, got the impression that they were waiting to get their lives back when she turned 18. They would never admit to that but she's suspected she was an accident. A happy accident. Like the pizza place.

Allison is sitting on a corner stool nearly hidden from the rest of the shop, her back to the street. Cafe Ine sits at the end of the Mohegan Lake Main street, a stretch of state Route 6. Next door is an old decommissioned stone church, St. George's. After the church, Rte 6 goes off into Yorktown. Yorktown, where Allison is wearing thin her welcome. They aren't entirely wrong. Maybe they are. Maybe they were so cold she ran off at 18 and married the first older man who showed her...affection? No, that's not Louis. Security? No, she's not going to blame them. She can't blame them for Louis. Louis would certainly have none of that. He did that all on his own. That was his game. Everything is a game to Louis, he doesn't do anything by accident. Everything is carefully planned out.

The coffee Shop has an Italian cappuccino look to it, if that's really how it's done in Italy. A lot of gold round rails, mirrors, maps of Italy showing the regional cured meats. The meat posters look suspiciously like they belong in a pizza place. The counter is near the door and there is seating and a stage beyond the counter. The stage is visible from the covered sidewalk out the big front window. It hosts open mics for poetry and acoustic performances. Earthtones, weed, the smell of Patchouli, caffeine jitters, the epitome of the 90's. *I mean would it kill them to say something nice once in a while?* Allison sits quiet and shy in the corner, glancing over her shoulder now and then at the passing cars. The Lake they all used to summer at is around the corner. Untold horrors that Allison recalls. Her family used to go there with Carol and Louis' families every year for Labor Day. Carol and Louis were always cranky about it because they share a birthday with the holiday that always overshadowed them. Allison starts to feel her face redden. She feels invisible. The girl behind the counter is never going to turn around. *Hey you barista!* she shouts in her head but the words just won't come out. Allison is nearly getting up to leave, unable to speak up, be seen, she starts to vanish before her own eyes. Panicked, she looks at her hand, frantically turning it around and around, palm and back, she's disappearing!

The girl behind the counter finally turns, "Allison!?" The girl shouts with glee. Allison's eyes open wide, her mouth agape.

"Oh my God! Natalie!? Hi!" she blurts out excitedly, snapping back to reality.

"I haven't seen you since high school!" Natalie moved to Yorktown shortly after her mother remarried.

"You look great!" Allison always thought Natalie was very pretty, most people do and she still is, just stunning. Her smooth caramel skin practically invites you to pet her and her thick dark hair is shiny and confident. Allison feels a deep resonating chill in her gut, *Natalie still looks so pretty and I'm an old used up...sturdy gal.* When they were kids, Allison recalls Natalie was a lot of fun, but she was also mega boy crazy.

"So you're a barista? How long have you been here?" Allison looks around the shop, recalling a simpler time, she and Natalie sitting cross legged and wide eyed talking about a play.

"Oh yeah, this place? Cafe Ine is fun, I work here between shoots, I do porn." Allison feels an involuntary twinge of embarrassment at the word. *Porn.* Natalie was so blase about it. *Of course she's in porn. For Entertainment Purposes.*

Allison met Natalie near the end of elementary school and were close friends through high school. Never even had one fight. They rode the bus together -- Allison in 6th grade, Natalie in 5th. In the summers they went to Drama Camp together. They could walk to each other's houses and often did. Both girls felt a deep connection, a closeness with each other that they were both desperate for. They just wanted someone to like them for them. For nothing -- no reasons, no favors, no conditions. These two young girls bonded in humiliations. They got the one thing from each other that they couldn't seem to find anywhere else: Unconditional Love. They were never in competition, never even catty with each other. They had a few physical encounters. They certainly practiced kissing and experimenting, boys might call it third base. Dry humping in front of the TV in the downstairs family room at Natalie's house, *The Breakfast Club* playing on the VCR. They would pet on the couch and giggle, made out playfully until it would spill onto the carpet grinding together, pressing panty to panty, skirts pushed up, scrambling back up on the couch, straightening dresses and coughing as a cover if the basement door cracked open. "Watching a movie…" Natalie would crack when her mother inquired "What are you guys doing down there?" Allison can still hear Natalie's mom in her mom voice. Louis had said they were just experimenting and Allison and Natalie didn't think of it as lesbian or even a relationship -- just practice. No different than brushing each other's hair or braiding it. Shortly after graduation they simply lost touch. Allison had married Louis and moved to Gore. That was about five years ago.

Natalie puts a coffee down in front of Allison and puts her hands on Allison's hands, leans close, looks in her eyes. "Well, what are you up to? What are you doing here at Cafe Ine?"

Allison sips her coffee, sets it down. "I was out looking for a job…" Allison tells Natalie how she had to move back to Yorktown with her parents, the quick abridged version anyway, leaving out a lot of the lying around feeling sorry for herself but she can't stop coming back to Natalie. *Porn.* She is so confident. Allison wishes she could be that confident. *Porn.*

"You really married that creepy guy from across the street? I heard that, I wish I'd been at your wedding, but he was creepy, Al."

"Yeah, get a few drinks in me and I'll tell you all about how the creep across the street married me, took me out of town, isolated me for a few years and then kicked me out to the curb for a student."

"A student?! I get off in a few minutes, we're going out for a drink, my treat," Natalie sings. They plan to visit the little Irish cop bar down the street at Natalie's suggestion while a small crowd appears outside. A girl breaks off the crowd and comes inside.

"Hey can we hang this flyer in your window?" She extends a piece of paper to Natalie. She looks it over and nods handing it back.

"Sure go ahead, do you need tape?" The girls shakes her head no holding up a roll and taking the flyer back. She gives a thumbs up to the crowd outside who all wave and smile and mouth thank yous while the girl tapes the paper in the window.

"They want some guy to stay in jail." Natalie explains to Allison.

"What did he do?"

"Killed a girl, like 15 years ago."

When Natalie's shift ends they walk to her car. Allison hurriedly lights a cigarette on the short walk. As they pass the hair salon next door Natalie points in the window. "Remember Courtney?"

Allison looked in the window then at Natalie, "From camp?"

"Yeah she works in there, her boyfriend does too, he lives down the hill from me, say they got this Chinese lady in there doing eyebrow threading, she's great, she can clean that all up for you…" Natalie gestures to Allison's eyebrows. Allison looks at her reflection in the window of the dark flooring place. *What's wrong with my eyebrows?* Natalie has already moved on in the conversation.

"We have so much to catch up on!" She's saying as she pushes the unlock button on her key fob. A shiny silver Mazda Miata blinks and beeps to life in front of Allison, "Come on, get in."

Act 1 Scene 6

COURTNEY is washing a woman's hair at a sink. Next to her a young boy, MARCO washes another woman's hair.
Beat
(Camera focus out window, fades back away from window) Outside Natalie and Allison walk past on their way to Natalie's car.

(Popular modern hard rock plays throughout the shop at an Avante-Gardely high volume. It's edgy and modern. Steve at the counter clad in a leather jacket is there for image as much as reception. A large glass tank at the front of the shop houses a rotation of edgy reptiles. A child favorite has been the chameleons, Sam and Ella.)

MARCO:
I think I'm gay.

"Are you coming out to me again?" Courtney doesn't look up from the shampoo she is lathering into her customers scalp. "You go in and out of the closet like you're playing hide and seek with your sexuality, Marco." Marco's pimply face reddens a bit and he shares a glance at his shampooee while shyly brushing aside a curl of dyed-blue hair.

"I think I have a crush on Steve's roommate."

"Bruce or Hemis?"

"Bruce. Hemis is too tall, not my type."

Steve is Courtney's boyfriend. He is the leather-clad receptionist at the front counter and a professional BMX rider. He's 27. He's been dating Courtney, who is only 19, for three years. Bruce and Hemis are Steve's roommates, both have also worked at the hair salon.

Bruce is a glass blower. He is small in stature with pale freckled skin and deep red hair. His sardonic wit is often politically charged and he likes to take mushrooms and LSD. In the future he will be mildly famous for 15 internet minutes for a viral video in which he sings a parody of Springsteen's "Born in the USA" as a song about artificial insemination.

Hemis is an aspiring actor. Tall, muscular, he works out and is also a semi-professional wrestler. They sell weed on the side mostly to friends for extra cash and free bud for themselves.

Steve has been riding BMX professionally since he was a preteen. Right now he is showing off at the front of the shop to a regular customer. Courtney and Marco seat their washes and Courtney takes the woman, rescuing her from Steve who is waving a magazine that he was showing her.

"He was showing me a ladies' magazine..." she tells Courtney with a hand over her mouth for modesty, "...with naked men in it!" she exclaimed.

"Did he show you the picture of himself? He's been waving that thing around all week." In this particular spread of Steve's, his hands are tied behind his back. He is on his knees, legs apart and a woman in six-inch stiletto heels is stepping on his balls.

"Don't you date him?" The woman asks. Courtney nods. "Aren't you a little *young* for him?" Courtney nods again and shrugs. Steve was too old for her when they met but Courtney didn't care. She was just getting out of a notorious school and vulnerable, volatile, self destructive.

He was, to quote from a treasured 80s movie, "outstanding in that capacity" as she, along with thousands of kids over the years, had been sent to this school for behavioral problems. Courtney had been sent there as a last resort by her deeply religious parents but behind closed doors, unspeakable horrors went on for years. Recently the school made national headlines as dozens of people from current students in their teens to alumni in their 50s came forward with personal firsthand accounts of the atrocities, from cruel intimidation to molestation.

It had never been a secret to Courtney that she was adopted but something changed when she reached her pre-teens and that knowledge turned a corner with her identity. One day the seed was planted, that nagging doubt, that unanswerable question: *Who am I?* The only shred of evidence she's had is a tattered old piece of lined stationary, once a childish and whimsical orange but has now yellowed with age. It has cartoonish smiling faces in the margins and a sloppy vague note written by a scared 16-year old girl. "Who am I?" a question unanswered by the cryptic letter from her birth mother, it became an obsession that manifested in wild behavior, sexual promiscuity, and an overall identity crisis. Courtney would change her hair color and style so often she started buying wigs almost obsessively. But no matter how many disguises she puts on she can't figure out who she really is.

Marco walks back to the sinks guiding two ladies, a woman in her late 30s and her 13 year-old daughter. Courtney and Marco each take one to a sink and start washing.

"You need to get Sheng Nu to do those eyebrows girl." Marco tells Courtney.

Courtney looks up from the young girl's wash. "That. That's why you don't have to keep coming out Marco, we know."

"Straight boys don't notice your eyebrows need to be threaded, do they?"

Courtney thinks for a second. "They might not notice if I had a fucking caterpillar on my forehead."

The older woman sits up a little and tells Courtney, "That's not usually where they're looking, honey."

"MOM!?" The young girl protests, embarrassed, but Courtney looks down with a nod, brows raised, she has to agree.

Drama Camp 1992

(overhead v/o Courtney, singing Anything Goes)
Interior: Auditorium

Young Elizabeth walks into the Jewish Community Center on Old Crompond road where drama camp meets. Her babysitter Allison encouraged her to come. Today is her first day. Elizabeth sees Allison by a table, she waves. Allison waves Elizabeth over. Seated next to her is the camp director. Elizabeth is noted and tagged, sent to wait on the stage in a line with the rest of the campers auditioning. Camp Director stands, walks to the middle of the first row, looks left and right taking in the new recruits, and familiar young faces.

(v/o stops)

"Never Break Character!" She enunciates loudly. "If today is your first day that was the first of many many times you will hear me say that: Never Break Character. That is my number one rule. It's also my number two AND three rules. Never. Break. Character." Allison is mouthing it along next to her out of drilled practice and admittedly, a little bit of sarcasm. Elizabeth notices and giggles slightly. Camp Director looks at Allison who stands straight faced, eyes front. Slight grin. She glares at Elizabeth when Camp Director looks back at the kids. She acknowledges Allison with a gesture, "Some of you know Allison, if you don't, here she is...been with us for six years?" She looks at Allison. Allison shakes her head, corrects,

"Seven."

"Seven years. This is her first year offstage, and she will be co-directing with me." A phone rings, once, twice. Natalie comes out from backstage with a cordless phone in her hand. She walks to the front of the stage.

"It's Courtney." She leans into the audience and hands Camp Director the phone. Natalie is dressed in an all-black oversized stage crew shirt. She notices Elizabeth, smiles, waves, mouths, "Hello," before walking offstage and into the audience.

'Hello? Uh huh....OK. OK, we'll see you next week sweetie.." She hands the phone back to Natalie and she leans toward Allison's clipboard, tapping it roughly with a chubby finger, "Courtney is playing Reno. They are on vacation, she'll be here next week." A few groans sound out at this news. "I thought she might want that part. Reno's a real...hit with the fellas." She laughs but then frowns at Natalie, rolls her eyes. Allison catches the look disapprovingly.

People conduct themselves with a level of inappropriate behavior that is deemed acceptable. We encourage it, frown upon it and still perpetuate it all at the same time. There is a constant emission of these mixed messages. The fact remains that Natalie's performance last year "Hadn't left a flacid man in the house." Someone had put with a dry distaste at the time. Natalie revels in her abuse. She invites it, quite literally. Less Jack Litman and more Hollywood Come Hither. A wink and a curled finger.

Elizabeth wonders how this Courtney gets a part without even an audition? *She must be the queen bee around here.* Elizabeth glances around at the grimaces. She might have to watch out. Fortunately Elizabeth also knows what she wants, which happens to NOT be Reno. Elizabeth prepared by watching the 1963 black-and-white movie a few times on VHS. She will be auditioning for the part of Hope Harcourt. The famous debutante, the object of desire, the prize between the two male leads. Sort of.

As auditions start, Natalie, banished to the shadows of the stage crew since last year's scandal, is begging Camp Director.

"Can't I at least audition?"

"No."

"Come on, just let me audition, you'll see, please, I want to audition for the part of Bonnie…"

"Absolutely not." Camp Director looks Natalie up and down, pictures stuffing her very developed...This and That into a skin tight flapper dress, curves pouring out everywhere. *They'd run me out of this town.* She shudders.

"Can I at least have choreography?"

"Fine. You can overlook choreography this year. And stage crew."

Allison is pointing to the clipboard. "Elizabeth." She tells Camp Director. Camp Director turns to the stage and calls for Elizabeth, who walks out on the stage. There is nobody else in the auditorium other than Camp Director, Allison and Natalie. Elizabeth pictures the seats filled.

Adoring faces cheer for her. The applause dies down, the spotlight shines warm on her face, she smiles, "Get on with it Margret." Allison nudges Camp Director.

"Elizabeth."
"Elizabeth."

(v/o Courtney Anything Goes refrain, big finish)

Act 1 Scene 7

Interior:Car-day

ALLISON sitting in the passenger seat, NATALIE is driving.

Her calm demeanor is a stark contrast to her driving. Unsettlingly calm for these speeds and maneuvers. She drives way too fast, as if she is evading police fleeing a crime scene, all while speaking calm and matter of factly. Allison clings to the door with her right arm and the side of the bucket seat with her left. She smiles politely nodding as Natalie happily chatters on about how much she loves her car. Allison is terrified. She looks Natalie up and down searching for corporate logos. Allison can see her and Natalie in the #18 car on a TV at the Hooters bar in Syracuse. Bubble Tits jiggles her ta-tas in Allison's face with her hands impossibly overfilled with frothy golden beer in half-gallon steins. Red baskets with red-and-white wax-paper tablecloths cradle mountains of steaming chicken wings, glistening with hot grease, dripping with spicy red hot sauce all around her. Allison looks around frantically, Natalie is oblivious to the hot sauce and blue cheese that appears to drip from and shower down on her. She's calm as can be.

"I got this car after my first film. They pay a lot of money, porn…" Car lights flash by at high speeds, horns Doppler away as Natalie weaves through traffic, dangerously passing in the turning lane. Allison gasps as a car barely scrapes by on their right, she can see right into the passenger seat, she can count the thread fibers in the seat cushion. Their car speeds past the number 8 car, the Exxon Mobil car, the Mountain Dew car. Another car spins out behind them and explodes in a fireball on the wall. Checkered flags rain down in a tornado…Natalie yanks the car into the parking lot at the last second.

"Allison!" Natalie yells, "Allison? Hello? We're here. I told you it was only down the road."

Act 1 Scene 7.2

Interior: Brodie's Pub, evening

NATALIE walks confidently across the room toward the bar. ALLISON follows.

NOEL:

My beautiful Natalie, how are you, my dear?

The bartender greets her as the girls sit.

"Why Detective Noel Hill, you're so sweet!" Natalie stands on the rail, leans over the bar and kisses the bartender on his cheek, teasingly close to his quivering lips, "This is my friend Allison." When he moves away to get them drinks Allison leans over and whispers, "This is a cop bar?"

Natalie nods. "I stop here for a drink a few nights a week on my way home, flirt with the cops a little, so, you know...I don't get tickets."

Allison's eyes widen, "You have sex with them?!" She tries to whisper but it comes out too loud and she looks around in astonishment.

Natalie giggles. "Well it's not like they pass me around in back or anything, I've hooked up with a few here and there, whatever comes naturally you know...?" Allison looks toward the bartender, on his way back with their drinks, Natalie shakes her head, "Noel? I could *never*. He's so sweet." She puts her hand on his cheek as he arrives and repeats, "Noel's so sweet." He blushes, obviously smitten with Natalie. Allison scans around the bar. Only a few people are at the bar, a few more at tables around the room. Allison can only guess but they look like families out for dinner at the pub. Dads, moms, two-point-four kids. Traditional Irish folk music plays from the jukebox at a respectable dinner conversation level. The bartender slides down the bar, tending to his customers who are Belly Up as he exclaims to one who came in after Allison and Natalie. Natalie sips her drink daintily glancing around with an air of innocence,

"Isn't this place cute?" She bats her eyes and spins away playfully on her stool, sucking out the last drops of her Sex On The Beach. She looks comically innocent as if she might just as well be drinking a Shirley Temple. She jiggles her ice and chest at Noel who is engaged with a Belly Up in conversation, about which Allison doesn't hear save for the last words he says before sliding back down the bar to take Natalie's glass,

"...from sperm to worm." The phrase strikes Allison with a curious wonder, wonder at how neatly the words and their meanings fit together, wonder if this burly tough looking bartender knows he is quoting showtunes, but mostly wonder at how fun of a phrase it is to say. She finds herself repeating it in her head, substituting words 'balls to dirt,' 'cradle to grave,' 'sperm to worm.'

Natalie puts her fresh drink down with a sip and caresses Allison arm, "OK, now tell me about Louis." Allison quickly puts her drink to her mouth to buy time, shakes her head, glances around for a hole to crawl into.

Natalie puts her hand on Allison's knee, looks deep into her eyes, "Allison. I'm in porn. You're way ahead on bombshells here babe, you're gonna have to give me more than 'I guess mumble mumble, divorce mumble mumble, other woman, mumble.' Come on girl, get mad! Tell me what happened to you."

"I guess it just starts to feel like it was all one big manipulation. I don't know, it's like I can't tell what was Louis pulling strings and what was just the universe unfolding on it's own. And I think that's what he wanted, that confusion. Maybe he did, maybe he didn't. And I'd never know and that would drive me nuts or something. He told me I was going crazy. Like medically. Certifiable." Allison lets out a long exhale and sighs, settles into her high backed swivel stool, "Sometimes I wonder if I am."

"So where does this other woman figure in?"

Allison rolls her eyes. "It's just so…" She takes a deep breath, "embarrassing."

Natalie raises an eyebrow. "Embarrassing? That's all on you girl. You know what the difference between factory pleather and those soft-ass real leather seats in the car?" She dangles her car keys, "Anal. I did anal in a movie for the leather seats."

Allison tries to steer the conversation in another direction. "Remember how Camp Director always used to say 'Never Break Char--'"

"Hush! Character, yeah yeah, you stay in character, you're still not answering my questions, who was this other woman?"

Allison looks around the room nervously as if what she has to say actually means anything to the other patrons. She sighs.

The bartender catches Natalie's movements in his peripherals. "You girls need anything, Nat?"

Natalie shakes her head playfully, "Not yet Noel, thanks sweetie."

"When I met Louis he was practically asexual. When he did start to loosen up the slightest bit it was like I was drawing it out of him, like I tapped a well. It didn't come fast -- not with me -- but it did sort of feel like I sparked a heat in him." Allison paused, calculated, contemplated. "But when we moved up to Gore he started changing more rapidly. One day he stopped cutting his hair. I mean woke up and declared it, 'I'm not cutting my hair anymore' and from then on didn't get another haircut, just like that, after how many decades of the same haircut, once a week. He started smoking pot and hanging out with students. Innocent at first, hanging around the common campus areas, reading or whatever. Then one day he comes home with a guitar. One of those hollow, light yellow wooden acoustic guitars. Bought it at the little shop in town. Declared he was going to play guitar and spent the next two weekends in his study reading books and plucking at the strings. He comes out the second Sunday night playing a few recognizable modern hits and some timeless classics, which he called 'standards' like a seasoned vet on the lounge act circuit. Then he started bringing a student home. A girl. The other woman. She had only turned 18 that past spring." Natalie sits riveted to Allison's story, eyes wide, sips her drink dry with a loud wet sucking noise. Across the bar Noel punches in the code in the jukebox to play a song called "Natalie" from a TV show that he always plays when she comes in. A more delicate and poetic man might call it unrequited love, an older father figure man and the beautiful young girl he is hopelessly in love with. He hears the empty drink and comes to the call, putting two more drinks in front of them. When Natalie reaches for her pile of cash he puts his hand on top of hers gently, "These are on me sweet Natalie."

Natalie bats her eyes and turns back to Allison. "So I had a husband, we're divorced too. We have two kids."

Allison nearly spits her drink out."You have two kids!? I think that's more shocking than the porn!" They laugh together.

When their drinks are empty and it's time to go Natalie takes some of her cash and leaves Noel a sizable tip, waving him over.

"We're going sweetie, thanks." She leans over the bar and gives him a passionate gentle kiss, half on lip, half stubble cheek. Natalie leans back looking coy, says, "Thank you." once more before looking at Allison with her *I Dare You* look, "Go on Al, give Noel a kiss." Allison leans over the bar pushing into Noel's personal space. She breathes in the essence of his aftershave, leans in close and kisses him full on the mouth, passionately but without tongue. A primal heat surges in Allison as she grabs his face with both hands still kissing him. Finally she leans back. "Thanks for the drink." She says cooly.

The two girls walk out of the bar in silence together. When the car door shuts Natalie bursts. "Oh my God, girl! I meant on the cheek! Fuck!"

Allison looks at Natalie with a sly grin,"Not two days ago would I have done that. This morning I might not have done that. Honestly I have no idea where that came from."

Natalie turns right out of the bar down the hill toward Peekskill. Allison points back in the other direction,"But my car…?"

"Fuck that, let's go to my apartment and party more, I'll bring you to your car tomorrow, it'll be fine at the shop." She drives into Peekskill and up into Eastland Apartments.

Eastland
Act 1 Scene 7.5

ALLISON and NATALIE stand before the front doors.

NATALIE:
There it is, Al, Eastland. Allison whistles as she scans the supposedly haunted old mansion and mutters,

ALLISON:
Take the good you take the bad…

"...And there you have the facts of life." Natalie finishes the theme. Beyond Eastland, the majestic Hudson river twinkles in the moonlight. Peekskill bay laps gently at the riverfront green.

"So Natalie, where's Tootie?"

Natalie laughs as though the connection never occurred to her, "My last Tootie moved out," Natalie smiles, "Say, Al," she says with a clearly devious innocence, "Why don't you move in with me?"

Allison loves the idea and is starting to suspect that idea did not just occur to Natalie. "I don't have a job yet..." She starts to point out.

Natalie's way ahead of her. "I can just get you a job --"

"In porn?"

"-- at Cafe Ine, silly." Natalie grins.

"But not in porn right?" Allison laughs.

Natalie laughs too, adds,"You should! But no, I meant the coffee shop."

Allison thinks about Eastland, they watched that show all the time. "Do you remember...?"

"Of course I do." Natalie smiles and both girls squeal,

"Green Eyed Monster!" That particular episode had rung comically true with the politics of the social construct at Drama Camp.

"Come on up, we'll have some wine."

A near empty wine bottle sits proudly on the table between them. Natalie on the loveseat, Allison sprawled across the sofa. She had held out some hope of getting back to her car and home to her parents house but after half a bottle of wine, Natalie's sofa is starting to sound like a great place to sleep. She didn't really want to go back to that house anyway.

"It's a sleepover!" Natalie giddily declares when Allison gets real and calls it.

"That's it. I'm drunk."

"It'll be like we're in middle school."

"I was not drinking in middle school."

"No silly, the sleepover part."

"Should I braid your hair?" Allison slurs with a giggle. "Hey! Do you have any Kool-Aid?"

"Oh my God, do you remember? It worked so much better on your light hair, only the dark greens and dark reds would stick to my hair."

"And then I would go home and my mother would say," Allison puts on her mom voice, "What's wrong with you, don't you want boys to like you?" Allison snorts, "It's not my hair, I'd tell her." She thinks for a moment, recalls, "Do you remember that time we went to Chuck E. Cheese?"

Natalie rolls her eyes. "They were so weird," she chuckles " sorry about that." She adds sheepishly.

"I could almost understand thinking we might not want to play any games, we were in middle school but your little brother wanted to play." Allison thinks about how Natalie's mother and stepfather had taken them to Chuck E. Cheese just for pizza and then they left without playing any games. "There's so many places that have pizza, much better pizza, and Chuck E. Cheese was kind of far, my parents were pissed, I didn't tell them, I didn't know though, why go all the way to Connecticut for shitty pizza…?" Allison laughs. "And they wouldn't let me call my parents!"

"I know!" Natalie laughs, "It was like we were kidnapping you."

"Wanna see a trick?" Natalie giggles getting up, changing the subject. She wobbles toward the kitchen. "Look at my trick." She says pulling a banana from a hanging fruit basket. She slides the banana right down her throat until only the stem is sticking out her mouth "Gloopheee" She muffles over the mouthful pointing to the bulge in her throat. Grasping the stem she wiggles it up and down a few times then pulls it out, holds it up with a smile, "Ta-Da!" Allison amused and a little disgusted can only laugh, "It comes in handy at work." Natalie adds with a giggle.

"Nat, you're so goofy, it's adorable. I don't think most people really know that about you."

Natalie smiles shyly. "People think I'm just a slut but that's not my personality. It's more like…my hobby." She laughs and Allison laughs with her. A good hard laugh. That and the wine makes Allison a little dizzy. Allison looks fondly on Natalie, thinking of school,

"Didn't you try out for cheerleaders squad one year?"

Natalie laughs,"Yeah could you imagine? Bee Aggressive! Bee E Aggressive!" She pumps her fists in the air and shakes her shoulders, swings her hips.

"Why didn't you make the squad?" Allison asks, as if she doesn't remember.

"You know. Those evil bitches blabbed all over school."

"No, what happened?"

"Oh my God it was so embarrassing, I tried to do my cartwheel move I was working on, remember it?"

Allison nods quickly giggling, holding it in best she can. "I remember you were like, obsessed with cartwheels," She manages straight faced.

"Right? I put together a whole routine with my special cartwheel move in it, I worked so hard on that for that tryout. So embarrassing, my cartwheel was so nice it was perfect but I misjudged and when I landed I banged right into one of those big grey garbage cans and fucking fell in fucking ass first!"

Allison nearly falls off the couch as she howls with laughter. Natalie playfully tosses a pillow at her. "So embarrassing." She repeats. "Remember how we used to practice kissing?" Natalie smiles, teasing seductively. Allison blushes, her heart races. This time it's Allison's turn to be embarrassed. Natalie makes everything sound so sexy. Allison stares longingly into Natalie's sexy mouth, imagines kissing her right now. She feels warm, flush all over as Natalie licks her lips in slow motion, she gets lost in it. Natalie is oblivious to it, breaks the spell as she clicks on the TV.

"Want to watch some TV?" Allison feels silly, laughs at herself, blinks away the fantasies. The wine is taking hold, taking over, pulling her under. The big fluffy couch hugs her, she sinks in, warm, drifting off to sleep on the couch, classic TV reruns sing her off.

'When the world never seems…" Allison sleeps, "To be living up to your dreams…" She does not dream.

Act 1 Scene 8

Interior: Living Room, morning

ALLISON wakes up on the couch, neck stiff. The smell of coffee percolates through the room.

Allison awakes to the rising of bile in her throat, darts off the couch to the hall bathroom. She barfs up the last few glasses of wine, her retching sounds hammer at her temples with long dry, hollow coughs echoing in the bowl, tearing out what feels like her esophagus. She shuffles out of the bathroom deflated and mildly humiliated. Natalie appears not to notice but Allison knows she had to hear, she can still now hear the toilet finish filling and that's not nearly as loud as she just was screaming into it. Nonetheless, Natalie is unphased, standing in the kitchen in her short nightshirt, stirring her coffee. She isn't wearing any panities and the bottom of her butt cheeks are peeking out. She hands Allison a steaming cup of fresh aromatic coffee. Allison surrenders to it, closing her eyes she inhales the scent, sips the nectar, sitting back down on the couch.

"So do you want that job?" I have off today so we have all day to hang out. I'll call Marc now and we'll talk to him when we go get your car." Natalie is too cheery for Allison's head but it would sure be nice to get a job.

"You can just tell him like that?" It sounds too good to be true and when things are to good to be true it's usually because it isn't. *Louis was too good to be true and look how that turned out.* Natalie saunters off into her bedroom to use the phone. When she comes back she announces, "You got the job, kid." She says with an ambiguous accent and a playful nudge.

"Doing what?" Allison plays along, "Distributing stacks of newspapers yelling 'extree, extree read all about it!'?"

"Come on let's go get your car and you can meet the manager, Marc. He totally has a crush on me." Natalie smiles and sips her coffee. Allison recalls fantasizing last night about making out with her, feels a slight tinge of embarrassment. "It's kind of mean, I know, cuz I do lead him on a little and shit." Natalie mimes oral sex, "You know...keep him on a leash. He loves it."

Allison smiles but decidedly does NOT know. If anything she's always been the one on the leash, not the one holding it.

"*I* want to hold the leash for a change..." She mutters to herself quietly. Natalie grins, Allison's not sure if she heard her and was grinning at that or not,

"He was trying really hard the other day…" She pauses, smiles, repeats "Hard" with a giggle. "He kept desperately pressing it up against my leg at the counter…"

"You just blow him!?" Allison blurts, the idea finally sinking in. Natalie is so casual about it.

"I mean, he's not really my type," Allison noticed a long time ago, back when they were kids, that Natalie's "type" was a broad term. "I felt his eyes all over me for like the first week I worked there, so one night we closed up and I was sitting on his desk." Natalie climbs onto the coffee table in front of Allison, "I admit it, I was showing off, crossing and uncrossing my legs," She slowly slides one leg over the other back and forth. Allison bites her lip and blinks awkwardly at Natalie. "He was all nervous and trying to hide it but he had nowhere to go." Natalie leans in close to Allison and looks hard and serious into her eyes, "I said to him, 'do you need help with that?' Just like that." Natalie swings her leg over Allison's head, puts her feet together and hops off the table, "I hopped off his desk and slipped him out of his khakis, I bent over and put it in my mouth. I leaned over and stuck out my butt like this," She leans over at the waist with her legs straight, knees bent back some, gives her butt a wiggle and pretends to fellate Allison as if she had a dick. "I only gave it a couple of strokes and I could tell he was going to bust so I let it fall out my mouth and he came on the floor." She smiles and takes a breath. "I gave it a playful little tap on the head and watched it bounce. He winced because it was all sensitive and I was like, 'Bye, see you tomorrow.' Since then I really just have to look at him with my mouth open -- you know, Blowjob face -- and he'll do whatever I want. I guess that's what I do right?" Allison can't help agree, the world pretty much gets what it wants from Natalie, always has.

Allison's thoughts suddenly turn to Natalie's stepfather and shudders at how creepy he was. She had always suspected...something. Like he...got what *he* wanted from Natalie.

They finished their coffee, put themselves together and drove at race speeds back up to Mohegan Lake. Allison gets her car and a job and while she's in the area grabs her bag from her parents house that she never really unpacked, leaving a note:

"Mom, moving in with Natalie, remember her? Got a job in Mohegan Lake, apartment in Peekskill, be back for the rest of my stuff in a couple of days. Call you later, Allison."

Act 1 Scene 8.2

Interior: Bedroom,day

ALLISON is standing before the
bed.

It has a crisp clean white fitted top sheet, no other bedding, blankets or pillows. A blanket is just another one of those things people take for granted until they realize they don't have one. Natalie said when her last roommate moved out she threw away everything she'd left behind, flipped the mattress and put on this one clean spare sheet. "She was gross, you don't even want to know."

Allison did not want to know. Actually she does want to know. She figures she'll have to pry into it later. "It'll be fine tonight. Tomorrow I'll have to go out and get some bedding." It will do. For tonight.

Allison drops her bag to the floor, looks around. Besides the bed there is nothing else in the room. A blank slate. Just like Allison. Not much, just her and her stuff. Not much. Just like Allison. She quietly undresses, dropping her clothes to the floor without care. She looks around again in her newfound nakedness. Naked, free, with nothing. She kicks her pants across the room and plops down on the bed, lays there spread eagle, her few possessions strewn about without order. Anarchy. Well, sort of. It's not exactly anarchy. She smiles. She slowly slides her naked body around on the crisp fresh sheet. *Natalie is in porn.* She imagines a repair man giving it to Inka. "There's yer problem, ma'am." She wiggles her hips trying to feel sexy. *Come fix my sink,* she thinks in a poorly imagined Russian accent. "I'm gonna fix your piping, lady." Allison finds herself kneeling on the bed humping Inka with her repairman's dick. Feeling silly she looks around the empty room. *What's wrong with me?* When she'd dreamt up the fictional porn identity it was not a real thing. People in porn weren't even *real* to Allison. She imagined that was how other people generally felt as well. They aren't real. Just out there. *For Our Entertainment.* But now, Allison is on the inside. Through the looking glass. Down the Yellow Brick Road. She knows a real person who is in real porn. She and Natalie grew up together. Either porn stars are real people or Allison's fake too. A cool epiphany panics her quickly and she glances in disbelief at her hand, turning it over. *I'm not disappearing am I?* Satisfied she's real and whole, she roots in her bag for a t-shirt and a pair of sweatpants, pulling them on. She goes out to the kitchen to see what Natalie is up to.

"So I start training you tomorrow." Natalie informs Allison as she walks into the room, "What do you want to do today?"

Allison looks at the bottle of wine on the counter. "How about some of that coffee?" Natalie sets about fixing a pot. Allison sits at the kitchen island, plucks a deck of cards out of a basket of oddities and shuffles absently. She looks down into a box of her stuff next to her on the floor. "Hey I brought my old Nintendo, do you want to play, uh…" She looks down, stirs around in the games, "Mario brothers, Tetris, Dr. Mario…"

Natalie turns around quickly at the counter, amused. "You used to love Dr. Mario, you were always playing that." She laughs.

Allison holds a cartridge up to her face. "I could never get the Nintendo Blow to work for me." She blows gently across the open end of the game.

Natalie grabs the game in a huff. "No," She scolds, "You look like you're blowing magick glitter off of a faerie's eyelash, you have to give it a good hard burst. *Booosh!*" She blows hard in Allison's face. A gentle spray of saliva leaves a few thin drops on Allison's face. Stunned she freezes, Natalie unphased dabs the drops off with her sleeve as if it were nothing and continues her theory, "You have to get the dust off the electric receptors that the eye reads on the game."

Allison realizes her bedding situation, if she is training tomorrow they better go shopping today. "You want to go shopping today? Since we can't go tomorrow now?"

Natalie smiles and nods emphatically at the idea of shopping. Allison is a crisp new naked doll for the dressing and while Natalie might not have put that kind of thought into it, despite sexism and marketing and patriarchy and feminism, sometimes some girls really do love to play dress up with dolls. They may also love pink. Allison is like a life-size Barbie on Christmas with a dream house to fill with clothes and accessories. Where to go first? Natalie wonders aloud mumbling ideas. There is one of those Mandy/Marshall/To-The-Max stores in the new Towne Center... that kitchy modern place next to the coffee shop...then there's the mall…Before Natalie can nail down a starting point for their shopping excursion the phone rings.

"Hello?" Natalie scoops the receiver, cradles it on her shoulder not breaking eye contact with Allison. She frowns slightly, "No there's no Jane Wenham here. Sorry." She shakes her head, "No problem." She hangs up and says to Allison, "Wrong number." It was all she had to say, and the memories rush back, flooding the room. Both Allison and Natalie light up and blurt at each other together, "Keegan!"

After all these years neither can remember who made the call, either Natalie or Keegan was trying to call somebody else and got the other instead. A wrong number. Natalie was always boy crazy, she's very flirty all the time with the boys and this was no exception. She got to flirting with Keegan and they decided to set a date. A blind date from a wrong number. "Horror movies start this way," Allison had protested but it was happening and Allison was going too. Keegan was bringing his friend so it was a double blind date. Natalie told Keegan to meet them in front of the mall in an hour. She must have had him worked up pretty good flirting breathlessly into his horny teen ear. They walked down to the mall as it wasn't far. The mall has a big two-story glass entrance and a theater inside under the food court. Allison sees two boys get out of a car a realizes that they drove there.

"I don't know...?" Was Natalie's thin excuse-slash-defense as the boys walked toward them. One was tall and skinny, somewhere in that awkward phase where he's not quite boy, not quite man either. Keegan was the taller one and more lanky than his buddy, who is actually named Buddy. the stockier one with shaggy blond hair. It's a little greasy and a bit of a mess. Buddy has the beginnings of chest hair and he tries to show it off with a button-down shirt, unbuttoned a little too far. He grossly picks at pimples in the sparse tufts of man on his boy chest. He puffs his chest out like it's muscle and he carries himself like he has more muscle than he clearly doesn't. Keegan's hair is darker, more neatly combed but just as greasy as his compadre's. He walks with a jerky rhythm, arms and legs jangling, still unaccustomed to his newly lengthened limbs.

Allison and Buddy are both anxious and awkward about the whole thing. Allison also quickly picks up that Keegan and Buddy have no idea that she and Natalie are in middle school. Natalie's going into seventh grade, Allison, eighth. Keegan and Buddy are obviously in high school, maybe 17 or 18. Buddy plans to vote in November, he'd said as much. The four of them decide quickly on a movie at the front entrance and duck inside. Allison wants to go see *Cry Baby* and Buddy wants to go see *Back To The Future III* but Keegan and Natalie just want to go make out and they decide on *Arachnophobia* since it's PG and starting now, despite Allison's protests about her own arachnophobia. Allison and

Buddy sit in uncomfortable silence and watch the movie, trying with all their might not to glance at Keegan and Natalie beside them. She practically leapt into his lap as soon as the lights went down, making out hot and heavy right away, groping at each other with a hurried desperation. By the time the opening credits end Natalie is on the floor blowing Keegan. His hands are buried deep in her panties. If only he could see they are Hello Kitty panties, he might start thinking she looks a little young, it's dark in the theater. Allison, terrified of spiders, tries not to look at the screen too much. She neither wants to be looking at the display going on next to her nor does she want to give Buddy any ideas. Then there were the three idiots in the theater behind them who kept screaming "Goodman!" at the top of their lungs everytime the actor John Goodman appears on screen. Natalie is furiously sucking Keegan's dick, every wet slurp echoes louder and louder, humiliating Allison, each loud suck pulling at her as if she was experiencing it the way Keegan was.

"That was crazy Natalie!" Allison blurts out, snapping back to present. "They were so gross!" She adds, laughing.

"I liked the attention Al," Natalie confesses coyly. She turns away as a far off look creeps quickly over her face, making her look younger and more vulnerable.

"Nat…?" Allison senses she'd touched a nerve, "Are you OK?" Natalie shakes it off and tries to put on a happy face but the residue remains. That's the best way Allison can describe it: There is a *residue* left on Natalie's face -- maybe fear, maybe sadness, whatever it was she can't quite place it but it was in that theater. Allison once again reverted back to thoughts about Natalie's stepfather, how she always felt a creepy feeling based on what she noticed as a kid but couldn't quite understand why. Now those hints and clues are pointing in bright spotlights with big neon flashing arrows. Natalie's promiscuity, her sexual aggression, all the attention she sought was a reaction. Of course -- it was a self defense. At least she *chose* to blow Keegan, plus all the other boys lucky enough to be in the right place at the right time with their eager penises to offer the pretty girl with stepdaddy issues. They didn't care that she was acting out just that she was putting out...who cares why?

"Still, I can't believe you hooked up with him, they were so…" Allison thinks about Keegan and Buddy standing there in front of the mall. *Greasy.* She laughs and snorts when she does. She covers her mouth and laughs harder, snorting again. Natalie laughs at Allison, snorting too, which makes Allison snort again and it starts all over. When Natalie can compose herself enough she adds,

"And then I saw him a few weeks later!" Natalie howls between fits of giggles.

"Right!" Allison had forgotten about the Second Sighting Of Keegan. Natalie's blind date was in the summer, early July. She was going into 7th grade and her orientation was at the end of August.

"We walked in as a group and he was mopping a hall right near the main entrance." Natalie recalls Keegan's working at the middle school with a grin, "I saw him and I was going to say 'hi' but when he saw me smiling he looked mortified because he realized I was just starting there." She laughs, "It's kind of funny, right?"

"Statutory rape? Yeah, it's hilarious." Allison deadpans.

"Fwop" Natalie tosses a dish towel at Allison.

"Fwop!? Oh my God!" Allison laughs, "I haven't heard Fwop in years!"

Fwop was one of those regional slang words. At first it had meant to be an imitation of a pussy fart. A queef. Through repeated use in the halls and passing it to siblings and babysittees it became a slang term for a girl in general, used around Lakeland High School and the Shrub Oak area. The more crass girls used it on each other.

"Fwop!" They yelled together laughing and smiling with glee,

"I think a kid in my class took credit for Fwop." Allison thought,

"I think a kid in *every* class tried to take credit for Fwop." Allison said, tossing the towel back.

"I think I got it from my Homeroom." Natalie admitted.

"It was all over my class." Allison said, "Then there was YOY..."

Natalie cocked her head to the side like when a dog hears a high-pitched noise. "You fucking fwop!" She laughs and throws the dish towel back, and adds with a smile, "Let's go shopping!"

Act 1 Scene 9

Interior: Car, day

NATALIE:

He gets me...

Natalie chatters on cheerily about her car but Allison is distracted by Natalie's maniacal driving. Her left hand is white-knuckled in a death pinch around the flare of the custom racing bucket, her right palm stiff armed into the door panel. The Miata sits so low to the ground Allison feels like she's laying in the street, floating at high speed. She pumps a phantom brake pedal with her right foot praying for it to work. Her left foot is planted firm, her knee locked straight. Driving with Natalie is a terrifying experience. Allison describes it as careening out of control, suspended in free fall. Crash and burn always feels imminent, like in a dream when you're flying over water, falling toward land. You can feel your legs try to run and brace for impact, your butthole puckers, you tense as you know that sudden stop at the end is coming. Then you wake up in a gasp. Allison isn't waking up. She falls back on a pirouette against the car as Natalie screeches to a halt at a light. She is happily describing her car's custom exhaust in great detail and with a matter of fact air about compression and power. Horsepower. Pounding. Roaring. Natalie's hand gently caresses the stiffly vibrating hard rubber knob on her gear shifter, rubbing her thighs together feeling the rumble in her loins.

"He gets me." She says with complete seriousness on her face, giving the dash a loving little pat. Allison trembles in anticipation of the light turning green. She recoils from the traffic signal as if it might strike her physically. Natalie is theatrically laying out the schematics of her race package exhaust.

"How do you know so much about cars?" Allison interrupts, confused.

Natalie gazes sheepishly over her shoulder. "I used to change the oil with my dad when I was little, before he moved…" Natalie turns away and looks intently at the red light. "I guess I've just always been a car girl." She adds as the light turns green. Allison's head snaps back against the seat as the Mazda leaps forward through first gear, then slams her again as the transmission chirps the tires into second gear. Natalie casually speeds through the narrow city streets. Allison winces as Natalie narrowly misses some parked cars. Allison can see pitting in the paint on the car door. She turns away and shuts her eyes tight, bracing for the jarring side swipe, the screech of metal sliding violently against metal, but it never comes. The car jerks, bouncing Allison back up straight at attention, pressing hard into the door and floorboards, gripping the seat tight.

Natalie is still talking calmly, "I guess that's how I met my ex, he was into my car. I came out of a store to pump my gas and this goofball was drooling all over it." Natalie pulls into a gas station and kills the engine, gliding to a stop in front of a pump. She yanks up the e-brake hard and says, "He was really impressed with my car knowledge but you know, it turned out that *he* didn't know as much as he let on." Natalie sighs it off and looks at Allison, "Do you want coffee or something?" She opens the door and steps out of the car without actually waiting for an answer. A couple of guys parked in the fire zone take notice as Natalie peels herself out of the low sitting sports car. She glistens with a sheen of sweat as she emerges from the hot radiating motor's cockpit -- her trusted steed, her lover, her daddy issues. Her hair swings around in slow motion as she shakes her head and stretches. Allison thinks Natalie looks like a car commercial, striding across the parking lot and breathing in leers from boys on the sidewalk. They're standing next to a black Firebird Trans Am parked in front of the store in the fire lane, puffing out their chests,

"Nice car." One croaks awkwardly as Natalie passes. She pauses in the doorway and glances back over her shoulder and the car and then the driver.

"You too. Bandit." She smiles with a wink and swishes into the store leaving the boys wanting more. She pays for her gas and proudly parades past them waving over her shoulder at them. She lays across the car seductively giving the boys a show. She caresses the roof as she pumps her lover full of fuel. When the tank's full she opens the car door and slides one leg in.

"Nice car." one of the boys stutters desperately, as if this hasn't already been established.

Natalie giggles and flashes a flirty smile, "You said that already." She slides back behind the tinted windows and shuts the door. "Boys are cute." She says innocently to Allison, who is busy bracing for take off. Natalie turns the ignition key, the Mazda's souped up engine begins to purr. Natalie was making more and more sense to Allison, now able to see the world through wiser and more mature eyes. More Jaded. Allison never met Natalie's real father. He lives in Pittsburgh. Natalie visited him sometimes and he sent her cards for birthdays and Christmases, called her once a week. But he never visited Yorktown. Allison remembers how happy Natalie used to be when she was going to see him or right after she'd talked to him. Then there was her stepfather. To even use the F-word -- Father -- makes her cringe. Allison is convinced, based on her grainy films of memory, that he abused her, can almost see it in Natalie's childhood eyes. And not surprisingly, she acted out. She confused the father-figure abuse and long-distance love and morphed it into a doomed quest for love through loveless sex and the confused ideals of sex, power and love. And control. Natalie's delicate feet dance and flutter on the Miata's tight pedals. Her whole body hangs off the steering wheel as she pulls against a turn. The car floats around a corner, drifting, swishing her fishtail like a mermaid gliding through the curling waves.

"You have to turn into the skid!" Natalie calmly explains the physics of drifting her car at high speeds. *Turn into the skid.* Allison hears echoing in the back of her head as she bounces hard off the door when the car rights hard into the straightaway. Allison shrinks into the seat as Natalie's foot sinks into the gas and the car goes faster and faster. It feels impossible that it can go any faster then it does. Every bump in the road floats the car higher off the suspension until the last little hill, when Allison is sure the car has left the ground completely. Then Natalie is standing on the brakes, commanding her bronco to stop at a light. The car rumbles quietly, obediently awaiting her next command. It tugs at the clutch begging for her to whip it into gear, begging for her to smack its rear end hard, it wants her to ride it, it wants her to beat on it, do it, do it to me harder. *I'm in control,* Natalie thinks, her soft hands gripping the rumbling wheel. She is in control of this big throbbing monster. She's the one doing the fucking. *Everybody wants to fuck me.* The car rockets forward, leaping at her command. She slams down on the stick, revving the engine higher and higher until it whines under her. Finally Natalie yanks the car into a parking space with a jerk of the suspension fighting centrifugal force as she pulls back on her lover, raising the parking brake authoritatively with a tightly clenched fist, curt and dominating. Exact. The tall glass entrance at the center of the mall is far away from them. Allison can clearly see plenty of parking closer.

"Why are we parking so far away?"

"I don't want anyone fucking with my car." Natalie replies naturally as she's getting out. Allison rises out of the car and looks at the mall entrance over the roof of the Mazda. She looks at where she and Natalie met Keegan and Buddy. Where so many teens meet in front of the mall to pair off and hide in dark theaters or dark woods to make out and explore the dark contours of the opposite sex, or the same sex in some cases, sometimes both at once, all...sexing.

"Come on." Natalie urges Allison from her daydream, "Let's go try on clothes movie montage style!"

Allison nods as they start walking, "You're a car girl. Huh. You're like a Mona Lisa Vito."

Natalie smiles, puts her hand out to stop Allison and affects a deep New York accent, "However, in 1964 the correct ignition timing would be four degrees before top dead center." She giggles, "I loved her, in that movie, she was awesome."

Cafe Ine
Act 1 Scene 10

Interior: Coffee Shop, day

ALLISON is standing at attention behind the counter.

ALLISON: (v/o)
Pay attention.

Allison watches as Natalie gives her the short tour and a quick tutorial on the cash register. Making change needs no introduction, just the mechanics and an idea of how it all works around here. Allison can learn how to make the fancy Italian foamy caffeine desserts later, for now all she has to do is take cash and serve the plain black coffee to the confused old timer who thought coffee was simpler and doesn't understand why it needs all the fancy copper steampunk contraptions or why all the sizes mean 'big?'

"What happened to small, medium and large?!" They always yell. *Small medium at large,* Allison giggles at the thought of a psychic midget on the lam, *you'll never catch me copper*

The shop is glinting and bright with brass rails, mirrors and big copper shiny tanks. The counter curves around, leaving a small waiting area for lattes to go or a short sunny conversation at a small table in the window. Around the bar into the seating area, tables sit at cozy angles. Across from the bar and along the wall of the seating area is a raised platform, penned in by more brass with more tables. In the middle an area with no brass rail serves as a stage with a stool and a microphone. The microphone has a little on/off switch, just click it on to speak. It's an exercise in free speech. People rant or read poetry, some rap, hip hop, a capella. Some people sit, some stand. Some play an acoustic guitar, a harmonica, a drum.

"This little shopping center can get surprisingly wild sometimes," Natalie is saying. Allison is looking around at the quiet show. A few people who all came together sit at a table in front of the microphone. One guy from their group slouches on the stool. He's dressed all in black, his jeans are shiny with grime and he's wearing a floppy black leather hat with a wide brim. It looks like one Jim Morrison or Jimi Hendrix might wear, and its owner looks well aware of that.

"This one's called My Mood Hat," he is saying with a tip of his brim. He reads terrible poetry from a tattered notebook, looking up theatrically when he thinks he's being edgy or is making some deep point.

"It'll get busier later, it's still early." Natalie notices Allison watching the dull reading. "The Hair Salon people get pretty wild after lunch and into the evening." Natalie points out beyond the hair salon next door. "All the way at that end is the smoked barbeque place and the other end is the pizza place for lunch."

The coffee shop attracts a certain type of crowd around the open mic atmosphere. When they were kids Carol called it her bohemian phase. After a week Allison decides this crowd has never grown out out of that phase. Carol was in that phase when Allison moved to Yorktown. She wore that stupid hat, declared it bohemian. What the hell did she know about bohemian? She went down that dark Poe poetry path for a while but that all changed quick, as it often does with pre-teen girls.

Then of course there's the foot traffic from the other shopping center employees. People at work are generally fueled with the nearest source of caffeine. A coffee shop in a roadside strip mall is guaranteed the clientele of the mall plaza at minimum, and the Mohegan Village Green Plaza is no different. "You get all the dirt on all the little inter-office romance scandals." Natalie advised Allison on day one and she did not disappoint. Except the BBQ guy, Gus Brown. He's a sweet man who's happily married and putting his daughter through college. He is the friendly and wholesome voice of reason, stationed at the end of the mall. A white-haired gentleman who likes to smoke meat and bow hunt, often with the character who owns the hair salon, Neil Rappaport. He's a tall broad man with a short pile of blond dreadlocks on top of his head. He likes a fashionable amount of 90's shock appeal, they play edgy hard rock music in the shop and he hires a staff of mostly alternative looking young people. He understands the importance of image and marketing.

During the day the open mic is a sort of a free-for-all. If nobody is there, you can step right up. At night it's more formal, with structure, time slots, and a host. Consequently during the day you often have a lot of droning amateurs and nervous first timers, the former of which Allison is tuning out right now.

"I first read this next one a few years ago in Peekskill at One Station Plaza, who remembers the spoken word scene from the early 90's...?" The stage voice drones, reading a cryptic and dramatic poem.

Natalie is off on a shoot, and Allison is working with people she has nothing in common with. They're all friendly enough but Allison keeps a distance. She imagines, looking around the shop, clientele and staff alike, that little home-wrecking tramp would hang out here. She probably even knows some of these people. They read dark, depressing, morbid suicidology notes, 'looking deep into shallow water' one of them said one day, feeling particularly pleased with himself.

Two young girls, both small in stature and clad in black with dark eyeliner, sit at a table near the window. One is hunched over the table, clutching a book with an intricate and precise drawing on the cover, the lines wrapping around the binding and onto the back. She holds it tight, hiding its contents from the world's prying eyes, hiding behind it her bad-attention getting chest, pouring her soul out onto the pages, guarding it from the world, a world she wants to understand her and share all her pain, her embarrassing secrets. She screams inside and it spills out of her in ink, splashing across pristine pages, staining it forever like a fitted pane of stained glass. It's the only way she can share these carefully crafted windows, scribed out in her spell books as she writes and rewrites and recites.

The two small goth girls pour over the chessboard, sipping coffee, talking about Shakespeare and poetry. "Roze, it's your turn." Chelsea, the perched girl, impatiently awaits her opponent's turn. The broody teen looks up from her book, out the window then at the board. She slides her rook across it and looks back out the window. Town looks different, light hits things differently after a few semesters out of town.

"Checkmate." She says joylessly. *Classic teen angst*, Allison thinks as she turns her attention to delivering a latte. She wonders if she'd been like that. She thought again of that little trollop, glancing around again waiting for latte guy to get his money together. Yeah, she would hang out here alright. She'd fit right in with the coven around here.

Sure, she and Nat practiced kissing in middle school. Natalie is a good kisser. Even when she was with Sonja they were discreetly private about their relationship. It occurs to Allison that her and Sonjia were mostly a secret. But these girls today, making out with girls in public, buying into the flannel and witchcraft and bisexuality market, It's all marketing. Allison shakes her head. A guy takes a sip of his coffee, smiles politely, pushes forward a modest tip and leaves but Allison sees something different. She sees him in cartoon form, stiff in a suit, a glinting jewel in his tooth, a damn pirate if you ask some, tossing dimes to the peasant children, laughing at his big fat marketing profits. *You bastard*, she thinks irrationally, scowling at his back as the glass door shuts behind him. *The damn Patriarchy. Selling sex and treating women like the help. The talent. No! Not even the talent. They respect talent, women are props. Hot, sexy...dripping with butter/fat/bacon/chicken/beer. Hold this. That's what she said. Why should this dick get the profits? The Dick. That's not the prize. The VA JAY, baby! THAT'S the prize. From the minute they come out they spend the rest of their lives trying to get back in. Why doesn't the vagina get more? These...DICKS. Strap on a fuckin vag, those things can take a poundin'.* She isn't quite there yet, but an idea is hatching in Allison. Clocked in, waiting on people for tips. Time, it was only a blink, the fat suit greedy CEO type, the sleaze, the Buffalo-style vagina, it was just a flash. She hears it, off in the distance, a glimpse. She's not there yet. *Never Break Character.*

Over her shoulder a couple of goofballs are at the mic. One is playing an acoustic guitar, the other is singing. He is careful of his pose and posture, singing with seriousness in his voice like it's a cause he is pleading for you to listen to.

"Who kidnapped all your children and dressed the little girls in t-shirts bearing logos like eat me I'm delicious…" He has an obvious pointless drawl to his voice. He had said before they started, "This is one of ours we rearranged for you here tonight…" To the amusement of their four or five friends who came with them. They're the only people in the cafe besides the chess girls since the cartoon CEO left.

"It's daytime," One of them joked. "We're in the band, Dicks" another heckled.

Interior: Eastland Apartment, day

ALLISON is sitting on a stool at the kitchen island. Natalie scurries about in the kitchen making breakfast. She puts a steaming cup of coffee down in front of Allison,

NATALIE:
That shoot yesterday was something, I'm not going to sit for a week...

She exclaims, rubbing her butt with a pouty face.

Leather seats, Allison thinks, stirring her coffee. She is still thinking about the shop yesterday, the broody girls, the fashionable bisexuality, her fat suit hallucination, Dicks raking in Porn Dollars while the stars ice down sore butts.

"Were we really so goth and broody when we were younger?" Allison asks, still watching the coffee swirl.

"Well, we weren't Goth. I didn't listen to the Cure, did you? Depressed Mode? Bauhaus?" Natalie wanders off in song parody, "Bauhaus, is a very very very fine house...Bauhaus. In the middle of our street..." Allison rolls her eyes at Natalie, "We weren't but other kids were."

"Like who?" Allison demands.

"Did you see Dead Poets Society?"

"No."

"Well, they did." They both burst out laughing, they can hardly remember why it's so funny, it just is. "Those dirty sweaters!..." Natalie howls and they both burst out laughing again, louder and harder. Allison ponders it, catching her breath, mulling it over, swirling her thoughts like mylar glitter snow. It's been eating at her, the marketing, the sexuality. She watches Natalie wiggle across the kitchen, her cute, damaged butt peeking out from under her t-shirt.

"You got paid a lot for last night?" She asks, still watching Natalie twitch her money maker.

Natalie unconsciously ignores the question, turning around suddenly, remembering a thought. "Do you believe in this idea of unrealistic body image problems in girls?"

Allison thinks about it. "Yeah, we're all pretty insecure aren't we. I mean boys had He-Man and the A-Team to look up to and I don't see no He-Mans or B.A. Barrackasisis...ses around, do you? And you know they all get up in the morning and flex in the mirror." Allison flexes and puts on a dumb jock-boy voice, "Yeah...lookin good, hey baby check out this dick."

"Yeah they do all seem pretty pleased with themselves...I was reading an article saying how that's part of this broader thing where girls have been sold this image that's ideal and something to aspire to."

"I can see how girls are taught to look good for the boys, while the boys need power to conquer, the girls need to look pretty for the boys, be a wife, a mother, have a family, a purpose. Make a baby, in fact make two, a boy to carry the family name and a girl to carry another womb for when mine falls out..." Mid-rant Allison remembers the flyer in her purse. "DUDE!" She yells, pulling a sheet of paper from her purse. "Last night right before I left a girl came in and handed me this!" She pushes forward a flyer of blue photocopied paper, slaps it down on the counter. "Doxy Reunion!" The headline splashed across the top of the page says, "This Weekend!" Allison taps the date excitedly, "They're doing a set at the coffee shop, it's been years!"

Doxy had been a popular local band when they were younger. They had achieved a modest level of national success, a ticket out of this podunk town, one might say. Morgan, the group leader, happens to be Natalie's cousin. Their big hit, the titular single "Doxy" had not yet made it to radio when they played Natalie's Bat Mitzvah. A dozen or so Yorktown middle school girls heard that year's biggest hit before anyone.

"Did I ever tell you how I helped Morgan name the band?" Natalie doesn't even wait for Allison's yes. "I opened the dictionary..." Natalie mimes opening a book and continues to recall every detail while Allison thoughts venture elsewhere. She'd heard the story so many times when Doxy was big, but now she looks at it with a wider lens.

When they were school girls Doxy logos covered their paper shopping bag book covers. They hung up pictures from magazines in their lockers the year Doxy was on top of the world and all over MTV. Then like most bands, Doxy broke up and the girls went their separate ways. Sometimes people move on to different bands or the stage, some people move into a shop and build clocks, some write books. The spirit of Doxy's music, especially with the local girls who looked up to them, was that you can be a strong, independent woman and get out of the town they grew up in and do so on their terms. Doxy was proof of that. Allison needs that right now, she realizes, she needs a bright guiding light. Her Aunt Catherine was always sweetly singing "Wish Upon a Star" when the North Star blinked on for the night. Allison needed this reminder of local pop culture, finding herself even more excited now than she was earlier when that girl handed her this flyer.

"Remember how it cool it was when they played your Bat Mitzvah?"

Natalie grins a Devilish grin. "My grandmother caught me in the bathroom with, um...I don't remember his name...?"

Allison shakes her head, "Nat, you don't even remember his name?"

Natalie shrugs with a sly grin. Allison suspects it could be a fake one.

Allison sees herself in denim shorts two sizes too small, her child bearin' hips stretching the unbuttoned shreds of faded blue tight enough to stay on her cartoonishly fat ass and short enough to show off her thong underneath. Her red flannel tied in an innocent cute little bow under her bouncy milk jugs barely contained in their barely legal plaid hammock. "Looks like two puppies playin' under a blanket," a creepy voice cracks out of a dank corner as she prances by barefoot past a little red barn with a bale of hay on her shoulder. "I'm here to fix your haybale, ma'am," a poorly imagined farm boy offers her a slab of penis and a money shot. Allison's farm porn fantasy blows away in a puff of smoke.

"Natalie, have you talked to your boys?" Natalie stops moving and sighs.

Slowly she puts down her coffee and leans against the counter opposite Allison. "No," She says weakly, "My ex won't let me." Natalie looks at Allison, knows she's avoided it this long and gives in. "He took them away and filed for divorce while I was in rehab. He put me in and handed me the papers, it was all planned. Porn was actually the last straw I guess. He'd planned to hide the drugs from the boys, that was bad enough but the porn became the deal breaker. He couldn't let his boys know their mother was a whore. He couldn't have a sex trade worker in his family. Porn actress, sex slave, vegas whore, Hunts Point hooker, all the same in his house. A shame to the family. And don't think I was alone stuffed in a dark family hall closet, same secrets, bunch of mother's little helping stepford ass..." Natalie's tangent had escalated into a scream, startling herself. She takes a long deep breath, "Sorry I get so...."

Allison nods it off trying to remain calm, but drooling on the inside for more. "Take your time." *Hurry the fuck up!*

"I'm trying Allison. I'm trying really hard. I'm clean." She glances at the empty wine bottles they've been drinking. "I mean besides wine." They both give pause to the idea that maybe they have been hitting the bottle quite a bit. They look around at the full containers of empties and at each other.

"We haven't seen each other in years, so maybe we've been drinking a lot of wine for a few weeks…?" Allison offers and looks to Natalie for more.

"But I'm clean and he still holds it over me. 'It's not good for the boys.' Like I know, Dick! The boys can't have my drugs!" Natalie is quickly screaming again. Again she stops, takes a breath, apologizes to Allison. "Plus he can't get over the porn but he won't even let me talk to them, there's always some fucking excuse, he just relays messages to them for me."

"You could quit porn…?" Allison knows this is ridiculous before she even finishes the thought.

Natalie bites her lip. "You know what? I like my job. The money is so good, it really is, it's ridiculous but I really do enjoy the sex. I do. I mean look at me. Big slut right? That's what everybody thinks."

Allison even doesn't bother with a polite protest here. Time to call it as she sees it. "I guess…?" She mutters awkwardly.

"I know, I do it to myself and I'm not always so proud of myself but when I'm working it's different. I'm the prize."

"The prize." Allison repeats.

"I'm the star. I get fucking paid."

"You do get paid."

"The best part? The best part of it? I'm calling all the shots. I'm in charge. Sure, there's a director, sometimes we even still use a script and shit but I'm in charge. Do this to me like this, I'm going to do this to you like this now, get the camera over here so you can see his whole dick, yes I'm calling the shots. I'm doing it and the way I want. It's those choices, that's what I love most. More than the money, more than getting paid to have sex all day, it's the power and the art." Natalie has a bright look of confidence then it fades back to the solemn, sad pallor,"It's mostly the drugs. He just won't trust me. I was being pretty irresponsible, self medicating, you know?" Allison nods innocently. "I accidentally OD'ed and one of the boys found me, nearly unconscious. He was really scared. That was it. He packed my shit, dropped me off at rehab, took the kids and left for Texas."

"That's not good," Allison cringes. "Was he ever OK with the porn?"

"Of course the wannabe meathead in him, he was cool with porn at first. It was hot, his own personal little slut, all this cash, he thought he was a fucking pimp. But then it started to get under his skin. It hurt his ego. He started getting pissy about shit, other shit, unrelated little things and then the bickering would lead to who's big dick I was on last and I could tell it was the thing that had been bothering him all along and not some dumb shit like I left a wet towel on the bed. Shit like that. He made a huge dramatic production out of our second boy's paternity. It was degrading. It's no excuse but it certainly didn't help my growing drug problem. You know what's funny? During that whole time, that rough few years, I was at this one shoot one day a few days before he shipped me off to rehab. I was getting tridented in this gazebo…"

Allison questions with her eyebrows. "Tridented?"

"Think about it, Tri. Dented." Allison puts it together and realizes boy's words for fucking are always violent. *Dent.* She looks Natalie up and down mentally counting the dents. She cocks her head sideways, configuring positions while Natalie continues, "I was on top of one, on my knees with one behind me and one in front." She holds up an empty wine bottle pretending to fellate it. "Some people call it Eiffel Tower." She shakes her head, "Somehow air tight full of dick was the most at peace I'd been in months." After a moment's contemplation in a happier time she composes herself with a brave and pretty smile. "I just have to accept that all I can do is keep doing what I do Allison. Time."

Allison, taking all of this in stride, holds up the Doxy flyer in front of Natalie, who almost spits out her coffee at the sight, pushing her mug away.

"Doxy!" Natalie yells out, "Right! We have a Doxy show to go to tomorrow night, I'm so excited! I haven't talked to Morgan in forever…"

When Allison gets home from work the next afternoon, armed with shopping plaza gossip and buzz about the show, Natalie already has a couple of glasses of wine poured and a bunch of old junk in a box on the island counter.

"I dug out some old junk!" Natalie calls, raising a glass as if Allison coming home was the starting gun. Ready. Set. Drink. They sip wine and giggle looking through old photo albums, middle school yearbooks and school binders covered with Doxy doodles.

Allison runs her finger over deep cut hard blue lines in a carefully doodled Doxy logo on a Supermarket brown bag book cover. The old grocery bag still holds the phantom textbook within its permanent creases. Small friction burn tears along wear edges threaten to lose the perforations. She handles the middle school relics with care. A decade ago or so the book cover, before it was a book cover brought groceries into Natalie's home, maybe canned peaches, maybe Matzos, who knows? Allison pictures the familiar Matzah box she'd seen in the Supermarket, the Star of David in the corner. Natalie didn't really want to be Jewish, her stepfather had insisted she and her mother convert. Allison remembers how Natlie hated her Torah lessons and how sad she looked. It was impressed upon her that she downplay her Hispanic and Latino heritage. They wanted her to act...white? Like a nice white Jewish girl. *Never Break Character.* Natalie tried to be a happy girl, even appeared to be, but one of her first real talents was hiding behind a pretty smile. Allison remembers another thing about that year, another transformation in Natalie. In reality it had been in transition since before they'd met but in the defining lens of hindsight...Allison runs her finger along the Doxy on the book cover, thinking back. She sees the dictionary, the girls sitting on Nat's bed -- cousin Morgan, Natalie, Morgan's writing partner MicHELLe. Allison wasn't there but she'd heard Natalie tell the story so many times. It was her time she touched greatness, as her dad would say, his little dad expression for when you meet a celebrity or contribute to something that becomes something. Great Adjacent. You touched greatness. It's for ordinary people. Civilians. Like an award for a non military participant. Natalie thumbs through the dictionary in her story. What if she wasn't happy back then? Sitting there sad, thinking, *Slut.* Why? It seems unlikely she found Doxy at random…

From Webster's New Collegiate Dictionary 1977:
doxy, \dak-se\ (possible origin dockedoll fr MD) 1. A woman of loose morals; prostitute 2. Mistress

"What does Doxy mean?" Morgan had asked, intrigued, "It sounds cool, I like how it flows."

Natalie read the definition to them, "'Women of loose morals'?! Yeah! Wear that like a badge." Morgan and MiCHELLe cheered in jubilant agreement, not noticing the pain Natalie was hiding. Through the corrective lens of hindsight Allison can see through Natalie's mask. *Wardrobe! Natalie's pain is showing!* It all starts to swirl in a tornado, the Star of David, the Doxy logo, the creepy stepfather, the rampant promiscuity, the brave faces and pretty smiles. She watches it all spin as she runs her finger down the Y.

She trails off over some faded doodles and looks up at Natalie. "Did your stepfather do something to you?" Natalie's big doe eyes widen over her wine glass. She slowly lowers the goblet and takes a breath.

"It seems obvious now doesn't it?" She says with a strange calmness. "It was all happening to me at once, Al. He and my Mom practically cut me off from my father and the rest of my family. They wanted me to be a nice little Jewish white girl, Allison, I mean look at me, that's not me, and then he started touching me too?! On top of all that? Allison, I didn't know what to do. She pauses. "Is it weird that I escaped into porn?"

"It's gotta be some sort of Spotonironic, oxymoronic."

"What did you just call me?" Natalie purses her lips and raises her brow. "Do you want to get some weed for tonight?" She says with a happy smile.

Allison puts up a hand, "Whoa, subject change."

"What else is there? My mother's husband touched me -- Ok, more than touched me -- and I acted out. I was starting to bud as a preteen and he was a letch. It started as touching, him touching me, then it progressed to him making me touch him, then, well, he raped me Allison. There I said it. He raped me. I was a little slut and now I do porn, but I'm cool Al, I promise, I had to get past it. I tried drugs and as you can see that didn't work out. Almost killed me but it didn't change it. I had to get past that."

"He didn't start out raping you right away?"

"He bought me dinner first, so to speak? It took him almost a year to escalate to sticking it in my ass. Never in my," She looks down, "Not with his dick, I think he was afraid he could knock me up and that would surely get him caught. I didn't want to obviously, I did say no every time. But he would threaten me and force me to." She shakes her head and rolls her eyes, rubbing at them, reddening, starting to well up, "I was just a little girl. What a monster." She pauses again, composing herself. She points her fingers at herself and waves them like conductor's wands. "Compose yourself." she says through a brave and pretty smile and they both laugh and break the tension. Natalie waves her hand, fanning her face now and breathing easier, her color returning to normal, her smile more authentic, "I really am past all that, Allison, it's sort of getting to me now talking about it but I'm OK, I had to find a way past it. He took away control, a lot of control of my life and I can't have that, Allison. I'm a free spirit, I'm a passionate Latina girl and I can't hide that. I need to be in control of me. And now I am. You know that old porn star, the really famous one, April Lynn? She once said that it pissed her off when people would call her a whore. A whore does something they don't want to do for money. She says, she never fucked anyone she didn't want to fuck, she says she would say, 'I'm a slut not a whore.' I love her -- she's a real inspiration to me professionally. My producer has been trying to get me into April's production company for months."

Allison is suddenly distracted by the clock behind Natalie. "We should start getting ready!" She says with a start and they put down their wine glasses and rush off to their rooms to get dressed for the show.

Doxy Reunion!

Interior:Coffee Shop

The larger-than-usual crowd spills out the front door and fills the short sidewalk under the strip mall pavillion. Allison and Natalie park around back in the employee lot and go in the back door. They perch up on the bar to watch as Doxy takes their stools up on the stage. Morgan and MicHELLe pick up guitars and lay them across their crossed legs, smiling big glad-to-be-back nostalgic smiles. They haven't performed together for years in their hometown where they played backyard barbeques and classmates' keggers and graduation parties. You could lose count how many times Doxy played at the lake on the boardwalk or in the bars on main street -- Ilsa's, the Triangle, Chumper's over on old Crompond road or the Gemini or the bowling alley out in Carmel. Before videos on MTV, before world tours and drunken brawls in foreign countries, before all the delicious glitz and glamour and tears and pain and vomit, before they became the jet-setting, flash-in-the-pan celebrities of yesteryear. Fifteen seconds. It goes by that quick for many of their one-hit wonder counterparts, and for Morgan and Doxy it was no different. From humble small town roots to the dizzy heights of debaucherous excess to the cold dark gutter of rock's rock bottom. Yet here they are now. Morgan and MicHELLe, anyway. The two that started Doxy. Two silly little girls on a basement sofa with a silly dream and no idea how to get there. They started where everyone does, with lofty dreams.

The lights in the coffee shop are bright and warm, evoking the warm hug of family rather than the stark naked heat of the arena spotlights. The glinting copper gives the room a gentle pink hue, some discreet miscreants fill the room with a mild fog and the tolerant late 90's patrons look the other way with a smile. Takes a toke. A wave of hush ripples out from the stage and all the eyes turn to the guests of honor, anxiously awaiting the big comeback.

"Good evening, Mohegan Lake!" Morgan yells, "I think everyone knows who we are here, right?" She beams in the amusement the merriment, the joyous noise unto "I'm Morgan and this is MicHELLe and we're DOXY!" The crowd swells, the girls begin to strum, begin to speak for a generation, an angry generation who just want to Rrriot and change the world for their sisters.

Drama Camp 1992

The following week the big heavy metal double fire doors swing open with the loud echoing metallic clatter and the clacking of hinges. Courtney, tanned from vacation, steps through and breathes in deep. It's Courtney's turn. She is here to make her grand entrance...a week late. Make'em wait. She's here to claim her right as the new head bitch in charge.

Elizabeth is on stage with Allison who is explaining to her a finer point of how Elizabeth's Hope should come across to the front row. Courtney strolls down the aisle, up onto and across the stage, sizing up the scene. Elizabeth is new. She can sing, probably the only other voice even close to competing with Courtney's. Pretty, but no confidence. Courtney can smell that. She fixes a cool glare on Elizabeth, watches her finish her song.

"Hi, I'm Courtney." She introduces herself when Elizabeth finishes singing. Her eyes are friendly but not so at the same time. Elizabeth is unsure what to make of it. She feels sized up.

A few weeks of rehearsals and Courtney and Elizabeth are becoming friends. Or at least friendly. Elizabeth is cautious. Courtney has managed to hook up with most of the straight boys in one dark corner or another and Elizabeth has stayed out of her way so it's working out.

Courtney walks across the stage. "When are you going to give up this stupid act?"

Elizabeth feigns shock. "What? Excuse me?"

"You're in love with him…" Courtney delivers Reno's speech about Billy, tells Hope he "won't stick around long, half the girls in New York are after him…" She finishes her lines, spins dramatically, exits the stage through the fake ship door. Elizabeth, per the script, looks off stage then out at Allison. "Where's my Billy?"

Allison repeats the question to Camp Director, "Where's Billy?"

"He's not showing up today, dammit I forgot. Does anyone know the part so Elizabeth can do this song?" Courtney comes back through the porthole,

"I do." Courtney and Elizabeth proceed to perform "It's Delovely" together.

After rehearsal they all pile into Camp Directors van to go look at dresses.

Allison and Natalie share a laugh about the van. Natalie taps Camp Director on the shoulder. "One year one of your kids was driving, she said the van had a bottomless gas tank. It was always on E but it never ran out and she never put gas in it!"

Camp Director taps the dashboard, "Still reads E, gauge is just broken. I put gas in it. I can't believe she never noticed the smell of fumes, she never was the brightest bulb."

"Oh she did, she'd always say, 'what's that smell?' I guess I only now realize it was fumes."

"Yeah she was running the van on fumes."

Natalie shifts her attention to Courtney, sizing her up. "I have a dress in mind, I hope I can find it up there, for the Blow Gabriel." She purposely pauses with a grin, "Blow number."

Hearing this, Camp Director wonders if giving Natalie choreography was such a good idea.

Camp Director pulls in the driveway up to a carriage house that's been converted into a huge walk-in closet. It's filled with dresses, suits, hats, a gorilla suit, and tons of wacky costumes, all hanging on racks in rows. A white wooden ladder goes straight up in the center of the room through a square hole in the ceiling. The crawl space above them is also full of dresses, they spill from the opening. Allison climbs the ladder, starts throwing dresses down. Dress after dress tumble silently out the hole heaping in a lacy pile. A dress floats down, rolling on the wooden rungs. It catches both Elizabeth and Courtney's eye. Both light up, each reach for the dress. They find themselves on either end of a taffeta tug of war, unsure what to do, neither wants to make a scene, neither wants to give up the dress either. Allison steps in takes the dress gently from both of them, holds it up for Camp Director and Natalie to see. "What do we have here?"

Allison and Natalie point out how it's too innocent looking for Reno, so Courtney gives it up without a fight. Elizabeth wins the dress but wonders at what cost. Was she being paranoid, or did Courtney gave up on that a little too quickly? She *has* proven in the past to be petty, conniving and vindictive.

They proceed to dress Courtney like a whore and Elizabeth like a conservative debutante. It's a powerful message they send to the young impressionable girls. Elizabeth is looking at herself in a nice sensible dress, then over at Courtney in a Reno nightclub dress, thinking it's for the best. Elizabeth is very self conscious feeling fat in her chunky phase and decides to accept winning the dress as a small victory.

(v/o Elizabeth sings the refrain, "It's Delovely…")

Steve Hamilton

Act 1 Scene 11

Interior:Living room, night

STEVE is sitting in an awkward bent position on the couch, his head resting on the armrest, knees up. His torso, bent in half just below the pecs. A fancy new laptop computer rests on his gut...

He blew almost a whole check from his bike sponsor on it. The screen is only inches from his face. A strange underground Japanese cartoon flashes on the screen, turning his face different shades of colors as the frantic artwork blinks before his glassy eyes, bizarre Japanime cartoon pop music, shaking in time to the action. His dick is poking out of his dirty ripped jeans, he pumps it in his fist full of hair conditioner stolen from work. The half-empty bottle lays open on its side. A glob of white goo is oozing out onto the carpet next to the couch. The room is otherwise dark, save for the small shaft of light from outside shining on Steve's sweaty, blank stare. The stiff tweed couch cushion springs squeak lightly in rhythm with Steve's beating fist. The magazine with his starring pictorial lays face down on the floor on top of a few other raunchy porns, some Polaroids and some Thrasher magazines. Steve's roommate, Ben, squints into the darkness as he comes down the stairs into the living room. He can hear the weird beats and noises coming from the laptop and a high-pitched voice in English coming from a boombox on the floor, precariously close to the slowly growing glob of conditioner. The voice is repeating over and over, "Three little skeletons hiding in my closet, three little skeletons hiding in my closet…" It takes a minute for Ben's eyes to adjust and see that Steve is furiously masturbating.

"Hey, Steve, I...uh OH! Dude! Put your fucking dick away! Why don't you have your underage girlfriend come over and suck your dick, you disgusting pig? What...did she have homework to do tonight?"

Steve just laughs, stuffing his lubed prick back in his semen-stiff trousers, in no hurry for a guy who just got caught jerking off in the living room at three AM by his roommate.

Not far up the hill, Natalie and Allison are laughing and stumbling out of a cab loudly singing Doxy songs.

"I dropped Courtney off at the Plaza for that show, Doxy…? Then she was going home."

"To do homework?" Ben persists.

One day Ben will land a credited recurring role as a background agent on a popular crime drama and in 2018 he'll take a role with the controversial Crisis Actors playing a paid protester at The Indian Point Nuclear Power Plant, but this weekend he'll be battling Bam Bam Bigelow at a civic center in rural Appalachia. Neither wrestler will know that Bam Bam's racist hick girlfriend of several years, Risa, while on extended visit to her New York family, while rooming with Natalie up the hill just last year, sucked Ben's dick for a twenty bag of kind bud. She'd offered him a blowjob at a party on their patio because at least Ben is white, not like her fat Jamaican blow dealer who was always trying to get her to suck his dick. It amused him whenever she would curse and hurl racial slurs at him. He was at the party and when he heard her offer Ben a blowjob he said, "Come suck my dick, Risa, I got something for you," then laughed a big belly laugh when she cussed at him and called him the N word.

"Were you coming down here to say something, Ben Hemus?"

"Why do you always call me by my whole name?"

"I could call you Benjamin Taylor Hemus."

"My middle name isn't Taylor."

"I could still call you that." Steve reasons ridiculously.

"I suppose you could. Yeah, what are you doing with all those video tapes in the hallway upstairs?"

"I don't have room for them in my room." Steve confesses.

"I think you have a problem." Ben tells him, walking past into the kitchen, slapping on the light as he walks through the wide opening.

The big house is one of the older dwellings in the old part of the city, just down the hill from the old former girl's school where Allison and Natalie live. The apartment patio overlooks a small park and partially occupies the original house's farm land, before City Hall or the hotel or the public housing, or the city for that matter. Like many of the large old pre-Victorian houses in Peekskill, the house is separated into three different apartments. Steve, Bruce and Ben's apartment with three bedrooms is the biggest. A small studio fits snug in the basement and a small two-room plus kitchen and bath occupies the back and attic area of the old house.

Steve's "problem," or one of them anyway, is VHS tapes. He scours the bargain bins, yard sales, flea markets and thrift stores for hidden gems. Growing DVD sales are dissipating the VHS collection Steve can ultimately hoard, since they aren't making those anymore and only motivates him further. It started with an innocent wall unit. Small. It held about twenty five tapes. Chump change. When that was full he got a bigger unit. More like furniture. It stood six feet tall, towering over

Steve who is only 5'5" in boots with heel lifts, 5'3" in flat sneakers when he's on his bike. The six-foot unit holds another 100 tapes, plus a few if he's creative. It wasn't enough. A few years ago on a BMX trip he saw a small Mom-and-Pop video store going under to a big chain video. In hindsight jokes on Big Chain Video right? Steve bought over 200 tapes from Mom and Pop, mailed them home in boxes from the post office across the street from the shuttering store. That was a few years ago and the hoard has more than doubled over a few times since then. Now Steve no longer bothers with racks or shelves or furniture, he just stacks the videos floor to ceiling like bricks in lines, videos numbering in the thousands, two and three deep in the older parts of his VHS canyons. Stacks surround his bed and a new stack waist high and two deep works its way out his door and down the hallway between Steve and Bruce's bedroom.

Bruce also works part time at the hair salon and apprentices with a glass blower who is an older trans-woman. They do a demonstration every year at the Renaissance Faire over the river in Sterling Forest.

"What are you going to do?" Ben calls from the kitchen fixing a late night protein shake, "Stack VHS tapes like cordwood...?" He continued talking but Steve can't hear him over the blender now. When it stops he's saying, "....take them to your parents house in PA?"

Steve puts his computer aside and goes in the kitchen, "They want me to come out there and pick up the boxes of tapes in their garage as it is." He tells Ben, joining him at the table by swinging his leg over the back of the chair. Ben sips his shake as Steve plops into the chair, the song from his boombox still playing in the background. "Three little skeletons…"

"You couldn't turn that fucking thing off?" Now in the bright kitchen Ben sees Steve's eye is black and blue, "What the fuck happened to your eye, Douchebag?" Ben jabs a finger in the tender swollen shiner growing around Steve's right eye.

Steve winces and recoils, swatting Ben's hand away. "Ow, keep your catcher's mitts off my face! After I dropped Court off I went to the bar."

"Hit on the wrong guy's girlfriend again?"

"Yeah." Steve smiles with pride because he is in fact proud of himself. "I put my dick in her hand." He barely gets out before he bursts out laughing.

"Again? Guess you didn't learn from the last time." Steve had to have reconstructive surgery on his face last time he put his dick in a girl's hand, a thing he likes to call The Surprise Gift. He used to do it a lot before last time. He was trying to chat up a young co-ed at a college town bar in Ohio to little reception. Not that he noticed he was striking out...Steve never sees that. Her cold and sometimes even rude responses did nothing to dissuade him. He waited patiently for the opportunity when she would put her hand in just the right position and he could lay his penis in it like he was serving up a hot dog. Just slip her the dog right in the bun, just lay it in there. Most times he just gets slapped usually with the same hand to his face, sometimes they smack his penis. He considers that bonus points. An OK, not best case but better than a face slap. Once a girl tugged it like ten times, teasing him about the size and speculating correctly that he was a two pump chump, which he happily proved, releasing on her arm on pump three. She was thoroughly disgusted and he loved every second of her revulsion. In subsequent tellings of the story he lasts longer in his version: "She whispered hot dirty talk in my ear and jacked me under the bar." Last time, the time he needed surgery as a result, she told her boyfriend who happened to be an offensive lineman on the Ohio state football team. He and his buddies rearranged Steve's face for him, hence the emergency surgery. He competed in a bike park freestyle competition a few weeks later with the protective mask and bandages still on.

"Hemus" Steve repeats in Ben's face over his shake.

"Stop breathing your stank breath in my glass. Why are you obsessed with my last name?"

"Hemus."

"Fuck you."

"It's your name." Steve persits getting up. He steps on his sock toe, pulling his foot out and leaves the yellowed dirty tube sock where he stepped out of it. He hops up on the counter, pushing aside a partially full dish rack and swings his foot into the sink next to Ben's blender and starts washing his foot.

Ben jumps up yelling. "What the fuck, asshole!?" grabbing his blender away from Steve's nasty foot water.

"I have to wash this gash every few hours, I don't want it getting infected, Dude."

"Do the fucking dishes first before you wash your fucking nasty foot gash, you disgusting fuck!" Ben stands there in the middle of the kitchen in his bed shorts, no shirt, his half a glass of shake left in one hand and the wet dirty blender in the other. Water drips from the blender in a milky little puddle on the linoleum tile next to Ben's foot. He's contemplating if he even wants to know how Steve gashed his foot, then decides against it.

Ben looks silly to Steve, who hops off the counter giggling at Ben. He is walking out the doorway when Ben adds, "And take your dirty fucking cum sock. Don't think I haven't seen you dump a load in your sock and put it back on you nasty fuck." Steve laughs, spins around, scoops the sock off the floor, not denying dumping cum into it. Ben already won't touch Steve's hand but he especially won't if Steve only has one sock on. In fact, Ben tries not to touch anything of Steve's or anything Steve might touch. Ben's world can feel pretty small sometimes.

Steve walks out of the kitchen with one bare foot laughing, a crusty sock hanging out of his jeans pocket. He calls from the living room, "Who fucking works out at four AM dude?" adding, "Do you have any weed?"

Ben leaves the kitchen light on and and walks past Steve to go work out in his room, "I have weed you can buy, you cheap fuck."

"Come on Ben Hemus let's smoke."

"I'm not going to smoke, I'm going to work out before work." Ben only sells pot to supplement his income between shoots and auditions. He doesn't smoke much and he's only a casual party drinker. He treats his body like a temple and a money maker at that. "You should work out too you lazy turd, you look like you can hardly lift your bike, don't you have a trip coming up in a few weeks? You're not twenty-one any more, Steve, you're almost thirty and you've been punishing your body, between riding and partying..."

"Don't fucking lecture me man, I'm a fucking legend in BMX man..."

"Whatever." Ben cuts Steve off disappearing up the stairs, "Fucking legend." He snorts laughing.

"I don't party like that anymore..." Steve says weakly but Ben's only response is his slamming door, followed shortly by the clink of his free weights ringing together, then thud to the floor. *Clink. Thud. Clink. Thud....*

Steve did have a pretty bad reputation years ago, always drunk, weeklong LSD binges, coke, whatever, Steve did it all. The LSD on bike trips solidified a certain persona on the BMX bike circuit that did actually approach what one might call 'legend' status to the chagrin of Steve's haters. But at the end of the day the guy rides a mean course. Tripping his balls off but his tricks put kids in the stands and sold merch. Kids want a Steve Hamilton signature bike. But they also don't have to ride around the country in a small van or share an apartment with him. To a spectator Steve is a spectacle. A show. He often rides with a big fisheye lens strapped to his forehead. "This is how I want to see the world, through a fisheye lens," he would explain meandering around a bike park before pulling an Olly into a sick grind or some spinning kicking flat land trick. Tripping on LSD, driving from bike park to bike park, riding every steep staircase, rail, basement door and landing dock, it distorts reality. They would often be filming each other, footage for their bike company's promotional videos. Steve would pick up roadkill along the highways, clean the bones and glue the skeletons to his bike frame and gear, anything to put on a show. The bean counters Steve works for are usually happy no matter what his publicity is, bad publicity is good publicity and hey, it's the 90s. Extreme is in and Extreme on Camera equals money. Unfortunately for Steve's roommates, teammates, van mates and anyone else he comes in contact with when he isn't on a bike, well, they learn to put up with his antics. Until they don't.

Steve plops back down on the couch, yawns, looks around. Looks at his computer. He looks at the stack of Polaroid pictures on the coffee table. He'd fed Courtney Ecstasy all night and when she passed out he took naked photos of her. Then of a few different people fucking her. He flips through them with a deviant smile. Bored. Tosses them back in a pile on the table, decides on TV instead. Clicks on the set with the remote. Drops the remote on the table, sits back, crosses one leg over his other knee and pulls off his sock. He quickly pumps another load into it watching the morning weather report. He puts his sock back on and shuts the TV off. He leaves the kitchen light on and goes upstairs to bed before the sun starts coming up.

Act 1 Scene 11.2

Interior: Kitchen,morning

ALLISON is sitting at the island, she sips her coffee. NATALIE pours herself a cup. Their heads still buzz with last night's excitement. It's an emotional hangover.

A little bit of wine hangover as well, as Natalie and Allison with some of the other baristas filled to go cups with wine in back. Moreso, they were still riding high on last night's joyous innocence. It's a good ache. Like that soothing deep muscle burn after a good rigorous workout. Sport, dance, sex… A good burn. They saw old friends and had others to talk about, old friends they promised to keep in touch with since signing yearbooks "K.I.T.!!" but they won't. They all have the same conversations every time they run into each other at the wakes until it's themselves in the box. Everyone around them is saying how good they look and how they should all KIT more and not just see each other at these things with their eye rolls to grief and hands folded in polite social prayer. Doxy was certainly no funeral. Last night was just about the opposite of a funeral.

"I feel so…" Natalie pauses, her big brown eyes gaze at the ceiling, "reset." She purses her lips tight and squints into her coffee.

"Reset?"

"Oh, I don't know," She shakes her head and looks up smiling, "All I know is I feel good."

Allison nods, both hands wrapped cozily around her mug. "I know what you mean. Refreshed. Right? Maybe? Good times. Old times, good feelings. I do sort of feel like a lot of old baggage just slid off my back last night. It's just not so heavy any more, you know?"

"Yeah…" Natalie nods, her eyes widen, she bites her lip. "Hey...So do you want to get some pot?"

"Natalie?!" Allison is taken aback by this. Neither of them has ever really been potheads, though they did smoke last night with Morgan and MicHELLe after the set. Allison thinks about it for a moment, "You know I've never actually gone and gotten pot. Every time I've smoked, I think you could count the times on your fingers, someone always just already had it. Yeah. Lets get pot. How do you get pot?" Allison doesn't even know where to start. "They don't put ads in the paper do they? They couldn't could they? How could they…"

Natalie laughs."I have a guy, Al. He lives right down the hill too. Hopefully Steve's not home. He's fucking obnoxious."

"Steve from the hair salon?"

"Yeah. His roommate. He works at the hair salon too but I don't think he's been there lately. He's a wrestler…"

Allison frowns in amused confusion at this, "A wrestler?" She gives this a little thought, "So I bet he's in pretty good shape, huh?" She laughs and Natalie does too, playfully smacking Allison's arm.

"Yeah you little slut, you should get laid!"

"By your pot guy?" Allison laughs. "Pothead."

"I don't get pot a lot you know. But sometimes you just want to take a nice big bong hit and lay back and smile at a ray of fucking sunshine, you know?"

"I'm just glad we don't have to drive around looking for a guy with a shirt with a letter on it."

Natalie spit snorts coffee onto the counter. "That's a rave. On TV. Girl, you really did get cut off for a while there didn't you?"

"Remember the U4EA episode?"

"Oh my God." Natalie shakes her fist. "That damn Emily Valentine!. Remember how jealous we were of them?"

"Yeah, over privileged rich twenty something year old high school students."

"And then all this horrible stuff happens to them." Natalie laughs.

Allison realizes she *was* cut off. That's what it was too, cut off. She knew it then, she can feel it now. That knowing. There just wasn't anything she could do. How? She could have walked out the door and got in her car anytime. Why didn't she? She was too busy playing Susie Fucking Homemaker to Professor Predator. Till Hussy Homewrecker came along. *Careful what you wish for.* Sheng Nu had told her one day while she was threading her eyebrows.

"You just might get it." She finishes out loud, daydreaming.

"Get what?" Natalie looks amused seeing Allison come back to reality.

"No, it's, OK, I," Allison collects her thoughts, "It's just a whole long weird train of thought. That's been happening to me. I go off in my mind into, I don't know where, this…"

"Vonderlande?" Natalie giggles, "Do you go off into Allison's Vonderlande?"

Allison laughs, hands on her hips, she teeters at the waist and puts on her Inka voice, "Ooh Mister Rooster your cock is so curiouser and curiouser."

"Dude, you're all over the place. Your Russian accent is terrible and what the fuck is Mister Rooster...?" She can hardly finish, she's laughing so hard, "Your rooster cock!" She manages to blurt out and continues to laugh. Allison gets up from her stool. *Never Break Character.* "New cup new cup, go down go down." She commands Natalie with a serious look, her Russian sex spy accent improving; slightly. She puts her hand gently on the back of Natalie's neck, gives a gentle tug, "Go down." She says again in a dead panned Ruski stare. "Down your hare hole?" Natalie smiles, kissing Allison quick and sliding off the stool. She smiles politely at Allison's pantied crotch and gives her butt a playful spank, stands up, hooks her coffee mug off the table, heads for a refill. "You really should start doing porn, Allison. That was kind of fun. Porn could use a few laughs. That Inka thing, it's silly but you could make it work. You're sexy Allison." Allison looks doubtful at Natalie then at her self. She doesn't quite see it. She feels big and lumbering. Lumbering. That's what she thinks of herself. Sturdy. *Child bearin' hips.* Meanwhile, Natalie is so cute and pretty. Guys like a nice little package. It makes their little package feel bigger and more important. Those poor little peckers.Those fragile little ego sacks and their magic wands they love so much they can't keep their hands off it. They're so proud of it and they want to show it to you but they also want to feel like it's big, impressive, irresistible. Allison realizes how long it's been since she's had any sex. No wonder all these Inka fantasies and the shedding of inhibitions. *I do need to get laid,* the thought hits her so suddenly that it shocks her a little. Steve's roommate Ben had been by the shop, she knows who Natalie's talking about. He is a strapping young lad...? "Yeah why don't you call that guy. Let's get some pot."

Natalie looks at the clock on the wall. It might be a little early to call most pot dealers but Ben gets up ridiculously early. Natalie pops the phone off the hook and cradles the receiver on her shoulder. She twists the long spiral phone cord around her finger while she scans the phone numbers penciled on the wall around the phone, dials.

"Ben?" She nods at Allison, "hey it's Natalie." She smiles at Allison. "Yeah up the hill." He asks her some code and she simply answers "Yes." Then, "OK we'll come down then." She pauses. "My roommate." She shakes her head at the phone, "No, Risa moved out a few months ago, wow has it been that long since I talked to you? No, my new roommate, Allison. She works at the Cafe. We've been friends since middle school." She smiles at Allison and sets the ball in motion, "Yeah, she's gorgeous, you'll like her." She covers the mouthpiece to hide her glee. She sees the excitement in Allison and plays with her a little. Ben is just telling her about a match he has coming up but Natalie acts as though he's saying something juicy just to rile Allison up. She hangs up still giggling.

Allison finds herself asking like a schoolgirl, "What did he say? What's funny?"

"Girl, you need to get laid."

"I agree but do we really think I'm going to go bonk a stranger at a garden party this afternoon?"

Natalie nods enthusiastically. "Yes, that's exactly what you're going to do." She practically shouts. "I know you haven't had any sex since you've been living here and that's already too long for me babe. And I know you didn't have any Good sex with the English Teacher." They both automatically sing together,

"An English teacher!" Allison thinks about it, the sex was barely, finally starting to show a heartbeat right around when Louis started hanging around that campus. That little trollop is probably getting fucked a little more properly than *she* ever had. *Good for her. Slut.*

"So am I wrong?" Natalie asks, hands on hips, waiting for Allison to answer. "Well?"

"No. You're not wrong., I guess it's just," She pauses, "Was I thinking out loud?" They have a good hearty laugh and set about morning-after coffee rituals. Still buzzing from last night, Allison bites her lip. It's about time she gets laid. Banged properly too by a young stud. *Young, dumb and full of cum,* she thinks, giggling while she picks out a careful outfit. It needs to look carefree and casual. No plans, lazy Saturday, oh this old thing? But easy access if Operation Boy Toy Plan works out. It's so hard being a girl sometimes. Party clothes can be so binding. It's really fucking counterproductive. That's the part Hollywood and porn don't show you: the unromantic removal of these torture devices women have to wear. To look good enough to take them off. Push the tits up and together, hold that cleavage right there, looks good honey, no breathing, breathing is overrated, you're fine, round out that ass, tuck in that tummy, zip this in here, with the help of a pit crew of course, strap on those heels, buckle 'em up nice. Let's see those sexy calves baby. Fuck, by the time we're done unbuckling, unstrapping untying, unhooking all these contraptions who's in the fucking mood anymore? Allison chooses a nice casual dress she'd gotten from the boutique by the shop. It has a trendy floral print and a high modest neckline. Allison's always been a little -- OK a lot -- self-conscious of her broad hips. Something about this dress that hugs all the right curves and hides all the right things that gives Allison a boost of confidence. She's comfortable and confident. It makes her feel sexy. She admires herself in the mirror then slides the dress back off over her head. She drops her bra and panties and grabs a towel, walks to the bathroom."Taking a shower." She yells.

Natalie nods and yells,"OK." not looking up from the article she got distracted reading.

Allison walks dry from the bathroom, wet hair up in a towel. A small dry towel hangs from her arm. She's still admiring her body as she walks into her room to slip on her sexy confidence dress. Allison feels the best she ever has about her body. Even with drop dead gorgeous Natalie in the next room. *We're a couple of hotties.*

She's seen Ben around before, she can easily idealize his abs in front of her. And his pecs, bulging from a workout, all oiled up and glistening. She runs a finger in her mind around his pecs and down his abs taking a close look as she does, feeling the heat from his tight package, exploring below the abs with her hands, stroking it up against his tight oiled belly, her sandal-strapped heel digs in tightly around his tanned buttocks. She pulls him in, swallowing him whole, she runs her hands down his muscled arms, they brace tight, she can feel the blood course through his veins. They pull together, bumping, grinding, moaning. Sweat flies, hair whips, sweat drips from them, boiling from hot skin as it splashes…

"Damn, I need to get laid." Allison blurts, shaking off the late morning fantasy. "I better get dressed before I need another shower." She dabs at some dampness with her dry towel and straps on a nice comfortable bra. It doesn't need to do much in the cleavage department. They're covered in this dress. It just needs to hold them out nice. *Here's boobs for you,* Inka offers. She gives her head a good tussle in the towel. Carefully Allison unwraps her hair and sits on the towel on the bed, holding her head to the side so as not to get wet from her hair on her dry back and she brushes her hair. When her hair is knot-free and mostly dry she slips the dress back on over her head, straightening it down over her bare hips as she stands. She likes the way the material feels on her skin and the exciting forbiddenness of no panties underneath the hugging dress. She runs her hands over her hips, around her butt and down her thighs. She breathes deep. Looking in the mirror she confirms it, anyone could tell she isn't wearing underwear in this dress. She breathes deep, watches her breasts heave. She feels sexy and likes it. She watches herself wiggle in the mirror rubbing her hands over herself. She coos, working on her Russian. "Very sexy lady," Inka purrs. *Never Break Character.* This is what she needs right now. No strings, no feelings or commitments. Just a good old fashioned Schtupping. A proper banging. *Proper,* Allison keeps thinking. Natalie was right, that *is* the right word. Proper. It sounds painfully British, "A good proper snogging my good lady." *Snogging. A good proper fuck.* This guy, perpetual and unapologetic bachelor, proud of his physique. Leaves town a lot. No strings. Right down the hill. Let's not get ahead of ourselves...a one night stand, no leaving a toothbrush. Maybe an open booty call, just a good...proper, banging. She pictures a screen door slamming shut BANG the spring pulls it in tight, one loud snap, no bounce to it yet like the older ones, that gentle smack, smack, smack of loose age and use. BANG! *Like a screen door, the more you bang them the looser they get.* Well, that's it then...Allison is going down there with all of Inka Cockneedo's confidence. Sans the terrible Russian accent. A sexy secret agent looking for love in all the wrong places. Good hard sweaty wham-bam-thank-you-ma'am sex. Sex that leaves you sweaty, panting, satisfied.

When they're dressed and ready they sit in the kitchen swapping out late morning coffee for early afternoon wine. Just a glass or two to loosen up Allison's inhibitions.

Act 1 Scene 11.3

ALLISON and NATALIE get out of the Miata and walk the sidewalk half a block to the house. A few people are out on the patio and from the street they can see movement in a window. BEN and a few other people are crowded in a corner around a guy with a raspy voice telling a story.

METAL MIKE:
...so I'm banging this broad in my room, her head is hanging off the bed, we're both facing the door...

He demonstrates their positions, "The door is cracked open. I thought I closed it, right, but I think nothing of it. Then I think I see something out in the hall and I guess she sees it too, she pushes me off and rolls over, squinting at the door. She pulls the blanket up over her tits and she's like 'Ahhh! There's someone out there, go look!' So I grab my robe, I wrap it around me, I swing open the door and there's fucking Hamilton, beating off. The fucking guy doesn't even stop but then he fucking looks up at me and he's like, 'What the fuck, dude?' Like I'm the one fucking disturbing him!" The guy telling the story is Metal Mike. Mike La Croix. He's the owner of Metal Bikes, a bike company that Steve has ridden for. He has short but shaggy bleached blond hair and leathery tanned skin. He's wearing leopard print leggings and a worn old black leather jacket hanging open over a loose fitting tank top. Everyone around him is laughing. Mike greets Natalie with a familiarity that suggests to Allison they know each other. Mike excuses himself from the crowd to say hello to Natalie. She only introduces them but doesn't explain to Allison. Allison looks around, recognizes Ben, smiles, sure he sees her look him up and down. Sure...because she wants him to see. Then she sees Courtney who waves. Mike turns back to Courtney to ask where Steve is. Ben moves from the crowd across the patio to greet them.

"Natalie, nice to see you." He takes her hand in both of his giant hands. Her delicate hand disappears inside his grasp. He leans forward in polite gesture, not actually kissing Natalie's cheek before offering his hand to Allison, "Allison, is it?" Allison nods, smiles allows Ben to envelope her hand, she offers in delicate gesture. His hand is big and warm. *Big Gloves.* Her dad used to joke, 'You know what they say about a guy with big hands?" Then he'd give a sly sideways glance and funny voice, "Big gloves," and he would laugh and feel very clever and risque. *If he only knew.* Ben leads Allison and Natalie into the house through the kitchen. Steve is mixing a drink next to a smoking bong on the table. Bruce is gearing up to hit the bong.

"Come on kill that shit, hippy, I can smell it getting stale." Steve snaps. Bruce gives Steve the finger right in his face and leans over, pulls the slide and huffs in the full tube of smoke.

"Metal Mike is out there telling everyone about the time he caught you jerking off outside his room."

"You believe that guy?" Steve was saying as they passed through.

"Funny thing is Steve still doesn't see that he's the asshole in that story." Ben tells them on the way up the stairs.

"I haven't seen Mike in a while…." Natalie is saying.

"Oh, You know Mike?" Ben is talking to Natalie but looking at Allison. She has his attention, she can see that.

"Who is this Mike guy?" Allison asks.

"He runs Metal Bikes, a company Steve rides for. He was just telling us about the girl in the story you heard. She was one of the Metal Chicks, models they hire for appearances and photo ops." Ben does his best impersonation of Mike, "Sometimes I end up banging these broads…" Allison giggles school girlishly. Too much? Natalie gives her a calming glance. *Play it cool girl, damn,* her eyes say. Allison can hear Natalie saying the words.

Natalie peels two twenty dollar bills out of her jeans pocket and lays them on Ben's desk. "You were saying you have a match, was it tomorrow? Who are you fighting?" Natalie smiles at Allison as she turns her back to Ben. Ben sits at his desk, puts the twenties in a drawer and pulls out a gallon size ziplock full of buds.

"We're leaving tomorrow, the match is in a couple of days, I'm wrestling Bam Bam Bigelow, you've ever heard of him? He was in the WWF for a while." Ben pulls a hand full of buds from the bag and lays them on a scale, "He's in another league now, semi pro. It's not gonna be Wrestlemania or anything, Its at this Civic Center near Pittsburgh…" Natalie tenses slightly at the sound of the word *Pittsburgh* but Allison and Ben don't even notice. Natalie hardly notices it herself but it affects her. She misses her father. *Pittsburgh.* It echoes.

She pushes aside the blue wave of sadness and gives Allison another smile, running her fingers lovingly through Allison's hair. "Doesn't Allison look sexy?" She says through a big mischievous grin.

Ben seals up the bag and hands it to Natalie. "She does." It's a flat but warm response.

"Is that you in your wrestling costume?" Natalie points to a picture on the desk but doesn't wait for a response. "OK I'm going to get a drink," she says ducking out the door, quickly adding, "You guys should hang out." with a sly grin, the last thing Allison sees of her as she slips out.

"Chief Big Bear." Ben is saying.

"Huh?" Allison looks back toward Ben, he is still sitting at the desk.

"The picture, that's the character I play, it's corny I know." Allison nods knowingly but she's still looking at the bulge in his wrestling tights in the picture. His arms glisten, oiled for the photo shoot. Feathers hang from leather bands tied around his biceps to make the veins pop out dramatically. Chief Big Bear is wearing war paint and a feather headdress that Allison thinks looks a little light for a chief. *Maybe it's his battle headdress…? Did Indian chiefs have a battle headdress and a …? Dress? Headdress? A Dress Headdress?* Not to mention Ben doesn't look Indian at all and it seems a little racist. Not maliciously. Kind of immature. She glances back at the bear bulge. Allison traces the bicep line on Chief Big Bear and asks,

"When did you say you were leaving…?" Casually making her way around the desk. Ben turns his chair to face her. She puts her knee between his legs, gently pushes his one leg away from the other then sits on his knee.

"Have you ever heard of Bam Bam Bigelow?" Ben asks with a hint of nervousness in his voice. Ben is only a few years younger than Allison but the nerves make him look even younger. It's cute. She likes it.

"Shut up." Allison runs a hand up his shirt, leans in, kisses him. He kisses her back, his hands run over her curves as her hands earlier. She notices his hands notice her nudity under her dress. It's exciting. It's hot to her. She knows that he knows she skipped the panties. She sits back with a wild look in her eye and unbuckles Ben's belt, pulls the bulge out of Chief Big Bear's jeans. She is not disappointed. The young man's heart pumps a rush of blood through Allison's fist. She rubs the shaft, slapping it against his belly just as she'd imagined. He tosses his shirt aside, she stands, hikes her dress up over her hips and lowers down onto him, it seems to have no end, she is seeing stars as he hits buttons that have never been pushed before.

Act 1 Scene 11.4

Interior: Kitchen, day

STEVE and BRUCE are still doing bong hits on the kitchen counter when NATALIE comes back into the kitchen. COURTNEY is now sitting at the table. She is breaking up weed on a paper plate. Courtney hands the plate up to Steve. He takes the bud from it, packs the bowl and slides it into the bong.

COURTNEY:
When is this British dude supposed to get here?

Steve puts on a Cockney accent and says,

"That ole bloke is a's'posedly coming through later ta-night love." Resuming normal speech, "He said he is OK staying here, I offered him the couch."

Bruce takes a long pull from the bong, slowly exhales and says, "He should stay at the Motor Inn, he's going to think you're a lunatic."

Steve looks at Natalie and clarifies,"Guy's coming from the UK to do an article on me for a bike magazine out there." Natalie wasn't impressed enough for Steve. "Say Nat, we should do a video together. You can come to a loading dock where I'm riding and we'll fuck on the dock…" Courtney stands up hard, shoving back her chair with a violent metal shriek against the floor. She throws the paper plate at Steve because it's the only thing there to throw.

"What the fuck, Steve!? How are you trying to fuck Natalie right in front of me?!" Courtney swings at him, grazing his head with her fingers.

Steve looks at Courtney with a calm confusion like it's some misunderstanding, "No it's cool babe, she's in the business too…"

"What fucking business, you're not in *any* fucking business, there's one picture of your nuts getting stepped on in a third rate raunchy *Playgirl* knock off…!" She's screaming in his face but Steve is only mildly shocked.

"But…?" He can't even fathom how Courtney doesn't see his logic, "No really Nat," He resumes unphased, as Courtney storms out. "It would be good for you, I mean we've seen all your moves, you're not getting any younger. I can give you a fresh angle. You know I'm the guy who started the Rugby shirt trend in BMX…? People would love to see me get my dick sucked…" Steve doesn't get to finish his thought as Courtney storms back in hurling a beer bottle at Steve. It connects with all the fury of a woman scorned, shattering on his already blackened eye, spraying the room with glass and beer. Bruce tucks the bong under his arm, slips off the counter and scurries up the stairs. Bruce wants no part of a fight between his roommate and his underage girlfriend that he lets drink in the house. Bruce has never approved and refuses to participate or even talk to Courtney in the house. Natalie runs out to the patio behind her hands, a good hard cry ready to burst from her face. Courtney resumes screaming at Steve and hitting him, swinging wildly with both hands until Ben comes running down the stairs, no shirt, pulling his pants closed.

"What the fuck is going on down here?!" He is yelling, pulling Courtney off of Steve. Allison comes down behind Ben. She's a bit more put together than he is. She slides past the scene wide-eyed to the patio, finding Natalie standing close with Metal Mike.

"What happened in there?"

"Let's just go." Natalie chokes out and grabs Allison by the hand, "Bye, Mike." she adds quickly over her shoulder, dragging Allison out the gate. Allison offers vague goodbye shrugs to the people she doesn't really know anyway. They duck through the hedgerow and out onto the sidewalk. Natalie walks with her head down, pulling Allison along. They get in the car and the doors slam shut. Natalie bursts into tears.

Act 1 Scene 12

Interior: Eastland, Kitchen, day

ALLISON is sitting at the island, looking suspiciously at Natalie. NATALIE somber, pours two glasses of wine. Allison absently shuffles the cards from the basket.

Natalie had driven home uncharacteristically slow, sobbing the whole way up the hill. For all that goes on in Natalie's life she still always seems like she has it together. *Never Break Character.* Allison has never seen Natalie break down like this before and isn't sure what to make of it. Natalie slumps onto the stool across from Allison, pushing a glass toward her and taking a big swig from her own glass. She takes the bag of pot from her pocket and drops it on the island counter between them. Allison deals out a hand of five-card stud, plucks two peanuts from the dish, puts them between them. She picks up her cards, gives them a look, puts two face down in front of herself.

Natalie sighs, scoops her cards up, "Do you remember how to roll a joint?" She asks solemnly, part sadness, part poker face. She takes two peanuts and tosses them in to ante, adds five more, pushes one card face down toward Allison. "One." She says flatly and stares out the window at the setting sun. "It all went so fast but it's been a long day." The Hudson river twinkles at her, Dunderberg mountain across the bay is ablaze of orange in the sunset.

"Do you want to tell me what happened in there yet?" Allison wants to give Natalie space, make her presence known but keep her distance while Natalie sobs. Allison slides one card at Natalie, takes two herself. She assembles them in her hand. Wasn't the cards she wanted but at least she's got a pair. A low pair. She tosses in the five nuts to stay. Natalie looks at her new card. The Ace of Spades. She grabs a handful of nuts, drops them on the pile slow, dramatically.

"That's intriguing." Allison grabs a similar handful and puts them on the pile. Natalie turns over her cards. AAA88

"Aces full of eights. Dead Girl's Hand," She mutters joylessly. Allison pushes her low pair facedown in the middle, pops a nut in her mouth. Allison ponders Natalie. *Fast cars, drug abuse,* she thinks, changes course, *I'll come back to that…*

"What did Steve say to you?" Allison asks chewing, adding, "and what was Courtney so mad about?"

"He was trying to fuck me. Right in front of her, that's why she was mad. I feel bad for her, it was kind of embarrassing. He was kind of rude about it but that's not so much it, it was something he said that kind of touched a nerve…"

"Natalie do you have some kind of death wish or something?" *Dead Girls Hand.* "You drive so fast…?"

"I don't Al, it's just…" She collects herself, "What am I going to do when I'm not…you know…?" She wants Allison to say it for her so she doesn't have to. She doesn't have to face it if someone else says it. "Allison, please say it." But Allison isn't going to. Natalie needs to hear herself say it. Not Allison or Steve or some sleazebag porn producer, "What am I going to do when I'm not pretty enough anymore?" She looks lost and sad. Like she just found out she'd been lied to for over two decades, that it was all a big fat lie. One tear rolls down her cheek. Her big brown eyes shine like window glass when the sun hits them just right, a twinkle in her wet eyes makes her look so young and innocent. Allison imagines it was how Natalie looked before they met. Innocent.

"I want to see my boys, Allison. I just want to see them." She had never sounded so vulnerable before. Allison refills the wine glasses and takes Natalie by the hand, leads her into the living room. They sit on the couch together, Allison holds Natalie in her arms, unsure what else to even do. Natalie weeps quietly without much to say, pausing periodically to take a dainty sip of her wine. She sits up, wipes her eyes on the back of her hands, puts the glass to her mouth, takes a small sip, holding the round goblet bottom with both hands. She sets the glass back down, puts her head back in Allison's chest and weeps.

After a long while she says quietly, "Allison I think you've been the most stable relationship I've ever been in." Then she is quiet again for a while, no longer weeping, just sitting, breathing. Hiding. Taking comfort, Allison provides it. Comfort. No more. Just an ear and a bosom.

Drama Camp 1992

Shownight. The auditorium is abuzz with excitement. Elizabeth is sitting alone in the dark wings amongst the curtains, going over some lines one last time as the seats fill in. Elizabeth can't help but think how she had imagined the Hope character, the romantic lead, the prize between the two male leads. She thought the part would be...bigger. Hope, as scripted, is underdeveloped and underused. She is little more than a plot point. She looks up from her script to see one of the *Anything Goes* townsfolk approaching. *Never Break Character.*

"Have you seen Courtney? Camp Director wants her."

Elizabeth points off into a dark corner. "Last I saw her, she was over there with Gabe." Both girls snicker at the delicious irony. It has not been lost on any of them as Gabe, Courtney's prize after a few false starts and broken hearts in the first few weeks of camp with a few other boys, is playing the Earl, the prize Reno gets in the end. It's almost as if Courtney planned it all herself.

Anything Goes is a pretty campy musical. The young amateurs deliver the corny jokes with ham-fisted clumsiness that can't help be charming in it's woodenness. Elizabeth and Courtney easily stand out as both have very good voices. Elizabeth learned a few valuable lessons rehearsing for tonight. Her voice is strong and at its best when it's near straining. Hope's songs don't leave much room for that -- they're dull, downright boring at times. "It's Delovely" is a fun and recognizable classic but Reno definitely has the better songs. Well played, Courtney.

Courtney stands center stage beaming in her spotlight. Reno's Angels whip away the preacher gowns. Camp Director glares down at Natalie next to her. Natalie grins, remains fixed on Courtney, awaiting the big dance. She worked really hard on the choreography.

"That is not the outfit I approved at dress rehearsal!" She hisses at Natalie. "What is wrong with all of you?!" She puts her head in her hand as the red lights dance across the stage, making it worse. Courtney is wearing very little, what amounts to lingerie. Audible gasps from around the audience haunt Camp Director, it's becoming a recurring nightmare.

She can swear she hears people whispering loudly, "Oh that one from last year choreographed this…" It's like a bad flashback. Fortunately Courtney's performance isn't nearly as shocking as Natalie's was. After all, Courtney's strength, besides a good voice, is in comedy. She makes it a little funny, it takes some of the edge off of the half-naked tween doing a stripper act on an alter belting out, "Blow Gabriel Blow!"

Elizabeth
Act 1 Scene 13

Interior:Bedroom, day

(fade open, close on Elizabeth's
face…(Applause) Camera pulls back,
widening on her)

ELIZABETH is sitting on the
bed.

A cold hollow aluminum can rocks back and forth, hand to hand as she replays the past few weeks in her head. Monica is chattering away in the other room, talking in that irritating backwards way she does, 'Meatloaf, which I love…' *Most people say 'I love meatloaf' dammit Monica.*

Monica has been living with Elizabeth's family full time for about a year now. She showed up one night, at 3AM with a suitcase and has never left. Elizabeth simply said, "Mom, Monica lives here now," and Mom was fine with it. Things like ass-backwards speech and where she squeezes the toothpaste tube are now full on annoying shit you can't escape. The honeymoon is over. They share the add-on bedroom built into half the garage, a common addition to the stock suburban raised ranch. The small apartment takes up a small bit of the downstairs family room too and since it encompasses the laundry room the girls are expected to move that along.

Elizabeth holds up the beer can, "Do you know where this came from?" Elizabeth knows where she thinks it came from. Ken was drinking Coors that night. She shudders at the thought and bites on her tongue to fight back a confusing array of disgust, fear, and anger. She had been one thousand percent sure she'd cleaned her room, scrubbed it almost as hard as she'd scrubbed herself after he'd...violated her. How could she have missed a can? It was behind the bed, but she's sure she moved the bed, she remembers moving it.

"Where did you find that?" Monica asks with too light a tone. Elizabeth is sure Monica knows. She was there. Nobody else drinks these Silver Bullets.

"Behind the bed."

"It probably fell back there when he was here and you missed it cleaning. I don't drink Coors, do you?"

"I guess." Elizabeth isn't convinced at all.

"Why were you moving the bed, anyway?"

"I just wanted to take care of a few things I'm not going to be able to do for a while."

"Recovery. Got it." Elizabeth looks around the room where a few weeks ago her...innocence was lost? Dignity? What she had of it. Her dignity. It wasn't lost anyway...it was stolen. Torn from her violently. She tried changing around the room but the real change, the big change is tomorrow. Tomorrow she gets her breast reduction. She will be someone else. That awful thing happened to her, these tits. After tomorrow they'll be gone and so will his stain. She knows that isn't really going to be true, she'd need a lobotomy for that but this is a good step. And it has its health benefits, her back and stuff at least that's why insurance will pay for it. They don't actually hurt her back much yet but they probably will, it's pretty common. Her mother had it done too.

She looks around the room disjointed, disconnected, as if life were over. That girl is dead right here on this bed, the life raped right out of her, gutted with weapons of destruction and deception. The light shines differently on this dead world, this old cocoon. Tomorrow she will molt the exoskeletal rack, her outwardly defining feature. *You must have missed it,* Monica's words ring in her head. It just doesn't seem possible. She pans around, noticing the last relics of childhood intermingled with the tweens and teen years, juxtaposed against this grey flaking reality like a disintegrating old wasps' nest. The bright happy colors of girlhood dolls and happy toys from happy times before tits and cliques, her teens, her goth phase, it all seems so old and long gone now. The dull color almost seems executed by cataract. What a difference a few weeks make. A happier thought penetrates Elizabeth's dark sense of humor, allowing her to laugh a little at Monica's expense.

"What the fuck was Ethan all about?" On the way back here a little while ago he'd abruptly insisted on them dropping him off at the gas station near the mall. Elizabeth bursts out laughing about it again. She had been making jokes in the car at Monica's expense. Her favorite target is usually Monica technically being Jewish. Her mother is, her father isn't and they were never practicing. She wasn't raised Jewish -- no Temple, no Torah, no Hanukkah or any other religious instruction. They're default Christians if anything, at least in December. Elizabeth had poked Monica and made her favorite joke about Jews being squishy when Ethan sat up between the seats and demanded Monica pull over. She pulled into the gas station and she got out, letting him out of her two-door car. A Lancer that she annoyingly refers to as Lance as if it were a family member. When she'd gotten back in the car she slumped in the driver's seat sullenly and muttered, "He broke up with me." It was only a short drive home from there and Elizabeth hadn't gotten to exactly why.

"Ethan is a born again Christian."

"So?"

"You made a Jew joke. He didn't know I'm Jewish."

"You're hardly Jewish but so what if you were? Is he some kind of anti-semite or a Nazi or something? Is he a Klansman?" Elizabeth is giggling.

"He said he can't be with someone who he couldn't be with in the afterlife."

Elizabeth falls on the bed howling. "Afterlife!" She laughs, "Squishy Jew." She cackles, kicking her feet laughing. Then her somber feeling comes washing back in, taking away the giggles in the strong undertow as her gaze falls on her pillow and she catches a flash of her face being pushed into it. His big hand on the back of her head, the ghost of searing pain lingers, she can feel him force into her ass dry and relentless. She can't move, the pillow is all she sees, cutting her off from the world. *Are these my last breaths?* Forced into the pillow where her head rested through childhood dreams. All she sees in this pillow now, are grown up nightmares. Virginity, stolen. She'd never had anything in there before, outgoing only. He stole that. She'd bled for three days her stolen ass cherry for a few more than that. Three days of darkness. No time for that though, have to shove that back down, things to do. She sits up quick shakes it off. Still a few things to do and her stomach begins to growl.

"I can't eat after 6pm so let's go get something now, I'm hungry."

"I think this is silly." Monica looks at Elizabeth's chest, "It's like slapping God in the face, lopping those off." Elizabeth knows Monica's been talking at work on her thoughts about Elizabeth and her breast reduction plans.

"Well it was silly of your people to kill the savior. Talk about a slap in the face, God's son, man." She shakes her head, lips pursed, "His son. Come on I'm hungry."

"Let's go get fa ja heetas."

Elizabeth looks at Monica with furrowed brow. "What?"

"Fa ja heetas."

"It's pronounced 'fajitas' you dim broad, it's Spanish, the J is…"

"I don't speak Mexican."

"Mexican?! Good God, Mon, I don't want to spend this life with you." Elizabeth snorts, "Can't spend the after life with you…!" She bursts into another fit over this.

Act 1 Scene 13.5

Interior:Doctor's office, waiting room, day

ELIZABETH is sitting alone in the middle chair.

She is thumbing through her thoughts and a celebrity gossip magazine pondering which celebrity boobs she wants. She pictures a barber shop but instead of pictures of hair styles it's all tits. A Boober Shop. *Pick a set of tits already, honey,* a mustachioed boober character urges her, sharpening a big over sized knife on a big metal rod. Back and forth from a famous actress shopping in sweatpants to her own middle school *Mean Girls.* An out of shape actor on vacation in the Mediterranean to bright flashing lights at the diner, Ken and Monica. The lights and the chrome of the gaudy restaurant changed, she's dizzy the lights are too bright, he's smiling that creepy joyless...dastardly, dastardly, that was it, he was only missing the big handlebar mustache and hooded cloak. Only instead of tying her to the railroad tracks he slipped something in her drink.

She turns a glossy page across her lap. A gorgeous woman holding a glass of wine smiles at her, smug in her gorgeous life, taunting Elizabeth. *Come live this gorgeous life of gorgeous luxury simply by sipping this gorgeous bubbly.* Elizabeth looks at the gorgeous woman's cleavage and then down at herself in her oversized sweatshirt. She's hiding inside it. Her cleavage struggles to stay contained in the biggest bras she can find and they aren't enough. They aren't classy like Gorgeous Bubbly and her Gorgeous Luxurious life. Fun bags. There to grope. In the dark. The chick with the tits. The big tits. Huge Boobs with the girl. Who? What girl? Elizabeth, behind the huge boobs. B00bs. A shiny page flips across her lap. The star of this year's big romance blockbuster cheated on, is getting divorced from, was cheated on by last years big action blockbuster hero. The caption beneath his photo lists other notable "conquests." Hers is captioned with who she's wearing and how she's wearing it.

Another glossy page of Elizabeth's memory flips by in her mind. What would her caption read? Was she asking for it? What was she wearing? Who was she wearing? Was it that little black dress? Wasn't that dress chosen for a reason? Did she lead him on in any way? What about him? Why is all the questioning aimed at me? Did you slip some shit in a drink?! Oh boys will be boys right? Burp. Crotch grab, spit. High Five. High Five. He keeps showing up wherever they are. It always seems like he's whispering to people then looking at her and high fiving. What could he be saying? Surely not 'hey I drugged and raped her' who would high five to that? What is he telling them? He certainly did NOT hook up with me, Well what was she doing wearing that if that wasn't what she wanted? I mean they're called Hooker Boots right? That all happened to the girl with the oversized tits. Well, she's dead. At least she ain't walking out of here alive. Elizabeth looks down at the shapeless lumps on her chest, pinned down, draped under sweatshirt.

"We're not both walking out of here girls, sorry, it's me or you. And it's gotta be you." Approximately a total of 12 pounds between them. Bright side? Every girl has that joke from Mother Nature of lopsided boobs to be self-conscious of. Some worse than others. Elizabeth knows a girl at the mall who has two distinct cup sizes. A full cup difference. Around the mall they call her CD. Behind her back of course. High Five. Elizabeth's doctor assures her a perfect match. Since they're going in anyway she can take a little more from the dominant boob and make her perfectly symmetrical. A big C/small D with a perfect cleavage line that can be harnessed and weaponized if she does it right.

A glossy page floats from one side of her lap to the other. A classically beautiful family of four sits in a classically beautiful park on a classic checkered picnic blanket eating classic sandwiches. The side effects sound worse than the disease the beautiful picnic people seem so happy and carefree about curing. The doctor wrote a lot of wink-wink words in the notes over the weeks in order to get this done. "Your back hurts right?" she'd say, nodding to Elizabeth. High Five. Her mom next to her nodding too, she herself just having the same procedure, tremendous weight on the back, there it is documented, it's hereditary. It didn't yet but she could see how it could easily start to, these huge fun bags hanging off her chest pulling on that bra line and lower back. *Sure whatever, my back hurts, does that mean insurance will pay? Because 'I got raped and want to be desexualized' isn't insurance worthy?* Economically viable. "What were you wearing?" The insurance agent wants to know before they pay out, after all, boys will be boys and if she was asking for it they shouldn't have to pay. To pay. Toupe. A big fat suit smiles "ting." Denied. A big rubber stamp on some numbered triplicate form for time savings, some official signed document, a notarized request for money. *Please sir, kin I 'ave s'more money to get my sex bags turned down so I might stop temptin' the boys so? They will be boys you know, they grope me in the dark and high five and ignore me in the halls.*

Monica ruined it at work. Elizabeth hadn't planned on saying anything. No "Hey guys, had my tits done." She was just going to take time off from work and come back a new person. Monica thought it was stupid. "Stupid." she kept calling Elizabeth for having the surgery. "Stupid." She went around telling people at work and all around the mall. It really, pissed Elizabeth off. It was a little embarrassing for one thing, plus it fucks up the idea of being a different person. That is what it is. She wants to be someone else. Someone different. If people don't recognize her around the mall, good. Nobody has to know. Her friends would know but that hot guy at the pretzel counter doesn't have to know. The guy who sold them smokes underage at the newspaper stand didn't need to know about her tit job. He's creepy already, now he's going to be looking at her tits even more. Somehow. She just wants to be someone different. Like Val Clarke. *Had the bingo bongos done.* She knew the year they went to see that play that she wanted to join Drama Camp. Now here she is sitting in the office waiting to get that done. Well, sort of. Not exactly what Val had in mind. Maybe some itty bitty titty chick in the next room will get Elizabeth's surplus titty pumped right into her chest. Like a Boob Redistribution Program. High Five.

She flips a glossy sheet of celebrities across her lap. A beautiful face covered in some hideous costume, a brave choice for a beautiful thespian to play an ugly monster and lean heavy on theater talent rather than beauty. A new character. A new mask. Elizabeth had chosen to play Hope Harcourt that year in camp. It was a new mask to hide behind. Chaste. Chased. *Never Break Character.* Camp Director told them all the time. Line? This waiting room could be outside a casting couch office. "Make up!" New character. *Take about half a tit off each, make'em even though, make sure they're economically viable.* Elizabeth is no stranger to putting her cleavage on display when she has to. Hell, she taught Monica to use it and it even works for her. Boys are so stupid sometimes. You can hypnotize them in that canyon. Fun Bag Canyon. The Grand Cleavage. They forget about your gross ass, your gross face. Your cottage cheese stretch marked gut or whatever part of your body you hate. Monica is gross. You can't say so, it's just girl code but she is. Elizabeth even suspects part of Monica's problem with Elizabeth's breast reduction is that she's going to look and feel better. Elizabeth is already "The Pretty One." *Nobody calls me the Smart One, even if I am.* Elizabeth would never say it out loud, as a girl who suffers from Former Fat Girl Syndrome, but if the shoe fits...

A matching set of celeb tits walks the catwalk, Elizabeth imagines herself doing a little turn, *What does she win, Bob? New Boobs!* This set of tits is a whole new identity. That's all we want, right? To be someone else. That girl with the tits.Tits Mcgee. Boobie McBoobtits. *That broad gets into ridiculous big-tit situations.* Big tits have a gravity of their own, outlandish nightmares are drawn into. Groping on basement davenports, hypnotizing tobacco venders, sleepy old vacations slipped in drinks. Big old titties, puts out, have a drink or four, lemme see them fun bags. Put butts in seats. Ass cheeks on movie posters, tits in submission, the hero gets the boobs, *What does he win, Bob? The New Boobs! oh and the broad they come with. Like taxes. Small print. Sign here, local and state laws apply. Be someone else. And the nightmares, they can hitch a ride on the jettisoned titty fat, see ya. Flotsam? Titsome? That's it right? All that boob? It's so much she must be slutty. Come here baby shake those titties. Hi, is the chick with the huge boobs there? No she got raped now she's gone. This is a new girl. One with average boobs. Ok, above average but not the hugest. Regular. Nice tits. Hypnotizing cleavage. Eyes up here buddy. That's it. It's confidence. That's what's getting weighed down. They're so heavy. It's hurting my back.*

When she had walked in the room was empty save for the woman behind the desk in the window. Now she's gone too. Elizabeth looks at the door next to the window. Any minute now a head will pop out and call her name, *You got the part. Come back behind this door and change your life.* Surrounded by nothing but metal frame chairs with the stuffed orange tweed cushions and backs. It's just Elizabeth in this room designed for waiting. *The Waiting Room. Sit here and wait. Read a magazine about Beautiful People. Here's a Highlights for your kids. Don't be a Goofus. Act right like a Gallant.* She flips a glossy memory and a paper page, one in her mind, one in her lap. This actress is unrecognizable and can't get work after an ill advised cosmetic change made her too average. Turns out the thing that needed fixing was her identity. So to speak. After surgery Elizabeth would hear from a lot of people, "Did you lose a lot of weight or something?" She had always accommodated her huge tits. First, due to Fat Girl Syndrome, she couldn't wear small shirts. And after living underneath big baggy sweaters, she'd grown into herself and people thought she'd lost weight. "Just about eleven pounds," She'll tell them with a smile. She probably has nothing to worry about with Monica going around telling everyone. People don't listen, let alone to Monica.

Is this…? Running? Running away from identity. The girl with the tits. In fact plenty of times it felt like Tits with the Girl. The Tits. They got invited to the basement makeout parties. Horny teen boys and their desperate boners. How did we not call those parties Blue Balls? Elizabeth was Belle of The Blue Balls. They were more than happy to suckle at the teats, slobber on her face in the dark. Horny teens dry humping in the shadows of the stank humid basements, hot with heavy breathing and fevered touch, fogging up the small windows from every corner. That's how it is. Always has been. They all heard their babysitters talk about the teen makeout parties on the phone when they thought the kids were asleep. They did it too. That was the old Elizabeth. In a short while she's going to be eleven pounds and one inner fat girl identity lighter. Elizabeth flips another glossy page of celebrity gossip. The room feels sterile. The cold steel frame chairs and the awful orange cushions, the awful orange fabric matches the awful orange carpet. *Does the carpet match the drapes?* Breathlessly whispering "unfinished basement" in a boys ear always makes them cutely awkward in the pants.

Elizabeth looks down at the red carpet parade of beautiful celebrities flagshipping designer designs for designers, walking display mannequins, barking and clapping for flash bulbs blinking and whining, lighting up accessorized smiles, waving at nobody and all the nobodies waving back. The nobodies all wave very enthusiastic open-mouthed smiles. They're already composing their time-they-touched-greatness story, "The time I met Gorgeous McBoobtits? Oh she waved to me, just me, we were the only two people in the world and now were in the same friend circle and you can connect yourself to her through me in the six degrees of Drew Barrymore game…" High Five. The time we touch greatness in our lives, we the plebes and our exciting brushes with fame. Elizabeth closes her eyes in anticipation of shopping next week. Bras that fit -- oh, the novelty!! -- and dresses that show off the hips she's finally grown into rather than hiding them beneath the Big Top. She tugs at her sweatshirt hem. *Step right up, ladies and germs!!* A circus theme grinds out its melody somewhere in the distance, *I'm a clown to you? I amuse you?* That dress shop in the mall where every girl in town has gotten her prom dress since the mall opened would be her first stop. She twirls in front of the mirror she's been before so many times. She twirls and a kaleidoscope of dresses flare off of her in a gorgeous carousel. Flashbulbs fill the air and she waves to nobody. "Who is she wearing?" Whispers float among the starbursts and delusional waves and wide smiles. She's going to try on snug little numbers in bras that fit, prom dresses, party dresses, confirmation dresses. It seems so long ago now, but this was the very dress shop where she found a dress to wear to Courtney's confirmation party. By that time they were Best Frenemies Forever but that social event would prove to be their first real platform to wage battle. The first little buds of confidence wilted as Elizabeth, twirling in front of the store mirror in her chosen dress, hears her mother barrel over with an armload of other options, "Why would you pick that out?? Your ass looks huge!" The mirror shattered, flying past her face in big shards and she is back in the room waiting. The Waiting Room. Flipping through glossy magazines full of shiny beautiful girls parading around in dresses, acting on screens and stages made up pretty for our entertainment. Putting butts in seats and selling burgers and cars and dresses. *Look how sexy the life of luxurious consumerism is. Look how sexy, look at her. The Pretty One. She's a real looker, eh? What's she sellin' 'cause I'm buyin' ah-woooo-ga! She's economically viable, get a look at those dividends honk honk squeeze, you'll get some milk out of those puppies. High Five!*

The woman behind the desk was gone, the woman who took her name and told her to sit and wait in the room for waiting and look through the magazines of what real people are supposed to look like. Soon that door will open -- *Did I get the part?* -- and a nurse will pop out and invite Elizabeth to come in back and be molded into a new person. That door will crack open any minute now and this will be her Big Break.

The door next to the window opens. A head pops out and poses the question to the otherwise vacant room, "Elizabeth?" Then again looking right at her, a fisheye lens close up tight on her face. Vulnerable. Alone. "Elizabeth?"

Act 1 Scene 14

Interior: Mall, day

ELIZABETH looks down at her cleavage and runs the buttons up. She looks in the mirror, gives her boobs a nudge and a jiggle. She puts her hands on her hips and twists side to side slowly, watching her new bust line.

Hot New Tits. She's never been able to wear a cute button down top before. Those little buttons could never hold back her old mammoth mammaries, but now they fit nicely. Just some playful straining on a button or two; for funsies. She adjusts the smart collar and tugs down on the hem to straighten the hang on her shoulders, smoothing the shirt tails out along the contours of her hips. With these normal-sized boobs dare she think she has a bit of that classic hourglass figure? It seems like a lifetime ago when she stood here in front of this same mirror. *Your ass looks huge.* She turns and looks over her shoulder at her butt in the mirror. That little girl looking for a party dress was someone else entirely. The doctor said to stay in bed for a few weeks and extend the heavy lifting ban even longer than that but after only one full day in bed, Elizabeth is bouncing back quickly, already feeling stir crazy. She feels fine, good, even the best she's felt about herself in quite some time. Four months ago The Incident happened. That would be how she would refer to it for years to come. Twenty years from now in therapy she will still call it The Incident. That was when everything changed. She spent the last four months second guessing everything since early middle school when Aunt Flow and her Overstuffed Fun Bags showed up on her doorstep. Those were rough years. They are for most people, especially girls. Girls without Fat Girl Syndrome and negative attention-seeking beacons of oversexuality. They certainly didn't help with frenemies taking artillery shots at the runways. Elizabeth had to grow out of that. She smooths down her shirt over her hips, remembering the Confirmation Party Dress. Until then Elizabeth had been no real threat to Courtney. But once boobs started growing, you know how boys are. You see one set of boobs and you want to see the rest of them. And once word gets around that a girl is willing to get groped in the dark, true or not, boys notice. Let a guy get to second or third base or even just say he did, people hear. High Five. Courtney was Queen Bee and all the other worker bees buzzed around her. Once bees start buzzing around Elizabeth's boobs, which pretty much equals "puts out," well now it's on. *Your ass looks huge.* She turns around again, examining her posterior. If anything, it's sort of flat. Even at her chubbiest pretween baby fattiest she never had much of a butt. Still doesn't, but the hips have come into their own, between growing taller and cutting back on the old canopy. She gives her chest another shake. This gives her a delicious grin, she likes this, it's manageable. A shimmy, a lip bite, a whole new persona. It's a whole new costume. *Hot New Tits.* A new character to play. *Never Break Character.* Elizabeth builds a whole new wardrobe for her new character. A smart look with a hint of classic pinup. Hope and Kim with a little Punk Rock Prom Queen. Classy. Chaste. Chosen.

"How lovely it is to be a woman…" She sings lightly, perusing new looks. Bettie Paige as Kim Mcafee. Each top and dress carefully frames her new bosom. "Lookin' good, girls." It's going to be their coming out party. Beautiful Newborn Baby Girls. Plump and round as a, well; a baby's bottom. Surgery was like their birthday. A new Life. That day, two days ago will be the anchor point. The girls. Their birthday is...her birthday. This new...character. With the Hot New Tits.

Why Don't You Ever Call Me?

Act 1 Scene 15

ELIZABETH walks confidently from the prom dress store with two big bags full of New Woman.

The sun is shining down through the big cathedral skylights. It's a happy glow. Sun beams lance over the balconies casting spotlights down onto the first floor tiles. Flecks of dust ride weightless through the rays of light, swirl and eddy in the wake of the casual shopper strolling by. The high glass ceilings and wide balconies give the two-story grand consumer canyon an open-air look and feel while completely inside, safe from the elements. On a rainy afternoon when the mall isn't so busy the sound of the rain running down the skylights is soothing and sublime. Sitting on a mall bench watching the water slide down the roof is humbling. In winter when the snow piles up one feels especially small. Today, the sun is bright. A light breeze floats by. Elizabeth still has plenty of shopping to do, thanks to Mom and Dad, so the plan now is to put this stuff in the break room and go into a few other stores until Monica gets off work. Elizabeth and Monica work in the record store at the east end of the mall with the catalog anchor store. Elizabeth was off today so she took a ride in with Monica. Tension has been building between them and it's weird. Monica can be sweet and helpful -- "Oh let me, you should rest." -- but then it also seems like she doesn't want to be seen with her. Since Monica blabbed about the boob job, work has been a little sour for Elizabeth. People…changed. *What has she been telling them?* Elizabeth has to wonder. That's the worst part too, that people know something and Elizabeth doesn't know exactly what. A secret she had, stolen from her. It's humiliating. It makes Elizabeth feel powerless. Across the corridor from the record store is the portrait studio. One of the guys in there is known around the mall as Hot Vince. They seem to always have a Help Wanted sign in the window which suggests a high turnaround, but they all say it's a great place to work. It's mostly art students working through school. Elizabeth thinks maybe this new character would get a new job, make new friends. New Life. Her white button down with the smart collar and smart blue stripes is a wear-it-out-today buy. She likes the feel of the new shirt on her midriff skin, smoothing down the shirt over her hips with the heels of her palms, a shopping bag clutched in each. She looks up to see two boys walking towards her.

"Holy shit," Elizabeth whispers, "It's Hot Vince." There he was with the new guy across the hall, who is really tall and cute too. Hot Vince is, well, hot but he's also short. A few inches shorter than Elizabeth. Being taller than a boy makes Elizabeth feel BIG and that just further fuels her insecurity. A tall one and a short one. Boys always travel in two packs like that. It's funny to Elizabeth, like perhaps it increases their odds. Something for most girls in a variety pack. A tall one, a short one, a rugged one, a neat one. Fat one, skinny one. It's actually a pretty good strategy. Having the two to compare tends to compel a girl to decide which one she likes better and choose that one when in reality she might not choose either had she encountered each one on his own. It's a neat trick. Human nature. Girls hunt in similar ways sometimes. Elizabeth sneaks a glance at herself in a passing mirror. She feels good. She looks good. The scent of cookie tickles her nostrils from the nearby food court. Good God, she is *hungry*. The two boys veer toward her, they approach with silly grins. *Boys will be boys.* New Guy speaks to her.

"Why don't you ever call me?" he says with a big sly flirty smile. He's cute. Taller than she'd realized from afar. Taller than she is which she finds intriguing, as she looks up to few men. When she does it makes her feel...safe? Whatever it is, she likes it and she likes the attention.

"Why don't you ever call me?" She plays coy and right into the set up.

"Give me your number and I will." He had that all planned. She is impressed. She was chosen. *How lovely to be a woman.* Elizabeth gives New Guy her number. "What's your name?"

"Elizabeth," She writes on his arm.

"I'm Bill, this is my friend Vincent."

Act 1 Scene 15.2

Interior: Dining room/kitchen, day

ELIZABETH is sitting with LOLA
DAVIS and LAURA HILL at Lola's
parents house. Her boobs are two
weeks old.

ELIZABETH:
It's the girls' two week
anniversary. She gives the girls
a jiggle.

Laura is rolling a joint. She holds it up and runs a finger along the bulge, "I can't get it to roll straight, they always come out pregnant."

Elizabeth looks at her cell phone. There is a code. She gave Bill her number a few days ago. If he is going to follow up and call her it should be about today. Since meeting Bill Elizabeth had to endure a disastrous and all-around awkward double date. One of the girls from work sort of blackmailed her into it. Chasey from work has the hots for Elizabeth's brother. A double date with her brother who brought a friend. For his little sister. Nobody except for Chasey was comfortable. This was a high price to pay for a fake ID. Awkward, mortifying double date for Chasey's ID so Elizabeth can get into bars who don't scrutinize cute girls is too hard.

Lola is talking about her vagina, "Her name is Shaniqua Davis. No relation. She's a big confident black woman."

"Your vagina has the same last name as you but you're not related AND your vagina is also a large black woman?" Laura looks at Lola with a quizzical and doubtful eye, lights her joint with a chuckle. She passes the joint to Lola and looks to Elizabeth, "How did Chasey do with your brother?" They call her Chasey at work because she looks like porn actress Chasey Lane, who happens to be her brother's favorite porn star, a detail Elizabeth could have gone the rest of her life not knowing, but it's also possibly the only reason he relented to the double date disaster.

"I'd guess not well since he spent most of the date furious at his friend who couldn't help drool over the girls." She gives the girls another jiggle. She's really getting used to this feeling sexy. "I dressed them up nice." She smiles, "But my brother isn't speaking to me now. I don't know why it's all my fault."

"Isn't she really short?"

"Yeah I guess she's pretty short."

"And isn't your brother kind of really tall?"

"Yeah, actually that was funny. She spent the whole night standing on chairs trying to be at eye level with him."

"Where's Monica?" Laura asks dryly. They've never clicked, Laura and Monica. "I don't trust her." was all Laura would usually say due mostly to a largely Southern upbringing. Laura has no use for Monica, she sees right through Monica's games and thinks she is a complete sociopath. The others barely notice, maybe because they see her more. Monica has a personality morphing habit. *Single White Female dangerous.*

"She's at work."

"Good." They all laugh. Maybe it just looks different from Elizabeth's angle. Her family took Monica in. They share a room, they're like sisters. *Were like sisters. She put me in his car.* Monica needed help and Elizabeth helped her, with makeup, dressing better, a roof. It was Elizabeth who showed Monica how to use her cleavage, which even the heaviest girls can use to their advantage. Horny boys have very short memories. But Monica harbors a deep, jealous resentment for Elizabeth. Maybe it's this that Laura smells but can never quite pinpoint. Monica's deep and twisted hatred manifests in a slow burn. A long game of deceit and torture from behind a smile. The smile of a friend. Of a sister. The student killing the master. *She had to have heard me cry for help, she ignored me* If Laura knew any of this she would be pissed but Elizabeth could never tell her,

"I saw Shannon Grace out the other night…" Elizabeth started to say.

"Ugh, I hate Shannon Fratelli." Laura interrupts. Elizabeth and Shannon Grace Fratelli were from the same part of the Bronx. Old family friends. Both families happened to move from The Bronx up to Yorktown around the same time. No doubt their fathers had the same land developer contacts. Elizabeth and Shannon aren't exactly friends. They basically grew up forced to sit at the kids table together. Since moving to a new town and having no other acquaintances, they became old alliances, even bad ones, which are sometimes better than having no alliances at all.

Lola laughs, "Remember when Shannon blew up Elizabeth's markers?"

"What?" Elizabeth laughs, "Why have I never heard of this before? What the fuck?"

Laura holds up a hand laughing trying to compose herself enough to say, "You went home because Shannon was trying to start a fight with you."

"Oh my God! I remember that! We were talking about our V-Cards, like when we wanted to lose them. She was being mean to me all night for like no reason."

"Yeah, that night. After you went home she found your backpack."

"That's right, I left it there and just walked home in my pajamas."

"She took out your White Out Markers and stomped on them and tried to set them on fire." Laura laughs, "Sorry I guess we were kind of in on trying to blow up your markers. Not that we took her side or anything, we just wanted to see shit blow up." They all laugh.

"I forgot all about that." Lola chimes in.

"I never even noticed when my mother got my backpack back from Mrs. Fratelli I forgot all about my markers. Those White Out Markers were all the rage that year. I looked all over for them."

"Fuck Shannon Grace, she said I was 'Busted.'" Lola offers.

"That's right! We were out at that Dicey place in New Rochelle." Elizabeth explains to Laura who hadn't been around for that one. "They didn't ask pretty girls for ID."

"How did Monica get in?" They all have a good laugh at this.

"Shannon Grace was there that night, she comes over to us and tells Lola she took a poll…"

"A poll? That's lame."

"She goes, 'We took a poll and decided you're busted.' Busted was Shannon Grace's thing that year. Everyone was 'Busted.' Then she told me, 'No Hot Guy Would Ever Want To Fuck...' me." Elizabeth adds. "Later she was sniffing around this guy I knew and I knew I could steal him from her so I hooked up with him in the parking lot. She was so mad." Elizabeth chuckles at this but then thinks about it and a wrinkle crosses her brow. "Really fucked things up for me with his brother though."

"What?!" Laura and Lola's eyes open wide.

"Remember I was trying to hook up with that guy, James? It was his brother. I was almost there too. But after I hooked up with his brother he wouldn't talk to me…"

"Deuce!" Lola yells.

"Ah, the one that got away." Elizabeth recalls fondly her metaphorical fish story.

"Deuce?" Laura asks.

"They did it twice" Lola clarifies, laughing.

"Oh!" Laura laughs with Lola and they both repeat, "Deuce!"

Lola asks Elizabeth, "Have you seen Becky?"

"Who? The Mad Stabber?"

Lola laughs, "She was always trying to stab you for some reason, wasn't she?"

"Yeah, she was!" Elizabeth laughs, "One time I was tickling her…"

"Well that would make me want to stab you." Laura interjects with a smile.

"I was sitting on her gut…"

"Her gut was huge. Probably still is."

"She had the biggest ass of any woman I have ever seen of any race. I was straddling her tickling her and she blew this huge fart! It was hilarious."

"She must have been mortified." Laura laughs.

"Yeah sixteen year old girls don't fart." Lola adds as her dad comes into the room.

"Mr. Davis!" Elizabeth and Laura yell out like school girls. They love Lola's parents and Mr. Davis is especially popular with Lola's friends. He's a happy fun dad with his corny jokes and warm safe dad hugs. Mr. Davis was and continues to be a genuine safe space to be around in a world deceivingly hostile to a young girl. Mr. Davis is one of the good guys.

"Hey girls." He greets them enthusiastically, "Laura Lee in the face how have you been kid? How's your Mom? Dad?"

Laura chuckles at his familiar joke, "My middle name isn't Lee." She blushes and protests like she did when she was a kid. They had never been completely sure what he meant by "in the face" but they had always assumed it had to do with Laura's dead pan brutal honesty. You can always count on Laura to tell it to you like it is. Mr. Davis made some corny dad jokes, played all the hits for the mini reunion, lightened the mood and took his leave, leaving them to continue to reminisce and and catch up.

As Mr. Davis leaves, Lola looks around mischievously making sure her father is gone. "I want to get a specimen." She says quietly. "I want to get a guy to cum in a jar and see what happens to it over time."

Elizabeth grows a grin, "How would he get it in there? Are you going to help?"

"I'll watch." Lola responds. They all laugh,

Elizabeth grins, nods, "I would watch."

Laura thinks differently, "I think you would help."

Elizabeth nods with a smile, "I would help...Oh shit, did I tell you about Ethan breaking up with Monica?"

"That guy is weird." Lola adds, "You would have hated him Laura."

Elizabeth recounts the story for them. Laura can't stop laughing, "The Afterlife!" She howls.

Elizabeth looks at her cell phone again and then remembers in mild horror that she gave Bill the phone number in her room. Monica's room. Lately Monica has seemed like she would try to sleep with any guy Elizabeth might be into. *I wonder if it's because I wouldn't kiss her?* She thinks back to the night they were drinking and Monica came on to her. Elizabeth had backed away and now suspects she is embarrassed by the encounter. She suddenly hopes he isn't calling. Not yet.

Eventually the conversation cycles back to Shannon Grace and the White Out Marker fire, followed by what they had initially been talking about -- losing their virginity. Naturally updates were in order as most of them had lost their virginity by now, being young adults on the verge of being able to drink legally. In another few years. Lola is the only one who is proudly still a virgin and weird about the whole thing. Her friends think she likes the way it intrigues boys: An adult virgin girl. Laura's tale is uneventful, high school boyfriend. *All my fault* echoes in Elizabeth's head. Her cherry popping had been less than legal. As well as a major source of tension between her and her brother. A nervous pang had hit her when Chasey said "double date with your brother." She had been shocked when he'd relented to go on the date. It had been his friend who took her V-Card, but a different one than the one he brought on the Double Date Disaster. Adam. They haven't spoken since Adam seduced his little sister. He went behind her brother's back and started talking to her around the block, or on the phone if he could get his little sister to call and ask for Elizabeth in case someone else answered. It was actually sort of sweet in a sick predatory way but big brother found out within the week and came home livid. At her. Why was it her fault? Of course he hadn't mentioned beating Adam up at school or the detention he had to serve for it. He didn't really blame Elizabeth but it felt that way to her. Like it was all her fault. Like she did something to lead Adam on. She looks down at her chest. *All my fault.*

"When was it for you?" Laura gets around to asking Elizabeth. She thinks back to the V-Card discussion sleepover and the Markers, the innocent middle school girls in footie pajamas, braiding pigtails, pillow fights, back of the hand kissing practice. They were so young.

"It was a few months after Shannon Grace set my markers on fire."

Act 1 Scene 15.3

Interior: Car, night

MONICA is driving.

Elizabeth has failed her driving test several times. An embarrassing amount of times. She has a new road test scheduled for a few weeks. Now if she can just get someone to teach her how to drive.

"We'll stop by the party, then we'll go up the street to Fulgums." Monica is saying. It's come to where Monica talking, forward or backwards, is annoying to Elizabeth.

"Why Fulgums?"

"The Greek is playing." The Greek is a guy in a bar cover band Monica has been trying to hook up with. Tensions have been rising between Elizabeth and Monica due to the growing pains of living together. Elizabeth feels Monica is ungrateful for her and her family's hospitality, unlike when she first moved in. She was polite and humble. But people get comfortable. Monica seems shifty lately too. Like tonight. She hadn't mentioned going to the bar after "stopping by" the party but she had intended on going all along. She could have said something is all. They are headed down towards the point just south of Peekskill. Their friend Dan is hosting a small gathering at his mother's house in Buchanan. Monica had tried to hook up with Dan only to find out he's gay, which was hilarious to Elizabeth.

"Your Gaydar sucks! I don't know how you can even call yourself a Fag Hag." She'd laughed. Dan seemed gay to Elizabeth but she just let Monica try anyway. Tonight he assured Monica that there would be straight boys to which she'd given him the "We'll stop by" line.

"Who?" Elizabeth demanded on the way. "Last time we were down here that guy Ty stuck his dick in my ear."

"I heard he moved to Pittsburgh with an exotic dancer." Elizabeth isn't listening to Monica though, she is thinking about that party. Ty might have been at that party with Bill now that she thinks about it. She had thought he looked familiar at the mall.

"Did anyone call for me while I was out with Laura?" She carefully leaves out that they went to Lola's house.

"In fact a very nice sounding young man named Bill called about an hour after you left. So where did you and Laura go?"

"Just out. Around and shit. What did Bill say?" She tries not to sound too interested. Hopefully he didn't mention being the tall handsome fella across the corridor at the mall, or Monica would be all over him.

"And where did you meet this Bill?" Monica sings with far too much joy.

"At the mall while I was shopping the other day."

"Where does he live?" Elizabeth doesn't actually know this yet.

"We just met." She folds her arms and leaves it at that.

Elizabeth and Monica walk into the small house with matching fake smiles. Once inside they go separate ways to get away from each other. Monica goes left toward some people in the living room so Elizabeth turns right and goes into the small kitchen. The kitchen has a classic black and white checkered floor and a lot of chrome and bright red fixtures. It looks very much like a 50's era diner and it only adds to the school girl whimsy. Dan and his Mom are good company. Trish and Dan are sitting at the small table talking. Dan welcomes in Elizabeth and she joins them. Elizabeth doesn't care much for many of Monica's new friends. She's also intrigued that Bill called. She never does mention him by name to Trish and Dan -- just that a boy she met called.

Monica is driving again. She needs to stop for smokes before the bar. They've both nearly forgotten how sick of each other they were a little while ago. Their talk is jovial party gossip. As they approach a traffic light a tall figure appears on the side of the road in Monica's headlights. As they roll to a stop he is next to them. Elizabeth looks out the window.

"Hey, that's Bill!" She immediately regrets saying out loud. No way to hide him from Monica now. Oh well. She rolls down the window.

"Hey baby, how much?"

Act 1 Scene 15.4

Interior: bar, night

BILL and ELIZABETH find a spot near one corner of the square bar along the window in front. Only one stool is available, the bar is packed. Elizabeth slides onto the stool at Bill's insistence, he stands beside her.

Near the rear of the bar a live band plays hard rock radio hits. Monica makes her way through the crowd so the bass player, whose attention she came seeking can see into her cleavage.

"What would you like?" Bill offers to Elizabeth, waving the bartender over.

"Hey Billy, how's your sister?" She asks as she approaches.

"Shot of whiskey and a coke." Elizabeth says in his ear just loud enough to hear over the band. He asks the bartender for the shot, the soda and a beer for himself. As she walks away to get their drinks he leans over and says in her ear,

"She's my cousin." She comes back with the drinks and Bill offers a twenty between his first and middle finger. She holds up a hand and walks away, "Thanks, Rene." He calls after her then turns his attention back to Elizabeth. Her hand drifts towards his on the bar. She looks up into his eyes. His are soft, kind, hazel brown. He's rugged but cute, almost boyish. Several people from around the bar have already given him a wave or a smile. Even the singer in the band notices him between songs.

"Hey Bill!" He calls over the microphone. "Can't miss you back there buddy, good to see you." Bill offers a humble wave, a shy smile, feigning embarrassment but clearly OK with the attention. Elizabeth finds herself excited to be next to him with all these people waving to him. *The Time I Touched Greatness.*

"Where were you headed when we saw you?" Elizabeth asks.

He chuckless silently under the music, shouts in her ear, "Here." They share amusement with this.

"Where were you walking from?"

"The Warehouse. I was watching Vincent's band practice, that guy I was with at the mall."

"We were at our friend Dan's mom's house…"

"You were just at Trish's house?"

"You know Dan and Trish?"

"Yeah sure, I know Dan and Trish!" Bill leaves out the fact that Dan is his roommate. They both realize at the same time what Elizabeth had suspected earlier: They were both at the same party at Trish's house about a year ago.

"Well your old roommate Ty stuck his dick in my ear."

"That sounds like Ty."

"And then he called me! I was like how did you get this number?! Because I certainly didn't give it to him. He put his dick in my ear! I ran away!"

Bill gives it some thought. "You know I don't think we had a phone in the house at that point, we had to walk up the block and across the street to use a pay phone."

"But why would he even call!? I literally ran away from him and his pecker he was waving around. He stuck it in my ear. Did I mention he stuck it in my ear? And more importantly…" She pauses. "How the fuck did he get my number?"

"He's fucking clueless sometimes. His version of all that was probably very different. He has a habit of embellishing his stories…a lot. Especially when they are about some girl he met who he swears is totally into him. No doubt he went home that night and told everyone all about this chick who was totally into him, lord knows how he got your number."

"I don't think I even told him my name." Bill nods as though that sounds about right for Ty. "One night after that I saw him at the mall, outside. I went out for a smoke, he was out there. He starts talking to me and my one syllable answers did not deter him in any way. He was sitting on the hood of what I thought was his car. It was nice, I think it was a Camaro or something, I don't know cars too well, but he obviously wanted me to think it was his but then some other guy comes out and starts yelling at him 'hey get the fuck off my car!' and shit."

"I bet he didn't even know the guy, right?" Bill laughs.

"Right!"

Bill and Elizabeth talk for a long time, having a good time, laughing and enjoying each other's company. The band, the crowd, they all seem to fade away into dull background static. It's just them in the bar as far as they're concerned. There is no time, just right here and now.

"How did they get the car out?"

"Petition."

Act 1 Scene 16

Interior: Car, night

BILL pulls into a spot at the deli right in front of the door.

BILL:

I don't think I should go in there.

"Why?"

"It's a long story. There was a fist fight…" Elizabeth's eyes widen,

"Well I'm not letting that go by, we'll talk about it later." She shakes her head, checks her reflection and goes inside to order sandwiches.

Some believe this deli is the center of the universe. It's known to be a pretty wild place. For a deli. She checks her reflection once more on the door on the way in. The boys at the deli pay attention to her. A bell rings her arrival as she walks in the door. She likes the attention. Who can blame a girl?

"Hey, what's going on?" Matty greets her as she walks in. From over Matty's shoulder Nads peeks through under the cigarette rack.

"Can we see your boobs?" This is not uncommon around here and they are always polite about it and Elizabeth does love attention.

"Give me a pack of smokes and I will." Elizabeth had pretty much counted on getting smokes for a flash. And who wouldn't want to show off the new stuff? These gals are…manageable. She's wearing the tits for a change, rather than the other way around like it used to be. After all, her doctor did beautiful work, these sweater puppies are handcrafted works of art. It's practically a sin to keep them hidden all the time.

"Who's that out in the car?" Nads grills Elizabeth while he grills her sandwiches. Matty puts a pack of cigarettes at the end of the deli case.

Elizabeth nods to the door. "I'm on a date. He said last time he was here he got into a fist fight or something, said maybe he shouldn't come…"

Nads throws down his spatula. "Bill is outside!? I love Bill!" He pushes past Matty and out the front door. "Bill!" He yells, sticking his head in Bill's window, giving him a big wet kiss on the mouth. Then he points up at the security camera on the front of the building, "It's not gay, there's a camera. It's art." He drags Bill from the car, "Come inside, who cares." Nads drags Bill back to the grill and continues cooking while he grills Bill like a father on prom night. "And where will you be taking Miss Elizabeth this fine evening young William?"

"We're going to eat sandwiches at the playground."

"The playground? Hey Matty maybe they'll see your girlfriend." Matty gives Nads the finger from the cash register.

"Matty's still pissing himself." Nads laughs, looking over at Matty. Bill looks over as well and assures Matty that he's feeling much better now and isn't going to start a fight again. Nads and Bill laugh at this.

"Is a playground picnic not a respectable date?" Elizabeth asks sounding as if she's joking but she's really not. She hasn't been on many dates before, besides the Double Date Disaster. Meanwhile Nads and Elizabeth keep glancing at the pack of cigarettes on the counter and each other.

"Fuck you guys, I wasn't scared." Matty holds up both middle fingers, "Come over here and pay for dinner, Mr. Cheap Date." Bill pays for the sandwiches. Nads wraps them up and walks them to Bill in front of the counter, handing them to him he gives Bill another big kiss and slaps him on the ass.

"You have her home by Nine now, ya hear? You kids have fun!" He tells Bill.

"Nine? Shit, she'll be home for breakfast." Bill gives Nads a big wink, lightly jabs his elbow in Nads' ribs then heads for the door, pausing to look back at Elizabeth who is still standing at the other end of the counter near the grill. And her cigarettes. She starts forward, stalling, holds up a finger.

"I'll be right out." Bill nods and ducks out the door to the car. Nads and Matty both turn their full attention to Elizabeth. She looks around quickly, the coast is clear. She gives them a big old eye full of the girls. Then she pulls her shirt back down, snatches the cigs off the counter and scurries briskly for the door.

"Thanks boys." She sings, "Bye." Waving over her shoulder. Nads and Matty stand at attention and applaud.

"Thank you." Nads yells.

Matty adds, "Come again."

Bill and Elizabeth are sitting on the swings. They sway gently, eating their sandwiches. They talk about where they're from, went to school, people they might know in common. She thinks he's cute, his charming goofy sense of humor is disarming in his shadow. She can't help notice his hands are quite large as is the rest of him. You know what they say? *Big Gloves.* She likes the way he looks at her, his eyes are kind. He thinks she's beautiful and she can feel that, she radiates in the glow of it. All she's wanted all this time was for someone to just like her for her. It always feels like...something else. Not this time. This time, right here, right now on this playground, on these swings it feels like someone genuinely likes her for her, for her beauty inside and out. She's not too tall, too fat, too chesty, too opinionated. She is her and she feels he genuinely likes her.

"How do you know those guys at the deli?" He asks her.

"We know a lot of the same people, school, shows, parties. Going to the deli, of course. What about you? How do you know them?"

"Same, I guess." Bill leaves out that his other roommate works there.

"What was that fight all about?"

"It was dumb. It was over a girl."

"That's not dumb."

"No it was. She sucked. She fucked around with one of the guys who worked there, Davis. I went down there, stormed in, Davis was sitting on the trashcan by the grill. I grabbed him by his hair, difficult with these mitts because he had a short little 'hawk. Two of his friends were there, they tried to help but I just kind of tossed them." Elizabeth laughs and on the inside swoons a little. It's silly and cliche but sometimes it's arousing when boys play rough, act big and tough. Sometimes. You can't tell them though, that's when they act like idiots. It's best if they don't know you're watching. "Bread and chips went flying everywhere." Bill conveniently leaves out the part when they bested him for a moment and held his head to the grill just as they would leave out the part about him tossing them around with ease when they tell it. Of course as getting to know you goes, everyone spends a third of our lives at work, some of us much much more than others. Some a lot less.

"So you work at the portrait studio now?"

"Just part time for a little extra cash. I work nights full time at a rehab out in Somers."

"I just put in an application at the portrait studio." Elizabeth had decided a new job was in order for a new life and left the record store.

"Didn't you work at the record store?"

"I did. For a few years. I wanted a change."

"So you're going to be working at the picture place then, huh?" Elizabeth thinks she detects a hint of nervousness in Bill's voice.

"Yeah, you think you can help me get the job?"

"Yeah...no, yeah, sure. Sure." As before, Bill seems uncomfortable.

She changes the subject, "Have you ever been to the Bomb Shelter?"

"Like a Cold War bunker?"

"No silly," She smiles, "That farmhouse basement on Croton avenue near the high school where they had punk shows."

Bill levels his hand over his head ducking under it. "I don't do so well in farmhouse basements."

She giggles, his boyish dimples are cute when he makes shy jokes about himself.

"You're a punk rock girl, eh?"

She nods her head side to side. "Side to side," She smiles.

"What?"

"Side to side. Punk rock makes your head go side to side. Metal forward and back. Head banging. "

"That's funny."

"It works."

Bill gives it some thought nodding his head side to side and then alternately back and forth. "I guess it does. Do you like Pantera?"

"I'm aware of them." Bill talks about Pantera, obviously his favorite band at length. How they, along with Slayer, saved heavy metal through 90's grunge and how they were one of the few bands that really made it past the Seattle invasion. He lays out a detailed analysis of their discography and how it relates to lots of other things.

"Like how everyone is a Beatle?" She thinks it's cute how excited he is about it though she's still thinking about how different music makes your head move differently.

"Hip hop makes your head go back..."

Inevitably as every first date conversation does it comes around to the Ex-Arena.

"I guess I've never really done much dating," She admits, "Seemed like most of the time it was just come over and hook up, play Nintendo and chill. That type of thing."

"You play Nintendo?" Bill looks excited at this thought.

"I slay Dr. Mario." She brags. "So what was her name?"

"Casey. Most of my friends hated her anyway. I don't know I guess I'm still a little shaken by it. Maybe not. Wary. Maybe?" He shrugs and smiles sheepishly. She nods.

"I know how you feel. I kind of got...hurt. A few months ago...it was different than that. I don't know, are you saying you don't want to go rushing into anything?"

"Yeah." He nods. Of course they both really want the opposite. They both want exactly that, actually. They do want to rush in, rush into love, to bed, to be loved, to not be hurt.

Of course X and Y chromosomes tend to handle things like that a little differently.

"So what about your ex?" How did he hurt you?"

"You know, I guess I really don't have an ex. A guy hurt me." She knows she's leaving out a lot of detail, "But we weren't together or anything like that." Desperate to change lanes Elizabeth happily leaps off the swing suddenly and yells, "Let's go on the seesaw!" Running off giggling in a come chase me zig-zag.

From the ground Bill looks up at Elizabeth with the moon behind her. "Why don't you have your driver's license yet?" He gently stands up lowering Elizabeth slowly then lifting his legs up and allowing his weight raise her back up again. They bounce lightly back and forth on their knees.

"Nobody ever taught me to drive. I keep failing the test."

"They give you a handbook, did you read it?" He laughs,

"Of course I read it you fool. The written test isn't the problem."

"Parallel parking?"

"Oh I fail before that part. But yeah, that too. Nobody has ever actually taught me how to drive."

Bill stands still and motions with a wave for her to get off. "Do you have another road test scheduled?"

"Yeah, in a few days, actually."

"Come on. Let's go to the parking lot. I'll teach you how to drive."

Act 1 Scene 16.1

Interior:Bedroom, night

ELIZABETH (in v/o)
With Bill's instruction I pass
my road test. He is a natural
teacher. I get my license and
the job, all with a little help
from Bill.

He got the job himself with the help of preexisting friendships on the inside. He gets her the job and now they spend most of the week together but he hasn't been around all weekend. *All for the best,* she figures, as she's learning the ropes of the business in her first few days, orientation and such. She meets new co-workers without Bill around to distract her. Or to protect her, for that matter. It's good for her to relearn to be out in the world, exposed without a net. Unrehearsed. No crutches. No understudies. When her new co-workers start calling her Lizzy she goes with it. New job, new life, new tits, new name. Lizzy it is.

Elizabeth finishes doing her makeup, straightening her hair and heads out to the car. Dad gave her a car for finally passing her road test. It's nice, used but in good condition. Generous. Also sensible. A little Dodge Neon. Bill hasn't been around all weekend but they spoke this morning, agreed to meet for lunch. She wants to drive so Bill said to pick him up at his parents' house in Peekskill. He'd vaguely mentioned living with roommates that did not sound like his parents. He says his parents are away and he was stopping by to check on the house and stuff. Feed the cats. It feels like he doesn't want her to know where he lives. Is he poor? Embarrassed by squalor? Sounds too wacky, too 80's sitcom misunderstanding to be the truth. Maybe he really does live with his parents? She thinks maybe she'll confront him about it later. They're going to see a movie. Classic date-date. Scary stuff. Either one can get cold feet at any time, spooked, run off like a frightened deer in the forest.

Bill is standing on the sidewalk in front of a two-family house on a tree-lined street across from a pet store and an ice cream parlor.

When she pulls up she excitedly asks, "Can we get ice cream later?"

As he gets in he says, "Why not we get ice cream now?" She throws it in park and he gets back out. She gets out and they cross the street together. Much of her life Elizabeth always felt too big. Lumbering. She's always been awkward about it but in Bill's large presence she feels comfortably small. It's comforting to feel small and safe, wrapped in a big warm arm. They sit on the patio and eat their ice cream cones on wrought iron tables by wrought iron railings. The patio decking is blue stone, neat and sharp. The iron tables and chairs leave white powdery scuff marks beneath their feet.

"Why don't I know where you live?" She says boldly with a lick of her cone. "Do you live there?" She points across the street where she found him, "With your parents? It's cool, a lot of people do."

Bill shakes his head, swallowing a big lick of ice cream. "I don't want my roommate to steal you."

She laughs. "No really, what is it? Is it a gross mess?"

"Yeah it's gross. We're slobs." She believes he and his roommates are gross but not that he's embarrassed by it, nor does she think that his roommate would be trying to steal her.

"You don't know this crowd." He laughs. "Their philosophy is try to bang your buddy's girl. If she does it, she's a ho and you did your buddy a favor."

As they drive away with their bellies full and their brains frozen Bill points to a house a few blocks from his parents "Used to live there with Ty."

"Dick in my ear?"

"Yeah that guy, some other people."

"Why don't you still live there?"

"Legendary party."

"They kicked you out?"

"By petition."

"That's what you said about the car."

"That was the joke because they really did petition the landlord to get us out after a huge three-day rager we threw. After which Ty put his car in the neighbor's yard."

During all this time together Bill and Elizabeth have been clear of their intentions. They are flirty, sometimes even aggressively but it's often among company and for show. Making a joke of it in a way so it's safe. In private, however, that show of affection has been slower, more intense like a long chess match. A coy game of cat-and-mouse with passion and desire. They've built it up with much teasing. In the theater a hand slyly feels a leg, a leg presses against a leg, a hand slowly touches a hand. A toe dip, a catch and release, a little back and forth dance. Hands settle, nestle together in her lap, he leans toward her, looms over her, she's safe in his shadow. They watch the movie but their hands slowly caress. Their lips crack with anticipation. She wants him to kiss her. He wants to kiss her. They let it simmer, facing front, faces red, hearts beat faster. Her breasts swell, heavy breathing, alert and perky aimed at his peripherals. He shifts in his seat, try to politely adjust, aware she's aware. She breathes a light whisper in his ear, a chill down his spine, he turns to her, she looks up at him, their faces lit with the warm melting reflections from the giant silver screen. He leans forward, her smile invites him, she accepts his lips on hers, they kiss for the first time.

Is it fireworks? Maybe. Elizabeth had not allowed herself to be this intimate in many months since the attack. Bill says he hasn't been intimate since Casey. Elizabeth has the correct impression that Bill is not one to be very open about feelings in the first place as they'd spoken length about exactly that. It feels exclusive. Since her old self, since the girls' rebirth they had not yet felt the gentle touch of sexual foreplay. They kiss in the spotlight of the movie alone in the dark, eyes shut, doors to the mind open. Flash. Bang. Fireworks. A crackling fire. The 4th of July. Bright starbursts silently ride across the rippling lake as the bright flash lights up the night sky. The boom hits you in the chest as sound, the crack of light in Elizabeth's closed eyes sparks from their hot mouths. She sweats lightly, her head spins. She feels like a schoolgirl on that metal spinning disk on the playground laughing, innocently smiling into the sun. Her hair blows back, the creak of the metal bearings squeak in her mind. She had not expected to feel this comfortable with a man the way she does with Bill right now. It's a warm, safe surprise. His big hands caress her body. She feels sexy, accepted. Accepted. She is enough.

Act 1 Scene 16.2

Interior: Portrait Studio, day

ELIZABETH is staring out the window into the mall, daydreaming.

Give a revolving cast of teens and young twentysomethings working through art school a photography studio and some free time and two things are inevitable: Interoffice Romance -- i.e., hooking up in the dark room -- and silly photo shoots. Bill and Elizabeth are quiet about flirting and dating, but not secretive. They hook up in the dark room, which Elizabeth thinks they are pretty obvious about. She sees her fellow employees' wondering eyes whenever they sneak off to make out in the dark room. He paws at her around the studio, she eats up the attention and paws back. They call it casual but the time they spend together is anything but. It feels as if they belong. The bond they are developing is very tight. They have become fast friends something neither had expected but both welcome and need.

It finally happens. He's been patient and that might be their downfall but she's ready. He needs to drop something off at his parents house it's a good excuse for them to hang out for a little while they leave his car at the mall and she drives to Peekskill.

"My parents are away." He says mockingly, "Gee Willikers would you like to see my Star Wars action figgers, Miss Lizbeth?"

"You're all over the place there, big guy." She lays a hand on his chest, just a touch. She parks in front and they go in. Bill takes an envelope from his shirt pocket and pins it to the refrigerator with a big magnet from the auto parts store down the block and a colorforms He-Man magnet he made as a kid. He turns her to him and gives her a sly grin and a wink,

"Hey you wanna go fool around in my old bedroom?"

"Thought you'd never ask." They hurry up the narrow staircase. Bare wood creaks under their speed. He's been very patient. She's needed him to be. He's accepted vague hits and understands he knows more than most, though it isn't much. Anyone save for Monica. Every word Elizabeth could bring herself to say she's said to Bill. He's not dumb. He knows. He can fill in the blanks. She feels he accepts it all. All of her. She even feels like she's in some sort of relationship.

In his old bedroom. they sit on the bed. He points out the elaborate pulley system he'd rigged up to lock and unlock the door. It's very cool and works well but it's kind of silly as the room is so tiny he can reach the door lock from the bed if he just reaches out. It's not even a stretch.

"You slept here? The bed's too small for you." She smiles, puts her hand on his chest, leans forward, "Goon." She says with laughter in her voice. She kisses him. He pulls her in to meet him. Slowly they undress each other. The signals are all going through. The stars align, words go unspoken. They move in rhythmic unison, becoming a starburst, rockets red glare, trumpets sound, Elizabeth lets herself go. Bill is enormous. He's big and meaty. Elizabeth had not been with a man since being violated by one and she had been afraid sex might be ruined for her. She even warned him, if she freaks out, but she never does. Oh, he's hitting bottom, but not freaking her out. She may have blacked out for a moment but she does not freak out.

In the afterglow they lay still naked, her in his arms, his back against the wall. His outstretched legs still reach the edge of the small single mattress. It's comical.

The front door opens and shuts downstairs. Two girls voices come in with the traffic then shut it out. The girls are muffled as they move around down there. Then the knock of their boot heels starts to come up the stairs. Their voices get louder and become audible as they get closer. Elizabeth is getting nervous. Bill doesn't seem to care. Elizabeth frantically follows the pulley system line, *IS IT LOCKED!?!?!* In the fog of war she can't see straight The boots stomp to a stop outside the door.

"William!?" A loud female voice hollers from just outside the door. The knob is already turning before she's even finished his name. Elizabeth, still naked, claws at the thin white sheet they're barely under. Her clothes are in a neat pile just out of reach on the chair beside the bed. She hurriedly wraps the sheet around her, it feels practically see through. The door slams open. A tall, broad shouldered, full figured woman fills the doorway, "William!" She yells and plops down on the bed, "Where are Mom and Dad?"

"North Carolina." Elizabeth is relieved the girl is his sister not a wife or something he hadn't mentioned. Sis looks at Elizabeth and asks right in her face,

"Who are you?" She appears to have no regard for Elizabeth's nakedness. Nor her brother's for that matter.

Bill finally interjects, "Elizabeth. This is my sister, Serena.

"Hi…" Elizabeth starts to say.

"Do you have a sister?"

"Uh, yeah I do, I, uh…"

"Well I don't like her." Serena asserts with no context and then turns completely back to Bill, "What are you doing here?" She glances at Elizabeth on that and then back at Bill.

"They needed help with the rent."

"But they're looking at a house in North Carolina?" Serena shakes her head. Elizabeth sits still, trembling, trying to disappear. Her shirt is just out of reach right behind Serena who is still just sitting on the edge of the tiny bed, which might be shrinking now that she thinks about it, like it's all perfectly natural. *HELLO!?!?! Naked Here!* She screams on the inside. Panic is simmering, she's mortified. *How can it get worse or any more embarrassing? It can't possibly, can it?* Of course it can because another girl, younger than Elizabeth joins them in the tiny shrinking room and she slumps on the chair right on top of Elizabeth's neatly folded shirt and pants. The second girl is mousey and utters a grunt at Bill. She gives Elizabeth a bored glance with no emotion. *Why isn't he making them leave!?* Elizabeth is screaming in her head. Of course eventually they do leave and Bill seems amused by the whole thing. Elizabeth starts to dress but Bill pulls her back. She giggles in his arms and surrenders once again.

Since then they hook up in the dark room at work, in her car, which is a real trick because it's quite small. His car too is comically small for hooking up in but they do it. They hook up anywhere they can. She still has not seen where he lives. And she's NOT going back to his parents house to have sex, sisters walking in all over the place just hanging out as if Elizabeth isn't naked as a Jaybird. Still, Elizabeth is content. Bill is nice to her and that's enough.

Act 1 Scene 16.3

interior:Photo studio, day

A young mom walks into the studio toting a young child. ELIZABETH is sitting on a stool behind a small counter. They politely smile at each other. She looks at the prices over Elizabeth's head, mutters something to the kid and hurries him out mumbling some unnecessary excuse.

The two high school kids working with Elizabeth this afternoon are at lunch together and it's especially slow. Elizabeth is content to sit and watch the light mall traffic walk by. It's just as well that the woman took her kid and got out of there, didn't want to pay these outlandish prices. The portrait studio is another dying industry in the mall. Laws of Diminishing Returns. Even with the ever young crew of minimum wage workers the costs of the products have to keep going up and the quality will only stay the same at best, if not decline in addition to consumer products putting better and better portrait quality products right in their phones. Such is the free market. Elizabeth doodles on the back of a discarded price list flier coupon giggling like a schoolgirl, *Bill + Elizabeth. Mr. and Mrs. Bill & Elizabeth Roberts. Elizabeth Roberts.*

Since Bill hasn't been around weekends Elizabeth spent a confusing evening after work last night with Dan and Trish. The three of them sat at the little kitchen table with a bottle of wine. When Trish tapped out first and went to bed, Dan went on a long tear-filled monologue slurring all the way about how he feels about Elizabeth, which is completely and heterosexualy in love with her. This only reinforces her insecurities about being lumbering and mannish. *What's wrong with me?* Elizabeth is staring at her transparent reflection in the window. She had a gay friend in high school who was secretly collecting her hair, keeping it in a film canister and he was stone sober when he clumsily tried to kiss her. "But you're gay, right?" she'd said, pushing him away. He even had a boyfriend at the time. It did not help Elizabeth's confidence to feel like a hot drag queen. A pregnant woman walks past the studio and Elizabeth thinks about the water treading conversation on the playground. They approached carefully, hypotheticals, very hypothetical, no scary commitments, just theories. *IF we had kids...?* The conversation arrived there innocently enough. The fact that "they would be huge" was the general and obvious consensus. "I think by six months there'd be a big old foot hanging down to your knee," Bill had joked. "Wearing a Doc Martin!" she'd added, careful not to sound too eager. Talk of having a baby is not the best way to turn a first date into a second date.

One of the girls from the night shift, Lauren, comes in. She and Elizabeth take some silly pictures with props.

"Bill said you hit him with your car."

"What?" Elizabeth feigns ignorance to Lauren's accusation.

"He said you were dropping him off at his parents house and you hit him with your car…"

"He's making a big deal out of nothing," Elizabeth waves it off.

"So did you hit him?" Lauren rolls her eyes with a smile.

"Well, yeah but…it was like barely and he was behind me I saw him in the rearview mirror and all of a sudden, I don't know how he got his goony legs all the way around the car and in front of me, he threw himself all over the hood all dramatic and in slow motion. Did he mention the part where he rolled over my little hood in slow motion?"

Lauren is laughing too hard to hear any more. "Oh my god Lizzy, you fucking crack me up."

Act 1 Scene 17

Interior: Portrait Studio, day

ELIZABETH has accepted that BILL isn't around on the weekends. He is very good at getting away with vague answers, damn those dimples. From what Elizabeth has pieced together he's been visiting an old friend from Peekskill, in Boston. This is true.

The night shift is starting to come in around the mall, portrait studio included. The studio is oddly busy with portrait work. Elizabeth had spent a really nice week with Bill. She had not expected to see him today or until late Sunday, yet there he is, walking in the mall. He seems slightly taken aback to see her behind the counter when he walks in. She is in the middle of ringing up a customer for pictures she took of a kid next to a big 2. Lauren comes in with Vincent. Some of his friends and people around the studio call him Velvet, his crossdressing stage persona. Elizabeth finds this silly. She calls him Vincent.

All three of them walk towards the back saying, "Hey Lizzy," as they walk past her. Bill slips by with a try-not-to-look look on his face. Her glare does nothing to slow him down. Elizabeth finishes her transaction and follows them in back. She finds them storing belongings for shift and talking casually.

"What are you doing here?" She tries to sound conversational rather than accusatory. She feels as though she's come off like an inquisitor.

"His *girlfriend* is coming from Boston." Lauren sings 'girlfriend' in a shrill falsetto. It punches Elizabeth in the gut. Her glare focuses harder, she feels like she might throw up. *Girlfriend? His girlfriend?* The words melt into her mind...what does this mean? I thought...I thought I was his girlfriend. Who the fuck is this bitch? That everyone else seems to know about? *Everyone but me.* Elizabeth reddens with anger and humiliation. She cannot forgive this. She will *not* forgive this. This absolutely cannot be. He lied. He didn't lie, but he wasn't truthful. He didn't tell her. He told them but not her. How did she not see it? How did she not realize she wasn't his girlfriend? *What's wrong with me? Why does he have two girls, why aren't I enough?* She shrieks inside, she can't stand the feel of her own skin.

"I have to go." She says flatly, turns and leaves. She can no longer stand there with this humiliation. It soaks her, she's dripping in it like Carrie on Prom Night drenched in humiliation rather than pig's blood. Pig's blood right now might be less humiliating. They all know. As far as she's concerned, they are all pointing and laughing at her. Their phantom laughter echoes down the hall after her, following her out the door. She walks slowly past the big floor to ceiling windows, she imagines them all following her, laughing, pointing and staring.

Customers walk by, all but oblivious to Elizabeth. In the store, Lauren and Vincent go about their business but Elizabeth can feel their eyes burning holes in her back. Prying, judging eyes, penetrating her and her red-hot humiliation. She refuses to cry, refuses to take even one glance back into the store. She just keeps walking. If she would look she would see they are not looking. They are not laughing or pointing.

She can't see Bill looking out, watching her go, knowing his role and how she can never forgive this. He knows he is watching the one that got away, get away. Bailey had sprung a surprise visit on him. He had planned to go to Boston this weekend, break it off with Bailey, and come home to be with Elizabeth. Even now he had planned to dump her, ship her back off to Boston and be with Elizabeth. She doesn't look back.

All the way through the parking lot to her car she doesn't look back. She doesn't cry. She gets in her car. Shuts the door. Grips the wheel. She cries. "What's wrong with me?" She whispers between sobs. She dabs her eyes on her shirt sleeve,takes a deep breath, declares a line in the sand. *At some point, you have to stand up for yourself*. She contemplates marching back in there and giving him a piece of her mind, but realizes she has not mustered nearly enough courage for that. What courage she has is thin and wavering. Instead she goes for the cell phone. She'll make it clear that this was it. Not before she gives him the chance to explain first. She wants to. A small part of her wants to be able to forgive this. Almost. With one number left to dial she almost loses her nerve. She almost doesn't call at all but she deserves an explanation.

"Why didn't you tell me?" If he answered almost any other way than the way he does she might have erased that line in the sand. Almost any other response. "I was afraid to lose you"? That would have been nice. She could get past that. But that wasn't his response. And maybe it is for the best, maybe it's good, maybe not. Maybe they will forever look back at each other as the ones who got away. Maybe. Maybe not, but she needs to stand up for herself for once. If not now, when? He doesn't answer well. Not at all. He mumbles but it is loud and clear like a little boy who knows he's wrong.

"You didn't ask."

Act 1 Scene 17.1

Interior:Diner Booth, night

ELIZABETH is sitting alone
waiting.

Once able to compose herself in the car she'd called Dan. She needs her Gay. They always make her feel fabulous. Usually. Save for the occasional drunken clumsy attempt to kiss her; those times make her feel like a drag queen. *Jackie Newmar, pleased to meet you.* Hopefully tonight they can continue to pretend THAT didn't happen.

Trish swings by and gives Elizabeth a water and a fresh straw from her apron. "Dan's on his way."

"The good stuff. You know I like a fresh straw." Elizabeth looks up at Trish through the glossy sheen of cried eyes. She carefully tears the end of the straw paper, gently taps the straw free. She slides the straw from the wrapper and sticks it straight down into the water, watching it submerge, her face low to the table. When it taps the bottom she holds it with her fingers and slowly sips the cool water. It's good to hydrate. The cold ice water chills the inside of her cheeks, she feels the coolness descend her esophagus in a distinct bubble. It washes into her stomach which she realizes is empty. She looks up from the water, Dan is walking in from the main dining room into the new smoking section. He's not alone. One of the guys who works at the deli is with him, the one she thinks is cute. He's given her stickers with Vincent's band's logo on it before. She looks down at her lighter. Vincent had put one on it at work last week. She likes the way he looks at her. They sit down both across from her. Deli Guy spots the sticker right away.

"Hey, didn't I give you that sticker?" She explains how this particular sticker came to be on this particular lighter. It amuses Elizabeth how deli guy calls Vincent 'Velvet.' She giggles at the mention and tells him it's silly. Trish comes back with waters for the boys and they all order chocolate cake. The boys have coffee, Elizabeth a cola. Deli Guy appears to be studying her face. Like at the deli, she likes the way he looks at her. His sleepy bedroom eyes are lusty and romantic. She feels desire. She feels desired. It's a cool salve on her freshest wound.

It turns out Deli Guy is Dan's roommate and they realize at about the same time that the guy she is talking about is Bill, who also happens to be their third roommate. *My roommate would try to steal you.* The fact that deli guy is that roommate is not lost on Elizabeth, despite her current mood.

"What's wrong with me?" It feels like she's asking for the katrillionth time today.

Deli Guy awkwardly blurts, "I'd do you."

Trish smacks the back of his head but Elizabeth doesn't mind the idea at all, thinking, *I'd do you, too.*

They sit for awhile, Trish making sure their drinks are never empty, Elizabeth and Dan chain smoking. The gay one tells her she's fabulous, the straight tells her he'd do her. Hell, he's even checking her out. It boosts her spirits. A little shot of confidence. Even if it's just a little sugary lust, empty calories for a quick burst of energy. A smooth little confidence pill. *I'd do ya.* It's cute. He's goofy, sort of nerdy but still cute. Sexy. She notices his arms folded across the table. Muscled but not big, just defined. Shaped nice, strong but sensitive. His hairy forearm gives him a manly presence. It's primal. Elizabeth finds herself focused on it. His strong arms. At one point she wants to lean across the table and give his bicep a bite.

Gay Jim and the Giant Limo

Act 1 Scene 18

Interior: Elizabeth's bedroom, evening

LOLA arrives, shortly after
ELIZABETH'S phone rings.

GAY JIM: (v/o on phone)
Put on something hot honey, skip
the panties and get your
fabulous asses outside in five.

Elizabeth had stopped by the deli accidentally on purpose to see him. She'd told him she had plans when he'd invited her to the bar. That had been true, not that they were any big plans. She was supposed to hang out with Lola and Monica. Plans easily broken or changed. Going to see him they would surely encourage and hopefully not want to tag along.

Monica is in the shower. Lola is on her way over. They're going to assemble here and play it by ear from there. Elizabeth could not have guessed where the night would take her, even if she were given a million guesses.

Shortly after Lola arrives but before they can make a plan Elizabeth's phone rings.

"Put on something hot honey, skip the panties and get your fabulous ass outside in five."

Elizabeth hangs up and looks at Lola, "It was Gay Jim, he said to be outside in five minutes in something..." She air quotes with her fingers, "...hot."

Elizabeth and Lola search through Elizabeth's wardrobe outfitting each other: adjusting a boob, tweaking a hair, a zip here, a pull on this, a tuck here. Monica peeks her head into the room, adjusting her own bust.

"Gay Jim is outside hanging out the sunroof of a big limo…?"

Elizabeth looks Lola and Monica up and down, checks herself once more in the mirror.

"OK let's go, girls." Lola shrugs and heads for the door.

Monica is curious. "Where?"

"I have no idea but I guess we're going there in a limo."

As they exit the house Jim is waving wildly from the sunroof. "Get your hot asses in here girls!" When they get in he hands them drinks. Jim has already been drinking.

"Where are we going?" the girls want to know, curious, happy to be going. They raise glasses as Jim finally shares the big reveal.

"We're going to Big Gay Christmas at Thursdays!"

"In Manhattan?" Lola asks innocently. Nobody notices and her question goes unanswered. Elizabeth directs them past the deli, she thinks they can probably load up on free smokes with all these girls dolled up, all this cleavage on display. The ten short minutes out of the way should prove worth it and they can pregame hard all the way over.

At the deli the three of them burst through the door with a familiar greeting.

"Heeeeeeey" they sing, entering in formation, weaponized cleavage forward. The deli crew is more than happy to trade. Jim strategically stays in the limo to increase the odds. Lola, the only nonsmoker, subs in to get Jim smokes. She tosses them to him as they climb back in and he hands them shots, they toast a successful heist before getting on the road.

"Hey isn't that the Deli Guy you were talking about?" Lola says pointing at the sidewalk.

"He must be on his way home," Elizabeth gets up and pushes toward the sunroof. As she moves she realizes how well the liquor is working. She rises up out of the sunroof, the wind blows her hair back, she catches her breath, waves enthusiastically, "I'm in a liiiiiiiiiiiiimoooooooooooooooooo!" She sinks back down into the backseat adding. "He looks very confused."

Monica pats Elizabeth's shoulder. "You can explain later."

With the Christmas season on full tilt coupled with an unusually warm December, Manhattan crackles with life, teeming in holiday shoppers and seasonal tourists. The big draw of the year-end showstoppers, from FAO Schwartz to Radio City Music Hall, Times Square beats like a neon techno heart. While one might expect Thursdays to be in that beating heart, it's actually about 20 miles north in White Plains.

On a quiet city street one building in the middle of the block bounces with a dance beat. Bright pink tinted light spills from the window on the otherwise dark block, every other storefront closed for the night. A tall broad-shouldered black man stands at the front door with a clipboard held daintily under his arm. He is wearing red patent leather thigh high boots, a tiny red thong and a little red velvet vest with fluffy white piping. He is wearing a comically undersized white Santa beard and equally tiny santa hat cocked sideways on his shiny bald head,

"Are you on my list girls? I'm checkin' it twice," He lisps, "Are you naughty or are you nice?" He waves his hand around at them, "ID's ladies." All three produce their fakes. He glances at them, glances at his clipboard and waves them through handing them back their cards.

"Are we naughty or nice?"

"Neither hunny, go dance."

An inner door behind the bouncer muffles the steady pumping beat. As the door opens for them the music grows startlingly louder. The bright lights spill into the vestibule as glitter floats in the air amongst the smoke and bubbles and fog machines blow thick crisp white puffs with the beat. Subtle streams of pot and tobacco snake through the fog in hints. Cigarette smoking in bars in Westchester county was outlawed earlier this year. The over-the-top winter wonderland Christmas theme makes for a surreal surrounding. Fake snowflakes fall lightly from above. "Feathers," Elizabeth yells over the music in Lola's ear, "Like in the movies." Catching a few flakes on her palm.

"Get down." Lola yells back. Elizabeth playfully tosses a handful at Lola and they laugh together as they push their way through the crowds toward the bathroom. Lola points back at Monica.

"She's in her glory over there." Monica is in the middle of Jim and a few other guys.

"She's such a fag hag."

The ladies' room is even smokier than the dance floor and packed with a confusing array of drag queens and lesbians. Elizabeth finds herself face to face with a very tall woman with large hands and an Adam's apple as she rises from snorting a long rail of coke off the vanity. She shakes her head, holds her nostrils, suppresses a sneeze.

"You want a rail, honey?" She asks Elizabeth in a deep, husky rasp. Elizabeth smiles politely and shakes her head no. A dance beat remix of Violent Femmes' "Blister in the Sun" pounds at the door, "Big hands I know you're the one…" Elizabeth smiles, pushes into a toilet stall. From behind the Hiney Hider she hears Lola turn down a line. She hovers over the toilet, dress hiked up around her waist. She hears two girls, presumably lesbians, are complaining about the crowd.

"All the fucking girls in here tonight are straight!" One says with disgust.

"Bunch of fag hags, all came with their gay guy friends." The other agrees. Elizabeth smooths down her dress and flushes with her foot. She exits the stall and deliberately kisses Lola full on the mouth on the way out of the bathroom.

"We don't want any trouble." She whispers loudly into Lola's ear, giggling as they leave the ladies room. They join Jim at the bar.

"Where's Monica?"

Jim points to a gaggle of guys. "In the middle of that steaming pile of gays."

"Jealous?"

"Yes!" Jim says with a big playful smile and a fake pout. "Drinks!" He shouts turning to the bar. He orders a round for the three of them.

Elizabeth throws back a shot and chases it with an overpriced squirt of soda with too much ice in a brittle plastic cup. In her other hand she nurses an overpriced mixed drink, also with too much ice in a brittle plastic cup. The hole inside of her which she aptly named Loneliness just won't seem to fill up with liquor. And not for lack of trying tonight. She put on a big bright smile and pulled up her big-girl panties, despite Jim's advice. The bright flash of the pulsing nightclub, the loud music serves to conceal but not diminish her loneliness. Surrounded by people, even the four friends she came with, she still feels completely alone. She looks through the alcohol blur at Monica on the dance floor, eating up the attention from all sides. Gay men love fabulous big-breasted white girls. Elizabeth hates Monica right now. She lifts another shot to her fake smile, indulging Jim who continues to sing loudly and hand out shots. *I bet his smile is fake too,* and it is. Elizabeth isn't the only one filling that empty well with spirits.

"Scomps!" He shouts through a sweat sheen and a red hue. Elizabeth knows Jim recently separated from a man, an older man whom he'd been seeing for some time. His brave face, the good times, it's all fake. On him, on her. Elizabeth wonders how many people in the bright loud smokey room are fake and hiding too. How many are out there dancing and drinking away the sad and lonely. Suddenly it seems ironic, all the drag queens around her seem like the honest ones, the only ones in the place wearing their inside pain on the outside. For all the makeup and booze and dancing it's the costumed drag queens who are the most honest. *Never Break Character.* The Queens and Monica. Elizabeth's thoughts drift to Bill and how he betrayed her. Then she remembers a new development: Bill's roommate. He's cute. She takes a savory long pull from her mixed drink. It's getting seriously watered down at this point as the ice has fully melted. She fights off a wave of depression. *I need a good story,* she thinks, looking around. *There are stories everywhere. I was picked up in a limo and dumped off drunk at a big loud gay nightclub full of queens…* Elizabeth notices a hot blond queen across the bar from them.

"She's pretty."

Jim glances over. "She's a bitchy tranny."

Elizabeth is intrigued. "That would make a great story," She tries it out, "...So I was making out with this gorgeous tranny chick." She waves the bartender back, "Can I buy the blond over there a drink? The one in the slinky red dress." Elizabeth takes her drink around the bar to try to chat her up. The room spins slowly as she walks, the liquor is clearly doing its job. *I better slow down,* her inner voice of reason cautions. She approaches and says "Hi," but all she gets in return is a sideways stink eye as the hot tranny walks away, rudely swinging her long blond wig at Elizabeth. She rejoins Jim and Lola on the other side of the bar, "You weren't kidding." She says to Jim.

"Told you." Elizabeth sets herself on a stool and stirs her expensive watered down cola. She decides to sip it slow and start to sober up. She doesn't take anymore of Jim's shots. She'll be heading to the Eye after they leave here.

Balloon Heads
Act 1 Scene 18.5

Interior:Car, night

LAURA is driving. ELIZABETH
shotgun. LOLA sits in the back,
leaning forward between the
seats. Laura kills the
headlights,

LAURA:
Hoods up, girls.

The decision to sober up and visit cute Deli Guy at the bar does not stop Elizabeth from shaking off a bit of the funk and getting lost in the debauchery of the evening. She even makes out with a couple of gay fellas in the limo before they leave, but she feels a little less alone in his company. She finds him cute, handsome, funny, and what might be the best thing is, he seems to study her with great interest, which is just the type of positive attention she needs. Whenever he's working at the deli she casually stops by for smokes and a chat. Invitations and attentions.

Today she and Laura passed him on the road walking. Laura mistook him for a deviant criminal, much to Elizabeth's amusement. They picked him up and hung out for a while, he helped them get some pot and he showed Laura a joint-rolling technique to eliminate the pregnant middle. Laura claims it a life changer. He invited her to a show. Flirting is at critical mass and this show might be just the catalyst they need to push that further. Elizabeth excitedly describes to Lola how it went and how she'd like for it to go.

Laura is driving. Elizabeth shotgun. Lola in the back, leaning forward between the seats. Laura kills the headlights,

"Hoods up, girls." Three hoods are donned as the dark car rolls slowly up the block. The car creeps to a stop in front of a lush, manicured lawn with a small garden in the middle. A bird bath centerpiece on a small brick path bisects two semicircle flower beds adorned with painted rocks and ceramic lawn ornaments. The passenger side doors creak open. Elizabeth and Lola burst out of the car, running across the grass, covering their mouths trying to hold in their giggling and snickering. Lola snatches a gnome and they run back to the car.

"Hooded bandits!" they howl with glee, piling back into the car. Laura speeds off laughing. Lola holds the gnome on the back of the seat like a puppet.

"We should take this little guy around the world and send them postcards and pictures…"

"Like that other gnome did?"

"Well...yeah." Lola poses the gnome to nod along, "Yeah send me around the woyld" She says in a deeper voice than her own, trying not to move her lips.

"Is that your gnome voice?" Laura laughs.

"Can you imagine," Elizabeth points out, "how much went into that prank? Like how much money that must have cost? That has to be the most expensive and convoluted prank ever." They all laugh. "And the gnome came home in a limo."

"They could've been a flight attendant."

"Well, none of us are flight attendants so he isn't going around the world."

"Aw man." Says the gnome.

"So what do you want to do with this one?" Lola turns him to face her, she tells him,

"Sorry buddy, I guess you're coming home with me."

"Yay." Says the gnome.

"I have a better idea." Laura stops the car, grabs the gnome, and throws on her hood. "Hooded Bandits!" She yells at Elizabeth and dashes from the car across a lawn. She places the gnome on the doorstep, runs back to the car, holding her hood against the wind with both hands. She crashes back into the driver's seat, grips the wheel and takes off.

"Let's go to the diner, Monica should be there by now." Elizabeth explains to Laura how Monica has been dating some guy named Dom for a few weeks and she and Lola have been stalking their dates, hooded-bandit style. Laura is immediately amused and game.

She pulls up outside the diner and they can see Monica and Dom sitting across from each other at a window table. Laura parks in the shadows. Hoods up, they cross the parking lot hiding behind shrubs and cars. Monica spots them and silently shakes her head behind the window. They enter the diner and make their way across the room secret agent style, hoods still up, hiding behind booths and tables and confused busboys. Amused and irritated diners shake their heads. The diner manager glares at them with a watchful eye but Trish smiles and waves him off. "Girls will be girls," she tells him sarcastically and ducks into the kitchen. He's not amused but he lets it go and walks away.

Dom is not unaware he's being stalked. On their last few dates, he'd noticed but said nothing. Today he finally offers Monica loud enough for his stalkers to hear,

"Monica, I can meet your friends...?" They emerge from their hoods and not at all inconspicuous hiding places, immediately crowding into the booth, Lola and Elizabeth with Monica, Laura with Dom. Elizabeth folds her arms on the table, serious, demure,

"And what are your intentions?" In a parentally lighthearted tone. Dom, taken aback but amused,

"Uh, well, soon I intend on eating cheese fries and gravy." Dom breaks the ice well and survives the invasion. They discover he, too, has a deep love for the Beatles, as do Elizabeth and Laura. Before long they are as if old friends. When Dom and Monica's food comes they get up to leave. Elizabeth says,

"Well Dom, you've done well, I think I can speak for Lola and Laura when I say we like you and approve." She gives him a thumbs up.

Laura adds, "I like you more than Monica." Monica gives Laura a hard glare. She knows full well Laura is not joking regardless of how she made it sound. Her scowl turns quickly back to a smile as Dom looks back to her.

Back in the car they can let their laughter loose. "Did you see her face?" Laura smirks, puts the car in traffic and heads for her dad's house. "Hey, I promised my dad I wouldn't stay out too late," She's staying with him through the holidays. "You guys want to go hang out there?"

"Is Noel home? I miss him."

"I think so. Plus we might be able to get some weed from my step mother."

"Didn't you just get weed?"

"Yeah, and I'll *still* have plenty of it if I smoke her weed." They all laugh.

The girls sit in a small circle around a low table under the slant roof in the partially finished attic. A bong sits in the middle, a smoking gun. A stray wisp of thin white ribbon rises from the charred bowl piece.

"My head feels like a balloon." Elizabeth playfully pats her head, "Like it's on a string." She giggles.

Lola falls backwards onto the mustard pile carpet kicking her feet laughing. "Come back Elizabeth…" She echoes, reaching for Elizabeth's elusive string.

Laura quizzically touches at her own head with both hands, "Balloon Heads." Then the blank Balloon Head stare leaves Laura and she smiles. "What's up with Monica's new friends?"

Elizabeth sits forward quickly. "Do you know what she told me? She only hangs out with them because she's the pretty one." They all share diapproving glares. On the inside, each takes a pause to glance around the room and can't help think what the present group dynamic is to the other two. Elizabeth breaks the pause with a laugh, "She started working another job at a video store. Remember that really short creepy guy, Marc from the coffee shop? He's the new store manager, she said he tried to jerk off in front of her!" They erupt in howls of laughter, "He looked like that guy, the singer, what's his name...?" She starts to sing, "She took the midnight train going any…"

"Steve Perry." Laura says,

"Right, oh shit! I just remembered this is the second time this has happened to her! There was that guy at the record store, Steve something…"

"Why…" Laura can barely get out before she remembers, "Ooooooohh, Elizabeth has a date." She picks up the bong and takes a hit with a pleased grin. Lola sits up with a straight face and new focus, looks at Elizabeth.

"It's not a date, he asked you if you wanted to go too." Elizabeth says to Laura.

"He only asked me because I was there, he asked YOU to go."

"Yeah but with another dude and some other chick."

"Who?" Lola asks, unanswered.

"Yeah, some other dude, some other chick, him and you. That's a double date. You could get that specimen."

Elizabeth grins mischievously, rubs her hands together, "I can't get into all that again," She waves off the idea, "he was just with some other chick that Bill of all people set him up with, I don't want to be somebody's rebound piece."

"Who?" Lola asks again, still lost.

"Her name was Sophie something…" Elizabeth waves dismissively, not noticing Lola's expression.

"No, I mean--"

Laura pushes Lola's head. "Balloon Head!"

"Ahhhh! I'm floating away…" Lola yells softly, then she sits forward again, "Who!?"

"What are you, an owl?" Elizabeth is giggling. They all burst out laughing for a few minutes in hysterical fits. They die down and their guffaws turn to sighs and catching of breath. Lola looks from Laura to Elizabeth back and forth and says, "But seriously...who?" and they all fall out in hysterical laughter again.

New Year's Eve
Act 1 Scene 19

ELIZABETH is standing behind the bar against the wall nearest the front door.

The actual bartenders are lined to her left, in a zone defense. When she'd arrived earlier she was too drunk. Self medicated and confused. She's OK now, drained, weak but no longer drunk. A little stoned. "Here, straighten out." he'd said, handing her a joint before returning to work, leaving her in the kitchen to recover. Since their Not a Double Date ended in sexual confusion it's been weird. But when she got here earlier he took her in and comforted her without question or hesitation. When they had sex in his van after the show last week she hadn't expected to stick around but when he'd said, "Where are you going?" it seemed absurd to leave. Of course she told herself all along not to do this again, not so soon. She can't afford to get invested or be hurt again. Not emotionally or physically. Not now.

The bar is full. Fullest she's ever seen it in the short time she's been hanging around the Eye. The band is loud, which would be fine if not for this headache. A soothing welcome draft of cool air rushes in the door as it slams open. Two ladies walk in, startled by the door slamming open before them with the wind. One of the bartenders, James, rises from his post on a stool by the door.

"Evening ladies." Natalie steps forward, placing a hand daintily on James' chest.

"You're not going to charge us to get in, are you? It's almost midnight."

"Well maybe I don't need any money." James slyly glances at Natalie's chest.

"Oh, you want to see some titties?" She turns around to Allison, "Should we give him a little show?" She purrs with a smile.

"I don't know," Allison ponders, "How much is the cover, five bucks? These four titties are worth way more than ten dollars. How many bands are left?" She smiles and steps forward, "Do you vant to see these teedies?" She purrs in the Inka accent, sliding her shirt up over her belly. She teases the hemline in a wave, exposing first one bra cup bottom then the other. James, normally confident, cocky and carefree, seems to not know what to do. He smiles, taken aback by these two very forward and very attractive ladies. Natalie gives his balls a gentle squeeze and swishes past him slowly, paying no more than a tease and a smile. They take the seats in front of Elizabeth and start to remove their coats before it dawns on Elizabeth that she knows them.

"Oh my God! Allison?! Natalie!? Hey!"

"Oh God, Elizabeth! Wow it's been a few years! You're like an adult now." Allison puts her hands on Elizabeth's "So, do you work here?"

"No, I'm just helping out tonight."

Natalie smiles. "Which one?"

"Which one what?"

"Which bartender are you dating?"

Elizabeth smiles, blushes, "We're not dating…" She says coyly.

Natalie laughs. "Which one?" Elizabeth points down the bar. Natalie squints, "doesn't he work down the street at the deli?"

Allison recognizes him right away and hopes it doesn't show on her face. *It's that little coed homewrecker's ex-boyfriend.* She brought him to our house -- *MY HOUSE!* -- when Louis insisted they come spend the night. In hindsight, Allison can't imagine how either of them let that happen. Doug Kinney couldn't have written a more perfectly darkly humorous college professor situational comedy. So cliche it sounds made up. Allison wishes it was. Just a made up story, dreamt up by a coke-fueled 80's madcap comedy troupe. She watches him now, handing out beers and lining the bar in plastic champagne flutes. Allison hopes he doesn't recognize her. He looks at her and doesn't seem to. He smiles but it doesn't feel familiar. How did they let that happen? *What were you thinking?* she shakes her head at the clueless bartender. Allison hears Elizabeth react appropriately to Natalie's profession but she is no longer here in the bar. She's back in upstate, western New York. Her and the dumb ol' bartender over there, his ex-girlfriend stealing Allison's husband right in front of them. *Poor kid. Dumbass. He didn't even see it coming,* she bets. *What was I thinking? Letting my husband befriend a teenage student. He brought her to my house!* Allison can see it like it was yesterday, she's reliving it, it's happening to her now all over again, the outstanding college-town pot she partook of definitely factoring in to her flashback. She can smell the comfortably musty old living room and the crisp autumn country air. She is sitting on the floor in her living room, proud of her house. She decorated it herself and was especially proud of this room. The antique carpet, the deep dark red and golds and black patterns. A Monty Python movie played on the TV. It had seemed the thing to do, immersed in our own ironies and sense of self-deprecating humor. *And someone please ask my husband, "Can I buy some pot from you?"* And we can laugh at the pop-culture fun of it all. Looking back Allison can't understand how she didn't see it.

Shortly after they moved to Gore, Louis picked up a guitar and of course, being Louis, had to become an expert at the hobby. Cut to him passive-aggressively asserting dominance over this girl's boyfriend -- an unsuspecting, gullible young man -- fumbling clumsily through some chords. "I don't really play...?" he tried to say until Louis and Heather just passed the guitar back and forth, and leaving the poor boyfriend out in the cold. He fell right into one of Louis's traps. *How am I letting this happen?* Allison is thinking, watching it all unfold again and again. Who knows where that night could have gone if that tornado hadn't hit. She hadn't seen it at the time but now with hindsight, it seems completely obvious Louis and his little girlfriend were trying to orchestrate some sort of swap or something. Something was definitely going on -- maybe not that exactly, and she'd never know for sure since the tornado put everything on hold.

First the power went out. Off went the TV and the British comedy and the lights. Then the wind. It was a low hum from far in the dark distance, across miles of farm fields, blacker against the black night, humming slowly, lumbering across the fields, indiscriminately tossing everything in its path. The 'clone digs a trench as it weaves across the loose dirt, meandering like a blowhard drunkard, kicking barns and tractors aside as it bares down on Allison and her perfectly decorated farmhouse. The huge dark demon stares her down in her picture window. Black on black, the funnel slowly coming for her, the four of them forget any ulterior motives. All they could think of in that eternity was each of their own mortalities and the whistling humming winds drawing closer. The house shakes like a freight train is speeding through it, shaking for what feels like hours. The windows rattle, chattering violently. Allison recalls thinking at one point, *This will be forever.* The tornado was going to scoop her up from her cute little farmhouse, with its busted front window and the cutely decorated living room, and throw it all up in the air. They'll look down on Gore Lake and Madison county and all those fucking covered bridges but it won't be the magical land of Oz they land in...won't be any fucking munchkins or Dandy Lions. It'll be sturdy Allison splashed across upstate New York clutching her husband, his mistress and her gullible boyfriend. His head must be full of straw to come here with her tonight...*If I only had a brain.* But there is no liftoff. No Oz. Allison's marriage lasted a few more weeks rather than get spit out of a tornado. The house stopped shaking but the wind continued threateningly for the rest of the terror-filled night. All four slept in a security square in the center of the living room, sleeping in restless dreamy stretches, each waking alone in the dark from time to time by the whistling hum of the distant terror.

Allison tries to inconspicuously hide her face as he fills the plastic flutes with cheap champagne. He leaves half of each bottle full for some reason. The music in back stops and the loud buzz of people talking rises through the bar. An amplified voice from the stage booms over the buzz, calling for drinks to the stage in the closing seconds of the 1990s. He makes some morbid Crypt Keeper-like wisecracks and the whole crowd counts in unison from ten seconds down with Dick Clark muted on the TV.

"Three! Two! One! Happy New Year!!!" The bar shouts in unison and the band breaks into a new song to ring in the new year. As the empty plastic toasts hit the bar, the bartenders each grab two half empty bottles, thumbs over holes, shake them vigorously, spraying champagne on the bar, the people, the walls, the band. Natalie stands up on her stool and opens her mouth with a laugh. When the champagne shower show is over, Elizabeth returns fresh and blushing from her New Years' kiss to talk with Allison and Natalie. She dabs at her sticky wet face with a towel. Natalie notices Vincent paying Elizabeth attention. She notices the bartender fella notice too.

"Looks like you could have two of those fellas." She grins.

From out of the crowd, Courtney appears at the end of the bar. Seeing Allison and Natalie she gives Elizabeth a smile, "Well look at this." She sings, greeting them. "It's like a Drama Camp Flashback!" She laughs. Waving her arm around she gestures to the bar, "And this place?" She asks and answers in song, *"Anything Goes!"* She gives Allison and Natalie hugs and kisses, climbs up on the bar rail and leans over to give Elizabeth a kiss. Courtney waves and starts out the door but not before she notices the look in Elizabeth's eye gazing down the bar. She follows her gaze to the end of the bar where it ends at a bartender. Courtney takes note. "Happy New Year girls. Good to see you!" She says, pushing out the into the night and into a waiting cab.

Shortly thereafter a fight breaks out, spilling from the stage out into the bar.

"Anything goes indeed!" Allison exclaims, "Let's get out of here." She tugs at Natalie, who agrees. They quickly gather coats and say goodbye to Elizabeth hurrying out the door before the fight can make its way down thc bar.

(v/o) Courtney sings refrain, Anything Goes, fades out

Act 1 Scene 20

Interior: Eastland apartment

ALLISON sips her coffee at the
kitchen island.

ALLISON:
You should sell your dirty
panties.

The Hudson river glows with the pastel pink orange sunrise. Natalie in her t-shirt and undies, fixes herself a mug of coffee. Allison watches Natalie's butt jiggle slightly with the stirring. The past eighteen months of deep reflective thought, soul searching, people watching, hallucinations and delusions, sex, marketing and greasy chicken wings dripping with Frank's Red Hot Buffalo sauce, it all culminates, ferments and tumbles from Allison in one ridiculous out-of-context word vomit.

"You should sell your dirty panties."

Natalie turns around from the coffee pot with a bemused look, answering in an unexpected way. "Say that again but in your terrible Russian accent."

"You should sell your dirty pan-ties."

Natalie giggles at Inka, "Where would I sell my panties? How?"

Allison holds up one finger and swallows a gulp of coffee, "Hear me out. Surely there are tons of guys who've seen several movies starring Natalie and in the beginning of those movies presumably Natalie is wearing clothes. Stay with me. What if Natalie's fans could buy those dirty panties that Dick Bigly pulled off her? You could put up a website, people go to it where they'll find a link, *Buy My Panties* or something, they click the link and there's a list of dirty panties, they can come in plastic bags for preserved freshness, maybe you can custom-order panties, they can ask you to wear specific colors or exercise in them. I bet there's a huge market for guys who want to get off sniffing period blood off a dirty pair of panties. You or I might throw them away but there's guys out there I bet who would pay good money, the filthier the better..."

Natalie laughs and waves her arms, then tries to put on a deeper boy voice, "Can you wear pink cotton for a day and then pee yourself..." She pauses for a second of hysterics, "mmm hmm Imma sneff them good an yank mah cran...." She bursts out in tears and loud uncontrolled bellowing laughter. She manages to squeak out, "That's sick!"

Allison won't let up. "Who cares? What do you think they're doing watching the movies? If they'll give you another hundred bucks for your dirty laundry why not take it?"

"That's actually pretty brilliant, Al."

The Internet was a scary new place even in the early aughts. The concept of social media is still half a decade away and at the moment it exists only in chat rooms and instant messaging. Websites at this time are the way of the future.

Natalie sits down, now more composed at the island. "I still think you should do porn too Al," She gives Allison a pinch on the boob. Allison winces, brushes away Natalie's hand.

"Oh yeah hot. A divorcee staring down her thirties. I'm sure there's a huge demographic."

"Sure there's MILFs."

"What's a MILF?"

"It stands for Moms I'd Like To Fuck."

"I don't have kids."

"So what, you're not a Russian spy either. Peter North ain't no handyman. I know girls who do incest porn. They aren't really fucking their brothers. Hugh Jorgan isn't a pool cleaner. I'm not a babysitter…"

"You were…" Allison says with a smirk.

"None of that matters is the point."

Allison continues to think modestly but is it modesty? Maybe she's just shy? No, that's not it either. She's actually in the best shape she's ever been in, her confidence at an all time high. *Maybe being in porn isn't so far fetched. It's taboo. That would get under Louis's skin.* She thinks, arguing with herself. *Why would it? Would he care? Mother would be mortified definitely but what would Louis care?* He might see it as part of his victory. She hears his voice say, "She went off the deep end, I was right -- she's crazy." Thoughts of this nature float around her head -- he won't care at all, he'll be devastated -- why does she give a flying fuck either way what that bastard thinks? If he's amused, vindicated, insulted or disgusted. She settles on he won't care and she doesn't care if he does and *he* shouldn't even be a factor and what is she even thinking, she's not getting into porn but she wasn't good enough for him so he doesn't even get a say and if she wants to do porn she damn well will do porn and he can go fuck himself, he doesn't get to be a part of my decisions…

"Well then maybe we should get a computer," Natalie says seriously after some thought. "A lot of the big stars are putting up websites now, I just read that." She picks a book up off the coffee table,

"My hero, April Lynn Baker, in here, her new book. It's her autobiography." Natalie holds the book forward for Allison to see, she reads the title out loud like she's never seen the words before.

"April Lynn Non Stop: Some Kind Of Woman."

"I'm almost done...you can read it after if you'd like. I'm fascinated by her, she's so beautiful and natural, no plastic surgery, I admire that, she's fifty and she looks her age, but she's so real and proud of herself. 'This is me,' she says, fuck you if you don't like it. I wish I was as confident as her."

"Aren't you?"

"No." Natalie shakes her head, "I put on a good show, though, don't I?" Allison has wished for Nat's confidence, *I'd kill for just one of yours...?* and how she too can put on a show. She has been a lot more confident in herself, and Natalie has definitely helped facilitate that. Maybe she could use some in return? It feels strange now that she thinks of it. Allison takes the book from Natalie.

"She's your hero, huh?"

"Oh yeah. It's my dream to work with her actually. Time's running out though." Natalie taps her wrist like a watch, "I can't imagine she has a lot of movies left in her."

"Maybe she can pioneer the GILF genre...?" Natalie looks at Allison sideways, "Granny I'd Like To Fuck." They both have a good laugh about it.

"Well I still have to go to work," Inka adds, "For now." and Allison heads off to the bathroom to get ready for her shift at Cafe Ine.

Later that day, Allison rides the elevator up to the apartment in a melancholy mood. Her shift was fairly uneventful except one minor event. The coffee shop is closing. In a few weeks Allison will be out of a job. Not that barista was a long term career choice, nor would it be a hard job to replace but she's been in a comfortable routine.

Maybe a good shake up is just what I need. As if my life wasn't shaken up already. She refuses to let this get her down. *There are other coffee houses.* She laughs. *Pouring coffee is no career,* she argues with herself. She is still in a bit of a daze as she comes into the apartment. She's greeted by an exuberant Natalie.

"I got great news!" She shouts, pushing a glass of wine into Allison's hand, quickly tapping hers against Allison's. *Ting.*

"That's great Nat, what's the news?" Allison tries to sound happy and enthusiastic and fails miserably. Natalie sees right through the charade. Her smile fades some.

"Hey, what's wrong, Al?"

"The coffee house is closing. They told us today. We're, well, I'm gonna be out of a job. It's really no big deal, I don't want to come in here and piss on your parade, what's your good news? I could use some."

Natalie is practically hyperventilating. "I got the call!" She finally blurts out. "April! April Lynn, my hero, she's doing a big gang bang film... it's supposed to be her last adult movie and my agent said she wants ME! To be in it! She personally wants me!" She screeches happily, "ME!"

"So you got the part?"

"He made it sound like I don't really have to audition, just an interview. I'm going to meet April!" She bounces, quickly clapping her hands, "Tomorrow! Oh Allison! You have to come with me, I'm already nervous!"

Allison agrees to go. For moral support. Allison is not getting into porn. She is only going as a grounding tether.

The rest of the evening is spent rifling through Natalie's closet, drinking wine and catwalking all over the room. Allison fondly recalls searching for costumes in the carriage house and Inka tries on some slinky dresses as well.

"My God, I've never been this nervous about anything. You'd think I was getting ready for a date." Natalie jokes.

Of course between the wine and the excitement the whole ordeal quickly turns into a meandering sidebar distraction. Allison had not realized how much Natalie idolizes April, listening to her recount the countless interviews she's seen and read. It's impressive how much Natalie knows about April's life.

Act 1 Scene 21

NATALIE hurries back and forth around the apartment.

Natalie is alight with excitement. She scurries around the apartment like a chicken with its head cut off, chattering non-stop. Allison considers switching Natalie's coffee out with decaf but they don't have any. And why would they? Decaf. Like beer with no alcohol. Why? Allison's grandmother always kept a small travel size jar of Sanka in her purse. "Where are you now, grandma?" She says with a grin as Natalie rushes by in a flash. *Well I'm right where you left me, sweetie... in the ground.*

Natalie is so nervous by the time they are ready to leave she doesn't even argue when Allison insists on driving. A relief to Allison who just didn't want to be pinned to the door of Natalie's Mazda, terrified for her life.

"This is going to be a big title," Natalie is saying in the car. "It could crack mainstream media. Porn is never in the mainstream unless it's a big deal. This is going to be a once-in-a-generation event." She goes on. "It'll be April's last adult film. It's gonna be huge."

"Where am I going, by the way?" Allison interjects at the bottom of the drive at main street.

"Oh go right and take 9 North, do you remember where the Bavarian Inn was?"

"That old German restaurant? Was?"

"It closed, yeah."

"Why? It was there so long."

"Oh, it's kind of extraneous but it turns out the family from Continental Village had owned the restaurant for a long time, but when the last manager passed away his sons just didn't want to run a restaurant anymore. So they sold it to someone who decided to tear it down and put up a totally new building styled to look like a sports stadium and it's going to be a high end sports bar with a memorabilia museum. Apparently they have one of the largest privately owned sports memorabilia collections in the country."

"What does this have to do with a gang bang flick?"

"I was getting to that, so somehow April and her people are leasing the space for this movie and there's going to be some big media circus surrounding it all. I don't know all the details."

"How does April figure into the restaurant deal, I don't get that part?"

"Me neither, she somehow has some relation to the family that owned the German restaurant."

"Yeah. It was."

"What was?"

"Extraneous." Allison pulls into the parking lot. Some of the compound is still under construction and the parking lot isn't paved yet. The curbs, sidewalks and barriers are in place but Allison drives in over hard packed item 4, the layer beneath asphalt that most people never see.

"My agent said to pull around back, there's an office or something, he said you can't miss it." Sure enough there was a small separate brick building with a small window. It stands apart from the main building, also brick. It has a flat roof and a green door. Allison thinks there is something striking, something oddly ironic about it but she can't place it. The whole area looks like something she can't quite place. It reminds her of the stadium she'd been to as a girl before they moved to New York. She was only there once and she's never cared for baseball.

"What's that stadium named after the gum?"

Natalie looks at Allison slant-eyed. "Do you mean Wrigley Field?" She giggles, "that's so girly, Al. Oh a baseball touchdown." She laughs. Allison looks at Natalie from her side view with a raised brow.

"I'll turn this car right around, Missy." She says, putting the car in park. The green door directly in front of them has a small piece of duct tape in the middle of it with a name on it in black magic marker. It says *April Lynn.*

"Can't miss it, he said." Natalie points at the tape. That's when it hits Allison,

"Oh that's right The Green Door!" She laughs.

As the door opens Allison has absolutely no intention of getting into porn. At all. Even with Inka in her slinkiest Russian red dress purring in her ear over her shoulder -- *Eef you should choose to accept eet ---* she has given no thought into entering the porn industry. *The meeshon is to extract, mmmm shall vee say...information?* No thought whatsoever. Not even while watching April's videos. Allison just so happened to see one. Or a few. At the video store, in the back room. She'd gone in not intending to rent a porno, but there she was, April Lynn. On a dozen boxes. Not even a fraction of her movies but all the award-winning performances. Not that Allison looked it up or anything. I mean Natalie was always talking about April. Natalie said she could read the book. Allison didn't bother mentioning she had read it already. *By any means...sexually.* Inka purrs. April Lynn, star of *Night Rider*, an 80's action show parody. Allison rented it. *Different Strokes.* April's rich daddy adopts two well hung black orphan men. What'chu talkin' 'bout indeed. Allison rented it. Twice. She'd had no intention of watching it. Either time. But she did.

April greets them herself as they walk into the small room. The room is a square, exactly as the outside had advertised. Allison absently thinks, *I thought it would be bigger…?* an impossibility she realizes. *That's Vat she said* Inka deadpans. Allison has no intention of being in porn.

April is sitting on the front of her desk, naked except a thin camisole. Her legs are crossed, the top leg bounces with no particular rhythm. A fuzzy pink slipper dangles from the bouncing foot swaying precariously as though it might fly off at any moment. But it doesn't. It stays on like magic. Allison has no intention of getting into porn.

April holds up a hand in a 'Stop,' points to her mouth, looking through them, says,

"Yeah it's fucking small….HA! Yeah, that's what she said. OK call me." April reaches behind her, hangs up the receiver, tugs a headpiece from her ear, tosses it onto the desk. "Bluetooth." She says to them, "Frickin amazing, right?" She holds out her hand to Natalie, "April Lynn, you must be Natalie?" Allison is struck by the sound of April's voice. She realizes she had not expected it for some reason. April has such a distinct and unmistakable Jersey honk to her voice. It's easy to imagine she's from a blue collar working class Irish-Italian neighborhood, maybe even Jewish? April is a brash and loud woman and it's kind of endearing. Her laugh is as infectious as it is obnoxious and it's just another small piece of her charm. She has a fun and trashy way about her and she always seems to be talking about fucking, her pussy or her tits.

April shakes Natalie's hand. They talk shop, titles Natalie's been in, what she will and won't do for money who's the biggest she's ever worked with.

April tells Natalie, "Not that you'll have to do much in this one -- glorified fluffer really -- but you'll get a ton of facetime on camera and in the tournament and all, like fuck the formalities, truthfully. Nat, I love you, I loved you as soon as you walked in. I knew I would, I have like a fuckin' sixth sense about this shit sometimes, ya know?" Natalie stands dazed, lost on how her hero just told her she loves her.

Allison nudges her and she squeaks out, "Tournament?" Weakly, and embarrassed on the inside. April rolls right on.

"Yeah, they didn't tell you? We're doing a big charity poker tournament with all the big dicks and tits in porn, real cheesy photo op shit, trot out some old legends and then it will all turn into a big light hearted gang bang. I'm bettin'," She winks and air quotes, "I'm a break me a record. We're gonna call it The April Eight Hundred or something, I'm not sold on that yet."

"April's Full." Allison blurts out quietly behind Natalie with zero intention of getting involved in porn.

April leans to the side, looks around Natalie at Allison, "Are you in the business honey?" Allison shakes her head no. April curls her finger at Allison, "Come here." Allison steps forward without thinking, without thought or protest. April uncrosses her legs, hooks one around Allison's waist, pulls her in, puts a hand on the back of Allison's neck with a gentle presence, "What's your name, girlie?

Inka Cockneedo. "Allison Vonderlande." She says with a Dorothy of Kansas meekness.

April smiles, "You *have* a porn name." She says amused. April is not shy, she's attracted to Allison, she pulls her in slowly. Guiding more than pulling. Affirmative not authoritative. A suggestion. Allison can pull away at anytime. If she wants to. No problem. Allison has no intention. *Russian spy babushka vodka...um; ski...* April kisses Allison full on the mouth. Allison lets her and kisses back. Natalie reacts as one might, big smile, wide eyes, hand over mouth in merriment and wonder. Allison runs a hand up April's leg, April rubs her hand on the back of Allison's neck. April stops kissing Allison, sits back, crosses her legs again, looks in Allison's eyes, "Do you want to be in my movie, Allison Vonderlande?" She asks in her softest gravel and lights a cigarette.

Natalie smiles and claps playfully as Allison says, "Yes. Yes I do."

Act 1 Scene 21.5

Interior: Eastland Apartment, night

ALLISON is on the couch, NATALIE
rushes from room to room.

ALLISON:
That looks hot on you.

.

Natalie is nearly as excited about Allison getting a part in the movie as she is for herself. For the rest of the evening and into the night she is literally and figuratively all over the place. Busy, busy, she can't sit still or stay focused on any one thing for long. First she's dragging out her collection of April movies. Allison notes how many rentals she could have saved. *Late fees,* she thinks picking up and putting down the box for *New Wave Call Girls*, the movie on the TV now. Natalie can't sit through the opening credits before dashing off to root through a drawer full of camera-ready lingerie. It seems no amount of wine can slow her down tonight. Rather than try, Allison lounges on the sofa in the living room with a glass of her own, the bottle nearby. She positions herself so the TV and Natalie can both be in view. Watch some porn, back to Natalie, occasionally saying,

"That looks nice on you," or "That looks hot on you." Depending on what's appropriate. Watching *New Wave Call Girls* admittedly for the third, or fourth time? This time it's research, she tells herself. *Fourth,* she remembers, the first time she rented it she watched it twice. Returned it late.

Natalie scurries through holding up two camisoles. "Which one do you think?" She lays them across the back of the couch and dances through the kitchen without really waiting for an answer.

"Think what?" Allison asks, not looking away from *New Wave Call Girls.*

"Are you hungry?" Natalie sings from the kitchen but before Allison can answer Natalie is already back in her room rummaging through a closet.

"I could eat." Allison says under her breath with amusement. On TV April is giving Steve Drake a vigorous blow job.

Natalie rushes by. "Nice form." She drops an old People magazine on the table, the cover claims there is an interview with April inside. Natalie fills her wine and huries back into the kitchen wondering aloud if she'd preheated the oven.

"What are you preheating the oven for?"

"I was thinking about making Chocolate Chip Pumpkin Bread."

"Do we have pumpkin?"

"No." Natalie rushes back through the living room picking back up the two camisoles still undecided and heads back to her room.

"Well there goes that."

On the TV a man says into a phone, "You want a Devil? I guarantee she's hotter than Hell…"

Natalie calls from the bedroom, "Can you believe April wants to use your idea for the movie title?!" At the interview April had mentioned they were calling the movie The April 800, since she planned on shattering the previous magical gang bang record of 500 set a few years earlier in Houston. When Allison suggested "April's Full" she didn't think anyone had heard her nor could she believe they hadn't thought of it first. Poker, full house, the innuendos write themselves. Allison had seen a movie a couple of years ago with John Malkovich in which he lays down a full house, Aces and nines. "Asses Full" he says in a ridiculous Russian accent. *Vell Hello Mister Malkovich.* Allison made a simple connection and substitution. April's full of 800 dicks. April's Full of Dicks. April's Full.

Act 1 Scene 22

Interior: April's office, day

APRIL, ALLISON, NATALIE

With nearly two and a half months until the tournement/gang bang Allison still needs to make money. Fortunately with the shop closing the other baristas are jumping ship like rats off a sinking...ship. So picking up extra shifts is a breeze. The shop would be closed for good about two weeks before Allison embarks on her new career and she's determined to snatch up every dollar along the way until then. She spends all her free time, or what little is left after picking up all those extra shifts, at the gym. Allison has always taken pretty good care of herself, take the stairs more, eat OK, sleep nights, drink water, but she figures if she is going to be in porn she wants to be *hot*, not just in pretty good shape. After a few weeks it's showing and Allison feels pretty damn good about herself. She and Natalie have already done a few promotional photo shoots with April.

April's production company is ramping up an aggressive marketing campaign for the film, now titled *April's Full.* They will need security. April has a lot of well-meaning although delusional and obsessed fans. Porn in general also has its share of opposition. Groups of people who are always looking for porn to protest. These groups can range from feminist groups to evangelicals and sometimes they actually clash with each other even while protesting a common enemy. The new owners of the soon-to-open sports bar didn't want word getting out fearing people might not want to eat high-end fried bar food at high end prices in a soon-to-be sex puddle. April personally wants to keep the former owner's name away from publicity, as her granddaughter's paternal grandparents' family had owned the german restaurant for generations.

The deal to sell the land had been struck at a family wedding and actually included from the start the deal to film April's final adult film, complete with the charity poker tournament. Even the idea to tear down the building and put up a big brick stadium was a part of that tipsy conversation hashed out over rented linen tablecloths. It's hard to pinpoint exactly how it all laid out across a big round table in a banquet room in the back of a quiet rural pub just outside Albany, New York. Open bars tend to cloud details like that. Nonetheless, while an unmemorable wedding band fumbled through wedding classics and ancient aunts trotted out on the dance floor for numbers like The Chicken Dance and Dominick the Donkey, April seized on an opportunity. When she overheard her daughter's baby-daddy's dad negotiating with a family friend for the restaurant on the tail end of a logistics and strategy debate about poker she interjected and made it into a contract drawn up by her sister's date, who happened to be a lawyer, on a rented linen napkin with a marker. One of those nice ones. Surely it was paid for later, on the catering bill. It was taken to a notary, drawn up legal, notarized some more, legalized some more, but in the end it would be a part of the deal. Not everyone at that wedding was thrilled by the idea.

By the time the last photo shoots roll around Allison is in the best shape of her life.

"You look great Al, like Anna Nicole Smith but happy. And sober." Natalie giggles,

"Thanks, Nat...I think?" Allison laughs, glances down at her chest. "I think she's...taller than me."

The media circus starts tomorrow. Allison and Natalie and the rest of the fluffers are in April's office for one final meeting. April addresses the room, sitting on her desk. A dull abrupt echo gives April's pep talk a surreal tone, Allison thinks.

"Listen girls, this is going to be a lot of fun." It still doesn't seem real to Allison, this world. Porn. How is she going to fit in? How is she going to stand out? She looks around at the other more experienced girls around her. How did she get here?!

The sun rises over Peekskill bay, the rippling orange-pink reflection in the river, Allison's view. The aroma of fresh coffee dances around Allison's head and in her nostrils in a peculiar way. The circus begins today. March thirtieth, in the year 2000. The future has arrived. The world had not shut down at the stroke of midnight, planes did not fall from the sky, ATMs did not vomit cash, no computer turned on mankind when the calendar read 0000. The world did not end. The new date for that is now sometime late 2012. It's the dawn of the new millenium and Allison's old life was too behind her. A radical new life. Allison ponders the definition of the word prostitute. *One who is paid to have sex, but* she wonders *if there's a camera doesn't that make it art?* Later today April will clear all that up for her and Allison won't even have to ask. In a few hours protesters, counter-protesters, deranged April fanatics, stalkers and a sea of security will be lining a short stretch of State Rte. 9 in

Philipstown along with a small army of the porn industry press corps. Not to mention the busload of aging porn legends, all vying for credited cameos. *April's Full* is sure to be a monument to the sex industry. A legend will soon retire and everybody who's anybody naturally wants to be part of it.

By 10 AM the State Police are directing traffic around the disturbance along the two-lane wooded Old Post Road. Natalie has to drive past three checkpoints, two security guards and three different protests.

"Are they on strike? What's going on here?" Natalie reads a sign shaking over her windshield, "The Adult Film Industry Light Crew Union? I've never heard of that before, why are they here?" On one side of the driveway the feminists are waving their own signs shouting, "Porn degrades us! Women aren't objects!" On the other side of the driveway Bible verses adorn the signs, shouts of shame sound more like, "Jesus weeps when you masturbate!" and "Hollywood Porn Fag Enablers!" The Adult Film Industry Light Crew Union marches in a tight circle along the length of the property. "April Hires Non-Union Best Boy Grips!"

April herself is standing on a porch above the main entrance, she yells back, "Best boy grips!? We call them fluffers!" Natalie moves her car slowly through the opening until a security guard hangs the chain back across. April turns her attention to the car, looking at Allison in the passenger seat. "Hey, park around back and come in the back door!" She winks acknowledging the innuendo, runs in the open door behind her to meet them. Natalie parks behind the main building. The little brick house where April's office was, now an empty utility shed, is to the side behind them.

As they enter the backroom, Allison notices it looks like a kitchen only empty. No counters, prep tables, cabinets, freezers or refrigerators. Just a thick industrial orange tile floor and stainless steel backsplashes but no sinks. No ovens or stoves are in yet either, just capped pipes and coiled wires stub out of the walls. The room is otherwise full of one thing: Journalists. Camera & Host Teams are going over questions and angling strategies, cub reporters talk into hand held tape recorders, make notes in notepads pulled from pockets, stuffed away in backpacks. Several look at Allison, look her up and down unable to place her. Some double take before deciding she's nobody and move on. Some greet Natalie by name. Ever the professional, Natalie politely obliges a few pictures, pleasantries and questions without slowing her pace, gracefully never coming off rude either. Allison follows through the crowd in awe of the spectacle. On the other side of the room a large man in a yellow security jacket opens the door for them. Allison and Natalie leave the tiled room of journalists and enter the main dining room. A large circular bar dominates one side of the room and everywhere there is a lot of dark stained woodwork. *Mahogany? Elegant,* Allison thinks, picturing the room full of men jizzing all over the place and onto the white linen tablecloths. Nattily-dressed well-to-dos are seated at all the tables, it's a full on dinner rush. They appear not to notice the naked men jizzing all over them. Offering fresh pepper. And jizz. *That's disgusting,* Inka scolds. Allison giggles and follows Natalie toward April seated at the bar, waving to them.

"Over here," April explains, "For the interviews I want the two of you here with me." She loudly slaps the leather cushions on the fancy high back stools on either side of herself. "The other girls can sit around us," She nods to the other stools, "They went down the street for smokes, with that crowd out there they should be back in a few years!" April laughs loudly at herself. She'd been made up and was pretty much naked when Allison met April. Now she's wearing sweatpants and a hoodie. Her hair is in a high ponytail and she's wearing no makeup at all. It occurs to Allison that April really does look every bit her age of 50. She still looks great, just more natural. She's had no plastic surgery, Allison's sure of that, based on the crows feet and slight double chin. Again, she still looks great and more than that, she looks happy. Without thinking Allison blurts out,

"Why are you retiring from porn?"

April chuckles, "I'm holding a damn press conference in few hours because I didn't want to answer that question a billion times but I guess twice won't kill me."

Outside a commotion stirs as the Evangelicals clash with the Adult Film Industry Light Crew Union over exactly why April is going to Hell. The debate is muffled through the thick windows and brick walls, but the reason is pornography versus fascism. April points toward the bathrooms, "And I ordered food, it's over there." She points at a spread against the wall in the far corner of the dining room, steaming on one table. It looks Italian.

Allison stands quietly in front of the impromptu buffet, balancing a soggy paper plate in her hand trying not to poke a hole in it with her plastic fork as she stabs at a meatball. She glances at the sea of tables but doesn't want to be the first one to get Marinara sauce on the crisp clean white linen. The dull roar of journalists muffled by the swinging kitchen doors has a distinctly different tone than the controlled chaos outside.

"Fornicators!" Someone outside screams, making angry eye contact with Allison's glance out the window. She turns her attention back to her stiff breaded chicken in a sea of steaming ziti, tries to saw off a piece with the side of her plastic fork.

In a few hours the room will be filled with a lot of well-dressed people having a serious discussion about the Porn Industry. A few hours after that the room will fill with the clicks and buzzes of a poker tournament. The oddities and contrasts of all this are not lost on Allison. Then there's the main event: April's big show, the gang bang to end all gang bangs. The goal is 800 dicks. Tearing the old record of 500 a new one. So to speak.

When April finally gives the nod to the large men guarding the door to let the press in, she is in her chosen spot at the bar, camera ready and flanked by Allison and Natalie. Other industry bigwigs who would be making credited cameos in the gang bang occupy the dining room tables in meet-and-greet mode. Many of them are already in or headed for retirement from the industry themselves. The line to interview April is organized in such a way as to snake the press through the dining room like cattle, giving them plenty of facetime with all the other stars. They herd the press like an amusement park line with April as the ride, which she is. At the end of the line they are pushed out the door to sign certain non-disclosure agreements. Being the wise businesswoman, April is not naive to the fact that the press isn't always her friend. The doors open and the crowd lurches forward but they are caught by surprise by the meet-and-greet cattle herd line. They shuffle their feet, trying not to step on each other's heels. As the line snakes around the tables the room fills with the sounds of a hundred dirty jokes, familiar greetings, standard answers, a perverted Row Your Boat in the round.

"I love this place, the entrance is in the rear..." To Allison, the outsider, it sounds a lot like a reunion of people who work together. Naked. "It is true I can suck my own dick, but I always wear a condom. I don't know where I've been..." April is sharp and witty as the press files past. When the room is filled, April addresses the room. She gives a short speech about retirement, calls her own speech a bore. She speaks loud and clear, slow enough so that everyone can can jot it down and move on. She had mentioned not wanting to repeat herself too many times. When she finishes her speech the conga line of journalists starts shuffling back up through the room, the hum of the dirty word salad winding back up.

April tells a group, "I'm not a whore. A whore will do things she doesn't want to do for money." She smiles proudly and declares, "I'm a slut." More seriously adding, "I've never fucked anyone I didn't want to fuck and I think when you see that on screen, it shows, I'm passionate, some girls were in it for the money or drugs or whatever issues, not me, I was in it for the fucking. I fucking love sex, man, Some girls out there, they're actresses, they turn it on and off and that works for them, some of my best friends in the business, but I'm me, man, I get out of makeup and I'm all over you in the green room, they were always running around after me, the makeup department touching me up, I'd be sucking dick in the green room, smudging my makeup before they put film in the camera," April laughs.

Voices in the crowd banter about April's career "...and of course, you remember our star April in the cult classic adult pirate parody, Release the Semen. April plays Jackie Swallows, captain of the Black Pearl Necklace..."

Allison listens carefully as April casually discusses her early career fondly, her philosophies on life, sex and business sense. It's April's business sense that captures Allison most.

"I started out as a nude model, the nudie magazines were getting really popular, that led to exotic dance tours, just going around the country stripping to promote the magazines." April describes road trips as "vans full of girls being fun people" in a casual candid manner as the press files by. "My agent laughed at me when they offered me a film and I insisted on control of things like script and actor approval, said it was unheard of but I stuck to my guns, I said if they want me they will agree to my terms. He thought I was fuckin crazy but I got what I wanted obviously," She waves around her. She beams with pride describing a childhood and teen life that was shameless. Free and open sexuality. It strikes Allison, she feels knots in her belly for a moment as she's struck with a tantalizing new outlook, *Sex and your body isn't something to be ashamed of.* "Sex and your body were nothing to be ashamed of in my house growing up, my parents were openly affectionate and sexual with each other and encouraged us to be secure and happy. And satisfied! Satisfied! Too many women see satisfaction as a rare and accidental bonus, not within their rights to even expect!" Not April. "I want to get mine! And I get off on getting other people off so it all works out great!" April laughs casually. She is the happiest person in the world. "...my tits..." April says 'my tits' a lot. And it sounds so natural, *my tits.* It never sounded natural to Allison. Tits were to be covered, they're called breasts not tits. Breasts are to be desired but not for Her Pleasure. Tits are for boys to play with. Oh yeah, and feed all the puppies. Tits are there to feed the babies. If you have nice tits boys will want to put babies in you because subconsciously your tits tell them you can feed the babies. The babies you're going to pump out for him. April's tits seem to belong to April. Allison looks down at her own tits. *My tits.* She sneaks a feel, looking around absurdly trying to ensure privacy in a room full of inquisitive people with pencils, tape records and cameras. They're all talking about copping feels and tits anyway, taking in all the spectacle and recording it for posterity. Some are recording for content. Amongst the press corps April's own crew pans and circles the room quietly, discreetly capturing candid moments. For posterity and content. Allison is sure not to be picking her nose or looking directly at the cameras when they are pointing at her, which is often as she is next to the titular character. *My titulars,* Allison giggles to herself. April had expressed not wanting to repeat her business matters over and over but she happily repeats with a smile describing herself, "I'm just really real. I can't friggin help it. I'm April Lynn Baker, I live life out loud, I used my own name in porn for fuck's sake, that's how real I am!" Allison is mesmerized as April describes the trappings of of film, be it porn or Hollywood, like a seasoned old stage sage, "Lots of girls get caught up in it, they get trapped in the costume." She whispers loudly behind her hand to Natalie as if she were sharing a secret, "Good thing my costume's my birthday suit, eh?" She nudges Natalie with a playful elbow and continues with the Hollywood lore, "And they put those masks on happily at first, that costume gets you what want, or at least what you thought you wanted. It gets you what you need, but it's all a trick. It's really a well known saying from old Hollywood folklore, The Marilyn Tragedy. OK, It's like this," She waves her hands signals a lane change, "What if I told you that you can have this mask, a whole costume and it's magic. It's such a good costume that nobody can even tell it's a mask and it's so beautiful that everyone just wants to shower you with gifts and love and affection, they can't help themselves, that's how beautiful the mask is. Would you wear it?" She asks rhetorically to her amazed audience, "Now what if I told you there's just one thing," She holds up one finger and winks at a youngish girl who stands entranced, nodding, pencil in hand ready to jot down the next pearl, "You're trapped in this costume. You can't take it off. Ever. Would you still wear it? One more thing," She glances back at the same girl, "There's always one more thing right? And this is the real tragedy..." She glances at the girls' pad and nods, *Write this part down,* she says with her eyes, "...and I can't actually tell you this one, this one you have to learn for yourself, because we always think we can be the one, right? The one who can change him or make something work that nobody else can, right? Shit like that? But we can't always, can we? So now it's on you -- the mask -- even after all the warning you thought 'Oh, that won't apply to me,' but it *does,* Honey, and now you can see the horror for yourself. You can't actually have the gifts the costume receives. You can eat the good food, but you can't taste it. You can make love but you can't feel it. And you're so beautiful it's a curse, they can't help it, they want to give it to you, they shower you in it. They drown you in gifts and affection and that's what you're doing in there, drowning because the mask can't cry but you can. But that's not what they see and they couldn't comfort you anyway because you can't feel the warm embrace of an arm, just a dull dead weight on your back. Would you still put it on?" She looks with a serious look at the young reporter then smiles big for the crowd, "Well, not me!" She proudly thumbs her chest.

As the line moves fresh new faces with pencils and recorders and a lot of the same questions keep coming up despite the speech. April takes it all in stride at times, sometimes just ignoring a repeat question and instead addressing the room with an anecdote. "I miss working on productions, I mean with directors and scripts and stories like *New Wave Call Girls,* I mean it was a *movie,* just with sex scenes. Like when you see a *Pretty Woman* or a *Fatal Attraction,* the sex isn't real, it's artsy, it's even sexy, but in porn we give you the sex. Sex is a part of the story too isn't it? I mean that's why you call a hooker right? Fuck, the hero always gets the girl, what do you think he does with her? Anyways I think that's one of the things missing in porn nowadays: the art, the performance."

A young dumbfounded journo stutters, "So uh, you're from New Jersey…?"

Act 1 Scene 22.2

Interior:Dining Room, evening

Poker Tournament

A big after party follows the...Allison isn't sure that was a press conference in the traditional sense. It was a bittersweet, mostly jovial event. Unique, certainly, but press conference doesn't really cover it. First off, it was more like a high school reunion -- everyone who was ever anyone in porn is in town for the weekend, but the energy Allison felt in the room was this unspoken dark cloud, like all this was somehow the end of an era. It's the end of April's adult film career though it feels like more than that and yet, it seemed like nobody wanted to talk about THAT. It's like they all know, they all see it coming, the proverbial writing on the wall. This is it...the last hurrah. April pulled the chute at just the right time and the rest of them are just going to have to ride out on her wake, or go down with the ship. So many metaphors. With the impending of the rise of the internet everything seems up in the air. Nobody seemed to want to talk about that yesterday either, beyond the entry level they were all at, websites and such. It's nothing like how it will be by the middle of the next decade. And nobody sees social media coming, not at this juncture.

The after party has gone on into the small hours and the porn industry does not disappoint Allison when it comes to throwing a party. She is careful to pace herself amongst strangers. She's distracted by the opportunity to glean knowledge networking. It's all so very much. By the end of the evening Allison hasn't even gotten drunk.

When Allison and Natalie arrive the following day for the tournament, anti-gambling protesters have joined the fray outside with the evangelicals, feminists and the light union strikers. Today is the big poker tournament and the sexual innuendo jokes will fly all night on repeat, likely to be repeated tomorrow ad nauseam. Variations of the phrase "All in on the nut flush" would be uttered more times in the next thirty-six hours than could ever possibly be counted by any conventional means. The whole adult film industry seems to be showing up and there is no press tonight. There's still easily twice as many people as there was last night even without the press and everyone is dressed like it's the Oscars. One familiar blonde with huge fake tits remarks how she "...hasn't seen so many of these sluts with their clothes on since the Wankies last year."

Allison looks around her table, down at her cards then slides them face down back to the dealer with a silent shake of her head. She and Natalie had been practicing their poker skills at the apartment, dealing each other hands over morning coffees and brunch mimosas. Lunch was usually eaten with wine. Dinner, wine. Allison realizes how much wine they've been drinking, shrugs it off. They watched poker tournaments on ESPN in the wee hours. Also with wine. Allison's life has certainly taken a bizarre turn between leaving Gore and now. She looks around. *OK no contest, not even close but this just isn't fair.* Porn Industry Charity Poker Tournament and Gang Bang is a really specific and particularly bizarre place to find oneself. *Two years already!?* Almost. It's all happened so fast. She hasn't heard the last of Louis either. Here she is, living in Peekskill, New York on the verge of an unknown journey onto the dangerous and misunderstood sex industry highway. She's drinking a lot of wine and studying...Poker? Allison's never been one to go into anything unprepared so over the last few weeks she's dove headfirst into learning how to play. Not that she didn't know the basics...who doesn't? She's read a few books from the classic masters, the 10-2 guy, some upcoming new hotshots she'd learned about from the late night ESPN card games. She looks down at a new hand, doesn't like it, pushes it forward. This time she looks around at the faces for reads. Somewhere in the room an aging starlet loudly jokes, "Oh my god I haven't been fucked so hard by two spades since I filmed *Big Blacks Little Blondes* a few years ago..." To the amused laughter of everyone in earshot.

Allison looks at another new hand. Strong. She antes, *limp in.* The strategy works as do a few more hands in a row. Allison finds herself with a sizable chip stack in front of her by the time they reach the first break. In a poker tournament like this when a predetermined amount of players are eliminated everybody stands up to stretch and the empty seats are filled, consolidating the tables. Allison doesn't have to move. She surveys the room, reading faces and chip stacks, studying. She is thirsty for all the chips. One important lesson Allison picked up is that poker is a game and the object is to have all the chips. Very simple. It's about the chips. Not money. You have to be able to separate those two ideas. In this case all the money is going to charity anyway so it doesn't matter and all the more reason to win. It's not about the money. It's about the chips.

The sound of chips clicking around the room commences as the break ends and it isn't long before the familiar jokes are flying free again. Outside two different religious protesters get into a shouting match regarding whether one can't climb the ladder to heaven with penis or poker chips in one's hand. You can not. They do agree on that.

"You can't climb to heaven with your hands full of penis!"

"No it's gambling that fills your hands full of dirty money and tools of ignorance!"

"Masturbating!"

"Gambling!"

"Masturbating!"

"Gambling!"

The man next to Allison acknowledges the protestors and jokes, "Sounds like my life in the 80's," with a grin, jabs her ribs gently with his elbow.

Across the room someone shouts, "All in on the nut flush!" in triumphant amusement. For, the trillionth time. Chips click clack click clack, cards shuffle shuffle.

"Oh shit I haven't seen someone get fucked that hard on the river since *Cleopatra Whore of the Nile!*"

When it so happens that Natalie's elimination signals another break and re-seating, this time Allison does have to move. The tables are condensed again and Allison's chip stack is in the top five. When she settles in her new seat, Natalie sits nearby to cheer her on. Somewhere in the crowd someone yells out, "Liquor up front, poker in the in the rear!" For about the gazillionth time today. It still gets the same laughs every time.

All Allison's studying pays off and she advances to the final table. Who actually wins the tournament isn't really important. What's important is how much money they raised for the charity April chose for at-risk girls. These potentially at risk girls are the real winners today. And Allison does a great deal of winning herself, in non-gambling related networking, gaining insight from the very intentional small talk she makes with the industry. And Allison isn't bitter at all with Ron Jeremy. He had the better hand.

April's Full
Act 1 Scene 23

Interior:Eastland Apartment, morning

ALLISON puts her feet on the
floor into a completely new
life. She passed the interview.

ALLISON: (v/o)
Did I get the part?

She schmoozed through orientation with ease. Maybe it's her sardonic wit, maybe it's her uncanny ability to shrink out of sight and existence. One may never know. Whatever the reason, Allison dresses in silent confidence. *Knock 'em Dead, kid,* Inka encourages. She contemplates the severity in Inka's voice and goes to meet Natalie in the kitchen. Natalie sits at the island in a daze, stirring her coffee, gazing out at the Hudson river with a goofy smile.

"Allison I can't believe this is happening." Natalie says without looking away from the river. "I mean I've worked with some of the people we've been rubbing elbows with the past few days it should be no big deal but it's all been so surreal, like a dream, like it wasn't really happening but today…Oh my God Allison!" She gushes happily.

"April is an inspiration isn't she?" Allison looks out to the river herself, Natalie nods agreement.

The girls ready themselves for the day and reconvene back in the kitchen. Natalie shuts off the coffee pot and glances at the calendar on the way out. "Why do you suppose we play pranks on each other on April first?"

"I thought it was that Pagan sect in the south of France, they celebrated April first as the new year even after everyone agreed on the January first calendar. They were ridiculed as fools every April first."

"So that means…Wait is that true or are you April Fool-ing me?"

"That's what my dad told me years ago, I guess I have no idea if it's true or not."

"Well I don't think I'm going to pull April Fool pranks anymore. That's mean." Allison feels a pang of dread in her gut. What if this is all an elaborate April Fool's Day prank? *Ha Ha Allison you fat cow nobody wants to see your sturdy ass get fucked you're not going onto porn,* Then Allison's Mother is chiding her. *I mean can you imagine? What will the neighbors think? The very idea.* She's much more sophisticated and Victorian than usual for some reason as she takes over Allison's inner monologue. *Well I never, the very idea, well it's just not done, a proper lady, pinky out.*

Allison clings to the bucket seat with both hands in her now routine death grip. Sure, the Mazda's catching some air this time as Natalie speeds across the Annsville Creek bridge. So what? Big deal. Happens all the time. She looks over at Natalie and down at herself.

Natalie is wearing a simple clingy and quite revealing dark blood red dress. Her lipstick and shoes match perfectly of course and her hair is twisted into a sensible yet elegant bun atop her head. Braless, Natalie's ample perky bosom teases at the plunging neckline seemingly on the verge of playfully tumbling out. Allison's confidence is high but she still feels Natalie outshines her. Allison herself is in a smart and sexy blue dress with her hair down, blown straight. Besides Natalie's lipstick both have on minimal makeup as they will need to be made up for the camera in a short while anyway. Allison gives herself another glance in the side view mirror. She doesn't feel like she looks a day older than the fresh face in her early twenties who left Gore a few years ago. *Don't tell anyone you're almost thirty, the penises'll shrivel up, worse than ice cold water. Thirty.* Shudder.

When Natalie is forced to stop at a red light Allison pulls down the passenger visor mirror, thinks she should have had Sheng Nu take care of these eyebrows. Too late now. She slams back in the seat when the light turns green and Natalie floors the Miata. Allison looks to the mirror again from pinned back to the seat and decides her dark choker really says, "I'm here to suck dick and chew gum and I'm all out of gum."

"What?!" Natalie laughs.

"Wha..? Nothing, what dick…?" This is when it occurs to Allison that she's given exactly three blow jobs in her life, none recently and one she didn't even get to finish. She takes solace in the idea that she's watched a great deal of pornography in the last few weeks and is reasonably sure she's going to be fine. Dicks are not complicated. As far as an entrance to hard core porn a glorified fluffer in a celebrity gang bang is surely the softest of landings. Allison looks back at Natalie and feels a little over dressed for a moment in her full set of undergarments. She knows there is nothing between Natalie's...That, and her leather bucket's besides that thin red dress. *Leather seats.*

Natalie eases the car between protesters to the waving direction of the yellow jacket security team. Allison notices there are more of them today. Protesters, that is. Now they've spilled across the highway and fill the narrow breakdown lane fifty yards in either direction across from the bar.

"Unfair wages!"

"What would Jesus do!?"

"Masturbators kill puppies!" Some racists are being dragged away by police screaming about Negros having sex with white women. They aren't saying Negro.

The kitchen is filled with naked men. The thick orange tile appears slick with the humid brackish atmosphere created by so many warm radiating naked bodies. Eye contact is extremely important in this room right now. Most of the men milling about in the kitchen are amateurs. Little to mostly no experience in porn besides watching it. Or acting at all for that matter. The kitchen is the corral for the extras, the seven hundred and seventy five or so dicks that aren't attached to a face and a credited cameo. Many are in over their heads, which they realized a while ago but there is no turning back now. Eye contact. Fifty guys in the kitchen all trying to maintain a semi-erection in a room full of naked men.

Occasionally one of the director's assistants pushes open one swinging door to coldly tell them, "Few more minutes and we'll start bringing you in about ten at a time…" Last time it was, "A few more minutes guys, we're just getting some camera angles set…" The time before that it was, "White balance issues…." Some of the naked sweaty semi-erect extras are starting to grumble. Some, with underlying misgivings, start making indignant declarations, offering up softly uttered ultimatums to nobody in particular. Nobody is fooled nor do any empty threats come to fruition. Nobody is leaving, not now. Men shift back and forth nervously from foot to foot, wet clammy feet march in place making soft tacky footsteps singing a soft tacky chorus. Semi erect penises, clutched tightly in one sweaty hand, half stroking, half protecting. Their postures are all similar, a sort of hunched over curl, another subconscious attempt to keep their weiners hidden from the world's eyes. That's one of the surefire ways to tell the difference between the amateurs and the few semi-professional semi erections in the room. The relaxed, upright and confident guys in the room are D-list adult film actors. They aren't big enough names to warrant a table or a credited cameo on the box, just a big enough face for a quick "oh shit it's that guy!" Experience in porn correlates directly to the erectness of both posture and pecker. Not that you can look down at another fella's semi-erect penis. *Eyes up here buddy. Eye contact. Not too much.*

By late morning the sun bakes through a kitchen window and the musk is ripening to an end-of-season boy's locker room with a disconcerting hint of pre cum. When Natalie and Allison burst through the back door, Allison recoils slightly from the thick atmosphere. It's as if someone threw a hot wet dirty wool cum sock in her face. She holds her head high and grins satisfied, feeling the power of looking hot in their tight dresses in a room full of naked, vulnerable men. Stiffening erections follow them through the crowd in a wave like divining rods. *Here pussy, pussy, pussy.*

"Hey Natalie." a few confident erections say in deeper-than-necessary voices over puffed up chests. They confidently swing semi-pro hard ons.

She gives one a harsh snap on the tip with a giggle, "Hey boys." She smirks at the wince as the pecker struggles to remain erect and ignore the sting. She smiles at all the dumb boy smiles and erections, amateur and professional. Chests and bellies sag in their wake as the swinging doors close on their hopeful hard-ons. The swing of the thick door pumps the musk around the room, giving it a fresh vigor.

"Gettin' ripe in here." Someone says right before the first group is finally invited into the gang bang. As the first group of ten naked semi erections are herded in, a new group of clothed, confident men are ushered in the back door into the kitchen and ordered to strip down. Their names are taken and a plastic bag is provided for their belongings. There is a tag for their name fastened to it for identification later. The bags are carelessly tossed in a pile in another room off the bar area. Outside, a large group of hopefuls fills the parking lot, talking big games about being discovered. Many hint at a hidden girthy talent in their pants. Several have mentioned something to the effect of, "I'm going to split that old slut down the middle."

Inside while the new group is stripped of underpants and bravado the room shifts to accommodate the void at one end and influx at the other. As the gravity of their new situation sinks into the newly nude they slowly curl into the death grip protection hunch posture. Slowly they warm to room temperature like a bag of pet-store peckers getting released into a tank at home. The scent of fresh nerve sweat wafts from the new dicks mixing into the room's musk. Just past the room of sweaty awkward semi-erections the main event is just about to get underway.

Allison and Natalie hold the distinction of keeping the on-deck peckers erect. April loves their elegant dresses.

"You two class up this gang bang!" She honks, climbing onto the table. Just last night it had been the table for the final poker showdown. Allison takes hold of her first pecker and strokes it slow, taking in the milestone of her first professional handy. She and Natalie each stroke an amature erection in each hand, smiling proud and elegant smiles.

"Get in there baby." Natalie releases a dick and gives his ass a playful spank. The shy amateur contest winner moves slowly forward to be the first of 800 dicks when he's pushed aside by an older man with the biggest dick Allison has ever seen. He's very tall, over six feet easily and he has a full head of coarse white hair, sprayed up into a gaudy disco era coif.

"I think I should have first go at her last time out, considering." He trumpets loudly. having been the first dick April took on camera so many years ago. Mr .Contest winner gets to go second. He's OK with that too.

And the gang bang is on. Cameras rolling, protests outside notwithstanding, the first of 800 dicks to be the last to slip ol' April the old Big Slick. April laughs nostalgically as she pulls Big Slick in by his oddly fit old man ass with Speedo bikini tan lines. Awkward fan boys and aspiring porn studs one after another clumsily climb onto the table trying not to look stupid on camera. Several with no clue what they're in for discover embarrassing things about themselves as they try to coax shrinking peckers into action with all the hot lights and directors and cinematographers looking at them.

"Come on son, stick your cock in the pussy, you've done this before right?"

"Let's go, you a virgin or something?" The cold unsexy humdrum job of filming porn can prove a death blow to an amature boner.

"Stage fright?" April teases.

Allison adds playfully, "Come on it's my first day, you're making me look bad dude."

April is less patient, "Back of the line in shame." She teases coarsely to that and any other pecker that can't perform. That walk of shame is one of the absolute worst walks of shame in the history of walks of shame. Walking back through the line of fresh dicks saying,

"What's wrong son? It's just a pussy." It's just no help at all to make a failed boner rise to the occasion.

Professional penises, are registered weapons with the sex industry, union cocks as far as April is concerned, no protection needed. Amateur dicks, unregistered penises need to be sheathed in condom by industry standards as well as state and local labor laws. Rolling on rubbers falls into the capable hands of Allison and Natalie from a bowl on their table filled with all colors and brands. A production assistant holds the unglamorous job of changing the bag of wrappers and used cock balloons every now and then and dumping more new rubbers into the bowl from the boxes of rubbers in the corner.

There had been some discussion earlier over the trash can to use. After consideration the small one was chosen over the big one as the thought of a big can of burnt rubber marinating in a sex juice slurry all day made the production team collectively gag. As each amateur dick finishes it's 15 seconds of fame, he tosses his scum bag in the trash heap of spent rubbers and sex slime, then coldly ushered into the room with the bags of clothes, hastily tossed in on the floor earlier. There they are left to bask in the surprise shame and emptiness while they squat down, naked, shivering and humiliated, sore pecker tucked safely into the mangina thigh cushions, picking through recycled grocery bags looking for their belongings. They find themselves searching frantically hoping to at least have pants on before the next flaccid cock comes in waving at him avoiding eye contact. Inside, a credited cameo jokes and high-fives April in that familiar way that only people who've shared history can share. It's alienating, from naked in the kitchen to dressing quickly in the dark shame room, it sounds like a real party, a real good time that you were just not going to be a part of no matter what you did. Once dressed and forgotten alone in the dark room full of tagged and bagged belongings with one more door to go through, *just sign here on your way out,* out into the real world, the sun bright in your eyes, the real world loud and harsh HD compared to the unreal and seedy world of pornography. As you walk out into the bright lights of life's harsh reality, to the angry shouts of various paths to damnation or salvation you ponder the uncomfortable poetry of the line of dicks on parade of which you were one, reduced to exactly that: Your Dick. Exploited, used and ashamed. Careful what you wish for. Ain't it funny? The only role for men here today is degrading, humiliating and all about their dicks. A parade of Dicks.

Only a couple of weeks later on April 18th, April's Full is available for download to paying members of AprilLynn.com and is available for sale on DVD. It's the first, last and only adult film April stars in that will never be released on VHS.

Drama Camp 1993

Elizabeth is standing alone center stage. "I'm auditioning for the part of Kim Macavie." She says proudly, loud and clear. Over the winter she took the Yorktown Theater workshop. With that experience under her belt she really has her stage legs now. Last year she made her stage debut with *Anything Goes*. Now, after drilling through Currer Bell's theater bootcamp, she's a salty seasoned veteran.

She stands awaiting her cue. Camp Director is visibly annoyed. Elizabeth isn't worried, she knows it's with Courtney. She'd humored Courtney last year, allowed her to feel like the big shot. Even let her pick her role. This year she refuses to put up with a diva. Courtney is very talented but she can be very difficult to work with and only getting worse in the last few years. Elizabeth did well last year -- Camp Director wants to nurture that.

Allison is trying to focus Camp Director, she points to the piano player and nods at Elizabeth. Camp Director had wanted Elizabeth to audition for the part of Kim. Elizabeth starts to sing the theme song, *Bye Bye Birdie*. The song wasn't in the original play, it had been written just for the movie. The 1963 movie had started with Ann-Margret singing the song alone in front of the curtain just as Elizabeth is doing now. Camp Director smiles. She leans over to Allison, whispers, "The '63 movie starts with Kim singing this just like this, let's do a version closer to the movie." She smiles innocently, "People like the movie." Allison nods, makes note on her clipboard.

"You already want Elizabeth for this part don't you?"

"Yes I do. Don't tell everyone till after though, let them audition, I don't want a repeat of last year."

"Courtney wants to play Rosie."

"I know she does and she'll likely get the part but she's auditioning this year, I don't want a repeat..."

"...of last year, I get it." Allison finishes.

Backstage Courtney is standing in Elizabeth's path as she comes off stage.

"I hear you did a Currer Bell workshop this winter."

"I did. Three in fact." Elizabeth is cautious. She knows through the grapevine that Courtney and Currer did not click well. A few seasons back she stormed out of a workshop and he blackballed her in his little circle. Yorktown Theater leads to his connections at the Westchester Broadway Theater, which of course leads to Actual Broadway. This cuts Courtney off from the bigger audiences she yearns for. All she really wants is applause and accolades from big crowds. Currer is flamboyant and bitchy. He surrounds himself with gay teen boys and fag hags, who are all also quite bitchy. Elizabeth learned all of this very quickly at Currer's workshops. For the sheer will to not incur the judgmental bitchy stares and side glances of Currer and his entourage was motivation enough for Elizabeth to rise to the occasion. They call a Currer Bell workshop bootcamp because it's eight hours of intense drilling one scene at a time, each in small groups and then performing them all in one variety show that same night. From what Elizabeth heard Courtney did not respond well to this method at all. She saw firsthand last season Courtney doesn't feel the need to practice. The look in Courtney's eye tells Elizabeth she's a little more of a threat to her now.

A few weeks into rehearsals, Elizabeth is laying on a prop bed on stage talking into a prop rotary phone, "Of course I'll always wear your pin." She pledges her loyalty to the boy who pinned her. She dances across the set, hangs up the phone, spins gaily in her makeup chair singing, "A skinny girl of thirteen...braces ear to ear...you could never be appealing…" Allison finds herself stuck on the song as Elizabeth sings. When she was thirteen Carol and her minions were relentless. Allison was a confused budding teen in that tough otherworld dimension between girl and woman. She had begun to bud earlier and curvier than Carol and her friends, a Cardinal sin, what a slut. Allison has noticed Elizabeth developing in a similar way, earlier and curvier.

Elizabeth is singing, "Now you're sixteen...you have that happy grown up female feeling…" She pulls on a big brown baggy sweater. They found one exactly like the one Ann-Margret wears in the movie.

Out in the lobby Camp Director is telling Courtney, "We're just going to have to cut 'Spanish Rose'."

"What?! Why?! I only had two solos to begin with, now I only get one?! That's bullshit, I'm the best singer you got…"

"Watch your mouth, young lady."

"You're not my mother!" Courtney yells. Camp Director shrugs, grins, holds her tongue.

"It's just not right, you're not Spanish." Courtney feels another sting, tries not to let it show, Camp Director knows she hit a sore spot. *Far as you know,* she thinks meanly, "I don't need the crap Courtney, people are getting really sensitive about that stuff, all this new political correctness." On stage Elizabeth wiggles out of her shirt under the sweater. Camp Director's smile makes Courtney think she isn't being completely honest but there isn't anything she can do about it.

"Well then I want to play Kim, Lizzy has more songs than I do…"

"Elizabeth is already doing very well with the Kim role…"

"I have a better voice than Lizzy, let her play Rosie." Courtney rolls her eyes, adding, "Or screaming girl number two." with a smirk.

"No Courtney." Camp Director turns and opens the door, 'The song will have to be cut and that's that."

Elizabeth is singing, "How lovely to be a woman…"

When Courtney doesn't follow Camp Director turns around, "Aren't you coming into rehearsal?"

Courtney rolls her eyes, "I don't need to rehearse. I've got my ONE song down." She turns to leave.

As she is pushing out of the lobby Camp Director shrugs turns to go, pauses only adding, "You're going to need to rehearse the Shriners Dance scene or I'll cut that too." Without turning around. She walks back into the auditorium, no looking back. She knows without looking that Courtney isn't going anywhere.

On stage Elizabeth is dropping her skirt out from under the big sweater. She stands there with naked legs and sings, "…You're what they're whistling at…" She is smiling, happily twisting her hair into a bun on top of her head. She dances across the set bedroom, "…to have one job to do…to pick a boy…" The words ring in Allison's head, *job to do, pick a boy…* Allison has been hanging out with Louis across the street at night. He's a good listener. She feels the taste in her mouth at the thought of Louis, wants a smoke. She has been very frustrated with her boyfriend,Tommy. He can be so cruel sometimes and Allison suspects Carol has her eye on him. In fact, she's sure she's caught him checking out Carol too.

On stage Elizabeth lays back on the prop bed, seductively sticking up one bare leg as she pulls on one sock, then the other, singing, "Things a woman knows…" Natalie waits in the wings offstage, one hand gripping a rope, the other she holding a letter from her father. She's been reading it over and over in secret for a week. It's a happy letter but she's crying. She misses him. Elizabeth tugs on her baseball cap, "How lovely to be a woman like me." Natalie pulls the curtain closed.

Buy Bi-Birdie
Act 2 Scene 1

Interior: Warehouse, day

ELIZABETH sinks into the dingy tweed secondhand couch under the blue tinted cloud of smoke that fills the room. VINCENT'S band is practicing in the corner room of the big brick warehouse.

It used to be a bread factory complete with a train platform for freight. Now it's a big industrial complex, sectioned off and leased out to dozens of entities including a recording studio.

A few people on the stage improvise a cacophony of instrumental jazz punk. They stare through their instruments in a haze, some hallucinating. High ceilings and thick brick walls distribute sound amongst the cloud in an unmistakable way. Under the influence of the constant flow of pot in the room it all seems so poetically perfect. The way the sun filters through the tall tinted windows, the way the train passes by the window so close you could almost touch it every forty minutes, if they're on schedule. The music, the room, the building, it all works very well together.

It seems every time she passes something to the left, something arrives from her right. Elizabeth is so high at the moment she's having a hard time remembering names, her own included and it's amusing. She giggles everytime she looks at someone and can't put a name to the face. She looks to her right expecting another joint or blunt but they've stopped coming. Finally. There he is. What's his name? Elizabeth giggles, racking her brain. *I came here with him.* An hour ago he told a random guy in traffic he was going to have anal sex with me...tomorrow. *Why tomorrow?* The poor random guy was probably thinking. Elizabeth giggles, loudly in her mind but in reality near silently. She looks right again at him. *He's cute,* she thinks. *What's his name?* She giggles. They'd cracked the code, so to speak, she and he. How do you avoid getting hurt? By denying your feelings. By "being friends" with so-called "benefits". Of course that old chestnut leads down a deceiving path and they've been at it too long already. *Chest. Nut.* A deceiving path of truth or dare. Inevitably in an effort to isolate oneself from pain, instead pain is invited in to dine at the table and everybody gets hurt.

"Mmph, bathroom…" He mumbles struggling to his feet and crashing out the door.

"What was his name again?" Elizabeth laughs looking to her left but she is alone on the loveseat. The other guy she came here to see is sitting on an amp onstage mesmerized by the vibrating strings on his guitar. He appears to be in a trance. "What's his name now?" She giggles. He loudly strums an eerie chord in a slow droning rhythm under the musical chaos from the other inebriated musicians. Another guy, Jon, walks in the room with a plate of burgers in one hand and a stack of two cans of beer in the other.

"Here's some burgers, you guys sound like shit." He puts down the steaming plate of browned meat and walks out sipping the top beer.

"What's his name?" Elizabeth howls with laughter at her horror, this isolated amnesia. She looks to her right, remembers he's gotten up and went…? What did he say? How long has he been gone? She giggles again and falls into a trance herself captivated by the ambient noise. Vincent strums his guitar, Elizabeth gives up trying to recall anyone's name. He had invited her to The Dock for a party but he and a few guys had eaten some mushrooms before she'd gotten here and now he's lost on the stage in the music and forgetting things himself. Forgetting he invited her to hang out, forgetting to talk to her, he strums his guitar. He hadn't even noticed she'd arrived. Nor with whom. With whom happens to be directly across the hall, awkwardly laying on the goofy romantic charm, trying to sabotage himself. Elizabeth, still alone on the couch, looks right again, remembers, *mmph, bathroom,* and looks past the vacancy at the green metal door he'd walked out. A minute ago? Has he been gone more like an hour? She groggily comes back to the small party. It is a party right? Vincent. Vincent, *that's* the guy on the stage, he invited her to this. He did call it a party. He said a small gathering. He said a few bands and grilling on the loading dock, some jamming. "Mixed up bands" he'd called it. The local music scene takes itself so seriously. Especially Vincent and his band. Jon with the burgers and their bass player, some weird older guy -- a local artist or something but not really talented at much besides being a creepy wannabe cult leader with a bunch of children followers. He writes dumb poetry and plays in a few bands. He seems to be a bit of a ringleader and knows everyone. Never a fan of poetry, Elizabeth sticks with calling him creepy.

She's coming out of the fog when the door opens and whats-his-name sits back down on the couch next to her, closer than before looking intensely forward, as if he's wearing blinders. She recalls everybody's name. She is looking right through him, boring holes in him with lasers, looking at the girl he brought in with him, sitting next to him perched on the arm of the small, shrinking loveseat. Courtney. A name and face Elizabeth could never forget. A train horn blares outside. Courtney smiles, smirks is more like it. When she speaks she sounds friendly but her eyes are not. Daggers shoot back and forth. If looks could kill he'd be dead on the couch where he sits, but being caught in the crossfire may have suited him just fine. Every subtle twitch of eyebrow, every silent moment, speaks volumes. Reams of scripts scroll by, side glances and rivalries, a chess match plays out in minute details and resting bitch faces. Lines in the sand are drawn and the dummy between them, just an extra. A sand bag for the big dress rehearsal. *A sexy lamp.* Elizabeth's glare steams.

> v/o Elizabeth:
> *How dare you*

> (With a glance smiles back),
> v/o Courtney:
> *He came to me*

> v/o Elizabeth:
> *I saw him first*

She fires off with a look that she knows is irrational. Courtney's bullshit technicality means nothing to Elizabeth. They're doing that Not A Relationship dance, trying to skip around the rules, trying to avoid hurt. *Well played, it's on.* Drama Camp rivalry boils to the surface, *Never Break Character. Who will be the romantic lead, did I get the part? Who will be the slutty comic relief, this time?* Those are the only two choices now. There will be no hiding in the chorus as a tree on this one. There are no Townsfolk. The big dumb male lead, clueless Deli Guy between them, is the prize. One girl gets the part. You can't have two female leads. You can't have two divas. Auditions start today. Right now. Courtney sat down only seconds ago, she speaks, her voice is friendly. Her eyes are not.

"Hey Lizzie." Outside the end of the train rumbles past the window.

Act 2 Scene 1.2

Interior: Warehouse, evening

By late afternoon the small gathering had turned into a big party that stretches well into the evening.

Vincent walks out of the small lounge and finds Elizabeth with an angry look on her face. People shuffle past from door to door down the industrial white block hallways from band room to band room. "Hey, where's--?"

"He left." She cuts him off, "With Courtney." She adds quickly with contempt. Vincent walks with her, letting her lead down the hall. He goes with her to her car, listens, quietly takes the keys, listens, drives, she talks, he listens.

"I listened to that whining bastard cry about some dumb slut who dumped him for her professor like fucking years ago…!" She vents.

"That bastard." He interjects at appropriate junctures.

"And this morning, I go and kiss him and you know how I don't kiss…?" Vincent nods, he knows she doesn't kiss. He's been listening. "And do you know what his dumb ass says?!" Vincent smiles, thinking about all the stupid possibilities, all the stupid things they've tried to coerce each other to say to girls.

"What did he say?" He says with sympathy, hiding his amusement.

"You kiss funny."

Vincent tries not to laugh, "That bastard." He manages.

"Who the fuck says that?!" Elizabeth drops her voice a few octaves and puts on her dumb boy voice,"'You kiss funny.' Fucking dick and he knows, he KNOWS I don't kiss…" She vents. Vincent listens. He drives, she talks. "Well fucking joke's on him, that bitch is going to Cancun for two weeks and he's supposed to go to New Jersey with me and some of the deli crew."

Across town above the Eye, Courtney basks in the awkward affections but it's nothing compared to the smug satisfaction that can only come from irking Elizabeth. *He's trying to pull some long game, he wants to wait,* bullshit.

"You know you don't have to wait with me?" She hints bluntly but he has his romance eyes on with a dumbstruck smile. Courtney laughs to herself, *I guess irking Elizabeth is the only satisfaction I'm getting tonight.*

Vincent drives. Elizabeth talks, Vincent listens. They drive past the bar. Elizabeth notes the light on upstairs. It both angers and intrigues her. Courtney infuriates her. They drive the block to the deli and Vincent goes in and buys a pack of Elizabeth's brand cigarettes. He listens to her while he packs the smokes, tapping the box against his palm. He's leaning casually against her car under the yellow spotlight over the deli parking lot. He listens.

"She's been pulling shit like this since we were twelve but she never really directed it at me before." Vincent pulls two cigarettes from the pack, puts both in his mouth. He holds his lighter up in a weird backwards grip and awkwardly snaps his fingers on the striker wheel a few times until it works. He holds his head sideways lighting both cigarettes, one over the other, then he hands one to Elizabeth. He suggests they go for a ride and talk more before he goes home. He drives. She talks. He listens.

Act 2 Scene 1.3

Interior: Hotel Room, New Jersey, day

ELIZABETH gets up from the bed,
disgusted.

On vacation in New Jersey the following weekend, it would be Elizabeth with the upper hand...sort of. She rolls her eyes at him with one hand wrapped around the shaft of his dick as he weakly declares loyalty to Courtney. She notices he doesn't try too hard to protest when she takes him into her mouth. She finishes him quick and leaves the room disgusted, not sure if with him or herself, or Courtney. Definitely Courtney. And him. And herself.

Elizabeth joins Jess on the second floor balcony. "It's like she's being faithful to him." She vents to Jess. "Give me a beer?" She asks, lighting a cigarette. Elizabeth doesn't usually drink beer. "I have a bad taste in my mouth." She adds, glancing at the hotel room door, Jess understands.

The salty air has a crisp chill. The sky is a deep grey, punctuated with darker ominous patches of angry-looking clouds. Lightning dances on the horizon far up the beach though it hasn't started raining here yet. Weather can be so funny on the coast. The rain is coming though. The white caps on the restless sea spank the beach a block east of the hotel with a lewd and greedy slap. Ugly seagulls aggressively stalk the trash cans below on the sidewalk.

"Where's Janel?"

"She went to get more beer. Said she needed it to tolerate these two idiots." Jess hooks a thumb toward the end of the balcony where Matty and Kev are playing a game they call Lust or Disgust. Elizabeth and Jess shake their heads at them, sip their beers.

"I mean he's acting like he's in some long-term relationship with her and they've only spent one fucking night together. He didn't even fuck her!" Jess turns her head slow and looks at Elizabeth, confused. "Right!? And I know she isn't trying to be faithful to him right now in Mexico at Spring Break, probably getting double teamed nightly..."

Beach Blanket Bimbo, Elizabeth thinks, creating a beach musical in her head. *Fun in the sun would you care for Bingo? I'll take two, more than one woman...from child to a girl gone wild, hop on this tour bus with a flash of my...smile! Check out my teeth! Hey, that's quite a nice set! Wink wink nudge nudge. While you're at it check out This and That. Didn't hurt my sex life either. Boys on the dock, sailors on leave, before shoving off come shove into me. High Five. Choreographed dance numbers all across the sand, put one empty drink down there's a new full one in my hand. Hose me down the sun in my face, a wet t-shirt trophy for winning third place. Oh, I love spring break…* Elizabeth rolls her eyes.

Jess shakes her head, nods at Matty, "This one won't even touch me."

A light sheet of rain finally moves over the hotel. A distinct storm line can be seen moving across the sea, the air fills with a mist that dampens everything, even seeping inside the room.

Janel climbs the stairs cussing about it, "Fucking rain, hoodies at the beach, bags getting wet…" She puts a soggy brown paper bag on the table between Jess and Elizabeth just ahead of the bag ripping from her hands in a soggy mess. "Who's fuckin idea was it to go to the Jersey Shore in March?" She plunges a hand into the bag, pulls out a beer, joins Kev and Matty at the end of the balcony, hooting at a girl walking by. "Hey baby, show us your titties!" She says with a slight buzz in her head. The girl looks up, confused, shakes her head and keeps walking.

"Disgust. Good one babe." Kev says to Janel with a high five.

Act 2 Scene 1.5

Exterior: Beach, sunrise

COURTNEY is sitting in a low
beach chair near the shoreline.

The hot Mexican sun shines warmly on Courtney's content smile. She sits in the sand watching the sun rise, pleased with herself. She'd spent the night partying along the beach with Spring Breakers despite being in Cancun with her parents. She looks over at them, they joined her for the sunrise not long ago. They choose to remain in weary denial that she hadn't come back to the hotel last night. The Guardians, as she's taken to calling them recently, to their dismay.

From the day she came home with them as an infant they had treated her as their own while never hiding from her that she was not. Now they are wondering if it would have been better for her not to know. It had never bothered her as a child, but somewhere in the confusion between girl and woman, as she went from Tomboy to Boy Crazy, it began to eat at her and she acted out in predictable response. With defiant behavior and promiscuity. There is no ancient text, university degree or instruction manual that can prepare someone to raise a girl through her teens. The rapid changes and identity struggles in teens is exacerbated in Courtney, her struggle for identity halted by a taunting hole in the story. By her mid-teens when Courtney's wild behavior became too much for them, The Guardians had put her in a fancy boarding school. It was supposed to be a great school, especially for girls like Courtney. It certainly was expensive enough and they had a sparkling reputation in the behavioral problem area. In the end the school only made things worse. They were later closed down with many staff members going to jail for some of the same horrific accusations Courtney had complained of. At the time they had chalked up the increasingly disturbing stories to her penchant for drama and fantasy. It was easy not to believe her at first. After all, she had landed herself in boarding school partly because of all the lying that problem childs are prone to. As a result of this, The Guardians foster a crushing guilt that only feeds right into her outbursts, then spoil her. They can scarcely bring themselves to say no to her at crucial times when it's the word she truly needs to hear, despite their best intentions. It's a vicious cycle and the sand between Courtney's toes here and now is top dead center. Funny thing is, she hates getting sand between her toes. She sips a mimosa despite the disapproving eye from her Guardian, aka Mother. Wouldn't she be pleasantly mortified to learn of Courtney's performance last night, competing in a wet t-shirt contest. She's slim, if not slight in build, and not especially endowed in the chest department so she's unphased by not winning. She hadn't expected to but it did satiate her desire for attention of the type. Two of her biggest supporters in the contest were eager to show her how much they disagreed with the judges decision. She allowed them to. Under a big Mexican full moon, she can still hear Natalie under her breath, "Tri-dented." The chilled surf had been a refreshing bath in the hot night air. Courtney smirks in recollection, lights a cigarette. The lighter attracts another disapproving glance from Mother.

"You promised you were going to quit that filthy habit."

Courtney pulls down her sunglasses and looks deep into Mother's eyes. "You know I picked up this filthy habit at *boarding school*." Mother winces as if stabbed in the short ribs. The surf laps lazily, inching closer to their feet, the tide coming in with the rising sun. Her retort isn't entirely true. Courtney started smoking *before* boarding school, but it became a full-fledged habit there. It had become a safety net of sorts. An escape. Escape from the abuse of the staff. They would steal off in pairs to console, conspire and smoke.

Dad finally says with a cheery deflection, "Let's get breakfast." The Guardians search their minds and the resort itinerary for ways to entertain and possibly contain their daughter. Perhaps even buy forgiveness on some level.

The Allan Family Academy had been renowned for its work with problem children and behavioral issues. Inside the walls of The Allan Family Academy, discipline was more strict and downright inhuman. When Courtney called home and reported her short stay in ISO they thought she was exaggerating, just being dramatic. But Courtney was *not* exaggerating, and she was not the only student at Allan Family Academy to mention the ISO room - a six-by-six box where the light stays on 24 hours and the AC blasts year round. Kids in ISO are left in their underwear and only given a dirty thin mattress and a small blanket full of holes at bedtime. Lights on. Kids enduring a stay in ISO could count on three meals a day which consisted of dry tuna and a stale piece of bread on the smallest, thinnest paper plate they could find. Bathroom breaks are all but unheard of. The strong piss stink attests to that. Courtney spent one day and one night in ISO. Some Academy students have spent up to a week in there shivering, freezing.

Cancun, on the other hand, smells like Pina Coladas, suntan oil and Courtney wouldn't mind a night alone with the cabana boy, bringing her and The Guardians another round of mimosas.

Later in the afternoon Courtney is sitting on the beach under an umbrella drawing on a sketch pad.

Mom pokes her head under the light blue canopy. "Are you drawing the ocean?"

Courtney holds out the sketch, "Robot." She resumes drawing.

"We're ordering lunch do you want something?" Courtney nods, agrees to the sandwiches they propose. She gives no thought to the Allan Academy, enjoying bar snacks on the Mexican white sand beach. She gives no thought to the other Academy alumni who alleged abuses from mental anguish to sexual assault, from not only other students but faculty as well. Courtney's parents may never forgive themselves for putting her there and Courtney won't soon forget her experience. Nor what it can do for her.

Act 2 Scene 2.0

Interior:Deli, day

ELIZABETH stands at the end of
the deli case staring red hot
lasers into the back of his
head.

He stubbornly refuses to burst into flames. A deep sad pain cowers behind a seething anger, both quenched under the wet blanket of hopeless impatience. It feels as though hours have passed since she walked in, though it's only been minutes. She'd called him earlier stating only that she needed to talk and that she would give him the short ride home. She shows up early hoping to gauge her thoughts on all this, considering the two new developments. For one thing he seems to have chosen Courtney for the part of romantic lead and Elizabeth has no Goddamn intention of playing comedic relief to Courtney. That's not how this is supposed to work. Courtney is the slutty comedienne. She doesn't get the male lead, she gets the jokes and the laughs. Elizabeth gets the love and adoration. *This is not the part I auditioned for!*

Elizabeth waits patiently, boiling, while he zones out on the meat sizzling on the grill. She waits, stares daggers into his back while he chops and turns and seasons the meat, periodically pouring on hot sauces before stirring it up and finally covering the whole thing in a generous layer of thick sliced yellow American cheese. He covers the long shaped meat and cheese with a long sesame seed bread. In New York it's called a wedge. Then he scoops the whole thing up off the grill with his spatula dropping it into a paper lined foil in his other hand. Elizabeth watches him bring his creation to the counter and hand it to the customer. Elizabeth listens as the guy with the sandwich, a black man, tells the deli crew a story about his white girlfriend's white college roommate and how she innocently, thought black people have tails. As angry and upset as Elizabeth is she can't help laugh hysterically with the rest of the deli as the guy waves his sandwich like a scepter punctuating his story with dramatic gesture. He delivers the story with the passion of a reverend; or perhaps a comedian.

When he finally gets off work and in the car with her it doesn't take long for him to realize what the unfortunate news is that's currently and quite literally developing within her. He finally has has the audacity to ask, "Is it...mine?"

She knows that he is insinuating that she's slept with Vincent, which she hasn't, but he doesn't deserve the peace of mind to know that. Though she and Vincent have been spending a lot of time together. Truth be told they may have begun having confusing feelings for each other. It happens, doesn't it? She'd cried on Vincent's shoulder when

Courtney 'got the part' and as it almost always goes, crying on shoulders leads to touching of other parts. Sadness and empathy are strong feelings, not unlike love and affection.

She feels stained, ugly and rejected. *Why don't you want me?* She knows what has to be done but she doesn't want it that way. *Tell me not to go!* She pleads with him to hear her thoughts but he can't. Nor can she hear his and if only they could hear each other's because he is screaming it too, *Don't Go!* But they can't. They can't do this, not now, not like this.

Elizabeth needs a ride. Though what she actually needs is for someone to just love her for her. She thought Deli Guy might have been that one but something went wrong, *Courtney,* she seethes.

"I just need a ride." She gets to saying, and he agrees. They spend the night in tears with all the sadness of breaking up even after all of their best efforts to not define themselves as boyfriend and girlfriend. Here they are in spite of themselves breaking up anyway. When the sun rises on Elizabeth's mostly sleepless night she leaves. And goes straight to Vincent.

Act 2 Scene 2.5

Interior: Vincent's bedroom, day

ELIZABETH:

That motherfucking goddamn sonofabitch bastard and his goddamn whore…! Elizabeth storms into the room. Vincent rises from the bed, standing to accept Elizabeth into a calming embrace.

VINCENT:

What are you talking about?

"He promised!" She sobs now, laying her head in the nape of Vincent's neck. It seems to fit perfectly, he being shorter than her, she just lays her head down. It's warm and safe. "He said he would give me a ride." She backs away to look at Vincent's face, she nods down at her belly, "I told him my appointment was Saturday and..." She imitates boy voice, "he says, 'oh, uh...I have a thing on Saturday...'" Her voice rises sharply to a hysterical shriek, "It's Courtney's fucking birthday!" She composes herself some, "He's throwing her a fucking party. Is there a more perfectly fucking poetic way to reject me so completely?! A goddamn *birthday party!?*"

On Saturday Elizabeth sits on her bed waiting for Vincent to pick her up. She holds her phone in her hand, glancing at it now and then hoping Deli Guy will call. *Call me now*, she thinks, *say you're through with her and don't go!* But he isn't going to call, he isn't going to tell her not to do it or give her a ride or give her the part. He's not going to call and wish her congrats on her abortion, nothing. She looks up at the jar on her desk, seething. *Your fucking seed.*

As Vincent pulls up in front of the clinic she glances at her phone one more time. "Bastard." She whispers lightly under her breath, tucking her phone back in her purse. Vincent is pointing, talking to her,

"I'll be right over there to pick you up when you're ready." Vincent puts a hand on her shoulder which says more than words could have.

Across town, Punk Rock Zombies is taking the stage at the warehouse, home to Courtney's birthday party. That sick twist of irony like a turning blade in her side is not lost on Elizabeth.

"Thanks." She mutters as she slinks from the car. Shyly looking at the floor. Elizabeth walks up the steps into the clinic.

Act 2 Scene 2.6

Interior: Warehouse, day

SERJ:

Hello, my name is Serj.
He puts his hand out to
COURTNEY.

"It is nice to meet you. I think you are very pretty."

"Thanks," Courtney smiles and points across the room, "You know that guy over there throwing me this party is my boyfriend right?"

Serj has been hanging around the Warehouse lately, trying to find a niche in the scene, get in a new band. His big claim to fame is having been the original drummer for a sort of local band from across the river that had struck medium fame with videos on TV and t-shirts at Hot Topics in malls across America. The band has since peaked and is now sinking back into obscurity, but his fifteen minutes being up doesn't stop Serj from telling anyone who will listen how he "pretty much invented their sound" and how quitting before they became sellouts was the "best decision of my life." Anyone who'd ever been into the band knows they kicked him out and could care less what Serj says. Serj is blissfully unaware of the fact that people don't take him half as seriously as he takes himself.

Serj looks over his shoulder toward the stage where her boyfriend is, "I know who he is. Come, let me tell you what my friend Velvet told me…" Serj leads Courtney out into the hall.

She looks around the room on the way out. "Hey, where is Vel? Didn't he just get here…?"

Serj leads Courtney to a dark corner, "He's late, you noticed?

"Yeah, so what?"

Serj looks around like what he has to say is of grave importance and secrecy. "Velvet told me he was driving that girl Elizabeth to…" He pauses and looks around again, "The clinic." He rolls his eyes for emphasis, "You know her, don't you?"

Courtney nods, "Yes, I do. The clinic? And it's…was…?"

"Your boyfriend's." Serj nods his head.

Inside the big room a tardy Vincent gets in his Velvet stage persona and climbs on stage. He and his band violently bash through an angry but abbreviated set of their heavy music and Vincent drops the microphone on the stage when they're done. It lands with a loud amplified thud and echoes the hollow beneath the wooden platform. A squeal of feedback punctuates the finality of the set. Vincent glares across the room, slowly descends the two stairs from the stage.

He accepts the back pats and accolades walking. He politely thanks them, disgusted as he storms out of the room. The rest of his band continues to play with little regard for the small party in their practice space. Courtney and Serj had come back in time to catch Velvet drop the microphone and now she gets on the stage and picks it up, tries out her voice over the music with a poem she'd written and rewritten so many times she recites it like it's second nature. The band humors her despite their continuing to play. When she runs out of ideas she sings a rousing rendition of "Happy Birthday to Me" over music that resembles nothing close to the Birthday song. A few people join her, hopping on stage much to the annoyance of Jon and the rest of the band who are just trying to practice. When the birthday singalong is through Courtney evades her boyfriend, leaving him to clean up the party as per the verbal agreement with Vincent's band for letting him have it. She ducks out into the hall, meets up with Serj and they steal away outside under the shadows of a wrought iron fire escape. Out in the dark parking lot Elizabeth and Vincent are sitting in Vincent's car. They watch Courtney sneak off to hook up with Serj and contemplate ousting them.

"Should we tell him?" They smile at each other in agreement.

"Fuck him."

Girlfriend?
Act 2 Scene 3

Interior: The Eye, evening

ELIZABETH is sitting at the bar.
VINCENT, on the phone, paces
behind her.

Elizabeth sits in her regular spot at the bar. She's annoyed with herself and with Vincent. She rolls her eyes upward toward the apartment. Most of all she's annoyed with...HIM. She'd noticed Courtney's car in the parking lot and she's noticed she isn't down here in the bar. No, Courtney is upstairs, stringing him along. Elizabeth heard it through the grapevine how Courtney had broken up with him a couple of weeks in. Literally two weeks. It's kind of her thing, but she's stringing him along, keeping him on the hook. Away from Elizabeth. That's the game to her. Vincent has been eating it up too. Bad mouthing him and being there for Elizabeth but he's… what's the word? Controlling. And mean. Not all the time, there is plenty of time when he isn't. *Why am I so subservient to the men in my life?* Vincent dictates what they do and when they do it. And he hasn't even tried to ask her to be a girlfriend. Sure he's fine with it when tears and venting leads to his dick getting sucked but he acts like he's doing her a favor, letting her suck it. Is it her or was she raised this way? She sees how her parents are and she thinks she'd been brought up. *Serve.* Serve up the sex on a silver tray, stick it in here then here. Repeat. Leave. Come back and do it again. Her mother's noticed the pattern. "Are they passing you back and forth?"

She hears the door to the upstairs apartment open. She doesn't look. The door to the bar doesn't open but the one to the outside does. From the corner of her eye she sees one person leave, probably Courtney. She can feel it, can smell it, even. Courtney stringing him along. Fuck him. That's what he gets. But she can't stay mad at him. She's not mad. She's hurt. So hurt that he cast her aside for Courtney. As much as she wants to be happy that Courtney is in turn hurting him she just can't. And here she is at the same time letting Vincent do...she stops to think about it. What is Vincent doing? Listening and taking her side? Being a friend with benefits, stringing her along, all the while making it clear how Elizabeth just isn't his type. A small part of her thinks Vincent just wants to hurt him. Vincent knows Deli Guy loves Elizabeth. He's torturing him by torturing me. Then she hears footsteps on the stairs. He seems to take forever to clomp down the flight in his big heavy boots. She viciously thinks how he's a fool in his logging boots, like he's a tough physical guy with an outdoorsy job. He's not. He just likes those boots because he thinks they make him look bigger and more intimidating. That and the the big steel toe is a weapon. "I'll fuckin' shatter a knee cap." she sneers in the dumb boy voice, trying to straighten his posture, getting up to his full height. The door opens, she stares forward, her expression is frozen in hurt anger. She doesn't look at him, she's short with her one word answer to his greeting. "Hi."

He looks miserable. Good. He looks happy to see her. Good. *Jerk.* Elizabeth considers playing cards, looks away toward the back room where a game is going on. Away from him. Vincent is behind her yammering away on his new cell phone, thinking he's important. Business. He's in a band and lives with his mother. Elizabeth looks back at him, Vincent's conversation with who cares about who cares is white noise behind her. She wants to laugh at Deli Guy for what Courtney is doing to him. She wants him to hurt like she does. She wants him to apologize. Seconds click by like hours. The tension in the air is thick and uncomfortable. Vincent's conversation becomes the only sound. Life stands still, it's as though for dramatic effect he pauses. It's dead silent for a beat.

"...no I'm at the bar with my girlfriend." The word punches time back into step. A train horn sounds.

"Girlfriend?" Elizabeth is as surprised as he looks.

"It's the first I'm hearing it too actually." She shrugs and looks away, *girlfriend?* she thinks. Just like that? I'm a girlfriend? Because he says so? Am I going to stand for this? Of course I'm going to, that's my role: Subservient.

Drama Camp 1993

The English Teacher Patient

Elizabeth twirls, turns, looks over her shoulder in the mirror. She's trying on dresses at the mall for Courtney's Confirmation party. She's wearing a straight-cut long blue dress with a floral print and a sheer layer cover. It's pretty, though shapeless, but very much in style. Elizabeth hasn't quite finished growing into her This and That yet -- her hips are downright dangerous, she has no control over her curves and her breasts practically have a mind of their own. This dress happens to hide all those curves and it's just as well, as Elizabeth is too young to fully understand how to wield such assets, besides the fact that they embarrass her.

"Why would you pick that dress, your ass looks huge." Her mother comments crudely. "Here, try this one." She adds pushing a red jersey dress into the small changing room. It's more of a classic style as opposed to the blue dress which is very modern. The blue dress looks much like the dresses the other girls will likely be wearing. Elizabeth just wants to look like the other girls, which she doesn't anymore. She looks more like a woman, while they still look like girls. Elizabeth shimmies the red dress over her shoulders, smoothes down the skirt over her legs. It's clingy and short, not too short, just above the knee. It has an Empire waist and actually is much more flattering for Elizabeth's figure than the blue dress. She turns around and looks over her shoulder in the mirror at her butt.

"It's not huge," She pouts.

It's a Friday night. The mall is crowded with teenagers. Allison and Natalie are sitting in the food court. Allison stubs out a cigarette in the ashtray and lights another one.

"I think Tommy is cheating on me." She says with a waver to her voice and chuckles inappropriately. Natalie acknowledges Allison's poorly hidden black eye and looks away.

"Is that all you want to tell me? Your makeup needs touching up." Allison's nervous laugh is a dead giveaway and Natalie recognizes it.

She laughs that way herself sometimes. "Why are you smoking so much?" She adds.

Allison takes a hard drag. "It's not like…" She sighs, exhales, "I should have headed for the hills after our first date. He's only gotten worse since then. Louis says he's just young but…"

"Louis? That creepy guy across the street?"

"Yeah I hang out with him at night sometimes. He's a good listener. He kind of set me up with Tommy in a way actually."

"And that's a good thing?" Natalie rolls her eyes. She doesn't care much for Tommy, seeing the way he treats Allison. "Yeah I can't believe you even went on a second date with him after what he said." Allison stubs out her cigarette and smiles. Both girls blurt it out together.

"Put it in your mouth or go home!" They both howl with laughter.

"Boy I know how to pick the hopeless romantics don't I?"

Down the mall corridor Elizabeth is leaving the store with the red dress. Natalie spots her, waves. Elizabeth waves back. "There's Elizabeth, probably got a dress for Sunday. Are you going?"

"I'm going to stop by. My mother insisted I go and bring her this cross pendant. Like she isn't going to get a million crosses. Are you going?"

"No I can't." Natalie smiles her face lights up, "I'm taking the train to see my dad for the weekend."

At the party on Sunday Courtney stomps around, placing demands on The Guardians and acts like a total diva. No one is surprised by her behavior. Courtney has been making out in the shadows of the theater with a different boy from the cast one at a time for a couple of weeks now. After sending out the invitations to the party she dated the boy playing her love interest in the play, Mr. Albert Peterson, for about two weeks. She then moved on to the boy playing Conrad Birdie. Another two weeks. All the while she was sneaking around with one of the Shriners from school, as well as a fourth boy from around town. He didn't come to the party but the other three boys did. Albert Peterson and Conrad Birdie are both still trying to win back Courtney's affection and fighting with each other over it. It hasn't gotten physical yet but it did come to push and shove at camp once last week. Elizabeth has been keeping to herself at the party. Besides Allison,

Courtney is her only friend there and they aren't very close. In fact Courtney has been keeping Elizabeth at an arm's length this whole camp session. They were closer last year. Today however, Courtney is too busy with aunts and grandmas and boy drama. Elizabeth, bored and lonely, thinks about calling her mother to come pick her up but then she notices Allison break away from a pack of aunts and neighbors with the same bored look.

"Hey, Allison are you leaving?"

Allison sighs, rolls her eyes. "I was thinking about sneaking out of here yeah."

"Will you give me a ride home, please?"

"Sure," Allison glances around, looking for an out, "come on."

The following week Courtney is singing "English Teacher" on stage at rehearsal. "You said a year, it's been eight long years, Albert..." She sings. Rosie has allowed Albert to string her along on a promise for seven years.

Allison leans over to Natalie. "Didn't Marilyn Monroe do a movie about how a gal gets itchy after seven years?" Natalie smiles. Camp Director is sitting in the fourth row just in front of Allison and Natalie. Each is watching the stage for their respective parts -- Natalie watches her choreography, wringing her hands, dancing with her head. Allison is critiquing the acting, Camp Director, production value. Allison whispers to Natalie, "Would you be waiting around for eight years?"

"I wait for no man." Natalie giggles. Camp Director glares over her shoulder and shushes at them.

Courtney swoons onstage as Rosie reminisces about Albert's old dreams of going to college and how he wrote poetry. "And in the 1953 yearbook under Albert Peterson's photo for favorite literature what did it say? Little Women." She gushes with a cutesey smile.

"I'm ruined in the music business," The boy playing Albert Peterson delivers at the potential release of such unflatteringly unmasculine information.

Courtney resumes singing, "...and become an English Teacher..." How happy Rosie could be if only she can be the property of a Pi Beta Kappa English Teacher. They could live in a nice little house in Queens that she would keep well. He would get that teacher's summer vacation, naturally. How proud she would be to have that life. That of Mrs. Peterson, the English Teacher's wife. Courtney beams. She swoons for that ambitiousness of a man, what she could make of him if only he'd apply himself. What he could be worth, what she could be worth by proximity. If only he had a Master's degree. Then she could be proud of her job well done.

Allison leans into Natalie's ear again, "Sure every girl dreams of getting a man OUT of the music business and into school. Those tweed jackets with the leather elbow patches. Hot."

Louis

Act 2 Scene 4

LOUIS drives. His young wife, HEATHER his passenger, their young son, BRANDON, strapped into a carseat, wide-eyed and curious in the back seat.

Heather had dropped out of school, but the damage had already been done. The grapevine whispers were months ahead of Allison leaving or Heather moving in. Louis had no choice, he had to resign as professor at the University. Heather was able to find a job near her parents down in Westchester. Louis agreed to buy a house in the neighborhood and promised to look for a job in the area also, though he is decidedly not in any hurry to do so. His hair is longer and far more shaggy than he ever would have put up with when he was younger. The campus gossip mill had already had its suspicions but when the town police pulled Louis over, dropping Heather off at her dorm a little too late one night, suspicions turned to speculations and outright accusations. People were saying he had gotten her drunk, which wasn't true. It's not entirely fabricated, she did have wine on her breath but they only let her have one glass, *we only let her...* Louis reflects on it, glancing at his current wife, thinking of the night he and Allison had Heather over for dinner. When you cook a prime rib to a tender pink, such as Allison had that night, you very well must have an accompanying red wine. *We aren't barbarians.* Allison had been wary when he suggested he was planning to invite a student for diner. *I think you'd like her.* She didn't exactly -- though she'd been civil -- and privately Allison had suggested that Louis was angling for a threesome. Imagine that...Louis and a threesome. There was a time when he'd thought Carol's sister should have been dragged off and tossed in a nunnery for cavorting the way she did. After seeing two guys sneaking out the back door of her house, surely they had been cavorting with Crissy, the slutty Adrian sister. And though he'd denied it in his suave, romantic way, he said it with *unless you're into it* in his eyes. The wine on Heather's breath was a careless misstep, spreading around campus pretty quickly and prompting the end of Louis's tenure at the university. He'd had that feeling in his gut as soon as the red and blue lights went on, filling his car with trouble. Louis knew when the cop said his taillight looked like it was out that the rumor mill had caught up with him. He knew damn well that taillight was lit. They pulled him over because he had Heather in the car. She had been saying they kept pulling her over in her own car too. She said she thought it was her Voodoo bumper sticker or because she was Wiccan. So cute. Like most girls in the 90's who read Moon Goddess and Faery Wicca, Heather claimed to be a witch, which Heather believed offended the town of Gore. She reasoned that the town doesn't choose to glorify their short hysteria in the manner that Salem, Massachusetts does. The town finds it collectively undignified, this is true but the town police of Gore likely couldn't give a flying squat what deity Heather identifies with. No, Gore's finest had been giving Heather and Louis a hard time because much of the town and campus already believed that the forty year-old professor was cavorting with a nineteen year-old student. Allison had already been a little young for Louis, much of the town is comprised of old family names, old family money and old family values. If you are going to be an adulterer you best have the decency to use the utmost discretion. A professor carrying on with a student is simply undignified. Discretion was gone, for Heaven's sake. Bathed in red and blue lights when the police told Heather to "go get some sleep" and for Louis to "go home to your wife," they had not even begun fooling around. Not yet. Thus far it had been platonic. Louis needed Heather to take the initiative so he could lay the psychological groundwork. Manipulating a nineteen year-old girl is as easy as you might think it would be. The proper balance of attention, affection, flirting. Small acknowledgments. Well-placed platonic innuendo compliments. Before you know it she's enamored and making the first move, or so she thinks. When Heather had leaned in to kiss Louis for the first time he had already been making the first move for months, luring her in, showing her the prize. Convincing her it was what she wanted. Now none the wiser for it he let her think she convinced him to sell the house in Gore. He sold it for a pretty penny in fact. She could find a job and be close to her parents and a school in Westchester would pay very well and maybe not have heard of Louis's indiscretion upstate.

Heather looks to her left at her husband, driving. He appears deep in thought and he is, thinking as he is now how all this played out since that night they were pulled over. A couple of short years ago his hair was a little shaggy. It was hip. Non-conformist. He was that cool professor on campus. Now he looks more unkempt. Less cool and more like he just badly needs a haircut. And now that she's really looking, he'd put on some weight. He has a gut and a chubby face that she hadn't noticed until now. Louis had always been lean and slender with proper posture. Even when he started to adopt the coolest professor on campus persona he still carried himself with a fit and kempt dignity. Now he just looks like an old slob. Louis and Heather had both been in a sort of denial about it, Louis sinking into the couch potato rut. The brilliant and ambitious mind Heather had fallen for was gone or at least well hidden. Definitely 'NOT IN' the sign would read, crooked of course if Louis worked at a Peanuts' walk-up Profesor stand. LECTURES 5 CENTS. THE PROFESSOR IS NOT IN.

Louis doesn't feel like a bum nor does he know that by the time he pulls in the driveway to his new home in Westchester that his wife is just realizing that she does.. Louis thinks he's in control, that this was the plan all along -- *my plans always work* -- but it wasn't. He's lying to himself now. He probably couldn't pinpoint where he'd lost his focus but he has. And to think he'd spent so long punishing Allison for stealing a fraction of his focus so long ago. Maybe he shouldn't have become a big pothead, sure it fit the image but it also probably dulled his mind, having been so straight-laced his whole life, burning out isn't sitting well with him. He doesn't see it of course, like Heather until recently, he's too close to it. As far as he is concerned he avenged himself with Allison. He tortured her for years and now Louis hears through the grapevine that she's fallen further into the sex trades industry. She must be in utter misery, completely disgraced. Louis pulls into the driveway of his new house with his wife and infant son. He looks to his right and smiles at Heather, "The professor is in."

Act 2 Scene 5

Exterior: deli, day

HEATHER gets out of her car.

They'd been in the new house a few weeks now. Maybe it's her growing disillusionment with Louis and his slow decline. Maybe it's the nostalgia factor, being back in town, she can't really put a finger on it. Something is nagging at Heather and she has to scratch that itch. She will have to go behind Louis's back, as he'd specifically forbade her to be in contact with her ex-boyfriend. Maybe in fact that was it. The fact that he forbid her that drove her to it. She'll drive up to that deli where he works, Roze brought it up in conversation, he's there a lot and they usually know where he is if he isn't. Heather packs up Brandon and heads to the car hoping to not even have to lie on the way out and she doesn't have to as Louis doesn't ask.

Heather parks in front of the deli and looks up at the sign and in the door, over her shoulder at Brandon. She gets the kid out and goes inside. The Deli Guy is behind the counter in a crisp white collared deli shirt over a black band t-shirt. His long hair is tied up in a bandana. He's smiling and his smile doesn't fade when he looks at her. She hadn't been sure how he might react to seeing her and now that he's OK with it she sort of wishes he wasn't. Not that she'd want anything bad to happen to him but that he'd still pine for her. It's silly. Silly and selfish but she has to admit when he wasn't over it, well, she liked that better than this. Nobody has to know.

She holds the baby up to him, "This is my son." Smart move holding up the kid, no do-we-or-don't-we? dance, no awkward hugs or kisses, not with the baby in the way, maybe some other time, Tiger. *Damn it Heather* -- she can't call him that. That would be too nostalgic. *Damn it Louis why am I even here, having these feelings now? Is this regret? I fell for the older professor and he turned into a crusty old bum after a few years and here's this...OK, ex-boyfriend who's also kind of a scruffy bum but at least he's in my generation for fuck's sake and my father used to say he was too old for me. So what do I do? Go for one fifteen years older?* "Do you want to hold him?"

He walks from around the counter, "Sure." He takes the baby, holds him on his side, looks the little boy in the face, "Hey there little guy." She wonders if he wonders the same thing she does. She knows this isn't exactly foolproof but it's pretty much all she's got and it's at least a decent hint.

"Well, I guess we better get going, Bran," She says, taking back the baby, "Louis doesn't really want me..." she regrets saying that much, "...talking to you."

His smug grin tells her he's pleased with that,"I bet." He chuckles slightly, "It was nice to see you." He pats the baby gently on the head, "Nice to meet you, little guy." Then back to Heather, "Hey do you remember when we parked out at Glenn's Cove and broke up and I said I'd give you five years to think about it...?" She didn't but she nods yes. He pulls a plastic toy ring from his pocket and says jokingly, "So you want to get married?"

"Kinda already married..." She holds up the hand with the ring. He laughs it off and tosses the toy on the shelf next to her, into a box off them. She didn't see him grab it though, how could he have known she'd be here? He can't possibly carry that around waiting for her to walk back in his life. It did sound like he was joking but now that she thinks about it he did say something to that effect when she broke up with him. Is he making a joke, keeping a promise? Boilerplating it? *Is that a glimmer in his eye? Is it hope? Is he still pining for her or is he just being charming? Damn his charm. Damn it Heather.* She says goodbye and hurries out the door. She thought she needed to know. Now she's less sure than she was before. Of what it is she wants or what the truth is. She spends the whole car ride deciding she's more confused about the whole ordeal than she was before. Louis will just have to not know she went up there.

"Where were you?" He asks, more matter of factly than accusatory.

She answers curt and annoyed, "Out!" She pushes past him, puts the kid down in a bouncer on the living room floor.

"OK." Louis is unphased, "I'm headed out for a little bit myself." Louis calls on his way out the door. He had forbid her to see her ex but it hadn't even occurred to Heather to forbid him to see Allison. Not that she'd obeyed nor did she think he would.

He'd had no intention upon leaving the house just now in running into Allison. It just happens. Louis had tired of asking suspiciously where Heather had been. Had he pressed it this particular evening it would have for once actually been true. He finds himself increasingly suspicious that she's sneaking off to see her ex, a prospect that shocks Louis. He never found the hapless ex a threat in the beginning when it was Louis who was the cunning predator, making a game of seducing a girl, simultaneously leading her to her own conclusions and turning her against him with a delicate practiced ease. Heather had been blind to the origins of the growing animosity she'd been developing toward her ex back home. A few well placed words of encouragement, backhand slaps at his expense, "you deserve better than that..." with a sympathetic shoulder at his callous behavior, "clearly he's not taking you and your feelings into consideration…" Surely the ex would cherish some revenge, some restitution of some kind. Surely he's figured out something by now. Louis can't have that. Perhaps a strict forbidding will drive her straight to him. He knew it would be risky but he also knows it has to happen. With any luck it will fuck with her head. If only he pressed today he might be pleased. Nobody had even considered Louis could run into Allison and Heather had no reason to think she had to worry if he did, Heather has no fear of Allison. If Louis could cast an omniscient eye he might be displeased to realize that as time has rolled away like concentric circles like ripples on a pond, from the time she left the farmhouse in Gore until now, Allison has risen from the ash puddle into a place of peace that she'd never reached before. In many ways she has Louis to thank for it. He drove her to the depths of the deepest darkest forest of despair where she found her inner strength. Or maybe she figured out sex sells and chicken grease slicks the wheels of marketing ad campaigns. On the other hand Louis has grown soft and slow in mind and body. And he doesn't see this in himself yet. Allison is going to see it right away though. When Louis leaves the house it was timed so that he was leaving when Heather was returning. It's part of a longer scheme to fuck with her head. Louis is not clear on yet on exactly how or why, as mentioned he's lost a step but doesn't see that yet. It's a plan in progress. He had not actually thought of anywhere to go, just to be sure to be leaving as she's arriving. So he simply drives over to the little shopping center at the edge of Peekskill, housing a supermarket and other typical strip mall spots -- Bank, chicken joint, laundromat, liquor store, retail chum, all the same stores as anywhere else. Louis parks in front of the chicken joint and walks the sidewalk, aimlessly thinking about maybe going into the supermarket. They might need milk, eggs and butter now that he thinks about it. He walks past the video rental place and a bar and turns up the ramp to go into the supermarket just as

Allison is walking out. They find themselves standing face to face for the first time in three years. Both are taken by surprise…

"Louis? Wow…I almost didn't recognize you." Allison, taken aback and mildly amused adds lightheartedly, "You look like shit." In saying so she realizes she hasn't given much thought to Louis at all lately, even less to how she might react to seeing him. She feels herself stand a little taller and straighter when she notices his grip on her has been gone. She finds it difficult to believe he's the same person or that he could ever have held any power over her.

"I hear you're in adult films now." Louis says, clearly trying to sound superior. Allison sees right through it with newfound vision. He thinks he's looking down on her, but he's not.

She smiles, "Technically only the one." She adds, "So far." with a wink. April has offered her more work, as she fully intends to continue to run her website and legacy from behind the camera from now on. Allison doesn't feel Louis is owed any of this knowledge. He can find out for himself. "Do you know the name April Lynn? She's a legend in her field."

"Yes of course…I'm conservative, not deaf dumb and blind." Of course by conservative he doesn't mean like those fellas down in DC. Louis finds them ridiculous, he's always voted some unknown party of "purple" as he would call them. No, by conservative Allison knows he means suburban sophisticated snobbery which is hilarious to her as he'd always held himself above all that. His parents, Allison's, Carol's, the whole town he felt were pretentious snobs and now he's one of them.

Allison laughs. "So what are you doing over here? Where's your student? Did she have homework to do?" Allison bites her lip, trying to keep the laughter to a minimum. This newfound boldness and upperhanded feeling with Louis is giving her a rush. She's almost drunk with giddy amusement. He's trying not to let her crack his stiff posture.

"She's home with the baby. We bought a house in Buchanan so Heather could be close to her parents."

"You sold the house in Gore?"

"We did."

"What about the university? Aren't you teaching…?" The apocalypse washes over her with the look in his eye.

"I, uh...left the university. I haven't taken a new position yet." A smile grows on Allison's face.

"You got fired for carrying on with a student didn't you?" Louis's stone face says "yes" though he says nothing.

Then he tries to claw his way back up to an upperhanded position. "Maybe I can direct a film with you and Heath…"

Allison puts a hand in his face to cut him off, "You might have had a chance at an awkward threesome the night you brought a vulnerable teenager into my house and fed her wine, but that's gone, pal, and you want to direct?!" She laughs loud and condescendingly, "How far the mighty have fallen, Louis. It's over, you have no power over me and I hope that poor little girl sees what a pathetic fucking weasel you are. Look at you, you're scruffy, fat and old. Your wife is twenty one, half your age. She's going to be running around on you like you're her babysitter in no time, pal. You have turned into the same delusional pretentious jerks like that whole town of Gore is, you said they were all so fake and now look at you." She can see she is hitting Louis hard and though he never shows any actual emotions on his face she can see the pain in his eyes. A tiny hint of guilt nudges at her and she begrudgingly lets up on him, softening her tone slightly. "I can almost say it was nice to see you Louis." She saunters into the parking lot toward her car, turning back to wave, "Don't keep in touch." She says with a jovial smile. Louis stands stunned for a moment, shakes his head, goes into the grocery store.

Allison sits in her car and pulls out her pack of cigarettes. She pulls out the last one and tosses the half heartedly crumbled box on the passenger side floor. She lights the cigarette and takes a few drags, looking at the box. She looks back where she just confronted Louis, back at the box, another drag and then looks at the cigarette. She remembers Carol giving her that first cigarette at the bus stop and how Louis used to give her cigarettes at night on the porch when she was upset. She looks at the cigarette in her hand and sees every single one she's smoked since that bus stop, all the same brand. Since the career change and the gym every day she's down to under a pack a day but for a while there after she left Gore, she was up to two packs a day. Same brand. Louis gave Carol that cigarette to give to her at the bus stop, she's sure of it now, with no proof at all. She takes another long drag, looks at it again and tosses it with a flick of her finger into the parking lot.

"No more. " She quits smoking cold turkey and shatters Louis's illusions. She drives home with the weight lifted from her that she didn't realize she was still dragging around.

Act 2 Scene 5.2

Interior: April's Office, day

APRIL has big plans for ALLISON and NATALIE.

Allison has big plans of her own. Allison sits in April's new office, not far from Eastland in a growing new industrial park area with a great view of the river. Behind the garbage incinerator plant. If you crane your neck to look downriver and across Glenn's Cove there's the nuclear power plant. April has a corner loft above a telemarketing startup on the second floor and a deli on the first. Elsewhere in the park is a gym, an electrical supply warehouse and showroom, a few business and law offices, accountants and a medical supply distributor. April's frosted business door reads an ambiguous ALB LLC and the door opens to a small nondescript waiting room. The office and studios are discreetly hidden from sight.

April thinks it's funny, "There's people right below us talking seriously on the phones about the cost of postage and no idea about the fucking going on right over their heads." She laughs.

"April, picture it...Nat and I play eighteen year old high school seniors, we're experimenting in the basement rumpus room, you can make a cameo, yelling down from the top of the stairs see if we want pizza bagels or something..."

"Al, you guys don't exactly look like teenagers."

"So what? I mean that's kind of my point, it's a statement about marketing sexuality and mixed messages about underage girls--"

"You want to make a feminist statement with porn?"

Allison has to concede some when she puts it like that, looking down, "I guess, I see..."

"You can still change the world, Al, you can. It can be done, you can make that statement, look, I've worked with the Randalls in Cali, I went to Europe to work with Erika Lust a few years ago, it's being done, Al and you can do it too, maybe do a second or third movie first, OK?" April pats the desk in front of Allison. "Don't get too ahead of yourself." April goes on gushing for a few minutes about the time she shot with Suze Randall in the eighties until Allison politely interrupts to steer them back to work.

"What about my Inka character?"

"That Russian spy whore thing? OK let's do a spy movie. Spy Humper?"

"That's funny, like the video game? What about maybe a comedy? *Spies like Us?* But you know instead of 'Like' as in similar it's Like as in like, you know what I mean? Like as in luuuuv…"

"I get it, stop!" April laughs. "Spies Hump Us?" She smiles, nods enthusiastically, "Yes I get it, that's great, you know when I started we used scripts and directors with vision…"

Allison recognizes April's speech. Sometimes it's hard for public people to turn off interview mode. *Marilyn Tragedy.* April insists they do movies even if they are short and mostly fucking. That's how the industry was when she started, she says it over and over, often. April often sounds like she's being interviewed, even in normal conversation. Allison also understands that *April's Full* will likely be the biggest splash in the last splashes of the old ways and the old world. She is going to need to be prepared for the next wave. For now she can ride out the wake of *April's Full* but for how long…?

Natalie continues to get work from her old agent but less now that they have been working with April.

"Where is Nat?" April asks as Allison flips through photos of potential guys to star opposite Inka.

"She has a shoot down in Long Island."

"For that guy? I don't know why she still works for him, he's so shady. I wish I didn't have to talk to him to get her in the first place, I almost passed over her because of him. Never liked that guy."

"She says she has to do a few more films with him, some agreement they had, he was a big help to her starting out, loyalty, yada yada." Allison points to a model. "He's cute, I could fuck him. Do you know him? Is he nice?"

April looks at the photo and chuckles, "Yeah he's a nice kid, you like 'em a little young there? Maybe we'll do a MILF stepson thing with him?" Allison nods, April makes arrangements.

Later that day Allison stalks into a living room set in a housewife apron and seduces a twenty two year old high school senior football jock. She helps him with some homework then she helps him with his boner, assuring him that his dad wouldn't find out only to have dear old dad walk in on them and join his son, *tridented.* Both men are comically the same age, Allison's junior. Allison finds she is quite alright with it and takes her co-stars out for drinks after the shoot up at that dive bar, The Eye.

"I always trust my gut, Al." April tells Allison over coffee this morning. After coffee, Allison does a girl-on-girl scene with a girl of a Gothic Genre. They model a short script and set after a book popular with girls in the 90s about the Faery Wicca faith. Allison still has her copy. Several activist groups find the video "problematic" online. The ensuing viral battle over those problems on social media in the future will eventually boil to the surface for a brief moment before a coffee chain steals the spotlight for a Christmas cup that isn't Jesus enough for social media.

After the goth shoot April is still talking about the old days and touring, "...in those days a girl needed content for her videos. A face on a VHS box was great. A lot of girls actually used the content to promote exotic dance tours and vice versa, it worked great…" April was among the first to see the potential. Content went from VHS to dot com and that's what they produce: Content. At a Dot Com. April still does publicity tours but she hasn't danced since the late eighties.

After lunch April takes a call while Allison looks through more photos of potential partners waiting out in the hallway.

April yells into the phone, No Shit! That's friggin awesome! thank you…! OK!...OK!" She hangs up the phone and slaps her hand down hard on the desk startling Allison, "I got the fuckin part!" April yells at Allison happily. It will be her first role in a movie that wouldn't be rated X. A minor role in a big horror movie by a rock star of a director which is a big deal to April. "Say, did you pick one yet? These guys are getting cold out there." She smirks. "It's so funny to me, there's no harm, I mean if they can't handle a half hour in a cold hallway next to two other naked men…" April laughs. She calls in three guys at a time, amateurs. It's cheaper than a casting call. Hot Guys Wanted. Guys always think they want to be in porn, it sounds great, fuck all these hot bitches. But most guys find out that it's not for them, they get embarrassed or can't perform. They catch feelings. That's the worst. When an amateur shoots a scene and thinks he's fallen in love is sad to watch happen. Some girls feel bad about it. Some of the toughest talking ones are the most likely to fall in love. "So I let them chill out there for a bit…" April jokes as to her method of weeding out the boys from the men, making them wait three at a time in a small cold hallway, naked. There is an endless stream of horny guys who think they can do porn. April sees this as a victimless and hilariously ironic crime to profit from.

Allison picks one but needs clarification on the scene April wants to shoot. "This one, but explain this to me again about the edge."

"No, it's called Edging. You jack him off till he's about to cum then you back him off a little, then you rev him back up to blast point and back off again. You do this a few times, really torture him then when you let him go he blasts a huge fuckin wad a mile high. People love high volume, buckets of cum, they love it. And it's all filmed from his perspective. They call it POV, point of view. That's what they want right? To see a hot chick jacking off their dick, I figure it's because that's how they picture it when they jack off anyway."

"You're a genius April."

"I wish I could take credit, not even my idea." April bows her head and surrenders.

Allison puts the guy's head shot she chooses on top of the pile, gives it a smack. "OK I'll jerk him off the edge."

"No, it's...whatever."

Lucky number whatever is led naked out of the hallway chilling area into the studio. Allison sits him on the couch and kneels in front of him. A camera over his shoulder focuses on her face and hands and his dick. She never even takes off her clothes. She brings him to the edge a few times and when she finally lets him release she aims him right at the camera. The young buck splashes the camera lens and douses his chest and belly in the most cum Allison has ever seen. Ever. Everyone's reaction to the final scene - Allison and April's amusement and the cameraman's horror - remain in the final cut. To date it's still Allison's most watched video.

Allison arrives for work bright and early one late spring day. She takes pause to look up at the old brick building on the way in today. Now it hosts April's office and the other offices but Allison doesn't know what the building was before. She does know that a vodka factory once occupied much of this bank of the river but she doesn't know if this building was part of the vodka complex. *Mmmm vodka,* Inka purrs. Allison pauses and reflects on her drinking.

On the first floor of the building there is a deli right inside the front door. The coffee isn't the best she's ever had but it's convenient. She's spoiled from the coffee made in fancy Italian copper urns. Allison walks into the deli this morning, there is one lady standing at the counter. Allison can see the young man behind the counter is having some difficulty. She recognizes him as fairly new though he doesn't appear rattled. He smiles calmly and shrugs at the woman who is quite agitated at this point.

Finally she blurts out, "Do you know how much longer this is going to take?!" She is practically shrieking and punctuates her frantic query with a nervous and quivering, maniacal laugh. Allison can't help think her question is strange, as he clearly has no idea what the problem is, how could he know how long it's going to take? These new card readers have everyone confused. Whatever the problem is, it seems to fix itself and he reaches for her card. The woman shoves her card forward with impatience, shifting from foot to foot.

The boy swipes her card and waits, "It's not working," he tells her, handing the card back. The young man has some type of middle eastern accent which is thick but not unintelligible. "It's OK." He waves her away.

The woman, looks at Allison in a panic. "What does he mean? I don't understand him…?!"

Allison is confused as she is having no problem understanding him, "He's saying it's OK, just go, come back later, give him the dollar."

The woman picks up the coffee looks frantically around at Allison and the counter guy, puts the cup back down, "I can just take it?!" She is still shrieking, "I don't get it, what is he…?" She picks the cup up again looking around like she's getting caught stealing, "I have to go! Should I take the coffee?"

Allison furrows her brow, a smile curls up on one side. "Yes. Take the coffee. He said it's OK, comeback later, it's only a dollar. Take the coffee." The woman is still tentative about picking up the coffee, looking around as though she still expects to be nabbed by police for shoplifting. Finally she turns and hurries for the door, looking back once more before disappearing out into the building lobby.

Allison shakes her head with the amused clerk. He pushes forward the two coffees Allison usually gets and she hands him exact change. "Take care." She tells him and takes her tray of coffees. The young man smiles and nods.

As Allison is waiting for the elevator her reflection waiting with her catches her eye like it's someone else. In many ways it is. She hasn't had the time lately to stop and think about that. The elevator door opens and she glides into the car, mesmerized. The doors shut and her reflection reappears. She continues to ponder the strange image before her as the elevator slowly rises to her floor. The girl in the reflection is standing tall. Allison always slouched as she was self conscious of her height. She isn't slouching at all anymore. The eyes looking back are decisive and authoritative. *Wvell, wvell, she certainly is authoritative,* Inka encourages. Five years ago the very idea that Allison could be in porn would have been mortifying. She imagines her mother WILL be mortified. Sex had always just been something that was done to Allison. In fact until recently, it was something that had only been done to her by three men, two of whom were boys and one a girl. And Louis was...not conventional. At first he had been rather robotic and dry, just like he is out of the bedroom. Of course without much to compare it to, she assumed that it was sort of dull, and Louis being Louis needed to seem like some kind of God. Now with more experience Allison realizes that Louis was adequate in bed, which is only slightly better than bad sex and honestly not even as good as masturbating. But after being on that college campus a few years, coupled with smoking pot, he did get a little better. But not much. Allison realizes she doesn't need affection from a man just a little deep dicking now and then. And Porn is a lot of fun. Sex is fun now for Allison, and that can really put a skip in your step. Allison is sure now that she is at least on some level bi-sexual. She does like men, but just sharing living space and affection with Natalie is more than satisfying on that side. It's not a sexual or even romantic relationship but far more than her marriage had been -- it is love.

Act 2 Scene 5.3

Interior: Eastland Apartment

NATALIE stands before the stove.
She pours a pancake into the pan
shaking her hips to the radio,
she watches the batter bubble.

NATALIE:

I don't know Al, you don't think
it could get weird between us?

Allison is still pitching the two of them reenacting their preteen makeout practice sessions. She is sitting at the island pouring syrup on her pancakes.

"You're a professional. I'm supposed to be one too now. It's not like...I mean, we've both done girl-on-girl scenes before..."

"But not with each other." Natalie chuckles, "Listen to me -- I sound like I'm trying to keep you on the hook in the friend zone." They have a laugh about it.

Every girl is familiar with the idea of having a...toy, for lack of a better word. Most girls have had one, one way or another at one time in their lives. The right boy comes along, he's romantically interested, she's not but he's nice and showers her with affection, so she corrals him in the friend zone. Friendly flirting combined with friendly reminders in the form of compliments. *You're such a good friend to me.* Like anything, it requires balance and, so the saying goes, when you play with fire you can get burned. It can become quite the complicated mess of emotions, promises, bold declarations. Many a crime of passion may have a ground zero in the friend zone. A girl is always in danger herself in getting attached and having feelings. Then things can get really cloudy. It's not usually a devious plan either, or even a plan at all. Sure there are some girls out there who do it on purpose, hold stables full of friend-zoned ponies at their call. Of course that often requires they occasionally go a little further than flirting. It takes more than cuddles and compliments at that level, but what's a little handy between friends? Keep'em interested, hopeful.

"This is completely different though Nat..." Allison wants to make a big deal out of how they look too old to be teenagers and at the same time make a point about how old men prey on young girls.

April thinks it's too political. "People want to have fun when they jack off Al," she'd said, "they don't need a lecture on being creepy they want to shoot a load in a dirty sock and go to bed." But Allison is persistent and her videos are doing well so April says "whatever."

Natalie has reservations. Allison thinks it odd, "What a change, I would have thought it would be me saying that, not you." Allison is surprised to even hear herself say this. "Especially you." She adds.

Natalie swings around quickly, "Why?! Because I'm a slut?!" She flips the last pancake out of the pan onto the stack, snaps off the burner and stomps out of the kitchen.

Allison slides off her stool in shame to go after Natalie, "Nat, no, come on, that's not what I meant at all..." She realizes as she says, that is exactly what she meant., "Come on Nat, I'm sorry, I didn't mean anything by it, you've just never been shy about it..."

Natalie opens her bedroom door before Allison can knock. "I'm sorry too." Natalie says softly wiping a tear from her eye, "You're right and you weren't being mean about it..." She looks as if there is more. Allison takes Natalie by the hand, leads her back to the kitchen, sits her on a stool, serves her a couple of the fresh hot pancakes Natalie just finished cooking.

"Is there something else? Nat, that was kind of, I didn't...Do you want to talk?" Natalie slices off a small pie wedge of pancake, dips it in a puddle of syrup, rolls it on the pat of butter melting on top of her stack. She puts the bite in her mouth and plucks an envelope from the basket. She hands the envelope to Allison. It's addressed to Natalie. Allison slides out a card. "Oh shit, Nat! I missed your birthday! I'm so sorry..."

Natalie holds up her hand, waves, shakes her head, cheeks full of pancake, "Mmmmph, mmph, mmmph..." She swallows, "It's not that," She says with a smile, "It was two weeks ago, we didn't see each other much that week. I had those shoots, you and April were busy, It's cool, I'm not that happy about getting older as it is." She adds with a grin, "I don't need you to remind me." She points to the card in Allison's hand, "It's from my mother. He signed his own name. It creeped me out. I've been a little down about it..."

"Why didn't you say something?" Allison puts her arms around Natalie, hugs her standing next to her stool.

"You weren't around." She starts to cry again, sobbing into Allison's bosom, "I don't mean to sound like I'm blaming you, of course you would have been there, you were busy, I was busy it was just..."

Allison rubs Natalie's hair gently, "It's OK I know what you mean, of course I was here the whole time, you just needed...I'm here now." They sit still in embrace, Allison standing for a long time.

Natalie pulls back slowly, turns in the stool to face Allison, takes both her hands in hers and smiles. "Thank you." She says softly. Then

Natalie's mischievous grin starts to come out like the sun from behind rain clouds, "You're right, Al, let's make out in the basement, it'll be fun."

Act 2 Scene 5.4

APRIL, ALLISON and NATALIE are seated at a small round table.

The small round table in April's office by the widow where they discuss plots and costume ideas. April and Natalie have been trying to subtly talk Allison into toning down her script, maybe not make so many references to their characters being underage girls, fearing it could be taken the wrong way. They point out how it can be interpreted with the opposite of her intentions. Natalie remembers the three guys they have waiting. "What do you want to do with the three guys in the hall?"

April now recalls putting three hopeful peckers in what she humorously calls the "audition room." If they do Allison's script they won't be needed.

Allison smiles. "I have an idea." She talks the three men into putting their clothes back on and helping her build a set with basement stairs and a door for April's cameo. All the materials were already in the studio -- a set of stairs, a doorway -- it all just needs to be put together like blocks. Allison has the men take off their shirts and she films it herself for cut in stock footage. Content. They unroll a hideous rumpus room carpet and set a dingy couch and old tube tv prop in place, all while Allison films them working. April and Natalie catcall and tease, flirting with the men while they work. As a reward for finishing, Natalie gives them a striptease dance while Allison films them, now naked again, masturbating to Natalie's performance. As per the contracts they signed this morning they will receive a copy of their scene on DVD and any royalties for DVD purchases or downloads. It's in the contract. Their video goes on AprilLynn.com, available to members for downloading. April had to commend Allison for the idea. Videos of men masturbating solo has been an enormous seller for AprilLynn.com and the overhead is zilch. Masturbator videos are easy. Just turn the camera around. Or add a second. It's all about efficiency. Men sit behind a window, watch live filmings and are filmed themselves masturbating. They were already here, "auditioning" in the first place. *Didn't make the cut son, how'd you like to watch, we film you too, royalties...yada yada, sign here.* Funny thing about guys: most don't read these contracts so well -- *Yeah, yeah where do I sign to see pussy?* -- and don't realize what they're getting themselves into. Videos of guys realizing what they are doing while they are doing it are particularly sought after by collectors. Videos where the sudden epiphany causes such a vicious mood swing he loses his erection and can't finish are a close second to videos of masturbating men solo when they do finish. It doesn't occur to many of them, until maybe later, that the people buying, downloading and masturbating to their videos aren't going to be the hot girl they are watching. Sometimes the ones that do read the fine print don't sign and leave right then and there. Others who read it and sign it and don't care who watches it, the money's green. The royalties aren't much but it's something. Plus, Content. You can always tell a Pro Boner. Posture.

While Allison and Natalie dress up the set and change into their costumes April settles up with the day's male actors. A modest check, a DVD and a business card with instructions on checking for and collecting royalties. Some of those guys who metaphorically lose their erections after the fact will often never check on their royalties. April can collect the interest on their money indefinitely. That part was her idea.

"You boys come again now." April quips with a laugh in her charming gravel voice.

In the dressing room Natalie braids one of Allison's pigtails. Allison's sitting in front of the makeup mirror applying lipstick and comparing braided verses not braided pigtails. They're wearing matching cheerleading outfits. Blue and gold seemed universal enough when they ordered them out of a cheer catalog.

"Do you think they know people order these for porn and cosplay?"

"When we order two, yeah they probably think something's up."

Allison decides on braided and Natalie does the other side for her. When she finishes Allison stands, faces Natalie. "You look great, Nat."

"So do you, Al."

It's perfectly natural for girls to hook up with their female friends -- It can be fun and comfortable. They walk in character, hand in hand to the set, smiling and laughing, joyously swinging their hands and hips in exaggerated arcs. Filming begins right away, April over the cameraman's shoulder. A few fixed cameras and a second handheld camera capture the room. Allison and Natalie sit together on the couch facing each other, one foot each on the floor, one leg folded underneath them. They paw and flirt finding impromptu dialog difficult to come up with. Tentatively they lean in together, kissing lightly at first in an innocent pucker. Slowly hands slide around each other in embrace, their kissing becoming more passionate. They stay in character. They take it slow, exploring their feelings and each others bodies inching further with growing nerve. Inhibitions melt, pulses quicken, the cameras disappear, memories and emotions fill the room, sweaters peel off shimmering braless bodies, short pleated skirts, teasing glimpses, hidden touches, slow revealing little peeks. Backs arch, legs intertwine. The room is as mesmerized by the passion as they are, it's wild. The intimacy makes even the professional crew a little uncomfortable. Allison slides off the couch wagging her rear at the camera. She puts her head under Natalie's pleated skirt. April takes her cue watching Natalie's face, slips into the shadows under the stairs. The basement wall is really just a black curtain in the shadows. She climbs the ladder to the platform and waits for Natalie's climax.

At the peak of Natalie's orgasm April opens the basement door, "You girls want pizza bagels?" She yells down the set stairs.

Never Break Character.

Allison and Natalie scramble to the couch to cover up, blushing in shame, all genuine, "Nothing…?! OK!" They mutter and cough, stuttering, "Thanks Mom!" together, hugging, laughing, tickling, teasing still, hearts pounding, adrenaline real, breasts heaving. The basement door shuts and they lean back in, the kissing working back up to breathless heavy petting, this time Natalie goes down on Allison, again April takes her cue from Allison's arousal, waits.

At the peak of Allison's orgasm April bangs open the door again, harder than before, yells, "Pizza bagels are done!" Again they jump, "Come and get it!" April adds as they struggle to cover up, still pawing at each other hungrily.

"OK we're cumming!" They yell together as scripted, giggling and hugging. They look into each other's eyes.

After a million years-long moment of awkward silence April yells, "Cut!" from the top of the stairs. Even April is uncharacteristically unsure. Allison and Natalie cling together in a sweaty breathless embrace. The stunned crew slowly shuffles out of the studio looking at the floor. April bites her lip and tries to look away walking past. She leaves them alone to process.

It got weird.

It Got Weird
Act 2 Scene 5.5

Interior:Eastland Apartment

NATALIE comes home to find ALLISON reading on the couch wrapped in a bathrobe, feet, up on the coffee table in slippers and under a blanket. Natalie sighs, slumps into the loveseat opposite Allison.

NATALIE:
Hey.

Allison and Natalie silently agree to do the most mature and reasonable thing about the giant elephant in the room between them: Ignore it. They politely avoid each other at all costs, toothless smiles and avoided glances in the hallways at home. In the heat of the moment nobody had given any thought to it. In the aftershocks it would be Natalie who would battle self doubt. Natalie has been struggling as of late with the idea of getting older, now in panic and paranoid retro speculation she scrutinizes every pinched inch and wrinkle on herself through the eyes of the men in the room behind the cameras. In her mind they are far harsher critics of her fat old ass when in reality, April's crew are discreet and strictly professional. But perception is reality. Up until now the silent unspoken order between them had always been that Allison is self conscious and a little jealous of Natalie. That's just how it was. Now suddenly it's as if their roles are reversed. It's jarring and confusing to Natalie. As far as work, she gets some from her old agent and isn't around April's office much. Behind her bedroom door, Natalie is slowly relapsing. By late summer Allison hasn't seen Natalie enough to notice her drastic weight loss but by fall Natalie quietly gets a hold of herself. By the time she runs into her old friend Metal Mike by chance in a supermarket she's again sober, mostly, not counting the wine and some weed on the weekends. She and Allison have still not talked about the shoot. The video and it's royalties are booming -- it's a site favorite and top seller -- but they have yet to address what happened between them and how it complicated their friendship. When Metal Mike suggests a casual double date, the girls agree, but continue to ignore the elephant.

Allison looks up from her book, lays it down on her lap smiling, "I feel like I haven't seen you all summer."

Natalie bites her lip and nods, "Me too." They look at each other silently sharing a telepathy that can only come with a close loving friendship. *Should we?*

Allison stands up and goes to the kitchen, "I've missed you lately…let's have some wine. Were you going to say something when you came in just now?"

"Oh yeah," Natalie jumps excitedly from the loveseat, joins Allison in the kitchen, "Do you remember my friend Metal Mike?" She asks, taking a full glass of wine, "We saw him, my God it feels like fucking forever ago, at that party down the hill…?"

"When you got pot from Ben?"

"Yeah, and you got something from Ben too." Natalie laughs.

"Yeah I did." *High five.* "Metal Mike, he was out on the patio?"

"Yeah he was telling them that story about Steve."

Allison laughs recalling the story, "Right! Steve was jerking off outside Mike's hotel room?!"

They laugh together, share a few glasses of wine and Natalie explains how she ran into Mike a few hours ago, how he wants to take her out, a friendly date. "Mike and I have been running into each other all over for years. It feels like we've always been into each other but it was never the right time, like I was married to my ex or he had a girlfriend or he was running around with the Metal Chicks, you know...?"

Allison sits watching Natalie talk, smiling, "You're so cute."

"Allison, what are we doing?"

"I don't know. I've missed you."

"I've missed you too. Are we lesbians?"

Allison smiles, "Do you know what Carol and her minions used to do to me?"

Natalie cocks her head to the side, "No...?"

"They did this one at a time, one would break off from the group, befriend me in private. We would hang out for about a week and then there would be a sleepover. Monday in school my newest friend would tell everyone at school I tried to kiss her and that I was a lesbian. A few weeks would go by and another one would do it. I must have fell for it four or five times." Allison pauses to reflect, empathize with her young self, "I just wanted someone to like me."

"When was this? I don't remember you hanging out with any of them."

"I guess I stopped falling for it right around when I met you and then we started hanging out."

"And I would make out with you and not tell everyone you were a lesbian." Natalie laughs.

Allison blushes. "Maybe I'm a little more lesbian than I think...?"

"Well I need you to go out with one more boy before you swear off them forever."

"So after years of bad timing now Mike wants to date you casually? What's up with that?"

"He's going back to LA in a few weeks, he's in New York on business. We aren't getting into anything serious and, I don't know, he's always been such a gentleman with me, I guess I never expect to be treated like that."

"Maybe you should. Expect it more."

"Maybe…"

"Maybe he likes you Natalie, likes you for you and not because he thinks you'll put out."

"Yeah, weird right?" They laugh at this sarcastic self deprecation.

"So Mike has a friend you want me to go out with? Is it going to be like the Keegan situation?"

Natalie bursts out laughing, "No, no, no, it's not going to be anything like that at all…I promise. I think you'll like his friend, his name is Brian. He has beautiful eyes."

"Beautiful eyes? He's fat isn't he?"

Natalie looks away with a smile, "A little. He's really nice." She adds quickly.

"I have to jump on the grenade again for you." Allison jokes with dramatic flair. "OK but where do you want to go? I don't want to do some lame dinner-movie-double-date at the Shake Shack and the drive-in like a couple of teenyboppers meeting some greasers on the sly."

Natalie notices a bottle of maple syrup on the counter from breakfast. "You know where we should go? Apple picking at Berry Hollow Farm." She holds up the syrup. "I got this syrup from the maple syrup farm across the street in the gift shop last time I went apple picking."

"When was that?"

"A few years ago. A nice old man walked us through this cute little orchard, he'd said the property was in his family for like hundreds of years."

Double Date at Berry Hollow Farm

Act 2 Scene 5.6

Exterior: Eastland Apartments, morning

ALLISON and NATALIE are standing in the crisp morning autumn air outside their building. A large tan luxury SUV pulls up in front of them.

Mike gets out of the driver's seat, Brian out of the passenger side. Allison notes Mike looks exactly the same as the last time she saw him except this time the pants look more like a cheetah pattern. Brian gets in back directly behind the driver's seat. Mike escorts the girls around the truck, opens the back door for Allison and ushers Natalie in the front, helping her up into the truck. He shuts both doors and gets back in the driver's seat. Natalie nuzzles into him across the front seat and they get cozy. Allison rolls her eyes. She looks to her left and her eyes meet with Brian's. He politely says "Hi."

He does have really nice eyes. "Hi." She says back adding softly, "I'm Allison."

"Brian." He extends his hand and meets hers, gives it a polite squeeze. A gentle shake, *not overbearing and not too limp,* Allison thinks. Brian doesn't strike her as a guy who would give anyone a limp handshake. Earlier Allison assumed nice eyes meant he's fat and Brian is a pretty hefty guy but he carries it well. Allison notes it's a little unfair how guys can be fatter than girls and still be attractive. He has a bushy beard and long curly hair that looked like it might go past his shoulders if it were straight but it sticks out in a wild mane. His deep blue eyes are kind, his boyish smile disarming. This is the first date Allison has been on besides that one night with Ben. And one night is far too generous -- more like a half hour, tops, including getting dressed. In the late afternoon. She can't help look at Brian through work eyes. No matter what a person does at work it can be hard not to bring it home. She sees Brian as a headshot and a cold naked guy in a waiting room. Sure, she'd do a scene with him, maybe depending on the other two. Funny how that illusion of choice works. *Does that mean I would sleep with him outside of work? Should I? Not on a first date.* Then she wonders if he knows she's in porn. *Did he go on this date because it was with two porn chicks? Is that how Mike described it to him?*

Due to human nature and how people act in groups it falls to Mike to be the unofficial leader of the group. His qualifications being he is the common factor among them. Mike tends to be the center of attention wherever he goes anyway due to his presence. He has a deep loud voice with a gravel bass and he's a pretty big guy himself, tall and broad shouldered. "So you want me to take you apple picking, Nat?" He looks in the rearview and over his shoulder at Brian and Allison, makes sure he has their attention. Allison understands. He looks back at Natalie, "You know what I think of apple picking?" Another glance at the rearview and back to the road, "It's a scam." He looks at Natalie again, "I mean if you want to go apple picking, Nat? I'll take you apple picking. But it's a scam."

Natalie shakes her head and smiles, "How is apple picking a scam?" She looks over her shoulder for support.

"Look," Mike puts a big hand up for effect, "I'll go for a walk in this orchard, ooo nice pretty, It's a nice walk." He bops and sways in his seat like he's walking, "and we're picking apples as we go, filling up our baskets, but plenty of people have picked apples before us so there's not that much low hangin' fruit, right?" He glances around the car, at Natalie, over his shoulder, at the road, in the rearview, back to the road, "So we're boosting each other up, climbing trees, picking each other up, doing all this work. Is there a ladder around anywhere? No. No? No ladder? Anywhere on this farm? You know there are orchards where they don't want you out there fucking up their trees, they do cider or juice or something maybe, I don't know, but those apples get picked too, you know by who? People who are getting paid and get to use ladders and carts. Do I get paid to pick these apples? No ladders, no carts, we're climbing trees, lugging around baskets, doing all this work? Do we get paid for it? No. AND now! Now I gotta buy these apples I just picked! This guy is going to charge me for my own labor!" Mike's loud gravel voice raises with his excitement. Allison thinks how much thought he's put into this, how much it bothers him. "So now Farmer Apple Asshole weighs the apples and tells you it's like fifty bucks! You don't want to spend fifty bucks on apples so how many apples do I get for twenty bucks? Twenty dollars you hear yourself saying, for apples! I mean twenty is still excessive but ole farmer apple sacks has you by the short and curlies, you picked apples, don't you want some? Fifty? Too much? Twenty? And you wind up with a small grocery bag, the same one, with the cute little handles, like you get in the produce section, a bag of apples you get at the store for like five bucks that someone else picked, got paid to pick, was delivered by someone, unpacked and put on a shelf by someone, five dollars at the store, same bag, I picked them myself on site, farmer apple dick didn't touch them, deliver them, nothing, twenty dollars!"

Allison is convinced, "Right?!" She blurts out in amusement.

Mike winks at Allison over his shoulder, "So what does Johnny Appleseed do with the apples you picked but couldn't afford? He's going to sell that bag of apples you picked to these lazy turd fucks who didn't even feel like picking apples today. And for the same damn twenty bucks!" Mike puts his hand gently on Natalie's knee and smiles warmly at her, "But I'll take you apple picking Nat. It'll be fun." He smiles with a hearty laugh and Natalie blushes. Allison can see the backs of Natalie's ears getting red, she can picture the coy smile she gets when she blushes. It's cute.

Brian leans to the center of the car and says, "I've been seeing self checkout lanes in supermarkets a lot more lately." He leans back and grins at Allison.

Mike booms, "Oh don't get me started on self checkouts!" With a big belly laugh Mike takes Oregon road out of Peekskill into Putnam Valley. As he crosses the little steel bridge over the Hollow Brook.

Brian taps his shoulder, "Pull into that deli, I'll get coffees."

Mike pulls into the deli and notices the tavern on the brook across the street, "We should have lunch over there after we're done getting scammed."

Inside Brian points to the coffee station nods for them to get coffees. He walks to the counter tells the man, "Four larges." The three of them pour themselves coffee while Brian pays for them. Allison watches Mike pour his coffee and wonders if he's making the connection that he's pouring his own coffee. Brian pours himself one and they all pile back into the SUV.

Mike sips his coffee, puts it in the cupholder and says to Natalie, "So I just take this road? How far?"

Natalie smiles, "All the way." She purrs, raising her eyebrows at him. Mike drives. They drive out into the woods up the side of a mountain for over fifteen minutes before Natalie points to a street sign, "Turn here." A short way up the road pavement stops. A dirt road continues up the mountain. They pass a small dirt parking lot next to a house. "That's where I bought that syrup, Al!" Natalie points to the house excitedly.

"It looks closed." Allison mutters, looking out the other window. Across the dirt path from the Berry Hollow Farm Market is a dark wooden sign. Allison recognizes the logo from the syrup they've been using.

"Go up this hill." Natalie tells Mike, points to a tree-lined drive and over a little stone bridge over the tiny mountain stream that babbles all the way down the mountain to the Hollow Brook. Mike turns up the hill as the SUV rumbles over the cobbled bridge, the tires singing on the hard packed dirt flicking over rounded rocks in the path. A small pull off on the left between breaks in an otherwise endless row of firewood appears. Mike pulls in next to another car. "That must be the girl I talked to on the phone." Natalie gets out and walks toward the car.

A girl gets out, "Natalie?" She shakes Natalie's hand,"I'm Aideen. Sorry we're not running this place on all cylinders these days," She leads the group across a small strip of lush green lawn toward an old rock wall with a wooden gate in it. Thick twists of woody roses cling in a violent-looking arch on a trellis over the gate. Inside the gate a long dirt lane curves away from them, lined with rows of apple trees. The orchard curls around the southface of the hillside. A walled garden between the house and the orchard is partially visible through the grapevines that grow out of control on the garden wall. Aideen hands them baskets and points to a cart, "You can pick as much as you want, use the cart if you need to," Natalie smiles at Mike, "There's a ladder around somewhere in the orchard too." Natalie giggles and pokes Mike in the ribs, "For twenty bucks you can take as much as you can stuff in your car." Natalie laughs loudly and pats Mike on the back, Allison and Brian join in giggling. "We're not doing much business from here last couple of years so these appointment apple picking trips, I figure we're not even harvesting this orchard anymore…"

Allison feels herself ask, "Who…?" Before she could think not to.

"My father passed away two years ago this month, Halloween. He used to run the orchard and the whole farm really but this is our house. With him gone my mother didn't want to be here, she moved to our property in Arizona. She's in a wheelchair and that house is all one level. She couldn't be here without Dad." Aideen waves her hand up at the castle rising out of the hillside behind the garden.

Allison looks up in awe, "Wow, it's amazing…the stone work makes it look like a real castle with a modern house built into it."

"That's actually exactly what it is." Aideen explains as they walk through the orchard. "As my father used to tell it, some great-to-the-umpteenth-power grandfather of his was a pirate who plundered the high seas and then came to Putnam Valley and built a castle. We're not all so sure how much of his stories were true. Then some other great great grandpappy of his came looking for it -- the castle," She points back as they are passing it, "Apparently his family also didn't fully believe all the stories, so he came here, found the castle and built a house in it..."

"The house you grew up in?"

"No apparently that house burned down, was rebuilt, burned down again, my father rebuilt this house."

As the castle fades away on the hill behind them Natalie pokes Mike in the ribs, "Say, Mike why don't you tell Aideen about the Apple Picking Scam?" She says with a wide innocent grin.

Aideen eyes open wide, she smiles at Mike, "Scam?"

Mike, blushing, waves his hand, "Na, it's not like that," He stammers, embarrassed and caught off guard. "You're alright, but these other orchards, they charge you, I mean, they like, you do the work..."

Aideen laughs, "Right?! We pay people in the commercial fields to harvest."

"They don't even give you a discount..."

"For your labor, right?!" Aideen laughs, "That was why my father always did small tours like this in the orchard. 'Take all you want!' he'd tell people and sometimes he wouldn't even bother to charge them, he had a way about him my Dad, people loved him..." She trails off a wave of sadness washes her out to sea for a moment, "Sorry, I don't want to ruin your day."

"No," Natalie assured, "I was here a few years ago he gave me and my friends a truckload of apples for twenty bucks and a kiss on the cheek. We all fell in love with him," She looks at Mike, "You would have gotten a kick out of him."

As they loop back around past the garden Aideen notices Allison peeking through the grapevines. "Not much growing in there, some of my dad's herb boxes are still kicking, his prize mint and some lemon balm. There is an onion box and a garlic box but most of the garden is just wild weeds now. Dad used to grow a lot of peppers. He loved hot peppers." Aideen turns her face into the sun with a smile, "When you were here," She says to Natalie, "Did he point out from here where the sun rose that morning?" Aideen points down the bluff into the saddles of mountains off to the east from the lookout, the break in the tree line, "He loved the sunrise, he would watch it and point out where it was coming up, making note of how far south it goes." Aideen points into the valley, "Right about there is where it comes up in late December. That's about as far south as it goes."

Natalie looks up at the late morning sun and traces back where she thinks the sun might have come up this morning, "Wow." She whispers in awe.

Allison walks with Brian, they make polite small talk. Allison has discreetly worked out that he knows they are in porn. She's waiting to see if he's going to bring it up and if so how? Why? The longer she waits the more she wonders, how has he gone this long? Don't guys talk about porn more than this when they aren't in the presence of porn actresses? Where doe she think this is going? *Vere do you think you're going?* Inka purrs but Brian continues to be cordial and polite. It's beginning to get maddening. It occurs to her that he could be under the impression that porn star equates to prostitute and that this is a sure thing. He's certainly not trying too hard. *How rude,* she thinks.

Natalie is asking Aideen, "...well do you believe it?"

"Believe what?" Allison whispers to Brian.

It's Natalie who answers, whispering back, "Treasure." Without looking away from Aideen.

"My father believed it. I believed him but either he found it and never told us or never found it or it never existed." She adds, "A lot of people in our family don't believe it ever existed, besides my father and sort of infamously two of his ancestors, the one who came here to find the castle and the one from around the revolution era, they believed, each one ridiculed and compared to the last."

They wheel the cart full of apples up to Mike's SUV. He's still thrilled by the story of the house. "So the first guy was an illegal immigrant?"

"Irishman in France illegally snuck on board a ship in a Parisian port bound for America, talked his way across the Atlantic in search of his great grandmother's castle. And her treasure." She adds, "The name he gave in America was Thomas Crowe but there is no record of him in

France or Ireland and we suspect he didn't use his real name. New continent, new life. It's as if the whole family is hiding something sometimes."

"Like treasure?"

"Like treasure."

"Do you believe he was a pirate?" Natalie asks.

"My great to the hundredth power grandfather? I don't know, the stories are pretty out there, it would be romantic, certainly explain the rebel streak in our blood." Aideen laughs at this as she helps load apples into the truck. She tries to refuse when she as promised only charges them twenty dollars.

Mike insists on giving her a hundred. "Consider eighty of it for the story." He blushes slightly, "and the humility." He invites Aideen to join them for lunch in town but she insists she has work to do thanking him profusely for the invitation.

A search for treasure is all the fantasy and conversation all the way down the mountain into town. You could miss the tiny town proper if you sneeze at speed as you cross over the bridge from Cortlandt Manor. The two main roads in Putnam Valley form a crossroads at the bridge. To the left a road winds up one side of the mountain, to the right, Peekskill Hollow road snakes off into the valley. Straight ahead Oscawana Lake Road winds up the side of the mountain to the north. As it passes Oscawana Lake it rides the ridge line into the mining areas of the old Philipstown expedition and Fahnestock State Park. Berry Hollow farm borders the park. Down at the bridge commerce clings to the corners. The tavern that caught Mike's eye this morning sits on his right on the bank of Hollow Brook as he comes down the hill. Diagonally across the intersection is the deli where they got coffee this morning. A closed down gas station occupies the corner across from the deli. A post office and the county sheriff's office next to that. Next to the deli is a small shopping plaza with a bank in an old Victorian era town hall building. There's a few store fronts, pizza, bagels, dance studio and a seperate building that was once a house, with a pharmacy and some doctor's offices in it. Across Oscawana Lake Road from the deli there is a building that looks as if it were once a barn. It's now a hardware store. Next to that is a liquor store as usual and some more doctors offices, insurance offices and a travel agency.

"This town reminds me of Northern California." Mike says as he rides through slowly for a place to park.

"There's a parking lot here." Natalie points next to the hardware store behind an empty shell that had been a video store until pretty recently.

A tall guy with long blond hair is behind the bar as they walk into the little tavern. A few regulars ignore them.

Mike asks the bartender, "Can we get a table?"

"Sit anywhere." He points into the dining area, "Take a nice spot by the window, you can see the Hollow Brook, I'll send someone right over." They take a rectangular table with a view of the brook. The only other people in the dining room are three older ladies at the opposite end of the room. They appear to be bickering casually. Allison hears without eavesdropping they are talking about Snow White and she pictures her snowglobe. The old ladies fade to white noise. Mike, Brian and Natalie sound distant. Flakes of glittery snow fill Allison's atmosphere.

"...want a drink?" Brian is waving at Allison, "Hello? You in there?" He says with a charming smile, nods toward the waitress.

Allison blinks, shakes her head, looks up at the young lady, "I'm sorry, I'm somewhere else, Can I have a beer please?" She takes their drink orders and walks away.

Natalie looks at Allison, taps her hand across the table, "A beer?"

"Something, I don't know, this place. Feels like a beer." Allison says with a smile. Brian nods,

"I would have a beer but I'm driving." Mike nods at Natalie with a wink. Allison studies Brian. Her assessment stands, nice eyes, charming, nice smile. He's polite, sociable, etcetera. She would sleep with him. After a third date. Knowing he's in New York on business and leaving for home soon and there won't be a second or third date makes that an easy decision. He also still hasn't actually, technically hit on her. He hasn't aggressively let the female know the penis is on the table. Here's the dick. It's an option. None of that. Maybe she's the proverbial grenade to jump on. *Oh God, I'm the grenade!* she overthinks. Allison is sure Natalie plans to fuck Mike. Allison has always felt like the grenade whenever she's gone out with Natalie and the Keegans in her life. Of course he was the only wrong number and the oddest circumstance. Boys and men of all ages always notice Natalie first. Always. Sometimes to a gross and scary degree. Predators. Allison thinks about how Louis is twelve years her senior. His new wife is twenty-one years younger than him. Lecherous faces leer at Allison as she strolls down creepy old man memory lane. Adults casting knowing, penetrating looks into her privacy. Violating her with their eyes. Allison thinks back to her teenage self with Natalie navigating a gauntlet of culminated catcalls through a dark Gothic mallscape, crazy eyes oogling over dripping fangs at them as if they were veal, milk-fed baby girls. *Predators.*

     The waitress startles Allison back to reality putting down the drinks adding politely, "Are you're ready to order or would you like more time?"

     Allison hoists her beer and chugs it, puts it down a little too hard. A burp sneaks out of her as much to her surprise as everyone else at the table, "I'll have the burger. And another beer." This begets a round of laughter and a round of beers for everyone on the house.

     She earns a second round of laughs when the waitress asks, "How do you want that cooked?"

     When she answers, "Rare."

     Back at the Eastland Apartment Allison sitting on the couch, Brian on the loveseat. They awkwardly try to avoid too much eye contact and struggle for light conversation while Mike and Natalie fornicate loudly in the next room. Allison pictures Brian as a headshot and weighs the cross country loophole to the three date minimum option. She shrugs off the Keegan Situation feeling and walks towards her bedroom, glancing over her shoulder at Brian. *Come and get it big boy* Inka purrs, "Come on." She winks and ducks into her room.

Act 2 Scene 6

Interior: Eastland Apartment, morning

ALLISON is sitting on a stool at
the kitchen island sipping
coffee.

Over the next few weeks Natalie's mood slowly darkens with the season. Allison hadn't noticed at first. After the date Natalie was in a pretty good place. Mike left for California a few days after to say goodbye and Natalie said it sounded like an afterthought on his way out. Not that she had expected any kind of call, much less a commitment. Or had she? Natalie and Mike had a long standing flirtatious friendship wound tight with sexual tension. For a few days she was fine. She was even chipper about the idea that his call sounded like an afterthought. It humorously emphasizes the idea that they aren't going to be a couple. That's when it dawns on her. Natalie is getting old.

This morning Allison is sitting at the island sipping coffee She has a piece of toast, a generous swath of cream cheese spread across it. A light coat of jelly tints the creamcheese. Crumbs crumble to the plate as Allison wipes her chin before reaching for the second piece. Natalie hasn't been up for coffee and toast with cream cheese and jelly for three days in a row now.

Allison's eyes are fixed on Natalie's bedroom door. As though she can see through it. "Nat. You up?" She says loud enough but not too loud.

"Yes." Natalie answers meekly.

"You want coffee? I made some. I'll fix…"

"No thanks." softer still.

Allison chews a bite slowly, swallows, wipes her mouth, sips her coffee, all without breaking her gaze on the door. "Are you coming to April's with me today?" Natalie doesn't answer. Nearly a full minute ticks by before the door slowly starts to crack open. Natalie stands in the doorway, hair disheveled, wrapped in a bathrobe. She shuffles forward, "Are you OK, honey?" Allison puts her hand on Natalie's shoulder. Allison need only look at Natalie's big wet brown eyes and knows she has a duty. She calls April right away, tells her they won't be into the studio today.

April takes it in stride, "We have editing and uploads and shit we can do today without you, I get it, tell her I can't wait to see her hot ass soon…no on the right more…" April trails off talking to someone else as she hangs up.

Allison hangs up. "I'm here for you all day."

Natalie sits in a slump on a stool and leans on her elbows. "Can you see the lines on my face?"

Allison puts her hand on Natalie's cheek, "Oh Natalie, your skin looks like smooth butterscotch. It's like you came out of an old man's cardigan." She puts on an old man voice, "Here ya go darlin' maybe I got a Werther's…"

This puts a temporary smile on Natalie's face as Allison searches the pockets of her old man sweater for a hard candy. "My grandpappy used to give me Werther's," She says happily, her eyes twinkle with tears, "No really, look here." She says pointing to her eyes, still smiling, "Look at these crow's feet…"

"Is this about Mike?"

Natalie looks away sheepishly. Pauses. "I guess, kinda." She says finally, "I'm getting old, Allison."

"You're in your mid-twenties, Nat."

"Late twenties, Al, and already divorced, two kids I can't see, my career is running out…" She trails off.

"Running out? Natalie, April just retired. In her fifties…"

"April Lynn Baker is a legend. I'm not."

"So we'll do something else, Natalie, we don't have to…" Allison realizes what she is saying, "Nat, you can do anything you're a great girl, if you don't want to be single anymore you could snag a man any time you want."

"Yeah because they all already know I'm easy." She sighs. "How much longer are they all going to want to fuck me?"

"Haven't you ever heard of Cougars?" Allison half jokes but sees Natalie's hurt through her big watery brown eyes. Allison realizes this was not the right thing to say, *I should have gone to work.*

At the Porn Shoot
Act 2 Scene 6.2

Interior: Eastland Apartment, morning

NATALIE sits at the island sipping her coffee with both hands. She's wearing a big broken smile that ALLISON recognizes as fake even as she wipes the sleep from her eyes all the way across the room. She goes with a nonthreatening,

ALLISON:
You're up early.

"I have one more film to do for my old agent and I can come work with you full time." Natalie's voice is shaky, they both ignore it. "Do you have a cigarette?"

"I haven't seen you smoke since middle school…" Allison instinctively goes for her purse, remembers, "Oh that's right, I quit a few months ago."

"Oh, yeah…" Natalie mutters into her mug, gaze still fixed forward.

"Where's the shoot?"

In the bathroom Natalie gives herself a pep talk as she brushes her teeth. She tries to smooth her face, the faint lines in her smooth skin seem to glow in her eyes. A shiver runs up her spine, a fear. She closes her eyes, takes a few deep breaths.

"I'm only twenty seven." She whispers to herself, "My skin is silky smooth, I'm young and pretty." She takes another deep breath and maybe just a little taste of courage. She slowly opens her eyes, calming down.

In the car Natalie tries to sing along to the radio happily but songs keep coming on that hinder that. She snaps off the radio as Mick sings,

"What a drag it is getting old…"

"Indeed, Mick. Momma could use a little helper too." She pulls over next to a bodega on Main street. She walks in right past the coffee to the cooler in back. She takes out a twenty two ounce Corona and places it on the counter with a thud. "Can I have a pack of Newports?" She asks, digging in her bag for her ID.

"Ten twenty five." The guy behind the counter slips the beer into a small brown bottle bag and slaps a pack of cigarettes down on the counter.

"Oh…" She had hoped to be asked for ID. She hands over a ten and exact change, takes a book of matches.

Outside she puts the beer on top of the covered trash can next to the door. She packs the smokes against her palm, it's been years since she'd smoked. She opens the pack and tosses the wrappings in the can. She pulls one out, laughs, "My wish," turns it around and slides it back it in filter first. She takes a different one and tosses the pack onto the trash can next to her beer and her purse, lights the cigarette. Her hands tremble as she tries to put the tiny flame to the tip. A few puffs, it's lit, she shakes out the match, tosses it in the gutter and walks to her car. As she opens her door she has to shut it quick and move in close to the car as another car speeds by a little too close. She finally sits in her driver's seat with a shaky sigh. She turns the key enough to put down the windows but doesn't start the car yet. Instead, looking around at the thin leather covers stretched tight over her bucket racing seats, she decides she doesn't want to blow ashes around and burn them. She smokes her cigarette then tosses the butt out into the street. She digs in her purse, just a little more. If one's good two is better, right? She starts the engine and pulls out.

When she finds the address her agent gave her she parks, shuts off the engine, opens the windows, lights another cigarette and opens her beer. She breathes deep, flutters her eyelashes in the rearview mirror. Her left eye droops slightly. One of her tells. Her ex-husband always knew when she was getting high when her left eye got droopy. *It's just a little bit,* she thinks. *Nobody will notice.* "I'm fine." She practices blowing off any accusation. Old habits.

As she walks in the door she sees two other girls have already arrived. They are considerably younger, she notices that immediately. They can't be more than eighteen or nineteen and seem like bratty kids. Little girls. Natalie feels sickened by how young they look and at the same time, old and haggard next to them. Their conversation sounds obnoxious, making Natalie feel older. Then they turn on her.

"Oh look, we get to work with a veteran." One says with a bitchy tone. Natalie does not take it as a compliment. She tries to ignore it but it stings. The producers fawn all over the young bitches but ignore Natalie, at least that's how it feels to her. They are motioning to her.

"And Nat'll play the MILF."

"What?!" Natalie is insulted. "I'm not old enough to play this bitch's mother…" She stops, afraid her words are a bit slurred. She rubs at her eye, aware of the droop. It feels drastic though nobody else notices.

"What's the difference, Nat? Nobody cares. They just want to jerk off."

"But I'm barely ten years --"

"-- A decade?" One of the girls laughs obnoxiously." You're a decade older than us, Grandma." This makes the other girl honk and snort laughing.

"Fuck you, you little cunt…." Natalie steps toward the girl.

One of the producers steps between them putting his hand on Natalie's shoulder, "Alright, that's enough girls, come on Nat," He says leading her away, "Let's go get you ready."

"I don't want to work with those two." She protests.

"It's fine, Nat, they aren't in your scene anyway. Come on, this way." He opens a door and ushers her inside. "Shelia will do your makeup and then we'll do the shoot right over here." He waves to the set and the two camera men who hardly look up from their cameras, give Natalie a polite wave. He brings Natalie over to the makeup station where Shelia the makeup lady is talking to Natalie's co-star. The producer says to Natalie, "Have you met Ted?" Ted is older, maybe mid to late forties. He's standing there completely naked and quite comfortable about it. His penis is enormous and though it isn't erect it's clearly quite thick and engorged. Ted catches Natalie looking at it, gives her a smile. She feels herself blush, can't help hope they don't want to stick that thing in her ass. It's not the biggest she's ever seen lengthwise but it's close and it's definitely the thickest. Ted's kind deep brown eyes are comforting, maybe a bit too much.

She shakes Ted's hand, "Nice to meet you." She says coyly.

"Same here, darling." Ted eyes Natalie up and down lustily, gives her a gentle slap on the bottom, "Go get ready, I'll be over here. I look forward to getting you naked." He says playfully.

Sheila leads Natalie by the hand, "This way, dear." She leads her away to her setup near a window before Natalie can react or answer Ted or Sheila. She glances over her shoulder to say something to Ted but he's walking away toward the bedroom set, his back to her. She realizes she doesn't know what to say anyway and mutters under her breath.

"What dear?" Sheila asks as she seats Natalie.

"Oh, uh, nothing…" She trails off.

Sheila starts to dab at Natalie's face. "Your eye is a little droopy dear, are you OK?"

"I'm fine." She shyly tries in vain to cover her eye with her hand, "Maybe a little tired," She offers a lame excuse, "Late nights, you know…?"

Sheila is unconcerned as she applies Natalie's camera makeup and sends her off to set. "Off you go."

As Natalie walks slowly across the studio floor she feels like everyone's watching her, though they aren't. She stumbles, regains her balance. The room seems to grow as she walks, she's getting nowhere. Ted and Sheila shrink away in both directions, the ceiling rises, the walls expand. Natalie shakes off some fog, feeling very small. She is intensely aware of her drooping eye. Her mouth feels as if she couldn't speak right if she tried. She's embarrassed and it feels like everyone can tell she's fucked up and though Sheila suspects, nobody else does and they wouldn't care if they did. This is porn, not daycare. If you need a little courage, hey…whatever puts food on the table. Lots of the girls get courageous before a shoot. Loosen up. Whatever they want to call it, that's up to them. Whatever it takes to get courageous, drink, drug, whatever they need to get up the courage to make that disconnect. Some girls, like April, don't need to, don't even want to. Natalie doesn't need courage for porn.

Natalie walks toward the bed, Ted is reclined against some pillows. The cameras roll as she walks into frame. She looks deep into his soft brown eyes and she starts to fall in, to see into them, she becomes colored with them, tinted in them. He pats the bed with his hand with a friendly inviting smile. His big hand makes the bedsprings echo a loud deep ring. In the dream time of his hand echo she is a little girl again -- innocent, happy, running to daddy, patting the bed, "Come on, Nat" she hears her papa say over two decades ago, before mom left and took her with, before he moved away. Her happy time with him…safe. *Oh God,* she thinks in a panic, *I can't fuck Ted,* having a brief moment of lucidity. But it's too late -- she is already climbing onto the bed, she can't speak, the words congeal in her mouth like a sour gag. Ted gently pulls her hair pulling her across his lap to pull up her skirt, gives her ass a rub and a smack before pulling her panties down to her knees and slapping her bare ass a little harder. Natalie starts to cry softly as Ted rolls her over, pulling one leg up over his head, he penetrates her. She sees stars as he splits her up the middle. It's definitely bigger now that it's hard. Nobody seems to notice or they don't care about her tears as Ted bashes into her. He says some lines, whatever the script said to further some loose plot to the scene. His words sound distorted to her, the room pulses with an air percussion. Did she even get a script? Is she saying lines? Does she even have any lines? Natalie can't recall, but nobody seems to care, she must be doing what they want. Ted slaps the stinging handprint, bouncing her off his tanned pelvis, his cock pounding her. A black hole blocks her vision, pulsing in time with his thrusts, dilating, contracting quickly with the rhythm. Ted's grunting grin disappears and reappears from behind the pulsing black hole. *What was this movie going to be called?* She can't recall. Hot tears streak down her cheeks. *Pop bangs wife and twin step daughters? MILF and the teenage girl scouts? Cheerleaders?* What fucking costumes did those little sluts pull? Those hot young girls Ted is going to fuck when this MILF is all used up? Did she even have any lines?

"Uhmphdaddy" She blurts out when he shifts her face into the bed and somehow finds a new bottom to hit. No one notices or cares, maybe they thought she was talking dirty but she's horrified and near hallucinations. Ted as her daddy, the one man in her life that never did abuse her, pounding away at her with a dick so big she swears she can feel it in her throat. He never abused her except in being so far away, why did he go? Why didn't he make mother stay; for me? She thinks, stars exploding with Ted's thrusts.

"I'm leaving you Betty." Ted is saying, "Consider this goodbye, it's your... parting gift." He says with grinning innuendo in his voice. He breaks the fourth wall and winks at the camera Roper style as he Parts Betty. The pain screeches in Natalie's head like a train skidding to a stop on the tracks. Ted sinks his massive penis into Natalie's ass. Alarm bells clang, a klaxon warns danger danger. Natalie swears she can hear the two bitchy skanks behind the lights and cameras.

"Are you cumming yet daddy?" They sing together. *They had lines?!* Natalie is sure she wasn't given any lines. *Why did they get lines?*

"I'm trading you in babe..." Ted delivers with a classic corny porn stiffness "...for a couple of newer models." He winks grotesquely again as he pulls out of Natalie's ass with a dry tear. Her asshole burns and swells out. Ted smacks the still stinging hand print again sending a fresh wave of shock to her fiery asshole. Hot tears roll down her cheeks, a sob escapes as Ted unleashes a torrent of semen over her shoulder soaking her ear and filling her open sobbing mouth. Far away and detached, she is at least thankful for Ted's professionalism in terms of taking care of his semen. Clearly he eats a lot of pineapple, she can tell from the taste. Ted is a courteous professional. However here in the moment in this room, Natalie's asshole is on fire, she is overcome with tears, utterly humiliated though nobody else in the room seems to notice. Or care. They carelessly move on without her.

"OK, let's get Ted cleaned off and fluffed up and ready for the threesome with the hot step daughters," Someone is saying, "Natalie can you move hon, we need to get this bed out of here, thanks babe…" Natalie gathers her things, sliding her burning ass off the bed. She can't look up into anyone's eyes, needing a little bit of courage. She hurries in a limp, urgency growing, clutching her belongings and clenching her stinging ass cheeks, she crashes through the bathroom door out in the hall. She barely gets to a sitting hover before her shaking bowels release. It feels like lava as it rudely rips past her swollen sphincter. She sobs loudly in the echoing tiled cold stall, digging in her purse, hot tears distort her vision, searing pain, she frantically searches. Finally her fingers find what she's probing for, her fingers wrap around it, just knowing it's there, that help is on the way is soothing. Courage. She swallows her courage, the black pulsing holes slow. Slows and darkens, more courage, she inhales, breathes deep, more darkness, slower still, the fire subsides to a comforting smolder, darkness, warmth swallows her, her hands slide down the stall, her sweaty palms leave a shiny slick trail. Tinted dirty water drips from her stinging asshole and splash beneath her. In her courageous fog she feels the water dripping, imagines it dripping over her, eyes closed she runs her trembling hands over her sweaty hair and face. She shakes her head, opens her eyes, takes a few deep breaths. Big mistake as it stinks like shit in here. Another wave of lucidity shakes her. Shamefully she stands up slow trying to clean herself with a big wad of scratchy one-ply commercial toilet paper. The cheap stuff dissolves mostly, no matter how much she tries to wad, until she runs out and is forced to settle for good enough. She gathers herself and her pride, straightens down her skirt, goes to the sink to wash her face and hands. Patting her face in the mirror she is suddenly shaken with a convulsion, vomiting violently into the sink. She looks again in the mirror, now crying from the shock and fresh pain in her throat from throwing up. She sighs, steps to her right and washes again in the next sink, wiping puke from her chin. She walks sheepishly out of the bathroom and past the closed studio door. She can hear those two little sluts screaming with delight as they no doubt take turns bouncing on Ted's massive cock. Maybe they're grinding their tight young pussies on his stubble chin, his nose up her tiny butthole, the other slut half standing over Ted, "That stupid little slut can't even take Ted's whole cock," she grumbles. Fuck those dirty skanks for calling her old. Natalie notices one of the skanks left her sweatshirt on a chair out in the lobby where she'd first seen them, recognizes the sweatshirt as the one that one slut was wearing. She snatches it off the chair as she walks by without breaking stride and puts the sweatshirt on her car seat so she doesn't get her wet shit water ass on her leather seats.

Act 2 Scene 7

Interior: Eastland Apartment, morning

ALLISON is sitting on the couch, one leg tucked under herself. Natalie's head is laying on Allison's lap. She sobs lightly.

NATALIE:

Allison, I'm sorry…

"Sorry? For what? You don't have to apologize to me, Nat. I owe you huge." Allison rubs Natalie's hair.

"I'm just having such a hard time with this…" She trails off, unsure of exactly what it is that's giving her a hard time. Her courage is wearing thin, the jangle of nerves inside her ringing like a dinner bell. The beast, it calls to feed. At first she ignores it, overcome with an inexplicable tangled web of sadness, "I feel lost, Allison." She breathes lightly, "Used up, like I don't...belong here anymore?" She questions her own words. "Like, I'm, I don't know. Through. My scene is over. I can just go."

"Well you know you can come work with April and I, now that your contract is fulfilled…"

"That's not what I mean." Natalie sighs. As of today, she no longer can see a clear path ahead in life. The road is opaque with fog. It's not any one thing -- her mother, her father, her step father, her babies, their father. Ted, Sheila, April. Porn. Natalie and her age -- the lines on her face, her expiration date, all at once conspiring against her, calling on the beast to come and make it all go away. When it gets so hard to not see any clear path forward due to the blinding pain, the demon promises to show you the way, promises relief, that sting and that numbness it brings. It can be so persuasive laying out clear-cut white lines in the fog, waving you in with the friendly warm smile of deception. When the jangle finally rattles too loud and Natalie can't ignore it any more she sits up slow, her hair stuck to her cheeks mixed in sweat and tears, her eyes puffy and red, makeup smeared in dark circles around her eyes. "I think I want to go lay down." She whispers, unable to make eye contact with Allison, who takes her chin in her hand, raises her head directing her eyes into hers. She wipes away some of the tear streaked mascara and tries to look into Natalie's eyes. Natalie gives only a moment's glimpse before turning away and getting up. She needs the courage for what she no longer even knows. And that's a part of the trick. When the smoke and mirrors, pins, needles and prickly pins make it all seem better you think that you know but you still can't come up with the answer that is the trick. Just one more to get you through...get you to where? Nowhere. That is the illusion when you can't see a path forward anymore and the beast takes hold, takes on the role of whatever you need. A father, a guide, it will simply tell you what you need to hear. With a smile. *I'll show you the way, my child.* But it's a trick. Natalie shuffles off in shame, head down, mood dark. Her curtains darken the room. A dim light prys through the thick fabric, her reflection in the mirror takes a bluish hue. Her eyes blurry through tears. She slides under the blanket, shivers. She's cold even though it's warm in the room. She wraps herself in blankets and the demons' warm embrace of lies, drifts off to a restless sleep. Her dreams are dark, too dark to see, the paths before her shrouded in shadow. Red yellow eyes peer out at her from the darkness. She twists and writhes, sweating, moaning, pulling away from the demon's long thin fingers. It sinks its black nails into her, clawing her back, tearing at her skin. She tries to pull away, then turns back. Warm crimson blood streaks down her arm and back as his nails rake over her, boiling her skin, clouding her in green fog as she rolls, moans, soaking her pillow and blankets. She moans in her sleep, a dull aching numbness stirs her, she blinks. She's awake. It's twilight behind the curtains. She can't tell if it's morning or evening. She sits up wiping sweat and sleep from her eyes. They feel sunken and heavy. She is less refreshed than when she lay down. She slides from her bed and shuffles to the door. Her mouth is tacky, tastes like sleep. She cracks the door slow. Allison is still on the couch.

"Hey Nat. You hungry? You want to get dinner?"

Dinner. OK, it's evening. "Let's order in." Natalie finds herself in a rare sweet spot. Courageous and numb yet awake and lucid. Somewhere after high and before the devil's dinner jangle. Natalie puts her head down in determination rather than shame and sets about putting out wine glasses, telling Allison, "I had a relapse." As she selects a wine from their collection.

"What does that mean…?" Allison is confused, not really in tune with any kind of drug culture. Carol's sister had a problem when they were young but it never affected Allison and neither Carol's parents nor Allison's would ever dare talk about such shameful things. Not in mixed company. Allison just has no frame of reference here.

"I have a drug problem, Al. I was clean a long time but I'll always have a drug problem. I've been using again, is what that means. I had a relapse. I, uh…I don't know. I don't know how it happened. I guess you never intend on it being a problem -- 'hey let's go ruin our life today' -- it doesn't happen like that, that's not how…I don't…I can't explain. It was just there. Wrong place right time. It does that. It finds you when you're vulnerable, like a living predator. It's hard to explain." She pops a cork and pours wine in two glasses. She empties one with a gulp and refills it. "I was down. After we went apple picking." She sits on the couch next to Allison handing her a glass of wine, she continues, "It's not like I thought there would be something serious but it was kind of an intense thing between Mike and I, we were close for a long time, always flirty, always into each other but the timing wasn't right so it was a really long buildup, I don't know...maybe I did kind of want it to be something. Something it was never going to be. Maybe I shouldn't have slept with him, but he was just there. I was down and he was...it was there, it was just there. I don't know if you've ever noticed, I don't know how many addicts you've known."

Allison nods slowly in agreement. She doesn't know any addicts. That she knows of. If she does, they have her fooled. She doesn't even make the connection to her own nicotine addiction. Society has a way of making some addictions socially acceptable.

"Every addict has a tell, see, because you can't look high. Nobody wants to enable an addict, not knowingly, so you try not to look high. Addicts have to people please, pleasing people will keep helping you get." She smiles, "Pleased. High. I don't know why I'm telling you this now, I'm breaking a code telling you, now you'll be looking for it but I have to get this off my chest now while I still have the nerve. My eye." Natalie points to her Left Eye. "My tell is my eye. My left eye droops when I'm fucked up." She sips her wine, shrugs. Allison thinks about all the times she'd noticed Natalie's eye drooping and not known what to think. "I guess I'm telling you this because..." Natalie chokes up, puts her fist to her mouth, takes a deep swallow catches her breath, her eyes brim. Allison waits, standing by, the panic subsides, "I ran into my ex husband not long after the apple picking date. I was high, he knew it." She pauses again, tears well up in her eyes again, she looks away, catches her throat, "I didn't even know he was in town. He knew because of the eye. He said I can't see the boys at all until I go to rehab again." She bites her lip, her face quivers "I'm scared. Just the thought of quitting gives me a panic attack."

"What...? What do I do? Allison is unsure.

"Don't trust me.." She hands Allison an envelope. "It's next month's rent."

"Your half?"

"No, the whole thing. Just in case." She looks gravely at Allison, "I can't be trusted." She shakes her head and drains her wine. Pouring another glass she says, "Order Chinese?" she says, picking up the phone.

Over Chinese food Natalie confesses in graphic detail the things her step father had done to her.

"I don't know if it's the wine or if it's because you truly love me."

"Maybe it's both."

"Maybe it *is* both but I feel so comfortable with you Allison, thank you for listening to me."

"Of course."

By the time they get to fortune cookies Natalie is cheerful. "What does yours say?" She smiles at Allison with a childlike awe in her face.

"Be your own boss." Allison turns the paper over for a mandatory look at the back, "Boss. I like the sound of that." She tosses her fortune away with a rehearsed casualness, hopes for help with Natalie from the cookie. "What's yours say?" Natalie cracks open her cookie with hopeful innocent look of a child on Christmas, Allison praying for good fortune. *You'll win lotto and marry a well hung billionaire.* Natalie pulls out the little white flag. Allison can count the crumbs hitting the table in slow motion, echoing like boulders spilling into a canyon.

"You will go on a trip." Natalie reads out loud. A bright wet shiny smile comes to her face, a tear to her eye as she places the fortune down on the table. "I have to go to rehab." She sighs as tears stream down her pained smile. *It's a nice smile,* Allison thinks. A bright shining hopeful smile.

Act 2 Scene 8

Interior: Eastland Apartment, morning

ALLISON is screaming...

She hears herself as though it's someone else. Moments ago she'd stood staring at Natalie's door and she knew. Somehow, she knew something, she didn't know what, she just knew. The lighting was off. Life was dull and faded, the color washed out. She'd stood frozen, looking at the door and somehow she knew: Natalie's dead. No need to check for breath or pulse, the grotesque death mask frozen on Natalie's sad, lifeless face as she'd opened the door said it all. Her big doe eyes looking up hopeful for help that would not come. The moment seems to last an eternity, Allison standing rigid in the doorway, she starts trembling. The dark room has a blue hue, a stale sleep and sharp death smell that picks at the hairs in Allison's nose. The smoking gun lays next to Natalie, her weapon of choice -- empty packages littered around her like the spent shells of a shotgun. The little packages of poison the demon craved. It won. It can be so persuasive, Allison never stood a chance. She just didn't have the experience. There is always clean up to do after the bright smile of admittance. If there is poison in the well it has to be flushed right away or it will call out, *eat me, drink me, shoot me, snort me, don't let me go to waste, just one more time, for old times sake. One for the road,* the demon coos in that romantic, persuasive way. Help you talk yourself into anything even though you know it's wrong but do it anyway. Allison sits on the bed, absorbing the scene, careful not to disturb Natalie in her awkward final resting posture -- precariously rigid, leaning half out of bed, neck slack, eyes fixed up. She sobs numbly, her hand cupped over her nose and mouth either to muffle her sobs or intercept the smell maybe a little of both., It feels unreal, thinking back to Natalie's terror, her sadness. It weighs down on Allison like rocks on a board pressing her chest like she's been accused of witchcraft in Gore during the witch trial hysteria.

"What should I have done, Natalie?" Her voice sounds mucus thick, the echo in the still room gives Allison a chill. She sobs loudly, lays her hand gently on Natalie and just sits, head down, eyes closed, crying. When she opens her eyes she notices a plastic bag on Natalie's nightstand. For some reason it catches her eye. It's a Ziploc bag. Inside is a pair of panties, Allison recognizes them as the pair Natalie was wearing yesterday at breakfast. Natalie was making coffee in her nightshirt and panties. She holds up the bag. Micro dots of moisture suggest they were warm and damp when they were sealed up in the bag. They had talked about selling dirty panties not too long ago. She was going to sell these, Allison is sure of it. She grins, wiping a tear away. Bag in hand, she goes to the kitchen, slipping the bag in her bathrobe pocket as she picks up the phone. The dial tone drones in her ear as she tries to decide who to call. She doesn't know how to get in touch with anyone who would be concerned. Reciever on her shoulder she dials 911.

"Nine one one what is your emergency?"

"Uh, I'm sorry I guess it's not really an emergency, I didn't know who else to call. My roommate's dead."

"Are you sure your roommate is dead, ma'am?"

"I'm sure." Allison chokes up, realizing again that Natalie's dead. A realization she will keep having before it feels real.

"I'm sending police and EMT's, ma'am, can you give me your exact location…?"

Drama Camp 1993

"That's right. To Hell with you." Courtney declares as Rosie, in Kim's bedroom taking her stand. "From now on it's going to be just me, Rosie, on the town, singing, dancing, drinking, having a ball..."

Camp Director looks over her shoulder at Allison, "Do you think we should change the drinking line? You know how sensitive people are getting about underage drinking."

Onstage Courtney continues while Elizabeth watches wide-eyed from her fake prop bed. "I wasted eight long years on that momma clutching, ass-prin splitting," Courtney grins at the word play joke, "Six foot tower of Jello...what did I ever see in him? It was rough from the start, broken dates, broken nails, broken hearts..."

Elizabeth as young, naive Kim asks, "All men can't be like that...?"

Rosie confirms, hardened, jaded by life, "Every last one. They're all the same from puberty to senility, Albert Schweitzer to Mussolini."

Kim ponders with midwest wonder, "I don't know why Ingrid Bergman ever married him...?"

Allison whispers to Natalie, "Nobody is going to get that joke." Camp Director shushes her. Allison defends herself. "Well, the reference is outdated." Looking back at Natalie she reiterates, "Watch, that joke is going to fall flat, nobody is going to get it."

The discussion attracts their attention on stage. Elizabeth breaks the wall and confirms, "Yeah I mean I get it but nobody else is going to..."

Camp Director shoots a finger stiffly in the air, bellows, "Never Break Character!" She stirs her finger in a circle motioning for them to move on.

Courtney continues, "Use them. Make them our playthings...." Allison looks over Camp Directors shoulder, brows raised. She can feel Allison's glare.

"Oh shut up."

"Sip from the cup of life, mix our potions full strength and drain it to the dregs. What do you think of that Mr. Peterson?!"

Elizabeth joins Courtney for the duet refrain, together they sing, "Broken dates, broken nails, broken hearts, what did we ever see in...?"

Kim is convinced. Bag packed Elizabeth leaps from the prop bed, Kim is ready to leave with Rosie tonight. Rosie of course reminds Kim she's only fifteen. "Juliet was only fourteen when she left home." Allison and Natalie giggle as Courtney delivers the Shakespeare reference.

"And look what happened to her."

When the scene ends Camp Director calls for a five minute break and tells Courtney to get into full dress for the Shriner's ballet. She has the stage crew bring out the table for the dance.

Allison leans forward, "I can't believe you're letting Courtney do the Shriner's ballet."

"For now." Camp Director is quick with glancing over her shoulder, "It's the next scene cut if she skips another one of my rehearsals and she knows it. In fact that's half the reason I've left it in."

Elizabeth joins them to watch adding as she sits, "Especially after what she pulled at the talent show a few weeks ago." Allison and Natalie grin, smiling and nodding thinking about the appalled whispers and lewd snickers as Courtney smirked her way through "I'm Just A Girl Who Can't Say No" from the musical *Oklahoma!*

Courtney steps out on stage leading with a bare leg in a sheer red dress. She approaches the Shriner's table.

"What better way for Rosie to get back at Albert then to do a stripper dance for a men's club." Allison remarks dryly.

Natalie waves her away, shushing. "I love this part." She's proud of her choreography, thinking she worked it out pretty well, considering neither Courtney nor any of the boys are really dancers. The boys sink suggestively below the table as if drowning. Hats fly, tassels twirl. Legs, feet, hands, arms poke out from under the table in all directions, representing the abstract orgy. The boys slowly rise and start to chase Rosie around the table.

Allison shakes her head. "And of course she only has herself to blame, getting this repressed men's club all hot and bothered…"

"Hush." Camp Director hisses but can't conceal her amused grin.

Natalie shushes them, "Wait, watch this." She points. Courtney falls from the table into the waiting outstretched arms of the six boys. They pass her around over their heads.

Allison can't help herself, "Look at them literally pass her around."

"That's nothing new for Courtney." Elizabeth grins.

Camp Director turns in her seat with a Devilish grin, "That's the other half of the reason I've left in the ballet."

Act 2 Scene 8.1

As ALLISON screams discovering NATALIE, so too does ELIZABETH scream in terror as VINCENT turns on her, strikes her.

Subservient and unquestioning Elizabeth slides seamlessly into living with Vincent at his mother's house in Yorktown. She lays in the dark of his bedroom, sunk down in the crack between the wall and Vincent's small single bed. He is snoring contentedly. She is sucking on her swollen lip, tasting the sweet stinging blood seeping from it. It all happened so fast, all of it leading up to and including this fat lip. She runs a finger lightly over it, feeling the contours of the split. The Ride seems so long ago now. How would her life be different if someone else had given her that ride? How different would it be if she'd never taken that ride? As it happened Vincent gave her that ride and she cried on his shoulder. It's practically predicated, it always leads to *I'm at the bar with my girlfriend.* Not that he'd asked her but then she hadn't questioned it either. Not long after she'd more or less just sort of moved in. Most of the time it feels like he is holding her hostage, keeping her around for rides. And revenge. Yet she can't leave. How did she fall in love with Vincent in the first place? She wonders this often, especially when he is calling her fat and ugly and punching her in the mouth.

She wasn't going to come back this time. It's been so many times but this time felt different somehow. There was a light of hope. A sparkle. Then Vincent's sister called. Could she please go over there to check on her mother, she couldn't get in touch with her and the mother was in the hospital, can Elizabeth please help. How could she not? The sister out of town couldn't get back for a few days, she was frantic, helpless. How could Elizabeth say no after all the time she'd spent under the woman's roof? On the way she couldn't help wonder if Vincent had been the one to put his mother in the hospital. The scene from a while back is still fresh in her head, how Vincent's mother practically begged Elizabeth to leave, to run. *They never change!* She had been reaching out, pleading as he stomped down the hall at his mother crawling away. He'd hit Elizabeth and when his mother finally tried to step in, he hit her too. Elizabeth had stood there frozen, unsure what to do. His mother stood up and pushed her, *Go!* she'd screamed at her, ordered her to get out. She had a terrible feeling what Vincent might do to her but she had calmed him down and all was eventually OK. *That time.* What if this time it wasn't? Vincent's sister said her mother fell, Elizabeth didn't ask if Vincent did it partly because if he found out and felt accused he might take it out on her. He's snoring lightly, rolling away on his side. The weight shift allows the bed to slide away from the wall a little, Elizabeth sinking deeper into the crack. The safe, familiar crack. She traces it all back to that ride. All his manipulation, abuse, it all started after that ride. But this time, this time was supposed to be different. She'd gone to friends for help. They stood up for her, they assured her, Jess offered to have him offed, but once she got here it's business as usual, how he needs her here now more than ever after all he'd done for her, after all his mother had done for her. He'd actually convinced Elizabeth to a degree that she had nowhere to go. She knew she could go home any time but still felt like she couldn't. After all he'd done for her. *To* her. How about *that,* Vincent? Elizabeth laughs nervously, covering her mouth quickly, not wanting to wake him. She shudders to think what her punishment might be for waking him. Vincent doesn't exactly have a nine to five job. He works at a bar, the Coachlight. He goes in at eleven AM. Day shift at a bar doesn't sound very lucrative but it's a bar full of local problem day drinkers. Most mornings, no matter how gently she tries to wake him for work, he calls her all sorts of vile names. Then there are the days a soft coo of "wakey wakey corn flaky" would be answered with a fist swinging at her face along with a blue streak of vile slurs. *Fucking fat cow dirty slut.* And that's just for waking him up to go to work. Come to think of it he called her a cow and threatened to break her face if she ever said anything like that to him again one morning at the Warehouse and they weren't even dating yet. *What the hell am I doing here?!* She should have stood him up that night, walked out and never looked back right then. She looks over at him, snoring, taking up most of his tiny bed. Most of her is tucked down in the crack. It's the only place she feels safe, if she's quiet. *Be quiet.* She recalls thinking that time at her house. *Be quiet.* She thought, as he wacked her in the head repeatedly with the Playstation controller. *I have to be quiet,* she'd thought insanely, not wishing to be heard by her family. It was her fault for leaning on the controller and starting the movie over. It had been extra bad as her cat had walked across the controller and restarted the movie twice already. They were watching 8 Mile. He beat her in the side of the head until she was nauseous and all she could think was not to make any noise and disturb her family. And Lord knows what they might have done to him. Why was she protecting him? He gave her a concussion with a video game joystick and she returns the favor with loyalty? Eminem was rapping about spaghetti and next thing Elizabeth heard was that familiar sound of impact, that hollow crack of the plastic smacking against the side of her skull. Her room got dim, she saw stars with each blow. She really should have been more careful. If only she had cried out, called to her brother or someone. Then again the first time Vincent had hit her, the very first time had been in embarrassment and frustration with her little brother getting the best of him on a trampoline with some theatrical wrestling moves. He's younger but quite large, much bigger than Vincent. He easily tossed Vincent around with the latest World Champion wrestling moves. Later Vincent took his loss out on Elizabeth. Even though the match had been all in good fun, Vincent's black eye wasn't fun, hers was even less. At least his was an accident. Elizabeth drifts off to an uneasy sleep with one knee on the baseboard radiator, her back to the wall.

Act 2 Scene 8.2

ELIZABETH is hastily shoving
things into a bag...

A bra, a shirt. Vincent is screaming at her, at this point she doesn't even remember why he's fighting with her. He goes off on her sometimes for so little who can remember from one day to the next? He tells her constantly how she trapped him in this relationship and how much he hates her. Elizabeth reaches for her keys. Vincent snatches them away,

"If you don't want me here why won't you let me LEAVE!?" She finally screams back.

He throws the keys back on the desk stepping between her and them, blocking her, screaming about how disgusting and disloyal she is. "I want to fucking kill you!" He screams in her face. He says he's going to kill her so often it no longer holds any water. It's just another thing he yells while he's smacking her around. And she's heard about enough of it.

"Why don't you just do it already!? I'm tired of fucking hearing it!" She yells in frustration. It's all so tiring, the fighting all the time.

"You fucking slut!" He shoves the phone in her chest, "Call him. He fucking cares. Let him come fucking get you." He screams. That's always what it's all about in the end. It's always about the Deli Guy. This poison, the jealousy, the fighting. It's exhausting. Elizabeth takes the phone. Maybe she will call him. He will come get her. So much of this fighting is about him anyway. She turns around and looks down at the keypad on the cordless phone. There is tightness in her throat. A pressure, a throbbing in her head. She's choking, she clutches at her neck. Vincent is pulling her scarf tighter around her throat. The room dims first, then it's brighter, brighter, almost white, her chest is hot and hard. She gasps for air but none comes. The room goes from a bright peaceful white to cool and dark. She crumbles to the floor. Vincent lets her fall, letting the scarf slide free from his grip, it slacks out from her neck. He watches her, she lays motionless for a few terrifying seconds then her chest heaves, she gulps in air in a sudden desperate long inhale. Her eyes snap open quick and wide then settle with her breathing. The room slides back into her view from black, back to a quiet ringing white light to a dimmer more surreal white haze. She looks around confused. Did that just happen? She feels her neck, she knows it did. The look on his face suggests it was real. He actually looks scared. Elizabeth is suddenly very tired. All this fighting, it's tiring. She lays down on the bed still dressed. Vincent lays down next to her. Elizabeth slides down into her crack between the bed and the wall and they both drift off into a nap.

Act 2 Scene 8.3

As usual, they're always so good at apologizing. It's practically normalized for Elizabeth. Of course she stays. It's been a few months since he choked her with her own scarf. She had to wear scarves since then for a few weeks to hide the bruises and friction burns. Hiding bruises is nothing new. The scarf look is cute. She's really good at hiding it by now and Vincent has gotten very good at his appearances. They even moved out of Vincent's mother's house into an apartment in Mahopac over an auto body shop. Their friend Tow Truck Joe works there. That helps Elizabeth feel a little safer. During the day. Vincent is building a recording studio in the space and acting very civil with Elizabeth, which she finds both amusing and suspicious. Suspicious because Vincent is conniving, amusing because she no longer cares. She wants to leave. All the fighting, all the jealousy, Vincent pushed her into his arms. Back into Deli Guy's arms. A girl can only be accused and punished for something she hasn't done so many times before she eventually just goes and does it. Vincent must smell it on her, she reasons. A couple of days ago he bought her flowers out of nowhere and last night he even wanted to have sex.

It starts with glances. Knowing looks, gentle innocent touches. A hand to an arm, legs touching under the bar next to each other. Too much eye contact. The world around them ceasing to exist. Vincent pays no attention to her at all. A girl needs attention. He gives it to her. If there is a video game to play or a guitar in Vincent's hands he pays so little attention that it happens right in front of him. Under a blanket in a room full of people or in the dark corner of the bar where no one is looking. It's exciting, they can be caught at any moment. A few months ago she took him into the stairwell just to make out.

He protested at first, "Vincent is my friend…" but all three of them know that it isn't really true. They hate each other and Elizabeth is the only thing keeping them civil and friendly. The excitement every stolen moment alone is, it's exhilarating. Strong hands on her -- gentle, sexy, not violent. If only she could find a way out. The courage to leave, to break free of Vincent's hold. He says she trapped him but it's her who feels trapped. Elizabeth this darkly amusing. It wasn't until after they moved to Mahopac that he dropped the pretext of his and Vincent's friendship. He was so cute afterwards, so paranoid of getting caught he obsessively hid the condom inside a Russian nesting doll of trash --

cigarette pack, fast food bag, used coffee cup, plastic shopping bag, buried deep but not all the way on the bottom in case it got dumped upside down lest it now be on top in a bag in a cup in a bag in a box right there in plain sight. That was the day Vincent brought home flowers and amore. After that they've taken any possible chance to slip away. One night right on the hood of Vincent's car in the parking lot while Vincent and everyone else were inside playing cards.

Last winter Nads was in town for the holidays and had gotten into some trouble. He'd been crashing in the apartment over the bar awaiting trial since then and the last week or two he's been crashing on the couch in Mahopac every few nights to break things up a little and help Vincent finish the studio. Elizabeth gets the feeling that Nads suspects something about Vincent and he's protecting her too. Tonight is his Going To Jail party. Tomorrow Elizabeth promises to drive Nads to court.

Act 2 Scene 8.4

Interior: The Eye, night

ELIZABETH:

You know I can't

Nads' going away party is an emotional affair. Everyone is drinking merrily and heavily. Between the bands and a large crowd the whole bar staff is busy. Elizabeth can see the pain in his eyes behind the bar where no one else can. On the outside, Deli Guy sings and spills beer in joyous celebration but his sad eyes scream 'leave him' when she makes eye contact. When Ethan passes out with his head on the bar they all cheer as Nads climbs the bar stool laughing, pulling out his Prince Albert and slapping Ethan's cheek with it. When someone passes out with their head on the bar the rules say you get a dick on your cheek. They usually draw it on with a marker. Deli Guy chivalrously hands Elizabeth the marker, deferring bartender's privilege to her. She musters all of her art school talents to lay a thick meaty cock across his face. When she finally gets the opportunity to be alone with him while Vincent is off dealing with the stage he breaks down. *Never Break Character*

"Stay with me tonight." Deli Guy pleads.

"You know I can't" It breaks her heart but she has to leave. She knows what she needs to do. She can end all of this, her pain, the physical and mental torture. His too. She's never going to let him have a normal relationship with anyone else anyway. She has to leave Vincent, but how? It's hurting her to leave the bar right now, to go where she doesn't want to go, be where she isn't wanted. Vincent has been cordial with Nads around, hasn't hit her at all as Nads would kill him if he did. That ends tomorrow and this party is all about that. Now they are leaving, Elizabeth, Vincent and Nads. Party's over. Courtney has been hanging around all night but keeping her distance from Elizabeth. Elizabeth has had her eye on Courtney all night. Watching her at the bar when she's asking for drinks. She looks down the bar and back at Vincent. Courtney can go have all the others, Elizabeth just wants these two. Doesn't even want one of them, the wrong one, the one she's leaving with. Courtney has noticed the stolen glances and pained looks. She's said nothing but she knows. She sees Elizabeth leaving, the look in her eye, the look in his. Oh and look here, Courtney notices her beer is almost empty. A sly grin crosses her face. A glint in Courtney's eye catches Elizabeth from the corner of her own eye as the door shuts behind her.

Courtney slides up to the bar. It's been a few years since they met at the Warehouse, she could smell Elizabeth all over him then and she can now too. *What are you doing to yourself, Elizabeth?* She thinks. *When are you gonna quit this charade?* She adds in the Reno voice, handing her empty bottle to him with a sweet look and bad intentions. *You're in love with him.* Elizabeth does have pretty good taste in men, he's pretty good looking. Don't know what she sees in Vincent but this one. Maybe she should have held onto him a little longer back then. He did throw her a nice birthday party.

"Can I have a beer please?" She purrs, sure to make their hands touch casually as she takes the cold wet bottle from him, innocent, meaningless, just enough. She can feel his attention try to follow Elizabeth out the door and she smiles.

Act 2 Scene 9

ELIZABETH sits excitedly in the big antique barber chair stretching out her arms on the armrests, legs straight, bouncing. ROZE is sitting in the chair next to her. CHUCK, the shop owner rolls up next to her on his stool, pulling on black latex gloves.

He snaps a glove dramatically and asks, "What can I do to you today, Elizabeth?" They all have a chuckle. Roze puts her hand on Elizabeth's arm and smiles.

"Independence day." Elizabeth declares. The first time it came up Vincent had made her feel terrible about herself, as usual. She'd only casually mentioned it flipping through a magazine. "I think I want to get a nose ring..." He hadn't even let her finish before launching into another one of his rants, ridiculing and forbidding her to do such a ridiculous thing. Threatening of course to break up with her if she defied him and pierced her nose behind his back. Somehow he even managed to suggest it would make her look fat, *Do these jeans make me look fat? No your ass does.* This time it's over and it's her doing. Their breakup needs to be final like he himself always used to half joke it would be. He could break up with her every month and she would come back so long as he had that hold on her but when *she* breaks it off it'll be the time it sticks.

"This is my Independence day." She told Roze and Lauren at Lauren's apartment that morning.

Without hesitation Roze said, "Let's go. I'll drive." Roze is a big advocate of empowering independence.

"Say, Chuck, why haven't you been around the Eye lately?" Elizabeth wrinkles her brow realizing this.

"I can't stand Vincent." Chuck deadpans, pouring alcohol on a small pad.

"Me too." Elizabeth thumbs herself in the chest and beams, "Let's do this."

Act 2 Scene 9.2

ALLISON in the passenger seat.
One man is driving, another man
in the back seat.

In her death, Allison takes on Natalie's spirit as a mission to keep Natalie alive, to keep all that was hers and radiate it back onto the world. Allison wants to keep Natalie's childlike wonder, the happiness in her heart, the perspective she once had. After the EMTs took Natalie, Allison had to go through all of Natalie's stuff to find phone numbers. Allison had to call Natalie's father in Pittsburgh and her babies' daddy. She called Natalie's mother. That one was the most difficult. It hurts Allison how Natalie had saved her and she couldn't save Natalie in return.

Allison saved the cookie fortunes from the night Natalie died and she takes them both to heart. Allison parted ways with April on the best of terms and put up her own website with April's full support and encouragement. www.allisonsvonderlande.com Allison framed Natalie's bag of panties and hung it on the wall behind her desk. You can see it in her profile picture in the background. She sells her own panties custom or stock, priced accordingly for every budget along with lots of other merchandise. Allisonsvonderlande.com will help over the next few years as pioneers in starting the cam girl industry. As well as front runners in the parody porn genre. A David vs. Goliath case against Allison which she ultimately wins helps catapult her website to success, inadvertently to the complainants best efforts. The Big Bad Wolf would appear monstrous in the public eye and be forced to concede opening the door to the flood of cosplay, Heneti and cartoon porn. She'll keep her favorite old snow globe on her office desk as a tongue in cheek wink and nod to her victory. A few years after that Allison will pioneer a green screen sex suit technology that enables her to provide very personalized content for her customers. It's an innocent enough idea but human nature's fantasies about fucking things it shouldn't will lead to a debate and lawsuit that will test the depths and limits of privacy and human decency. It works out fine for Allison but the debate will be swept aside when a seventy year old Christmas song becomes problematic and the internet turns on it. That all happens later.

Presently, late in 2005 Allison finds herself retracing a barhopping adventure with Natalie that seems ages ago now. She is partying with some car salesmen in Cortlandt Manor. They went to the little Irish cop bar where she and Natalie went for their first drink together. They've been to the Spanish bar down the hill. Allison suspects one of her car salesmen buddies stopped there for something other than a drink. The music was loud, sweaty little day labors grinding shamelessly on sweatier half-naked girls on a checkered dance floor. They didn't stay there long. Allison tried to check her car compatriots for a tell but they aren't trying to hide their inebriation. They pull into the rough dirt lot next to the gas station, home of the dive bar Allison and Natalie had stopped at that New Year's eve.

Allison walks in the Eye with a guy on each arm. She sits at a stool near the middle of the bar. Her car salesmen flank her standing in a territorial position around their female. Boys are funny. Allison is surprised when she turns to the bar and recognizes the bartender.

"Wow, Elizabeth, hi!" Elizabeth walks down the bar, greets the car salesmen by name. One asks for a Scotch the other a beer.

"And whatever Ms. Hart wants." the Beer adds triumphantly. Both take their drinks, leave an impressive pile of cash on the bar and go into the ladies room together.

Allison frowns her eyes, smiles, points after them, "Why...are they going to the ladies room?"

Elizabeth is unphased. "Everyone goes in there."

"There's two toilets?"

"I doubt they are going to take a piss. You want a drink, Allison?"

"Yeah, I'll have a Captain and Coke and why don't we let these guys buy you a drink too?"

"Oh no thanks. Can't." Elizabeth pats her stomach leaning back her other hand supporting the small of her back, "Knocked up." She hooks a thumb over her shoulder at the orb on the wall, "Maybe if there wasn't a camera, right?" She jokes, "No really though. Pregnant."

"Oh, how nice. Is it that guy from here, when I saw you a few years ago?"

"Well yeah, but there's a whole fucking book about how I got from then to..." She pauses, thinks, "..now."

Allison laughs rolls her eyes in reflection. "I know what you mean." She thinks about how long ago that seems now. They both do. Elizabeth thinks how much drama has led her to here and now, how reliable is he going to be? He ran off with Courtney the first chance he got before, all these girls laughing in the background when he called from California this morning. He'd sent her right into Vincent's arms and that was four years she could have done without. She still has the phantom pains of Vincent's abuse.

"So what have you been doing since then?" Elizabeth asks, setting Allison's drink down.

"Porn." Allison gives the shock time to settle and then gives Elizabeth the abridged version of how she got from then to now.

Elizabeth rubs her belly, taking in the story, thinking, "April…? That's a pretty name." Elizabeth thinks a moment, "Did he call you Ms. Hart?"

"I told them I was the Queen of Hearts when they asked me my name."

Elizabeth chuckles. "Didn't even question it?"

"I doubt they really care what my name is."

"So...what about Natalie? What's she up to?"

Allison's face twists, she almost whispers, It's still difficult to say and it still takes her by surprise. "Natalie passed away a few months...wow. Almost a year ago now..." She trails off. Elizabeth gives thought to where she was then. Scary.

Allison and Elizabeth talk about Natalie, her bubbly personality, how sweet she was.

"She only saw the sweetest things about a person."

"And she always looked great." Elizabeth adds with a smile.

"You know when I first ran into her she still looked good. Her hair and makeup done. It was like she was posed."

"I always say there is never excuse to not look your best. You know now that I think about it, I think I got that from Nat."

"That sounds like her."

They talk about Natalie's issues, which only leads to them thinking and talking about their own, similar issues. Allison noticed early on in camp that Elizabeth was developing the same way she had, both of them suffer from body image issues and subservience to men. Allison combats the latter these days by being a dominatrix in porn. Elizabeth tells Allison about the play they did the year after Allison moved to Gore. They did *Li'l Abner*. Elizabeth was a perfect fit for Daisy May as a thirteen year old with hips and boobs. They tied up her flannel and popped that budding rack up. They practically had their own spotlight. They stuffed her hips into some short short Daisy Dukes and she sang a song all about how she was washed up past her prime at eighteen because she hadn't landed a man. Courtney had no longer been at the camp.

"Do you know I ran into her while we were doing Li'l Abner, and this bitch acted like if she had been in camp I might have gotten the part still but only because I had boobs and she didn't. Still doesn't. She made it out like she could get whatever part she wanted on her talent but all I had was boobs."

"She really was a mean little girl."

"She fucking still is."

Act 2 Scene 10

Interior: Car-night

ELIZABETH alone looking at a lake.

Elizabeth is sitting in her car, gazing out at the familiar old lake once again. The lake sparkles silently with the street lamps reflecting in the rippling water. There is a light breeze. She's sat here in this parking lot so many times, when Vincent would throw her out. Or chase her out. That was all behind her.

She looks down at her belly, "It will be OK, little April, we'll do this together. You and me." She panicked back there at the bar. It all happened so fast. One minute she was battered and bruised at the hands of Vincent. Then she was rescued….by Vincent's best friend. It got so complicated. They had been friends since elementary school when Vincent lived across the street. Best friends, across the street. To Elizabeth's observation they hated each other but neither of them knew it. Or maybe they did. "They do now, Right April?" Elizabeth rubs her belly. Deli Guy had wasted no time once he'd rescued her from Vincent, no time at all, nailing her down. Knocking her up. All these terms are so aggressive. A Hostile Takeover. And then what does he do? "Oh, I'm going to go to California with Nads to help his brother's band on the road for two weeks and write about the trip in my column…" Run off with Nads to write about the west coast punk scene and leave me here knocked up and alone. Her own parents are out of town and don't even know she's pregnant yet. He's already taken off. "And what does your other Grandma say? Let's just say I don't think she has much faith in Daddy,"

At least the lake is consistent. *What was I thinking? He's not reliable! God knows what he's doing out there.* Sure he said something along the lines of an opportunity he'd likely never get again, nodding at her belly. *Opportunity to do what? Be a glorified roadie with a pen?* He's not even a decent writer and the *More Sweet Music Magazine* he writes for is a *free* paper. He takes it all so seriously but it's a silly hobby. *I mean who does he think he is? Almost Famous? It's all happening isn't it? All the little punk rock girl groupies, God knows what him and Nads, fresh out of jail, are getting into.* Elizabeth is not exactly brimming with confidence. In him or herself. He's off in California, her parents are out of town. She's lost all of her old friends to her abusive ex. She is alone and afraid and there is nobody to talk to about that. She looks down. A tear bubbles from her eye. The street light twinkles on the lake and in her watering eye. She grips the steering wheel with both hands squeezing, she rocks back and forth fighting back against crying. Elizabeth thinks for a moment, composes herself, starts the car. She needs a friend. An advocate. And she knows where to find one. Vincent alienated many of her friends but she has built-in friends that he can't touch. *Friends in law.* Deli Guy might be irresponsible and untrustworthy but he has a lot of friends who think of him as family, *so they will think of her that way too.* She rubs her belly as she drives out of Yorktown past the Eye and down into Peekskill. Not far from the river up on a hill overlooking Route 9 and the train station on a cute old city block not far from a brick paved spiral road that at one time was painted yellow. Yes, *that* yellow brick road. Not far from the Peekskill Military Academy. A Jacobethan revival neighborhood with a working class view of the Hudson. Elizabeth stops and pulls over on the opposite side of the street. The lights are on, it's not too late. Her heart pounds. She rubs her belly, "We need a friend, kid." She whispers. She gets out of the car. This part of Peekskill is fairly quiet. The faint sound of traffic in the distance below her on Route 9 is light. The street lights hum loudly, tinting the grey concrete yellow. The sun has since set between the mountains across the river. She can just see the tops of the spires on the Bear Mountain Bridge. One hundred and fifteen year old planks give warmly under her feet as she climbs the porch steps. The boards creak with her stride across the porch. The ornate wooden door before her, she knocks gently on the curtained pane of glass. A moment later the curtain whisks aside, eyes open wide in astonishment, the door whips open,

"Elizabeth! Come in, what are you doing here?" Roze welcomes Elizabeth into the house.

Act 2 Scene 10.2

Interior: Living room, day

ELIZABETH

I'm sorry...

Roze, Bill and a bunch of people Elizabeth doesn't really know at first glance, are gathered in small groups. Roze has a few friends over. Elizabeth walks across the threshold slowly. Shy. She can hear voices in the living room around the vestibule wall. She can't completely see them all yet. She wants to turn on her heel and bolt out the door, "I'm sorry," She stammers, "I didn't realize you had people…"

"No, come on in, there's always people here." Roze explains leading Elizabeth into the house, "Believe it or not I grew up in this house. I was able to buy it just a few months ago…" Roze is telling her as they enter the room. "You know when? Shortly after we went…" Roze points to Elizabeth's nose ring.

A few people are scattered around sitting in the large sitting room. Elizabeth doesn't know any of them except one. Bill. Bill's face lights up at the sight of Elizabeth. They have remained friendly. Bill only recently moved out of the apartment, but they have seen each other plenty. This context is surprisingly new, outside the bar with none of their usual buffers around, their history aside, the otherwise room full of strangers would be unbearable without him.

Mercifully there is an empty spot next to him on the couch. Bill pats the cushion loudly with his big hand, a big smile on his face, "Elizabeth my love, come sit over her with me," He brushes off the cushion and sneaks in a swipe or two on his mustache. Elizabeth chuckles, sits, Bill puts his warm loving arm around her, comically putting his leg over hers. He makes a show of awkwardly searching with his other hand for an acceptable resting place for it on her lap, grasping her hand briefly, mocking a boob grope and finding a few risque places for his hand on her thigh and knee before resting his hand on her lap, "How are you doing with Bebe Daddy out of town, do you need me to come back around, help you out..." He winks and nudges at her ribs playfully, "...if you know what I mean…?" He winks and nudges her some more with great comic exaggeration. Despite Bill's asshat way of making himself the center of attention, they talk as though they are alone in the room. Elizabeth realizes they have not had this intimate a conversation in a long while. She wonders had she been hasty choosing that moment to grow a spine. Perhaps she should have given Bill a chance to redeem himself, possibly explain? *No, what am I thinking?* She shakes off any lingering romantic what-ifs. *Explain what? What was he going to explain?* How he hadn't planned to get caught? How he planned to break it off with Bailey that night so he could be with Elizabeth? What if he was? She looks down at her belly and up at Bill, *For fucks sake if this kid was his there would be a foot dangling out of me already, our kids would be huge!*

"Who are all these people?" Elizabeth whispers in Bill's ear. Partly because she wanted to know and didn't want them all to hear. And partly, admittedly she likes to see him squirm a little. Her hot whisper tickles his ear and down his spine. He likes that and she knows it. He knows she knows it. She knows her whisper in his ear sends tingles right down to his co...xis. It's not wrong to want to be wanted, is it? A little harmless flirting, that's all.

"...I had sex with her baby's daddy…" Elizabeth hears a girl's voice say in the kitchen.

"What did that girl say? Did you hear that? Is she talking about me?" This angers Elizabeth and at the same time, it's humiliating. As much as she wants to jump up and run into the kitchen she can't, the glances, as she repeats the story over and over it seems to anyone who will listen. *I slept with her baby's daddy.*

Elizabeth is boiling to defend herself, looks at Bill, "Why is she telling everyone that? Did she?" She thinks frantically, panicking on the inside, she pulls closer to Bill.

"No, she didn't." Bill assures, "I know who that chick is. She drove him home one night a couple of years ago. He took her in the other room for a little while but she left after only like a half hour. He came into the kitchen and I tried to high five him," Bill puts his hand up and nods at it. Looks at Elizabeth, back at his hand, back at Elizabeth until she goes slowly to hit his hand, misses when he pulls away, "He left me hanging, says, 'I didn't fuck her.' I asked why, he said he put a movie on, they sat there for a few minutes and he tried kissing her and then he just stopped. Said something wasn't right, told her to go. Now she's saying she fucked him? That's fucking funny." Bill starts laughing, "Isn't that what he was supposed to do to her?" Elizabeth believes this is true, that was how he'd told the story himself, Elizabeth recalls, recognizing her from that night and they had talked about it after.

Elizabeth's eyes open wide, she slaps Bill's arm, "That girl! Her sister tried the same thing with Vincent! We all went to see Battery, not all together but we saw them there. She was going around saying she fucked Vincent after the show but he left with me. I drove him home. Where we lived together."

"I remember that."

"Why is she lying to these people I don't even know, I don't even know *her*!" Elizabeth is immensely perturbed, wanting to grab this girl and punch her mouth so she can then defend herself. They will all go the rest of their lives thinking some girl they met that time at that small gathering in Peekskill, that one girl slept with that other girl's baby daddy. They might even think it was recently, which it wasn't, and it wasn't even because he didn't fuck her. Elizabeth wants to run to the door and catch everyone in the house on the way out to set the record straight, *he didn't fuck her and it was like two years ago anyway, have a nice night* she would tell them with a hearty handshake and a pat on the back. *Yup, never happened, thanks for coming*. "Why is she even bringing that up?" She trails off and sinks under Bill's big hands as he massages her shoulders and neck.

"You know if it doesn't work out…?" He rolls his eyes down at her belly.

Roze smacks him on the shoulder, "Stop trying to pick up pregnant women."

Elizabeth spends much of the following week and a half at Roze's house. The girl telling lies did not come back again. It was of little consolation to Elizabeth as many of the people that were at Roze's that night have been back and all agreed that girl is kind of crazy. They all easily believe Elizabeth when she tells them her side of the story but the damage is done. She's mostly satisfied but it will still eat at her just a little, way in the back, *I fucked her baby's daddy* How many other skanks are going around saying that?

"And every time I talk to him on the phone there's girls laughing in the background. What am I supposed to think?" She vents to Roze. They are alone in Roze's studio, Elizabeth sists on the plywood floor watching Roze paint. There is something that doesn't sit right with Elizabeth every now and then...it nags at her even though she hasn't really seen Courtney since Nad's incarceration party. But there was something about the look in Courtney's eye when they were leaving that bothers

Elizabeth. A glint in her eye like she was up to something. That doubt sits in the back of her mind, taunting her.

Act 2 Scene 10.3

Interior: Roze's House

ELIZABETH sits snuggled into
BILL'S chest on ROZE'S couch.
Roze on the loveseat. Elizabeth
hangs up her phone, drops it in
her purse.

ROZE:

He's home?

Elizabeth nods, "He's coming over here now, that's OK, right?"

"Of course." Roze looks thoughtfully at Elizabeth, adds, "What's been going on with you two since he's been out there?"

"I've been intentionally vague with him, I didn't want to do anything or say anything too drastic."

"How's that working out?"

"I think it's worse. He sounds pretty frustrated with it."

"Well, he's concerned about you." Roze nods at Elizabeth's belly, "And the baby."

Elizabeth looks away bashfully, "I know it's just...he hurt me, going out there like that, leaving me here. Again."

"Didn't he discuss this with you?"

"He did, I guess, I mean it didn't feel like a discussion, it felt more like, 'I'm doing this."

"Is that what he said?"

"Well, I guess not, he asked my opinion but I couldn't really say no, he felt like he'd never get this opportunity again with the baby. That was how he put it -- 'When the baby comes… Like it's my...her fault, this." She rubs her belly, presenting it, "Which was all his idea. Then he runs off to California with Nads."

"Does he know you moved out of the apartment?"

"Most of my stuff is gone so maybe he noticed that. I don't know if he's stopping at the Eye, he sounded like he was coming here straight from the airport." As if on cue, Deli Guy appears walking up the front steps.

Bill pulls the curtain aside with a finger over his head, craning to see from his lounged position, "Yup, he's here." Elizabeth sinks defiantly further into Bill. He says hello to Roze at the door, old friends embrace. He looks in, sees Elizabeth comfortable and content. Bill's face is upturned in not quite a smile, but a cross between kidding and apology. He looks at her. His smile fades, his excitement to see her dulls, she takes all the wind from his sails, he looks hurt.

Elizabeth steels her reserve, "Hey." She says cooly. Too casually, avoiding eye contact. Too cool, above it. Beyond it. Cry me a river, build a bridge and get over it. He wants to embrace her but she won't let him in, gives him no opening,. *Yeah you're here, no big deal.* His temperature rises, glaring at the seated pair. Here he is wanting to hold her, tell her all about his adventure, and she won't let him. He's confused, angry, frustrated. The awkward silence between them is thick, heavy, agonizing. Finally he storms out. Roze and Bill stare at Elizabeth with stunned astonishment. Elizabeth struggles to change the subject.

Bill offers his prophecy, "Wait till he gets home." It hangs in the stagnant air, time stands still like they are waiting for it.

Her phone rings, breaking the tense silence that seemed to linger since he'd left. "I moved out." She answers the phone, quietly. His cry of frustration fades away, there's a crash and the line goes dead.

Act 2 Scene 10.4

Interior, Car-evening

ELIZABETH is driving.

Over the next few weeks Elizabeth needs time to reflect. Scared and alone, it's all a lot to process. He's ranting at the deli to anyone who will listen about his "crazy baby momma." He's certain she isn't going to let him see the baby now. Her sister says she should stop giving "The Emperor" such a hard time. Every time she's seen him he's cloaked in a hood and "looks like the Emperor from Star Wars." Last week he dropped a bunch of her stuff off at Roze's house, leaving it in a heap on the front porch. Elizabeth hadn't noticed it and most of got ruined in the rain. They had fought on the phone, all he wanted was to check on her, see if she needed any rides. She is certain he doesn't see the irony. Doctors appointments or whatever. She makes it difficult without even knowing why. She left those boxes of stuff at his house on purpose to keep the connection. She didn't really want to leave, and planned to go back all along, didn't she? *Right?* She just needs time to think. Things with Vincent hadn't even finished playing out yet and he already wanted to start putting babies in her...she deserved some time to think, didn't she?

Elizabeth pulls into a spot in front of the hospital. She's only a few weeks into her first nursing job. As she kills the engine her cell phone rings. It's Vincent. *Oh God I don't need this shit right now.* She answers anyway.

"OK, you can come back, I want you to come back but I'm not raising someone else's kid." He tells her, quite presumptuously she thinks. She recognizes how he's trying to make this about him.

"No. I don't want you in my life anymore. This is what I want." She knows it's true as she says it, *this IS what I want, isn't it?* It feels good to be the one saying "I don't want you" for a change. Vincent hangs up with a huff, his last ditch effort going nowhere. Elizabeth realizes, *Now I have to fix this...if I can. Am I being unfair to him? what have I done?"*

Thoughts swirl around her throughout her shift. It feels good to take the power back, or have any to begin with for that matter. Elizabeth has never really had any power with any of the men in her life, least of all Vincent. When he hung up she expected to be heavily affected and distraught, as she's accustomed to after any ordeal with Vincent in the past, but thankfully she feels none of that. She feels good. She feels good about herself for a change. *I'm making the choice this time.* She assures little April as much as herself, rubbing her belly. For the first time *she's* in control. That's the whole of it -- she's the one with the doing power. She rubs her belly again, "We'll get daddy back, baby." She thinks back to Vincent's pathetic plea disguised as an order, fiddling with a seam on her steering wheel. It's slowly dawning on her, her nail stuck under a loose thread, *I'm not raising someone elses kid though. Fuck him.* She rubs her belly, "We're a package now." She says with a smile, realization dawning on her face, warming her like a sunrise, she casually picks at the loose thread, "No. I don't want you anymore." She says again. That was the time. Vincent said it would be, for all the times he cast her out she would keep coming back every time until the time when she was the one saying 'I don't want you.' That was when it would be for good. That time has finally come.

That night, Elizabeth walks into The Eye. There is a girl sitting at the end of the bar where Elizabeth likes to sit next to the opening. Elizabeth sits next to her.

The girl looks at her, recognizes her from the pictures on the wall next to them, "Hi, you must be Elizabeth. I'm Alain." Elizabeth gets the feeling she had just been talked about. Alain nods towards Deli Guy, conveniently holding court behind the bar. "We went to high school together. I was a couple of years ahead of him." Without looking at Elizabeth, he puts a soda down in front of Elizabeth and a beer in front of Alain. Alain pushes her cash forward on the bar. He holds up a hand refusing the cash and walks away. "When he was a freshman I was a junior." Alain explains, "I was dating a senior. He was beating me up, in private, of course." She takes a sip of her beer, places it back down daintily. "I see this poor guy walking down the hall one day, his hair was all shaggy and he was wearing a metal band shirt. I grabbed his arm and said, 'come with me,' walking past my boyfriend." She stopped held up a hand, "Ex-boyfriend. I took him outside and gave him a sip of my vodka and a smoke."

"Your vodka?"

"I put vodka in a juice bottle from the cafeteria, anyway, he helped me get past that, I'm sure he was terrified, poor kid, he was scrawny in ninth grade." She chuckles at him with a warm smile. He smiles back but still won't look at Elizabeth, "My ex was one of those big, scary seniors and the singer in the school's big metal band." Alain looks down the bar, Elizabeth following her gaze. She can see his frustration. He saved Alain. He didn't even know he did, he barely knew he was saving Elizabeth. He did save her too. Sort of. In a bumbling sort of way.

Outside it's starting to rain, light but steady. Elizabeth listens to Alain talk about old times at the Eye when she worked here. Alain is telling Elizabeth about a fist fight at the Eye a long time ago. A Rebel, a Joker, a bunch of Cycle Tramps, they all came with Pete from Chumper's, a fight broke out, Michelle the bartender was pregnant and a few guys, Andy and Big John T were protecting her. Elizabeth looks down at her belly and thinks about how he wanted her to leave the bar a few months ago while a band was filming a video for a song about being Lionhearted. He's been a little protective and she can't blame him. She hasn't exactly made his life easy, even if he deserved it sometimes. That all has to change now. He'd been calling and asking about the baby without being a stalker, talking about the 'us' thing. Not trying to pressure her, not too much. He didn't really want her seeing Vincent and who could blame him for that? He wasn't even really mad when Courtney called him from the Coachlight and told him Elizabeth was down there doing blow, drinking Michelob and flirting with Vincent. He even said when she picked up the phone, "I already know the answer to this but humor me, were you…?" Obviously she wasn't. "I don't even drink beer. Or do blow, why would I start now, at six months pregnant?' Elizabeth knew Courtney was just being petty.

Alain is talking about people Elizabeth doesn't know. He brings Alain another drink. Still won't look at Elizabeth. He'd had a very frustrated sounding fight with Roze on her porch a few weeks ago. She's been quite an advocate for Elizabeth and nobody can call anyone out or talk them down quite like Roze. Most people have a hard time saying no to him but she always has his back even if he needs tough love. Elizabeth had been eavesdropping on the fight, found it funny when he awkwardly blurted out an accusation along the lines of Roze suddenly likes Elizabeth better. "I don't even know what I'm saying." he defended himself when she called him out on how childish and stupid he sounded. Elizabeth looks at Alain, she's telling more old-time Eye stories in a quiet calm monotone. Her posture is proper and Elizabeth can see how she probably looked like a girl in a heavy metal video in the eyes of a dorky high school freshman with that sparse dirt mustache he was trying to cultivate. Oh yeah, Elizabeth has seen those pictures in his photo albums he tries to quickly flip past.

It's not very busy in the bar tonight and even Alain leaves pretty early. Elizabeth slips out and watches people leaving from the car. The lights in the bar finally go out. A few minutes go by before the lights go on upstairs in the apartment. He's sitting silhouetted in the window, talking to someone in the room, she can't hear. The apartment window is open but the car window is not. It's raining still, the rain sliding down the windshield makes the view an unstable blur. She's scared. Can she really count on him this time? She gets out of the car. He looks down at the sound when her car door slams shut. Elizabeth stands under the window looking up.

"Can I come in?" She asks, the rain drops hide her tears. He is looking down at her, stonefaced and quiet. It feels like forever. *Say Something!* she screams in her head.

"I'm scared!" She confesses, the rain streaking down her face, her sad eyes looking up in the rain, blinking. He looks hurt, unsure. He must be scared too.

He takes a deep breath that she thinks he might blow her away in a mighty huff and puff but he sighs, "Come on up."

Act 2 Scene 11

Interior:The Eye-night, raining

ELIZABETH walks slowly up the stairs to the apartment.

He takes her in out of the rain. Shelter from the storm. He listens with patience, surrenders, surrenders himself to her. To the child growing within her, his baby girl. Elizabeth feels it. He understands that he needs to be patient and he is. When he takes her to dinner for her birthday it's a kind gesture for the mother of his child, not a plea for their reunion. She can feel it, his sacrifice.

Then he gives her the ring. "Save this for your...our daughter." He says with acceptance. The ring shines like a bright star in the dim light of the booth in the themed chain steakhouse. He hands over the gift "for the baby" with a wise faith and it works. A surrender to faith. By the holidays Elizabeth realizes that it is time to move from this tiny apartment. This tiny hot apartment above the loud smokey pirates den might not be the best place to have a baby. By the end of January they've found a new place not far away to start a new family. Only a few blocks from the Eye can be very far away, time and space warp around the center of the universe.

Courtney walks into a nearly empty bar. It sings like a song and dance number in her head, *This place is mine.* She can smell it. She sits at the bar next to a young guy, Bobby, who has been hanging around trying to get bands on the stage. The bartender approaching her is new.

"Hi, I'm Kevin." He tells her, "What can I get you?"

"Can I have a beer?" She puts a bill on the bar in front of her, looks to the guy next to her, "Are there any shows this week?" Courtney had been trying to get Serj to help her start a band. They've been on and off for years, times like now she questions why they are on. He's still riding out his claim to fame story about having been in some band that got fairly big a few years ago after kicking him out just days before they were to sign to a major label.

"Where's Serj?' Bobby asks Courtney.

"I don't even know." Courtney rolls her eyes and just when she is thinking old Serj is about as good for her singing career as an English patient, a couple of her old friends walk in. The Eye is creepy like that -- it always seems to provide what you're looking for.

They sit at the bar, have a few drinks and talk about the old times and the not so old times, as you do sitting at the Eye. They chat with a few of the bar's regulars, Johnny Rotted from Punk Rock Zombies and a guy they call Potso. Back at the Warehouse, Courtney would sit in and sing a few songs with the band.

"I'm trying to put together a new band." She tells them.

'Are you planning on having Serj on drums?" Potso asks.

"You know, I was going to...we've been looking for people to play with," She looks around, "But I think I don't want to be in a band with him, you know? He can go be an English teacher."

A few hours, a few more drinks and some phone calls later Courtney has a new band. She goes into the ladies room and tags the wall with her black magic marker.

Act 2 Scene 11.2

Interior: Oregon Road Apartment, day

ELIZABETH is sitting in the rocking chair his mother gave him from the baby shower.

He is standing in the middle of the room looking around at the piles of stuff. He looks exhausted and overwhelmed. "That's the last load -- man, those stairs." They just moved to The Locust Hill from The Eye into a little two bedroom on Oregon road. It's a colonial house converted to a three-family apartment building. They live on the second floor. "We're going to have to move...where are we going to put all this stuff?" He's overly OCD about the efficient use of space and storage which Elizabeth finds endearing. He smiles, "Do you still have that jar?"

Elizabeth laughs, "My mother threw it out when they moved. I can only imagine what she thought, it was growing colonies."

He laughed with his flirty grin, "Gross. But that was hot." He loves to jerk off in front of her and she loves to watch him, she always had. She had been pretty sure she could get that sample when she brought it up. It seems like a lifetime ago. He volunteered right away when Elizabeth mentioned it was a thing she and her friends talked about it. She knew he would. When he asked her if she wanted to watch she was casual about saying yes but in her head she really wanted to. When he asked her if she wanted to help it sounded rehearsed. Of course she helped.

Elizabeth bites her lip and changes the subject. "Who's working the bar this weekend? Are they having a show?" She knows he's concerned about this as well. The bar, the bands, his stage, it's all sort of been his baby for a while but now with his actual baby on the way he's had to step back from that and doesn't like to give up control. She's learned that he's a bit of a control freak, which explains the stacking and sorting OCDs. She realizes her own father has a bit of a controlling personality and it's the one way he's like her father. She found a guy who is almost the opposite of her father in so many ways. Except that one. Go figure. *We really look for our father in a man don't we?*

"Bill got that guy Kevin from the videogame store to move into the apartment and take my shifts. Isn't it funny how he looks like Kevin Spacey?"

"Are we sure he's not Kevin Spacey?" He walks to the window and looks out at the Hillside Cemetery across the street, "Come outside with me." Elizabeth says, standing slowly, hand on her lower back.

"I wish you'd quit."

"The doctor said the stress of withdrawal is worse on the baby than smoking."

"Yeah, yeah, you've said."

Outside they sit on the front steps while Elizabeth has a cigarette. A family of four lives on the first floor. They have one young kid and an infant. The mom pulls in the driveway. She gathers the infant and with the older kid in tow, rushes past them covering the baby looking at Elizabeth in horror.

Elizabeth exhales a long stream of smoke, motioning to the mother. "Kind of dramatic, don't you think?"

"I know, you're outside. You aren't blowing smoke on the baby."

"She's totally judging me. Did you see that look? And wasn't that kind of rude the way she pushed past you? You were even trying to get up and get the door for her."

"Yeah, she wasn't having it."

"Can we smoke a bowl? The doctor said I can, that it doesn't cross the blood brain barrier and it will calm me down, she said I should smoke weed instead of cigarettes."

"You should. What do you think she'd think?" He hooks a thumb over his shoulder at the first floor with a snicker. 'Let's go upstairs and smoke under the hood fan over the stove."

For the last few weeks leading up to April's arrival they are in their own little world. Nothing matters except for their growing little family. They go for a ride on a nearby dirt road per the advice of an old wives tale. With the baby imminent she finds herself calling him Daddy. This reminds her of her own parents and grandparents calling each other mother and father or grandma and grandpa. It's like a rank. Once achieved that's your title. One is always referred to by what you are to the smallest of your tribe.

All her life and especially the last nine months Elizabeth has always heard that childbirth is the kind of pain you forget. These last few pushes she no longer believes it.

"...Those goddamn liars!" Elizabeth is screaming.

"Push Elizabeth! You're doing great!" The doctor is saying enthusiastically.

"There is no way I'm forgetting this pain!" A flash before her eyes, a montage of every time she's heard a woman in her family from her great grandmother to her mother and aunts say *pain you forget*. In a detached moment of lucidity, Elizabeth points to the TV and explains to the nurse what's going on in the *Law and Order* episode, "I've seen this one recently." She chirps in a chipper casual tone.

"Push!" The doctor is encouraging, the nurse discreetly wipes away the feces squeezing out of her.

"They don't tell you that either. Oh you forget the pain do you? Did you forget to mention you SHIT YOURSELF GRANDMA!!?" Elizabeth screams while she bears down to push. "Like a GODDAMN toothpaste TUUUUBE!!!!!!"

"Push!" Elizabeth can't help think how mortified she would be under normal circumstances to shit in front of strangers, yet here she is, sweating, screaming, feet in the air, slinging an Exorcist-worthy string of profanities at a room full of strangers, in her vagina like they are sharing coffee and scones at a table in a delicatessen casually talking about their day at work. The snip sound of her taint as it gives way under taut pressure to the surgical shears. And there he is, soon-to-be-new daddy, faithfully holding up a sweaty cramping leg ignoring the shit and blood, staring in awe at his daughter being born.

He looks up from her crowning vagina to her flush sweaty face with a big dumb smile, "You're doing great." He hardly even winces as she digs her nails into his arm. He calmly brushes hair from her face, "You're doing great." He whispers again, still calm.

"Fuck you, you did this to me!" She screams hoarsely despite her weak smile. He doesn't take it personally at all.

"Push, Elizabeth...you're almost done!"

"Ohhhhh...I'm gonna remember this pain! I'm gonna remember this! Imma 'member it good! All this charade telling girls you forget the pain, it's all a big sham, a flim flam I tell ya! A big joke, all the moms are in on it! Oh sure...tell her it doesn't even hurt, tell her you forget all about it...well not me! No sir! I'm telling everyone...!"

"Push!" The doctor tells her and then there's a white light, a massive release and a ringing silence. It's bliss. She almost doesn't notice him stumble through the corny jokes he'd rehearsed for nine months waiting for this moment, how long he'd waited to say "Put an extra stitch in for me, Doc," when they sewed up the episiotomy. She mostly misses his nervous performance. All she notices is the pain has gone away, fading like a morning dream.

Then it seems like she can't speak, she hears nothing, "Is she OK?" It feels like forever, time stands still nobody answers her. A chill of panic grips her spine with icy fingers "Is she OK?!" She repeats with more urgency and a little panic in her voice. It's like she's gone invisible. They can't see or hear her, she's about to scream and then a small warm bundle is weighing down on her chest. Big blue eyes looking up at Elizabeth. "She's perfect." Elizabeth coos with a dreamy smile, brushing a sweaty clump of hair off her face.

"She is." He says softly. Elizabeth forgets.

Act 2 Scene 11.3

Interior: Hospital-evening

ELIZABETH wearily wheels herself
down the corridor.

"Man…they fawn over you for nine months…" she's grumbles lightheartedly, "…and as soon as you squeeze that kid out it's like you don't exist." Proud poppa beams down a goofy smile into the rolling hospital bassinet twenty paces ahead. He's imparting advice to his newborn daughter, likely some silly thing he's overthought and rehearsed since the day she told him she was pregnant. Still, he could wait up for her. "Hello?! I just had a friggin baby here…"

Over at the bar, Courtney walks into The Eye with Serj in tow. On again. He's justified her new band without him as a good thing -- they can concentrate on different directions. He's putting something together, auditioning people to join him -- ex-members of low-level has beens. Courtney confidently with the upper hand flirts openly with a guy at the bar to get under Serj's skin. Serj sits a few stools away and strikes up a conversation with Kevin behind the bar.

Next to the guy at the bar is Gene from the band Battery, he nods to Courtney, "Hey Court, this is my big brother."

Courtney smiles, lays her hand in big brother's. 'Nice to meet you big brother. You guys want to smoke?" She produces a bowl from her pocket, "Packed and ready." They all three get up from the bar and go out onto the back porch.

Kevin feeds Serj a few too many shots and he begins to pour his guts out to Kevin. When Courtney comes back in Serj stands up with a sudden jerk, accidentally knocking over his stool in the process. He sputters something incoherent in the jealous boyfriend tone. Gene and his brother come in behind Courtney and Serj points at big brother.

"You!" He says clearly. Serj then tears off his shirt like a wrestler and charges forward in a clumsy march. Big brother laughs, easily batting Serj to the side. He crashes head first into the brick wall under a thick wooden shelf.

"I'm a United States Marine, buddy -- I kill people for a living. You sure you want to do this?" Courtney scoops Serj up and drags him out back, nurses his black eye. No hard feelings. But that doesn't stop Kevin from spreading drama with his new favorite toy: social media.

Act 2 Scene 11.4

Elizabeth rocks in the chair in little April's room, reading. April should be up soon.

Daddy pokes his head in, "Hey I'm going to take a quick shower. What'cha reading there?" He asks as the book cover in her hands catches his eye. She holds it up for him to see the cover fully.

"Fresh in my Freezer, by this chick Gail Bohun. She draws a bunch of comics, graphic novels and shit. She wrote this book about the problematic themes in horror and horror music…"

"Keep you fresh in my freeeezer…" he sings, walking away. "OK taking a shower." He calls as the bathroom door shuts behind him, clipping his voice off.

Elizabeth reads some more until she hears the baby. "Oh you're awake?" She coos to April. She's quietly gurgling happily in her crib, "Did you hear your Daddy?" Elizabeth asks, her lifting her up. "Who needs a diaper change?" She sings, lifting the baby up and swinging her around and over to the changing table, "I do, I do Mommy," She says for the baby, "Weeee." April soars around the room, plants down on the changing table with a giggle. Elizabeth lays her down and sings to her while she goes about changing her diaper. "She's a baby. Whoa whoa whoa she's a baby, talking about, the little baby," She sings, "Ahhhh Tom Jones!!" She shrieks in whisper, tossing the wet diaper into the trash like a bra onto the stage, "See, get it?" She smiles at the baby, 'Cause the diaper is like your, because ladies used to throw their…Never mind," She pokes the baby's nose. "I don't know why, they just do, they want to have the sex with Tom Jones, they just do." Elizabeth carries the baby into the kitchen, where he's at the table breaking up weed on a paper plate. "Look who's up from her nap." She announces, lays the baby across his lap. "Here, Daddy."

She begins to prepare dinner while he tells Elizabeth about his day. He's taken a job with Rabid Mike, snaking drains in supermarkets. "I swear the meat department treats the floor drain like a trash can…" He's complaining, describing in graphic detail the look and smell of dirty water backing out of a floor drain clogged with fat and rotting meat scraps, "And don't even get me started on the grease trap…!"

Elizabeth intervenes, "Yes, please don't." looking down suspiciously at the meatloaf she's about to put in the oven.

It's warm for early spring and warmer in the second floor apartment. When Elizabeth had put little April down for a nap she had been in just a t-shirt. When she got her up she took off the sweaty t-shirt, a tiny baby sized white tee with a little blue Ramones logo. She changed her and brought her out in just her fresh diaper. Now she is laying across Daddy's lap where Elizabeth laid her face down.

He rubs her back some after breaking up the weed then rolls his after dinner joint. "Oh man, I got weed on the baby." He says casually as he twists the joint. He lays the joint on the plate and brushes off her back, picking her up and looking into her face.

"Do you hear yourself?" Elizabeth asks him but he seems unphased by how ridiculous he sounds.

Instead tells the baby in his soft daddy daughter voice, "I banged your mom last night."

Elizabeth gasps, "Don't tell her that!"

"What's the difference? She's barely a month old, she doesn't know what I'm saying." To the baby he adds, "Do you?" In the soft daddy voice. He hates living here in this apartment, Elizabeth can tell. She knows. She knows him better than anyone. It's not even just that he says it -- it's his mood, posture, mannerisms. She can tell by the way he carries himself that he feels like a guest here. He can't seem to get comfortable and she can't blame him. They can barely walk around barefoot on the carpet let alone have sex in their own bed without a broom handle hitting their floor from downstairs. "They make me feel like an intruder in my own home!" He complains after dinner as they huddle under the hood fan over the stove to smoke his after-dinner joint.

"You got weed on the baby you friggin pothead." Elizabeth giggles, trying to hold in her hit passing him the joint.

"At least it's just weed." he says and hits the joint. "It's not like I got blow on her." He gently taps the ash into his special pot ashtray, "I hate that I have to stand under this fan. I'm a goddamn grownup, I want to smoke pot at my table or in my dad chair. I feel like I'm in middle school." He takes another pull and passes it back to her.

"Do you hear yourself?" She asks him again.

"What? It wouldn't be a problem at all if I came home from work and had a few beers or a glass of whiskey, would it?" He doesn't wait for an answer, she knows not to bother, he's on a roll. "It sure was a problem when my dad did. Nobody smokes a joint and then goes and beats up their wife and kids." He takes the joint from her and absently rubs the ash into the ashtray twirling the joint between his fingers, "I have a decent job, we pay our bills, we pay rent to live here, why can't I do this?" He holds up the joint for her to see as if she doesn't know. He misses living over the Eye and she knows this. Even though this was all his idea and he would never admit it, he misses that life and a part of him still wants that life. He lived like Peter Pan into his thirties and while he's a good and loving father, he just needs time to adjust to adulting, she assures herself, noting how he has said he had been left unsupervised for a long time. Now that he's gotten her stoned, Elizabeth goes down to the front steps for a cigarette. She doesn't see the difference but he insists she smoke tobacco outside. Just as well, Elizabeth gets a little uncomfortable around the baby when she's high. He's unphased by it. Pothead.

Outside, Elizabeth is sitting on the step smoking, flipping through a Pennysaver, the local classifieds that comes in the mail. She can't help but notice it's gotten a little slimmer lately due to the internet. People are even getting online to some degree on their phones now. The wealth of the world's knowledge, right in the palms of their hands. Elizabeth looks at her cell phone laying neatly on top of her cigarettes, back at the paper in her hands. She flips past the ads to the rental exchange. An ad for a four bedroom down in Montrose catches her eye and she calls the number on impulse, leaves a message. She lights another cigarette, thinks about the ladies room wall up at the Eye. The talk between her and Courtney has been silently escalating but last time Elizabeth went up there by herself, he did promise such rewards for giving birth, she had noticed graffiti in the bathroom in black magic marker. It said, "A mother doesn't act this way." She recognized Courtney's signature tag style right away, she knew it had to be meant for her. Elizabeth realizes with Courtney's band she has a stage to perform from. This leads Elizabeth to think she needs to get back onstage. Since she stopped performing in drama camp musicals she's been victim to too many assaults, both physical and emotional. It had snowballed there for a while, hell it was an avalanche of crumbling confidence. She needs to challenge herself. She needs an outlet. She needs to get back on stage. Just a few years ago she couldn't even sing in front of three friends with their backs turned and the lights off. Despite that vivid memory, Elizabeth wants to start a band. She stubs out her smoke, collects her stuff and walks briskly up stairs and into their apartment, declaring, "I want to start a band." The door shuts behind her and she walks to the center of the living room.

He is sitting in the chair with the baby in his arms. He looks down at the baby and back up at Elizabeth, "Now you want to start a band?"

She's shuffling through a drawer, pulls out a notebook, "Yes." She sits down in the chair next to him and starts to write words on the first blank page in a notebook with a few doodles in it. She had been drawing in it at Monk's ill-planned coffee house.

He points out the time she had a hard time singing in front of him, Vincent and Monk, "...With our backs turned and the lights off..."

"That's going to change." She says defiantly, without looking up from her notebook. "I wasn't always like that, you know..."

Bill had seen the end of their reign over the Eye coming to a close from a mile away. It happens. When this room became available to him he saw it as an omen. Life changes, and the more it changes the more it stays the same; but it doesn't. You can't go back. There's no going home. People do what people do and then pair off and make more people. You can't hold onto your heyday if you need two hands to handle the present. Bill had been singing in a band for a few years now but he'd wanted to pick up the bass guitar. Munky moved out of this room and as a result out of the band. Bill picked up the bass and the room for one low price. When Elizabeth moved into the Eye it hurt Bill. He would never say so -- he loves them both and would never hurt them. He also didn't want to watch them pair off and make more people. He can be supportive, he just doesn't have to watch. Only to move into this little room and watch a young family grow anyway. Bill smiles at the thought of it, plucks out a rhythm. Music is just like an engine to Bill. It comes natural to him. He also realizes it was their reign over the Eye that gave them the music scene, something that none of them were willing to let go of. Knowing Big Daddy was going to have his hands full with Elizabeth and the baby, Bill had one more move up his sleeve. On his way out the door he turned Kevin on to the place. Bill knew Kevin would see the opportunity and keep it going for them. The music scene that is. They needed someone on the inside. Bill is sure Kevin can be that guy on the inside. Bill knows Kevin from the videogame store in the Cortlandt Towne Center. He was perfect for their needs, and bringing Bobby with him will keep the momentum going. Bill is still not sure what to do about Vincent.

He hasn't been around much and Bill isn't sure how he's going to react to seeing him. Not much scares a guy Bill's size but Elizabeth running out that door into Bill's arms, fleeing, that look of terror in her eyes, that was scary. He'd heard here and there about Vincent in court and his new band through the scene but he hasn't been coming to the Eye and he downright avoids Bill. Someone had to look after the bands. So Bill brought in Kevin. He suggested to Mike that Kevin run the bar in Pete's absence. Kevin recognized quick that the only time the bar makes money is when there's a show. So Kevin does exactly as Bill wanted. This cramped little room in his friend's house though? Especially since the baby from the growing young family isn't a baby anymore and is a kid with opinions and personal space issues, which are now invading his.

Act 2 Scene 11.45

Interior: Oregon Road Apartment-evening

Elizabeth addresses April in her
swing as she pushes the vacuum.

"Big hard-working Daddy guy will be home any minute." She says over the vacuum. She's a little nervous. "We're going to meet Daddy's buddy from the old days. Daddy will tell you tales of the old days one day. Over and over." She says with a smile at the happy baby. Daddy comes home as expected excited to see his old friend. Randy hasn't lived in New York in about as long as Elizabeth has known daddy. "Apparently when they grew up, well, Uncle Randy became what Daddy calls a Metro Sexual." She grows more nervous waiting for their guest. Butterflies flail in her stomach like it's a house party inside her. She is nervous about impending judgment or approval...something she can't quite put her finger on.

When Randy arrives at a decent hour he brings with him gifts. They take the milestone pictures for Daddy's photo album. His photo album has always been and is of growing importance to him, now with his family growing. Randy is pleasant enough with Elizabeth, though a little dry. Maybe he's nervous too, maybe for similar reasons.

Then he hits her with, "So is this really his kid?" Elizabeth can't tell if he's trying to be funny, trying to because it isn't fucking funny at all and now she isn't sure how to feel about old roommate Randy. And she is sure he's looking at her like he thinks he recognizes her but can't place where from. Then it hits her. *Good God don't recognize me! Of course these two metalhead chuckles went to see that movie, he looked at me the same way once?*

Act 2 Scene 11.5

Interior: Large Kitchen-late afternoon

ELIZABETH SETS IT ALL UP.

Everyone is happy. She has her family, baby and daddy, for love and safety. She has Bill to feel chaste and Dan to feel fabulous, all under one roof. In the shadow of the Indian Point Nuclear Power Plant but it's in a cute little neighborhood. They're like a regular Nuclear Family. OK. not quite *regular*. She has a band as an outlet to pour out her rage, anger and humiliation, and a bottle of pills to take the edge off once in a while.

Even found time to get married. Went out and picked up a modest cut cream white dress with a plunge-y but classy neckline and matching low-heel shoes, which she calls her Gettin' Hitched Shoes. She looks back to when he proposed. Sort of. He didn't really ask so much as command. It was sweet. She could never forget it. They had gone to Wendy's on a burger run. He turned to her romantically and demanded, "Marry me."

And of course her storybook answer, "But it smells like French fries and I have a boyfriend." Storybook. A year and a half later she's ditched the old boyfriend and had a baby so she figures it's about time. She makes some calls. She looks down at her sparkly ring which she loves. Dan and Daddy pull in and come up the steps, in the back kitchen door. They have been working with Rabid Mike and the plumbers together. "Hey Dan, Hey Big Hard Working Daddy Guy, how about we get hitched Friday?" She holds up the shoes, "I got these Getting Hitched Shoes already so…" She smiles, throws her arms around his neck gives him a big kiss.

Another milestone moment, she could never forget his romantic storybook answer, "Uh, OK." Swoon. Storybook.

Dan, hand to mouth gushes gaily, "Aw. I love weddings."

Friday Bill and Roze come to serve as witnesses along with Dan and Elizabeth's family. That's what they call the best man and the maid of honor at town hall: Witnesses. They stand before the honorable Judge McCarthy.

They say, "I do." They sign here. They can now file joint taxes. Storybook. The American Dream.

In the parking lot they decide on The Colonial Diner on Old Crompond Road to take the wedding party out for breakfast and hand April over to grandma and grandpa.

Over breakfast Daddy tells their small party about how when he was twenty one he'd stood before the same judge, "That time he gave me two weeks. This time he gave me life." He puts his arm around Elizabeth, howling with laughter. Elizabeth isn't a fan of that joke. She can tell it's going to be one of those goddamn stories he tells all the fucking time. She rolls her eyes, shakes her head.

Roze hoists an orange juice, "To the new Mister and Misses. So where are you going for this Honeymoon?"

Elizabeth beams, "We're going to Boston for a Laser Zeppelin show."

Roze chuckles, "So romantic."

Three hours later they are pulling up in front of the hotel. "Sixty-nine Boston street, Here it is." She points with a grin.

He grins too. "So we're going to have to sixty-nine in Boston on Sixty-nine Boston street, right?

"I think we have to." They never got to that Laser Zeppelin show. Storybook.

The following week, in reality all that has changed is Elizabeth's last name and they're just fine with that. Elizabeth arrives home from band practice and flops on the couch under Bill's arm.

"Did you decide on a band name?" Daddy asks from his desk chair. He's watchful of Bill's arm and sly grin.

"Oh I had a name from the start, they all knew that. It's called Fwop."

"It's called what?" They both laugh. "What the Hell is a Fwop?"

Elizabeth laughs, "It's a word from high school."

Bill laughs, "What's that? Never set foot in one."

Daddy tries to recall that one. "That doesn't sound like any vocabulary word I remember from high school."

Bill reminds him of his ageing statue, "That's because it's been so long since you were in a school."

"It wasn't a vocabulary word you two dimwits, It was a made up slang word. At first it was a queef or rather the sound a queef makes. It evolved into just slang for a girl, like bitch or slut." She puts on the dumb boy voice, "Look at this Fwop ova here."

"Oh" Daddy adds, 'We had Yoy in middle school."

"What?"

"Yoy. It was our regional made up slang word. Legend has it some girl was really stoned up on the rock back when there was a big bronze moose up there and for some reason and she couldn't stop laughing and saying 'why oh why' over and over. Why oh Why. Yoy. It became a generic response. Yoy. It was lame. 'Hey check out my new sneakers. Yoy…'"

"Yoy" Elizabeth then goes on to explains the life cycle of Fwop at her high school. While she does, a flash passes by her, a fleeting memory, Natalie was babysitting. She was telling Elizabeth all about her cousin's band Doxy. Elizabeth gets it now, sees in hindsight Natalie's pain. None of them understood it then. Vincent never called Elizabeth a Fwop but only because he wasn't familiar with the term. He called her everything else, anything that would hurt. Fwop sums up everything he ever called her to cut her down, fat slut, dirty skank, sloppy whore. Well he can't cut her down anymore. She's taking all of that and forging it into a big fat shiny badge heated with her channelled anger. *I am Fwop hear me roar where all my Fwops at?* Elizabeth sees Fwop as the feminist equivalent to a racial slur. *You can't use that word -- only we can use that word.* She feels a sudden pang of guilt, that sadness you feel when you think of someone from long ago and then recall their passing. Natalie. Elizabeth looked up to Natalie and now she can see why. If Elizabeth can just make everyone happy then everyone will love her. No pressure. She starts to build the Lizzy Fwop persona. A look, a personality. A rival. Courtney.

Up at the Eye, Kevin wipes the bar in front of Courtney and the guy sitting next to her, Bobby's friend. She is telling him with great amusement how what a coincidence that her band name is Remote Control just like his old show.

The guy looks confused, "I didn't host Remote Control, that was Colin Quinn. I think you're thinking of the guy who hosted Singled Out. I know that's supposed to be the joke here, but I'm not him either, I uh…" He looks around for confirmation.

Courtney waves him off, "Whatever, TV's Chris Hardwick, we're just going to call you Cupcakes from now on anyway."

"What? Why!? I don't…OK whatever, Courtney." Cupcakes motions to Kevin for another round of shots with a small circular gesture on the bar between the three of them.

Kevin obliges, without getting off his seat on the beer cooler, "Right away Mr. Cupcakes." He reaches into a cooler, pulling out a bottle of Jagermeister. "This bottle was 'purchased' with buybacks." Kevin winks with the use of air quotes, bottle still in hand. He pours the shots, puts the bottle back under the bar, and hoists his shot waiting for the rest of the group to follow suit.

Courtney and Elizabeth wage a war. The kind of Girl War that's done silently. Women are so much more dignified in war than men. War fought with style and accessories. A look, an attitude, social status. The wounds they inflict are mental.

Elizabeth has no problem getting her band on the stage at the Eye, it's as easy as asking. They wage a war of words from the stage in not so silent ways, calling each other out in dramatic fashion of the live punk show backdrop to their shit talk. They wage a war in black magic marker on the bathroom wall and on social media platforms, with mascara, lipstick, strategic bandanas and cleavage, and crowd pleasing challenges to thunderous applause. A war of social hierarchy. Classic queen of the hive. You can't have two divas. There can be only one.

Act 2 Scene 11.6

Exterior: The Eye-night

ELIZABETH and JOHNNY ROTTED
(from the band Punk Rock
Zombies) are standing outside
the bar listening to a mutual
friend tell a story.

The storyteller will remain nameless
for reasons that will soon become obvious.
This is the scandal that rocked the Hudson
Valley.

The Great Swedish Fish Scandal!

"I worked at Blockbuster in the new Cortlandt Towne Center. So we had this machine that we used to shrink wrap videos and games that were coming out of rental circulation. Naturally we sold them at a discount. One day I noticed that I had a talent with the shrink wrapper, like I mean factory sealed...you couldn't tell the difference. I was curious if I could fool anyone so I took an empty box, a box from a game we were still renting, because we saved those. So I took one, I threw a handful of Swedish Fish inside and sealed it up in the shrink wrapper. I hold it up I'm admiring my work, I think it looks pretty good. I showed it to some co-workers they all agree they can't tell the difference. This gives me an idea. So on my dinner break I walk across the parking lot to the Walmart. They sell games. I go up to the courtesy desk and returned the game. No questions asked, easier than I'd even expected. I had a story, too -- no receipt, a gift from grandma, she's old yada yada she loses things, nothing, they didn't even ask one question. So then I hit the game store in the Towne Center, there too, no problem. I go up and down route six -- Caldor, K-Mart, Kohls, anywhere they sell games and movies, I take empty boxes from Blockbuster, we throw out boxes by the box load, boxes nobody was ever going to account for, it was perfect. I started going to Poughkeepsie, White Plains, over the river, Nyack, Middletown, Woodbury. I had other people doing it...splitting the money with me, a whole network out there returning games and movies with candy inside. But now, but now, all these boxes, these returns, they're going back on shelves. People are buying them, taking them home expecting to play Mortal Kombat and getting a box of candy. So now people are bringing them back to the stores all over the place." The storyteller pauses for dramatic effect. "Now I'm curious." A sly smile grows on the side of his face, "I grab a box, cut it open, take it over to Walmart. The first one I went to. I show them, I say 'I bought this here I got it home and candy', I dump out the Swedish Fish and they say 'yeah that's been happening we don't know what that's all about.' This of course is hilarious to me. But now Christmas is coming and I can feel the heat coming down. I'm making really good money, so there is tons of games out there wrapped up and hidden in closets, I just know it. I start noticing cops and security guards hovering around courtesy counters and game departments everywhere I go, see because they have no idea at this point where this all coming from because it's all over the place, but it's everywhere I go now, I have to go to three or four places before I feel like the coast is clear and I can make an exchange. And remember...I have all these other people out there doing this too, so I tell them if you aren't comfortable just walk away, ditch it, whatever you have to do it's no big deal and if you do get picked up, if you tell them anything it's fine, you can even implicate me, just tell me what you said so I know. I told your girl Courtney," He winks and points at Elizabeth who squints and growls a little at the notion of Courtney being her girl, "I told her just tell me what you tell them if you get picked up. That's all, I just need to know. So Courtney gets picked up returning a box of candy over in Yorktown. She tells me she didn't tell them anything but I know she's lying, she must have told them everything because a detective came to Blockbuster and picked me up. He brought me across the parking lot to the barracks right there in the Towne Center. Oh he was hot, Detective Hill, I'll never forget him, I was right under their noses the whole time. He sits me down in an interrogation room and he's trying like Hell to get a confession out of me. I mean he's got her story and he knows it's me, he *smells* it on me, he knows I'm his guy and he knows I know, he does, but I'm deny deny deny up and down because I know he's got nothing solid, just Courtney's word against mine and his hunch. He's trying to scare me with numbers -- hundreds of complaints, thousands of dollars, the works. All he wants is a confession, and he's not getting it. Then he overplays his hand and I see my out. He wants a confession so bad so he drops his offer too low, down to one count. One game. It's worth ten bucks. A wrist slap, he says, if I confess to one. And I jump on him, I say, 'Well, if I refuse and it goes to trial, couldn't I go down for all of them if I'm convicted?' He smiles and nods, thinks he has me, and I say, 'Well, I know I'm innocent but I could still lose a trial so I'll cop to one, where do I sign?' All the wind went out of his sails when he realized he got nothing just a little appearance ticket and no real confesion. I signed so fast. So Detective Hill leans back and starts to laugh and I don't get it, I was like, 'What's so funny?' He says, We've been calling you the Grinch around here, I'm just picturing all these kids all over the Hudson Valley opening up their Christmas presents and all this candy pours out.' Man, if I knew what Courtney said I might have been able to get away with it all, not even cop to one but either way there is nothing they can do to me now. I mean, I basically got off Scott free. "

"That bitch has been talking shit about my baby," Elizabeth seethes, Courtney's latest move in their cold war has been to spread the rumor around the bar through clueless Kevin that April is Vincent's baby. "If she were here right now I would punch her in the face…" Elizabeth looks up toward the road, "Speak of the Devil." She pounds a fist in her hand as Courtney comes walking toward the bar. Elizabeth storms over to her swinging her fist, "I'm gonna kick your fucking ass," connecting with the side of Courtney's face.

Inside the bar, Bill's reunited band, Gun Bunny is launching into the seminal, pun intended, hit "Little Boys" in which Bill and Munky do a duet as a priest and altar boy. Bill poses the quandary, "…if they're under eighteen, it's not adultery…?"

Elizabeth takes another swing at Courtney with a left, connects and holds onto a fistful of hair. She then swings with a right, still holding a tangle of hair in her left. Johnny Rotted and Block Buster guy start to slow clap as Elizabeth drags Courtney across the rough dirt lot kicking and screaming until a big chunk of her weave pulls out, bandana and all, giving Courtney the to scramble to her feet and get away, leaving Elizabeth holding what looks like a trophy scalp.

Johnny Rotted is on his phone, "Yeah right in front of the bar…you're where?" He is saying into the phone, then looks up. A car's headlights approach from the east coming from the deli, Courtney slinks off and is hiding behind a gas pump, no doubt licking her wounds.

The car speeds by, whoever Johnny was talking to leans out the window and yells, "Courtney is a cunt!" Much to Elizabeth, Johnny and Blockbuster Guy's delight. Elizabeth goes inside triumphantly to find Daddy and show off her trophy.

The fight was over before Kevin knew there was a fight. He is busy at the business end of the bar entertaining a corner of underage girls he'd gathered. Even the shadiest of regulars are getting uneasy about the girls Kevin has been bringing to the bar. There is underage and there is Under Age. At least nineteen, twenty year olds are adults, but sixteen, seventeen? That's just too much. Or too little in this case. Kevin is laying on a creepy display of Romantic Father Figure as he jokes and flirts with the four teenagers. Cupcakes has taken to calling the end of the bar "Kiddie Corner." Elizabeth bursts through the door flushed red, puffed up with adrenaline, eyes wide darting side to side. Her hair is wild and flying free, something she rarely allows. In one hand she holds aloft a black-and-white bandana with a mat of hair tied in, dangling from the knot like ribbons as she marches. Gun Bunny is doing their self-titled theme song for the second or third time, as is their odd set ending custom, when Elizabeth makes it through the throng to the front of the stage where Daddy is watching the band from the steps, as usual. Elizabeth grabs his hand, drags him outside to show off her trophy and tell him what he missed, which Kevin notices and decides this might be something he ought to investigate. He politely excuses himself from his young guests and follows Elizabeth outside. On his way around the bar he gives an extra wink and a smile to a petite nineteen year old named Kristen. He's made his choice for the night. On his way down the bar he realizes how often he still feels like an outsider at the Eye even though he lives and works here. The old clique that lived and worked here still hangs out here. There is history with these people that he just doesn't have. He looks back at Kiristen before he pushes out the door. Outside he takes in the recounting of events but there is no situation so Kevin quietly slips back inside. He gets back behind the bar and pours himself and Kristen shots. He is hoping it's her tonight. When he invited her he told her to bring friends and she did. Young girls where they don't belong make friends fast. Kevin knows how it's done. It doesn't take long to put together. The two best ways into a nineteen year old girls panties are booze and attention. Shower a nineteen year old girl with booze and attention and she'll think it was her idea to seduce you. Some girls like drugs which are easy to come by at the Eye. If what you want isn't here already it'a phone call away. Kevin likes his booze. He'll smoke some weed with you on occasion maybe take a toot of blow but booze is his mainstay. Promises of booze and drugs and all the attention they can handle and the teenage girls will stroll right up the stairs and into the predators' jaws. Maybe Kevin is starting to believe his own bullshit. There is something different about Kristen.

Act 2 Scene 11.7

KEVIN is wiping the bar in front
of COURTNEY.

He puts down a glass of wine. Fallout from Courtney and Elizabeth's fist fight divides the small music scene that centers around the Eye. Musicians are funny. Very rank and protocol, it's all very political. It's like a cross between the military and a daytime soap opera. When Elizabeth put her band together she intentionally chose people to play with who were happy to align against Courtney. Some of them blame her for breaking up their old band, which she now fronts a remnant of, having replaced them. The drama was practically built in. Kevin had put a computer behind the bar recognizing the rise of social media. He sees it as a way to bring people to the bar and that's working well. Especially with underage girls. The fight has tensions up around the bar and Kevin is looking for a way to mitigate the damage. He doesn't want to scare anyone off with familiar sounding rumors of old. It's been difficult to shake the reputation of the old Eye being a rough place. Just when he's starting to build a good steady crowd of his own. He almost doesn't feel like an outsider anymore with all his new crowd around him. Too much drama is no good though. A little drama is good for business, but this fight might be too much.

Kevin looks back down the bar at Courtney, "What about you in a thong?"

"Excuse me?"

"You could pose in a thong for a flier, you know...to make peace. A peace offering."

"A piece of my ass?" Courtney smiles, "Sure. I'll pose for a picture in a thong *and* her band's tshirt." She laughs, "That should work great." She knows exactly how Elizabeth and her crew of Hatin' Ass Bitches will react if Kevin suggests this. She stops laughing but grows a shrewd and mischievous smile, "Sure. Go ahead. Suggest that." She insists with a serious look, nodding at Kevin's computer. She sips her wine. The door opens behind Courtney. She looks in the mirror in front of her at the young girl walking in. The girl makes a beeline for the stool in front of Kevin. Courtney shakes her head, "*She* looks too young." She says quietly sipping her wine, minding her business.

Since moving into the Eye Kevin has used the bar to great lengths to draw girls to his lair. Feeding them alcohol, drugs and compliments works out for him. A dangerous amount of underage girls have Walk of Shamed down those stairs and slunk out into the harsh, judgmental morning light of the Eye's unforgiving and unsympathetic parking lot. It always seems harsher at sunrise when one wakes from a bender and contends with the What Have I Dones. With enough tequila and blow most everything seems like a good idea. Kevin capitalizes on this and when he's gotten what he wants he never misses them when they slink out and never come back. That usually happens when they realize the dark underground is just that: The Dark Underground. Not at all the glitz and glamour that Hollywood and Disney make it seem. But Kristen has now been Kevin's favorite for a few weeks. She never did that walk of shame, she stuck around. Kevin figured she would wake up disgusted with herself and flee like the rest but the novelty of being bad hasn't worn off her yet and Kevin fears it is he who's starting to like her. Suddenly it's he who is under the spel, finding himself hanging on her words. He sees her as mature, an old soul, all the lines of creepy old man bullshit are backfiring. He's caught in the blowback. He sees it. It's not just a line. He believes it. She is sitting at the bar in front of him, her wide-eyed innocent smile drawing him in. He's falling in love with her. Somehow a statutory date rape habit turned romantic courtship. Flirtatious bartender eyes start to look more like love sick puppy eyes. Unfortunately for Kevin, the smell of desperation starts to break the spell on Kristen. Those dang pesky primal senses like smell and sexuality. Getting fucked up and messing around with an older man has been fun and exciting up until now but the cartoon popping heart bubbles around Kevin disintegrate the illusion. He starts to gush in a way that is a lot even for him and Kristin can't help think that it's getting too serious. By the end of the night she isn't even staying. She's quiet about it, a little creeped out by Kevin's rapidly growing clinginess. She sneaks out while the night and she are still young and he has his back turned, facing the register. The bar is still busy. It's not even the end of the night. That's when the outside lights go out and the outside doors are locked out and the private Eye party begins. Kevin has practically weaponized the Buy Back policy and cooked the books in such a manner that Mike and Pete's lawyers and accountants can't detect any loss. That's when the booze is free and drugs are plenty. Kevin looks at the clock, it's not even midnight. A pit sinks in his gut looking at the clock as he just catches Kristen duck out the door. The door puffs closed indifferently behind her. It heaves slightly as she opens the outer door. Both doors settle back in the stops and the pit in Kevin's gut sinks deeper and he feels the cool panic wave of an addict. His eyes dart around the bar, he needs to call her cell, why do all these people need a drink right this second?

He hurriedly drops a beer in front of Cupcakes, "Right back…" He mutters on the fly. Cupcakes isn't going anywhere. Kevin uncradles the phone, dials and ducks in the kitchen, closing the door behind him. He leans against it in despair. She doesn't answer. He ducks out the door, dials again, no ring, straight to voicemail. The phone is off.

Later upstairs Kevin sits at the kitchen table completely sauced and near sobbing. Monk is sitting with him shaking his head.

Monk rolls a long joint in an extra long paper, lights it, 'Pull yourself together, Man." He snaps at Kevin in frustration, "Look at yourself, she's a teenager, Kevin. What do you have to offer her? Your daughter is older than her, for fuck's sake." Monk takes a long pull from his joint, offers it to Kevin, hitting his shoulder with his fist, the joint in hand. Monk lightens his tone, "Here man, take a few tokes and mellow out."

Act 2 Scene 11.8

ELIZABETH punches the red phone icon on her cell and slaps the device down on the table

ELIZABETH:

That bitch!

(She screams.)

"No thanks." She'd told Kevin in restrained anger to the offer before hanging up. "That fucking pervert just wants to take pictures of her half-naked slut ass…"

Big Daddy tries to joke, "I wonder if it was as easy to talk her into a thong as it is to talk her out of one…"

Elizabeth shoots him a look and adds, "Can you not keep reminding me you fucked her?" He shuts up, turns in his chair, goes back to working on his column. Kevin called and he probably even felt like it was his own idea but Elizabeth knows Courtney knew exactly what would happen, she knew exactly how Elizabeth was going to react, *that bitch.* Even with Elizabeth's confidence the highest it's been in…well, forever, and the bruises on her knuckles still fresh black and blue, Courtney still has a strange power over her, a way of intimidating Elizabeth. "I can't wait for that bitch to get fat and ugly and people stop letting her get away with everything, you know?" She looks at confused Daddy, wary from the line he just crossed, leery of incurring any more wrath today, "Yes, OK?" Elizabeth sighs, "She's gorgeous and that's why she gets away with half the shit she pulls." Elizabeth has always felt like she has to work harder at it than Courtney.

Kiss and Makeup
Act 2 Scene 12

Interior The Eye, night

ELIZABETH sits down at the bar between MONK and CUPCAKES.

They are talking about the band Kiss. Elizabeth has never cared for them. With or without makeup. Kevin is on the other side of Cupcakes completely hammered.

Cupcakes looks at Kevin concerned, "Aren't you supposed to be working?"

Kevin leans over at Cupcakes then leans past him and looks at Elizabeth, she looks at Kevin, he points to her, "You're Belize." He slurs at her, "I'm Switzerland. You're Belize."

Elizabeth frowns, shakes her head, squinting, says, "Wha…?" She starts and gives up, shaking her head. Monk and Cupcakes conversation about Kiss has expanded to include Twisted Sister. Monk is saying how he knows them from the club scene in lower Westchester and NYC back in the 70's and early 80's.

Elizabeth chimes in, "There's a weird joke in my family that Dee Snider is my sister's real father." Elizabeth laughs, feeling the need to clarify that he isn't, probably not and it's just a joke. Though her mother has said she's met Mr. Snider, but she's a celebrity magnet. Elizabeth looks back at Kevin, through Kevin at the door, through the doors into the parking lot. She can still feel her fist crashing into Courtney's face, the rush, the satisfaction, years of feeling like Courtney's understudy, even though they never competed for a part. She's still always felt like second fiddle to Courtney, that smug fucking slut. Hitting her felt about as good as sex. Love and hate are such close emotions.

Elizabeth recalls the last time she spoke to Allison here at the bar. She had done April's Full and worked with April Lynn for a while then gone out on her own. She was talking about sex and fried chicken and turning things around, how she uses boys, brings them in enticing them with what they think they want, drag them down to the depths of their own depravity, *A lot of guys are not ready,* Allison had said laughing.

Monk is back on Kiss and how Gene Simmons once said "…something along the lines of nothing attracts a crowd like a crowd"

Kevin is sprawling around on the bar gushing in sentimental slurs, "If you don't have anything nice to say come sit next to me." He slushes with a feminine swish of his glass of whiskey.

"Sex and fried chicken…" Elizabeth whispers to herself, "…attracts a crowd…" *Come sit next to me.* "Kiss and make up, Twisted

Sister…" She's muttering. The door swings open with a slam. Courtney stands in the open doorway. Courtney and Elizabeth lock eyes. Stare each other down.

Courtney moves slowly into the bar. She stops at Elizabeth's back. Moves around the end of the bar, Monk between them. "We done fighting?"

Elizabeth nods, "Are we?" She asks, hooks a thumb over her shoulder, slides off the stool "Come on." She leads Courtney to the back door, steps back to Monk and whispers in his ear, "Monk, do you have a joint I can borrow?"

"Sure kid," Monk fumbles with his cigarette pack, slices out a joint.

"I'll give you…" Elizabeth starts to say but Monk waves her off, bows his head humbly, "No, no, no, kid, it's OK take that, it's fine."

Elizabeth takes the joint and Courtney out back to the picnic table, lights the joint, takes a long pull, hands it to Courtney.

She takes it and snickers, "Drama Camp all over again." She hits the joint.

"I didn't smoke pot in Drama Camp." Elizabeth says dryly, takes a puff, quickly adds, "It really hurt me when you wrote he should have hit me harder on the bathroom wall."

Courtney's smile fades, she turns away, takes a puff of the joint, she turns back sheepishly, "Yeah. I'm sorry that was…you know what's fucked up?" Courtney takes another hit and hands it back to Elizabeth, "Right after I wrote that, I went to Florida with Serj, we stayed with his dad. He slapped me right in front of his father, I looked at him like hey motherfucker aren't you going to say something? His fucking father says to me, 'What did you do to deserve that?' You believe that fucking shit?"

"Vincent's dad slapped me once." *They never change.* Elizabeth hits the joint, hands it back, "We should do a show together. Our bands." Courtney's eyes light up immediately, she can see the possibilities, their feud, the fist fight.

It has the scene divided, but that just means they have their full attention, "It's perfect." They brainstorm ideas, lineups, flyers a good campaign strategy, Courtney adds congratulations about Elizabeth's marriage, "I heard you guys ran off and got hitched." In her old show tune stage voice, adding how she wants "to find what you two have…"

Elizabeth asks Courtney, "What's the deal with you and Serj?"

"Well, it's been a long time of off an on but now it's off and it's going to stay off because he's moving to California. I'm not." They talk candidly and open like old friends about relationships and putting on another show together.

Act 2 Scene 12.2

ELIZABETH is sitting in the living room chair, looks up startled.

Elizabeth and Courtney booked a date with Kevin for the Eye's stage. They plan artwork for the flier, a theme for the show, the two of them even working together has built in controversy. Social media is all abuzz, it's perfect.

"Fwop vs. Remote Control

with Punk Rock Zombies

to collect the bodies"

The flier is posted all over town and in the bar, but throughout the planning stages as usual nobody told the drummer anything. The drummer in Remote Control, unaware of the truce between Elizabeth and Courtney, takes the flier as a threat and becomes very defensive. Courtney of course takes to social media to ride the waves of drama that she thrives on. The show is off, the show is back on, bands are breaking up, friendships are on the rocks, the drama threatens unrelated friendships as truths start exploding out in anger about who slept with who and whatnot. Kevin takes to the helm of the social media mothership and pokes at the quivering festering pus-filled fight bubble. If you poke at a blemish long enough, it blows up on you.

"That's it. Let's go." Daddy looks pissed. Elizabeth gets the impression that "let's go" was a courtesy and he is going now with or without her. She grabs her shoes and hurries out the door with them in her hands, barely getting the car door shut before he is chirping out of the driveway, jerking to a stop in the road and rocketing forward wheels. "Enough is fucking *enough*." he is yelling now, pissed. He's stayed quiet long enough, Kevin is going to pay for this, this is the last straw. "I'm gonna kick the fucking shit out of that bald-ass creepy son of a bitch, loving middle school drama fucking, drama, fucking...." He trails off losing the point, yelling in a blind rage, working himself up, speeding all the way. He makes record time, kicking up a huge cloud of dirt and skidding across the rough dirt lot in front of the Eye. Hardly shutting the door behind him he stomps in the front door. Elizabeth hears him saying something about peace at his house and Kevin fucking up his bar as she pulls on her other shoe and hurries in behind him.

Elizabeth flings open the door and rushes in. Several of the bar stools before her have been toppled in his wake, pointing in the direction of his fury. She makes it in the door just in time to see him rounding the corner of the bar.

"...kick your fucking ass!" He is yelling, cornering Kevin, who looks as though he is trying to hide under the bar and behind a beer cooler, a grown man trying to escape Daddy's fury. Elizabeth can't help feel a little turned on -- Daddy, breathing heavy, veins bulging, muscles throbbing, sweaty with adrenaline. She loves his arms.

Jay the Doorman and Monk come running in the back door. Jay grabs Daddy by the shoulder, looks in his eyes, breaks the tunnel vision, takes him out back to blow some smoke in his face. Elizabeth sits down at the bar and chuckles at Kevin.

"Can I have a soda, Kevin?"

Kevin's eyes wide, his bald head shines with a glisten of fear sweat. He's pale white and catching his breath, "What the HELL was that about?!"

"He's had it with the bullshit around here, all the drama. I guess this was just the last straw. He's been quiet, watching and listening. You know Bill asked him." She points emphatically in the direction of the back door, "He knew, Bill knew he'd want someone looking after this place, for some reason, don't ask me why but he loves this fucking dump." She is still pointing at her husband outside, choking back a tear as she thinks of him, her husband out there, his chest heaving, sweat running down his face. "And he thinks you're fucking it up. You're fucking up his bar Kevin. Get on your social networks and smooth this shit out. That fucking drama is between her and I, the show is on, now cut it the fuck out." Elizabeth looks sternly at Kevin and puts her finger in his face, " And I know you helped her spread rumors about my daughter, saying Vincent is really her father. And If he," She points out the window. "hears you said that, he'll fucking kill you. And next time maybe we'll all let him."

I Went to a Fight
and a
Punk Show Broke Out
Act 2 Scene 12.5

Exterior: The Eye-evening

ELIZABETH steps out of the car, her foot hits the dusty parking lot.

Courtney scored a few extra last minute drama points with the short-lived controversy. *She always was good at that,* Elizabeth thinks, shaking her head. Come show night the little skirmish was last week's forgotten news. Luckily. As any music scene soldier will tell you, negativity spreads fast. One whisper of the word cancelled can spread faster than a thousand photocopies. And that's back when they made flyers the old fashioned analog way with magazines and markers, a pair of scissors and a roll of Scotch tape. And of course a copy machine. Kevin spends plenty of time promoting the bar on the phone and social media, sending out text messages and statuses. The little drama show seemed to be for in house entertainment purposes only..

Courtney and Elizabeth sit in front of mirrors at their homes, strategically applying makeup and designing hair concepts. Wars are fought on many levels. No amount of truce can put a stop to the war they wage. It's as though they derive an energy from each other, a strong intense energy. Love and hate can be so close sometimes. If they were in a stage production right now their mirrors would sit back to back center stage, they would sing a heartfelt duet about their hate and admiration for each other and some secret pain or plot twist. But this is no play.

Elizabeth steps from the car in her black and white shell top sneakers, low tops of course. She strides across the parking lot feeling good. Her denim capris hug her curves, she runs her hands over her hips as she walks. She feels sexy. A blue halter top tied behind her neck shows off her shoulders and sternum. She runs her fingertips across her clavicle, smiling at him walking next to her. He refers to her collarbone neck area as her *this.* He likes her *this,* and she likes to show it off for him. *This and That.*

It's not Elizabeth's first show with Fwop but it's exciting in a way, perhaps more than the first. She still has to prove that she belongs on that stage. To whom she's not sure, maybe to herself. Besides, Courtney's not the only one who should get to enjoy the spotlight. She gently taps the nose ring, a sort of nervous tick, or a tap for confidence. A Dumbo feather. No wait...Dumbo's an elephant, can't have that -- middle school fat shaming echoing down a long dark hallway. Linus' blanket? Fuck it -- It's Betty Paige's fucking bullwhip. Now let's show these fuckers there's a new goddamn queen around here. Well, maybe not new, but still young and beautiful queen, here to retake her throne. Elizabeth steps in the door with a strong confident flare. Early. There is nobody in the bar to see her Grand Entrance. She laughs to herself and joins her band backstage.

Meanwhile in Yorktown Courtney throws her arms around Serj's neck, he's decided to stay and she is excited for tonight's show. She's choosing a dress to complete a look, a sort of gothic Stevie Nicks, punk princess pinup. A black dress with red piping, matching high top sneakers and a matching bandana in her hair. She thinks of the old black- and-white one Elizabeth tore off her head a few weeks back and rolls her eyes. She gives the knot a final tug, snug around her ponytail and spins around, twirling her skirt. On the drive to the Eye Courtney and Serj talk of the future. When they made up last night and they talked about moving to Brooklyn together and getting a place, something in three or four years of on and off they had never done. He shrugs off whatever he was running off to do in California and Courtney accepts it. Serj even hinted at starting a family of their own. Courtney smiles. Then she gives thought to how she had deflected attention onto herself by making her bandmates feel attacked by the flyer. She smiles at this thought, satisfied. As Serj pulls into the Eye, the smile quickly fades with the memory of getting punched in the face and being dragged across the lot. She walks into the bar happily bouncing her skirt, cautious but not unpleased with herself either. Elizabeth is equally cautious in being too friendly with Courtney. "Hey, Lizzie." Courtney tries to sound calm as she enters the back room. The bar is starting to fill up quickly and the marketing ploy Allison called Operation Sex and Chicken worked perfectly. When she shows up late in the evening after the bands, she says as much. Courtney and Elizabeth start the night standoffish and suspicious but with each drink together they slowly revert back to old friends, noticing at one point that of all the people in the bar, they've know each other the longest. Courtney shares her and Serj's plan with Elizabeth, telling her how happy she is for her and how she can't wait to start a family with Serj like Elizabeth has. The deeper in conversation they get, the further from the party they drift from the lights and prying eyes to the darkness and shadows. The darker it gets around them the closer they get to one another. How close love and hate can be sometimes...the heat, that fire, alcohol fueled, inhibitions gone, adrenaline high. The crowd's cheer still echoes from the rickety beer-soaked brick pile, high on sexy adulation. Chests flush red, intimate lusty caressing, warm heat. The party inside roars with raucous debauchery as big parties at the Eye tend to do. They slink back out of the shadows straightening their clothes, wiping proverbial feathers from the corners of their sly grins. With guilty looks and knowing glances they share smiles across the bar.

Elizabeth whispers sexily into Daddy's ear what she's done with a devilish grin, "Don't tell anyone," She slurs, adding how Serj is not cool with it like he is. Daddy always says to her, *It's not cheating if it's with a girl.* Just the thought of Elizabeth hooking up with another girl gets him hot and bothered. She loves to turn him on. It's cute how he can't think straight with an erection.

She knows she is going to get it good when he looks at the clock with a smile and announces, "Look at that...barely 1 AM and we did all that." She sees his intention is to start getting everyone out. Kevin is passed out with his head on the bar. They'll need to get him and everyone else out of the bar before they can leave.

Daddy puts a beer down in front of Cupcakes who takes a big swig and points at Daddy. "This guy...he told me once 'Nothing good ever happens after 1 AM' and he was dead on." Cupcakes takes the rest of the beer down in another gulp and announces "I'm getting out of here before a fight breaks out or some other stupid Eye-type shit." He hops off his stool, pausing to stop the sway, "Sticks the landing." He gives Kevin a pat on the back of his bald head on the way by, "Later Kev. Slow down buddy." Kevin groans back in his sleep and snores. When he leans back in his chair and his head bobs back and his mouth hangs open. Courtney, inspired, pulls an old flyer off the wall and on the back draws a big meaty cock. Really veiny. She cuts out the dick and holds it next to Kevin's open mouth. They take pictures and post them to the Eye social media pages. You can scrub marker off your face but now with social media you can't scrub dick off the internet. There's a new lesson in town: never pass out with your head on the bar, especially at the Eye.

While Jay the doorman and Monk help Kevin up the stairs. Daddy declares, "We are not fucking with Kevin's drawer." He locks the money up, looking up at the camera with a thumbs up and says, "Kevin can come down here in the morning and deal with that. I'm not counting his money." A few people linger around drunk and spent. A general air of the party being over hangs in an uncertain cloud. Small groups of people searching for an exit strategy, making after bar plans at diners or other bars, most of which are futile gestures. Broke and hammered they start to filter out into waiting, reluctantly calling cabs or risky Designated Driver's cars.

Just as they are ready to leave, Courtney and Serj start getting loud, arguing. "You fucking whore!" She protests, but he continues with the rush of insults. She sobs while he screams at her that she "...is going to Hell!" And with that he storms away to his car.

"You fucking liar!" She screams, standing by the bar entrance with a cloud of dust swirling as Serj speeds out of the parking lot, leaving her all alone.

Elizabeth walks slowly across the parking lot. Only a few weeks ago she traced these same steps to punch Courtney in the face. Now her arm embraces her instead.

"He's gone. He was never staying. He lied to me." She looks at Elizabeth in tears, "I was going to tell him tonight that I'm pregnant."

Louis

Act 3 Scene 1

LOUIS is driving. He is towing a trailer. His son, now a few years old, strapped in back. His wife HEATHER beside him.

He is moving her out of town, moving his family. She's taken a job in a town he'd intentionally put in her sights. He planted the seeds. Louis reflects on how he's gotten here. It seems not long ago he'd moved his family to town. He did it to be close to Allison though that hadn't gone quite as planned and also to put Heather near her ex-boyfriend. He immediately forbade her to see him, knowing she would have to if he made it forbidden fruit. It would fuck with her head and enable Louis' usual manipulation, which it did. It all worked. The only snafu is his disappointment in Allison. She really should thank him for all he'd done to her. He did push her over the edge, after all. Had he not she never would have had the opportunity to land on her feet. *You're welcome. Shame about Natalie, if only she could have taken Allison down that path with her. She managed to beat the game. Bravo Allison.* Heather, on the other hand, she's right where he wants her. Louis carefully magnified her ex-boyfriend's dramatic post-breakup scene. He put a hope out of reach, knowing her nature so well. He read it on her face the day she disobeyed, the day she could stand it no longer. That was the day she went to see him. He knew she had doubt and he played into them. He knows she's had doubts about her son's paternity. By forbidding her to see him he helped feed that doubt. What girl doesn't like having an ex on the hook. That slutty chick next door growing up used to do it all the time. Louis watched it from the porch, she had a parade of hopefuls on the hook. The more pathetic ones she didn't even have to touch, though that never stopped her if the mood struck. Louis watched with amusement on more than one occasion when one young man, erection at the ready would be knocking at the front door while one was sneaking out the back. It was as if she had one of those pick-a-number systems like they have at the deli. Teen boys lining up to take a number and get a plate of her nasty roast beef. Willing is so attractive to a desperate horny boy. Meanwhile her older sister was a frigid bitch, never had a date. Even took her cousin to prom just to go and she didn't want to do that, her mother made her. Then of course there was their little sister. Louis looks back with an emotion that might resemble fondness. Carol. The little bitch. Ruined his tenth birthday. Still, she was about the only person Louis could even stomach, let alone talk to growing up in Yorktown. Boring milquetoast stepford suburbia. Pretentious posers. And when their kids run away or get busted with drugs or have unsafe promiscuous sex they shut up and ship them out to boarding schools like that awful Family Academy. Louis recalls with a chuckle reading about that school getting shut down recently. So many of his stupid parents' friends and neighbors sent their entitled brats to that hellhole to get harassed, molested and tortured. Anything just so they wouldn't have to actually do any real parenting. Louis hated them. All of them. His parents, their friends, their neighbors. Louis is, after all, a complete sociopath. He plays chess with people's lives for little more than amusement.

He looks over at Heather. She was only eighteen when he lured her away from her old life. He's been manipulating her ever since. He'd scoped out the Delaware town they are headed for now when Allison was still his wife. He's happy to be leaving again. He'd hated moving back to Westchester but he had work to do. The Westchester people, the traffic, the people. God how he hates them all.

Louis looks at Heather again and has an epiphany. Her ex-boyfriend, he'd seen him before when he was much younger. He was friends with little Vincent. Louis' mother sent him over to watch Vincent and his friend, a goofy kid from Vincent's old neighborhood with a big head and a dirty red sweatshirt. They were playing Empire Strikes Back on a fluffy white carpet that stood in stupendously for Hoth. Louis still has no idea how much his influence on Vincent had affected Elizabeth. He would be quite pleased to know. Tickled. The seeds he planted in Vincent so many years ago...that wasn't hard at all. His father was a drunk and his mother cold as ice. Louis recalls really liking Vincent's mom a lot, for that stoic coldness. Very practical. Reserved. Not that his own mother isn't practical and reserved but Vincent's mother's was unmatched in the neighborhood. Now that he thinks of it, she might have been the only other person besides Carol in all of Yorktown that he liked. He looks over at Heather navigating. She loves a good road trip. He's happy to get away from her family. She hasn't realized that one yet, how far she'll be from them -- her parents, her little sister, aunts, uncles and cousins. They're like the cast of Drowning Mona. Louis can't stand them but Heather is going to realize how close she is with them when she's so isolated a few states away. It's that isolation that he's counting on, he knows her well. Reads her like he read her file when she was his student. He knew she'd made an attempt. He knew her isolation up in

Gore and the confusion with her love life led her to the depression that she's prone to. It's easy to see.

Act 3 Scene 2

Interior:The Eye-night

ELIZABETH is singing karaoke.

She finishes her song and sits back down at the bar next to the new guy that's been hanging around. Becky and Mel brought him in, he works with them at the Renaissance Faire. They call him Krowface.

He's talking to Cupcakes about Kevin's new trainee, Betsy, "...With the glasses and the big boobs." Krowface gets up to sing a Dead Kennedys song, declaring his "pipes are on fire tonight." He sits back down when he's done and takes a big swig of his beer. Elizabeth gets back up to sing another song, she's looking around the bar waiting for the track to que up. The bar isn't very crowded, just a few of them, huddled around the karaoke. There's a couple of people out back smoking pot and a small group of non-regulars by the door. Outsiders. Elizabeth stands tall. For maybe the first time in her life she isn't self-conscious about her height. She feels statuesque rather than awkward and her voice is full and loud. A far far cry from Monk's lake house in the dark. She begins to belt out a Sex Pistols song with a sneer and a spot on Johnny Rotten accent. Her voice fills the bar. In fact it dominates the bar. When the song ends she continues to talk into the microphone to Cupcakes, Krowface and Roze.

The karaoke guy tells Elizabeth to stay up there and do another song, putting on an Aerosmith classic for Elizabeth to sing. While the track is queuing up Elizabeth is still talking into the microphone. A girl near the door walks across the bar and gets in Elizabeth's face.

She says, "You don't have to scream. We can all hear you."

Elizabeth puts up her middle finger and says loudly, "I will fucking kill you." It booms from the speakers just before the music stars. Elizabeth starts to sing and doesn't hear the girl getting pissed off. Krowface and Cupcakes and a few other people hurry to escort the girl out.

Kevin asks Krowface, "Who is this chick?"

"Total noob."

The girl bursts out into the parking lot hot. Steam is shooting out of her ears like a boiling teapot. She's stomping around in the parking lot, kicking up a bunch of dust and screaming, shoving her friend around. "I'm gonna beat the fucking brakes off that bitch!" A crowd of regulars stands between her and the door.

Cupcakes tells her, "Yeah, it's best if you just go."

Jay the doorman tells her, "It's not going to happen."

"Yeah, Elizabeth will kick your ass." Kevin adds, which elicits a roar of laughter from the bar regulars. Krowface spits out a swig of PBR. He gives a snort and a chuckle, swigs the rest of the brew. He drops the empty can and steps off the porch. The girl is standing next to a van.

The guy she came with is trying to convince her to get in, "Come on, we should just go." But she isn't listening to him.

She is still kicking dust and ranting about, "Kicking the snot out of this bitch."

"Look...you're just going to have to leave," Krowface tells her. He's only been hanging out here a short time but in that short time he's grown very attached. "Best dive bar of all time," he would tell people. It feels like home to a wandering Hellraiser. Like he found his people when he walked in the door the first time. His long lost tribe. He points to the small mob between them and the door. "Baby, that crowd is never going to let you back in there and if they did she would beat the fucking mustard out of you."

She isn't interested in his opinion though and her boyfriend is having no luck with his soft urging, "Come on let's just go." She is flailing her arms and kicking up a cloud of dust, spinning in circles carrying on.

Krowface smirks, tries again, "Look baby, you gotta leave."

She spins around fast and screams in his face. "Don't fucking call me baby, I'm gonna fuck that bitch up!" A little bit of her spit sprays on him and he can smell the rum and coke on her breath. He calmly wipes a drop of spit from his cheek with a single finger, a smile on his face.

He grins mischievously, steps out of her way and waves her through chivalrously, "Well then, I'm gonna keep calling you baby till you take off that fucking diaper, hike up your ovaries and go break off a piece of that ass." He gestures toward the door as if to invite her back in, and that's when she lunges at him. The Boyfriend Whisperer can't react fast enough to stop her and he whiffs through her dust outline in a vain attempt to restrain her. She swings her angry fist, punching Krowface square in the ale hole, knocking him back a step. The boy finally catches up, puts a hand on her shoulder, pulls her back. Krowface wipes his mouth on the back of his hand. Looks at the spot of blood, feels the sweetness on his tooth with his tongue. He throws his head back and laughs into the night sky, turns and walks back into the bar.

Back in Yorktown Courtney tosses in bed uncomfortably. She gets up and sits in a chair. It's been five months since Serj left. She decided after much agonizing to keep the baby. She wants nothing more than to hold her. To have a real tangible blood connection to someone. She'd isolated herself for the first few months. Elizabeth was the only person she'd told and though she didn't specify it was a secret, Elizabeth left it up to Courtney to tell anyone else. She wants to keep it. She wants a family. When she announces her decision Elizabeth of all people is the most supportive, even offering to give Courtney rides to doctor appointments. She gives no thought to that detail this time. Earlier today Elizabeth came over and brought a gift -- a beautiful soft furry faux leopard print baby blanket. Courtney holds the soft plush to her cheek and rubs her belly.

Meanwhile, back at the bar, Elizabeth is sitting with Roze, Monk, Krowface and Cupcakes. Kevin is showing Betsey how to close out the cash register.

Cupcakes is sharing his opinion on *Friday the 13th: Jason takes Manhattan*. "Let me tell you. Jason takes Manhattan. Part eight. The charming story of six twenty-eight year-old teenagers from Crystal Lake New Jersey who embark on their senior prom in March of 1989 from Vancouver on an old oil tanker party ship. During the trip the teachers and principal manage to get the entire graduating class *and* the entire crew of the ship brutally murdered. After the oil tanker explodes they scuttle the ship and manage to get completely lost somewhere in the ten fucking miles between New York and New Jersey port authority for at least an entire day and night in a row boat. At some point one of them manages to look slightly to the right and says, "Hey guys I found New York Fucking City, we're saved!" Immediately after making landfall, I shit you not, they are robbed, almost raped and 'banged full of heroin' by a couple of Spanish dudes who are apparently in the business of giving away free dope. It's cool though: because Jason hates rapists and drug dealers. They manage to re-group and call a cop after getting lost in back alleys filled with leaky barrels of toxic waste for an hour or so. The cop of course gets his shit wrecked in short order. Logically the girl wasted on smack steals his abandoned cruiser, runs it immediately into a brick wall, killing another teacher. Afterwards they crawl out of the fiery wreckage and talk about their feelings for a while. The movie devolves from there." Cupcakes sips his beer to applause.

A short while later, the door swings open and Allison walks in with two Route 6 car salesmen.

Somehow Krowface and Elizabeth had gotten from *Friday the 13th* to theater. As Elizabeth sees Allison approaching he is saying, "Yup, those are the masks of theater…"

"Oh look, she went to that drama camp too." Elizabeth waves, "Hey Allison."

Allison leaves the car salesman at the bar near the door, telling them, "Why don't you boys sit here and fight over who's buying me a drink," with a smile waving over her shoulder as she walks towards Elizabeth. She gives Kevin the hand-drink motion to get her a beer, nodding back at her escorts, they got it.

Kevin nods politely, "Of course, my dear."

"They find out you're in porn and suddenly they want to find out what they're made of." Allison whispers to Elizabeth, hooking her thumb over her shoulder. They giggle.

"Allison, this is Cupcakes, Roze, and Krowface."

Allison nods, pauses, draws her focus on Roze, points a finger, "Don't I know you…?"

Roze initially thinks, "I don't think so?" But then it hits her. "Wait, didn't you work at Cafe Ine?"

Allison nods with a satisfied grin, wagging her finger, "Yes I did, that must be where I recognize you from."

Elizabeth clarifies, "My friend Roze here used to be friends with your ex-husband's wife, Heather." Allison feigns confusion, looking around the bar cautiously, "Relax, Al…I realized a long time ago you would rather my husband not recognize you. I respect that. He's home with the little one anyway." Allison breathes a sigh of relief. It seems silly to her now and she smirks to herself briefly but she still doesn't want to make that connection, in fact especially now that she's doing so well. "Heather tried to kill herself." Elizabeth adds bluntly, never one for subtlety in such cases.

Allison's eyes open wide, mouth hangs open, "Because of Louis? I bet…"

"I think so, Roze says she's been on a downward spiral for a while. He refuses to work, she has two jobs and she still has to come home and do the housework and most of the parenting. She's said it was a mistake leaving her ex, my husband, and Roze says she thinks she can have him back with the snap of her fingers, so I have no love lost on her but as a girl I have to feel a little for her." Elizabeth pauses, hammers home, "A little."

Allison nods, "He's a predator. I learned that in the last few years of therapeutic hindsight. And he's a schemer. He wanted me to think I was crazy, it sounds like he's trying to break her too. I guess I feel the same way. She didn't set out to maliciously break up my marriage, he did. And I'm glad, I needed that spell broken, I couldn't do it myself, Hell, he started working on me when I was like twelve."

Elizabeth nods in agreement. She knows all too well about breaking the spell. "I told him to call her, even though I don't really want them talking."

Allison agrees, "It's the right thing to do."

Elizabeth purses down her lips, nods in agreement, gently smacks Allison's arm, changes gears to lighten the mood, "I was just telling Krowface here about drama camp,"

Both girls chant with a smile together, "Never Break Character." and laugh.

Elizabeth adds, "He's an actor."

"Oh?" Allison looks at him and back at Elizabeth.

"Hey, you know what I was reading recently? Remember when we did *Anything Goes*?"

"How could I forget, that was my first time in the director's chair."

"Well, originally Hope had more songs, like four or five. Apparently they cut out a bunch of her songs and cut down the character."

"I'm not surprised." Allison thinks about it, "You can't have two female leads. I bet the first Reno was the big star and she probably insisted they cut the part down, she can't allow herself to be upstaged by the young unknown starlet on the rise. You can't have two divas." Allison puts on her best Ethel Merman, "That little hussy isn't riding up on my star!" Elizabeth giggles. "Did you ever read *Valley of the Dolls*?"

Elizabeth nods, "Helen Lawson does exactly that at that opening night in

New Haven. Now that I think about it, I wonder if that play was inspired by *Anything Goes*…? Time period is right...."

"No, it was *Hello, Dolly!*"

"Anyone else I think I would be surprised, but you, of course *you* knew that."

"I have an embarrassing amount of knowledge of musicals. But yeah, *Anything Goes*? Clearly written by a man."

"A very gay man though."

"Still not a girl."

"Speaking of drama camp have you spoken to Courtney?"

Elizabeth sighs with amusement. "Let's see, since last time I saw you, she and I got into a fist fight in the parking lot, we might have hooked up out back, I'm still fuzzy on that. And she got pregnant." She adds quickly with a smile "It's not mine.". "The guy left, doesn't know she's pregnant and she decided to keep the baby. She's due in a few weeks."

"Talk about drama camp." Allison laughs, then furrows her brow and looks at Krowface, "Did I hear you say the masks of theater?" He nods, she looks at Elizabeth and says, "Have you ever heard of the *Marilyn Tragedy?* April told me about it, it's a well-known secret in Hollywood, an affliction, you get trapped in the mask." She shakes her head, "You can't become someone you're not, you have to be true to yourself, real with yourself and frankly, a little selfish. You have to love for you first. Look at me. I was raised to look pretty for the boys and hope one with a good family crest would make me his wife, hopefully not hit me too much. Fuck that." She points down the bar at the car salesmen, "I picked them up at Brodie's. I'm going to let them buy me some shots and let them think they're talking their way into my studio tomorrow. They'll argue all night about which one is going to chicken out and which one is going to teach me a thing or two but tomorrow morning when they're sober neither one of them is showing up. We're doing a Ball Torture Cow Milking Table." They all stare at her mouths agape at this. "You've heard of a milking table?"

Krowface looks around at his peers and says, "I think I know, I'm a pervert. but why don't you explain it to them."

"Well it's simply a table with a hole in it. Guy lays face down, junk through the hole and a chick milks his cock. We built a table with a…"

She pauses thinks, ...a cover, a cowl, that's it -- a cowl and a headstock. The cover is painted to look like a cow. We stick his head through the hole in the cowl and hang a bell around his neck." She giggles a little "It's like those cutouts you stick your head through get your picture taken at the carnival." She nods at her captivated, slightly disturbed audience, "Well his head sticks out and he looks like a cow," She smiles, "It has little cow ears and horns, anyway the cowbell humiliates him a little since we'll call him Bessie and shit like that. We stick a butt plug in his ass with a cow tail attached to it." Her audiences eyes grow wide, "The tail wags up and down with his dick, see she's under there squeezing his balls like his cock is a pump sneaker, you squeeze a set of balls like that for a while and the dick gets really hard. It pulses and shakes, it's funny. We did one a few weeks ago, this chick she's squeezing this guys balls for like two hours, she collected a cup full of pre-cum..."

"Two hours!?" Cupcakes can't even comprehend that.

"It's called ball torture, yeah two hours of blue balls. When she finally lets him out and lets him release, she gives him a few strokes and he dumps about a gallon of goo on his own belly." Allison adds proudly, "Yeah there are a few fetish girls out there using my Cow Milking table. I get cuts of those videos. Innovation is the key in any industry. Porn is no different."

Elizabeth laughs, knowing Allison's website, "Boys always think they have what it takes for porn until it's go time." Elizabeth says to Cupcakes and Krowface with a punctuating nod, adding, "What?" to their shock, "That's what Allison says...?"

"I do." Allison nods.

Act 3 Scene 3

Interior: Maternity Ward-morning

COURTNEY is sitting in a chair in front of a desk. Her parents behind her a hand each on her shoulders. A woman in a smart pantsuit whose name is on a plate on the desk with an important title.

Courtney is tired and pale. She has no makeup on her freckled face. Her hair is unbrushed. It was a tough birth and in the end they did an emergency C-Section. She clutches the baby to her breast wrapped neatly in the blanket gifted to her by Elizabeth. She looks down at the girl. *She has my eyes.* Courtney hasn't heard from Serj and has not tried to contact him. She looks up at her guardi...parents, who nod approvingly. Courtney leans forward, takes the pen and writes her and Serj's names on the birth certificate. The woman slides the certificate in an envelope and pushes forward another sheet of paper.

Courtney points to a box with the pen, "I check here? She can know?" The woman nods, Courtney signs, a tear in her eye. It's her only concession, it's the only way she can live with herself, not after what not knowing has done to her. The woman slides that sheet in with the birth certificate. Courtney's mom hands her an envelope. Courtney takes it, hands it to the woman, "I wrote this, can you put it in there too?" Her voice hitches. She puts her hand to her mouth and shuts her eyes tightly. Then she hugs the baby tight and kisses her forehead, "It's for the best." She whispers and hands the baby to the waiting nurse. The baby is wheeled out in a hospital bassinet into another room where a waiting couple will meet her for the first time.

Drama Camp. Showtime

Elizabeth and her two male leads lead the townsfolk in the famous "Livin To Do" song and dance number onstage. Allison joins Natalie in the darkness. Natalie, clad all in black, awaits her cue at her curtain rope. Allison is jittery. Natalie doubts it's show night jitters as they are two-thirds through the show at this point. Allison as stage manager has had an easy night in fact, with the production running smooth and stress-free. This is what they practiced for.

Onstage, the boy playing Conrad Birdie sings his part. He doesn't want to go to the army, seeing how he has all this living to do. There's all these chicks. And chicks are for kissing.

"He's *surrounded* by high school chicks." Allison points out routinely to Natalie.

She ignores this, asks instead, "Are you OK?"

"Yeah." Allison whispers. Her voice is shaky.

"You're barely holding it together Al, and the show is running fine." Allison glances around nervously, out into the front row. Louis came. He's sitting front row. She feels a calm. She feels a taste in her mouth. She calculates if she has time to duck out the fire exit for a few puffs. No -- she doesn't have that kind of time.

Onstage, Conrad considers going AWOL before leaving for the army, favoring partying with high school kids at the local small town malt shop. Elizabeth shakes her frilly pink top, just like Ann Margret in the movie. There's older men out there and Kim wants to run off to find them. She has living to do which means getting wild, breaking some hearts and drinking. Kim wants to get drunk with older men until her own father doesn't recognize her. Hugo is fine with this, discovering he is free to go get other chicks' phone numbers. After all, his old rival Conrad says there is an abundance of chicks out there just for kissing.

Allison bites a fingernail nervously. "This dance number always feels like it drags on to me." She glances around the audience, looking for reactions.

Natalie nods, "I know, I always thought so too, even in the movie." She shrugs, "I guess they're doing it well though, considering." Considering this group of kids this year doesn't have many real dancers among them. "Think anyone out there is upset about the underage drinking references?"

Allison glances around the audience again. Maybe. "Nah." She waves it off. Onstage, Conrad Birdie is being arrested, accused of statutory rape or at least being implied as such. "The script just glosses over that like it's not a big detail but don't you feel like it should be a bigger deal?"

"I know, it's not like they left the Icebox." Natalie shrugs.

"And Kim just throws him under the bus doesn't she?" Allison giggles. On stage Mister McAfee hears his daughter telling Hugo how she had been humiliated as they're walking off together reunited and it's all he needs to hear to press charges.

"That's all I need to hear!" He declares, finger in the air, ordering Birdie's arrest.

The stage clears in a flurry of townsfolk, leaving Courtney center stage with her Albert Peterson. "The NEW Albert Peterson!" he declares forcefully. "A woman's place is in the home. In the kitchen, barefoot, speaking only when spoken to!" Rosie of course swoons, being put in her womanly place. "Tomorrow you show up at the train station promptly at six-thirty AM, and bring your documents, Rosie, because I'm going to make you my wife," Albert Peterson demands on his way offstage practically as an afterthought that he loves her. Courtney stands center stage, smiling. Allison sees it...both girls win their prizes, get to *be* prizes. That's their prize. They get to be married. They're chosen. They get to be Missus. Courtney is joined onstage by the girl playing Albert's mother. It's the classic stand off, old as humanity. A mother and her son's new wife. Her replacement.

"The woman I will soon call..." Courtney's smile falters slightly, "...Mother." She manages to say without a voice crack. Natalie pulls the curtain closed. Courtney briefly joins Allison in the wings long enough to gripe, "It really sucks Spanish Rose was cut." Allison smiles, tightly, trying to look away.

Eyebrows raised, she garners some sympathy, "Yeah...?" She trails off weakly. Allison looks away her gaze, lands on Louis again and realizes, with the show night excitement to distract her, that Tommy didn't come. She really can't take his abuse any longer. Not at all. She knows what she has to do but she's scared. She has to break up with him. She looks again at Louis. She craves a cigarette. Natalie pulls open the curtains. She taps Allison's shoulder, snapping her back to reality. They giggle together at Conrad in drag. Albert's mother joins the two boys onstage. She comedically mistakes Conrad for Rosie. Then she tells Albert he can have three mink stoles when the train cuts her in pieces. The audience howls with laughter at her dramatic suicide attempt joke. Again, the stage clears, leaving Courtney and Albert Peterson to perform an abbreviated rendition of "My Rosie" leaving out all but one of Rosie's verses, but she wins her prize. Her English Teacher. He's moving her out to the country, gone and taken a job without a moment's discussion with his future wife. He's taken a job teaching at a school and they in fact prefer he have a good wife at home. In Courtney's one short verse she gushes happily about how she has been chosen. Albert goes into the big finish. Jazz hands. Courtney takes the hat from his head, hides their faces for the big kiss in the spotlight. Natalie pulls the curtains closed. As the curtains swing shut Elizabeth burst from between them to enthusiastically sing the theme song written just for Ann Margret and they close out the show just like the movie.

Epilogue

After *Bye Bye Birdie,* Elizabeth and Courtney don't see much of each other until a couple of years later when they both see a flyer for an open audition. Director Jacob Samedi is casting for an indie horror film. Both audition. Elizabeth would score the lead roles, playing both the dead mom and the prostitute. Courtney would win the role of Becca, victim number two. It would be the first time in their tenuous friendship that Elizabeth poses a threat to Courtney.

The movie is based on actual events, a horrific tragedy that happened at Mohegan Lake. A man abducted several prostitutes over the course of a day and night, killing all but one. The survivor, played by Elizabeth in the movie, looked like the guy's dead mother, thus also played by Elizabeth. It was a bizarre story.

The Georgia filmmaker, Jacob Samedi, took the tabloid stories of the incident where the survivor blurted out some delusional babble in shock about zombies and witches. He turned the real life emotional tragedy into a B-Horror Zombie Slasher Flick. *Dead Hookers In The Lake* would be universally panned by critics and audiences alike. The crew would be so ashamed of producing the movie that they would swear an oath at the wrap party to deny the movie's very existence. The Oath of Denial. Twenty five years after the film's release, Keith Baylor, the hair and makeup artist on the film, and Dory Wulftemp, the actress who played "Skank", would co-author and release the tell all book, *Filming Dead Hookers In The Lake: The Worst Horror Movie Ever Made.* That book would ironically go on to be a bestseller upon which a movie was then made about filming the original movie, essentially recreating much of it. Of course due to the success of the book and movie the original movie would see a massive surge in popularity and gain a cult following like a *Rocky Horror* meets *Evil Dead.* Even then, Courtney, Elizabeth and the rest of the cast will still deny to your face ever having made the film.

Recipes

Graveyard X-Mas Cookies

Oven 350
Cream, 1 cup sugar & ½ cup Oleo
Add 2 beaten eggs, 1 tsp vanilla
3 cups flour, 3 tsps baking powder, 1 tsp salt
Add all those alternatively w/ 1 cup of cream
Chill, roll out with flour, bake and frost

Chocolate Chip Pumpkin Bread

3 cups white sugar, 1 tbsp cinnamon, 15 oz pumpkin puree, 1
tbsp ground nutmeg, 1 Cup veg oil, 2 tsps baking soda, ⅔ cup
water, 1 ½ tsp salt, 4 eggs, 1 cup chocolate chips, 3 ½ cups flour
Oven at 350 combine ingredients bake 1 hour.

Hot Pepper Sauce

2 lbs peppers
3 cups dist. White vinegar
2 teaspoons salt
Chop peppers (wear gloves!)
Simmer ingredients 10 minutes (careful not to inhale fumes)
Let cool
Process in blender till smooth
Put in glass jars
Age 3 months.

Sources and inspirations:
"Dance 10 Looks 3" song from A Chorus Line
The musicals Anything Goes & Bye, Bye Birdie
The Facts of Life
Growing Up Female With A Bad Reputation:
Slut! By L. Tanenbaum
Mean Girls written by T. Fey
Snuff by C. Palaniuk
J. Malkovich in Rounders
Zack and Miri Make A Porno
Cam Girls by S. Dunne
Hot Girls Wanted on Netflix
After Porn Ends and After Porn Ends 2 on Netflix
Adult Film Star and Legend, G.L. Allen
Adult Film Star and Legend,The M. F. Hedgehog, R. Jeremy.
Peekskill in Pictures on Facebook,
My Facebook friends.
life
And JER, my muse.

The story about Krowface getting punched in the mouth is a
retelling of his own account from Facebook of getting punched in the
mouth by a chick who really wanted to fight my wife. I was not there that
night.

The Jason Takes Manhattan monologue was written, also on
Facebook, by M.C. Cacace, the original Cupcakes, my own personal
C.Hardwick. You don't need any context for that.

(Grass Cutter Diary 6:23:17 ...and the grandfather took a bite of his apple...")